THE
HEADMASTERS

PRAISE FOR THE HEADMASTERS

"*Mark Morton's* The Headmasters *is a brilliant science-fiction debut from one of Canada's best-loved nonfiction writers. This compelling YA novel is a spot-on updating of Robert A. Heinlein's classic* The Puppet Masters *for the new millennium, with intricate world-building, a great science-fiction puzzle, and—ironic for a novel about suppressed memories—a main character you'll never forget. I loved it.*"

ROBERT J. SAWYER, HUGO
AWARD-WINNING AUTHOR OF
THE DOWNLOADED

SHADOWPAW
PRESS

THE
HEADMASTERS

MARK MORTON

THE HEADMASTERS
By Mark Morton

Shadowpaw Press
Regina, Saskatchewan, Canada
www.shadowpawpress.com

Trade Paperback ISBN: 978-1-989398-84-5
Ebook ISBN: 978-1-989398-85-2

Front cover designed by Tania Craan

Shadowpaw Press is grateful for
the financial support of Creative Saskatchewan.

CONTENTS

To Farley, whose brown eyes first met mine at the Winnipeg Humane Society, as if to say, "Here we are, at last."

And to my wife, Melanie Cameron, from whom I have learned that the soil loves the rain, and the rain the soil; the wind loves the trees; the song loves the robin; roses and red are in love.

ZARA'S MEMORY

Bear takes me in again   to the heap of stones   and it's back
again
the hissing the head the eyes the fangs
i bring one hand toward the crack to lure it out
its head darts out i seize it with my other hand   draw it forth
with two hands now I squeeze its throat   to crush it   crush its
life
its eyes blink at me without concern   darts its tongue and tastes
the air
i grip it harder arms quivering won't give up
unrelenting waiting for it to struggle to flail to gasp for air and
die
but it doesn't
Bear waits and watches me   yawns   waits
bands of red begin to stain the yellow sky Bear sniffs the air: the
slackening is ending
i've stayed too long   all around me the desert place begins to
crack   split fissure
a rumble like thunder   then heap after heap of stones dozens
hundreds   thrust upward

through the clay then stop silence   clouds of dust hang in the
air
slowly settle i wait i watch   then from each heap a snake crawls
forth
they slither down the stones to the surface
of the desert place   they slither to the middle
converge in a writhing mass
time to leave   i tug Bear's ear   we try to slip away unnoticed
but the snakes   the writhing mass   surge suddenly toward me
they've sensed me know i'm here
i break into a run with Bear
feet pounding the dusty clay
but the snakes sweep after me   reach my heels
wrap around my ankles
i trip and they swell over me   enveloping entangling
my hands weighed down   they push into my mouth my nostrils
i can't breath
i'm going to die

PART ONE

CHAPTER 1
HARVEST

They did the coupling in the Ward on a metal table with straps. I told Ivy and Knot I didn't need the straps. I wasn't going to fight what I knew had to happen. I lay face down on the scratched and rusty surface of the table, my head sideways on the stained pillow, and waited.

Out of the corner of my eye, I could see Knot reach into a dirty nylar bag and pull it out. About as big as a big man's hand. Black and glinting like the shell of a water beetle. Shaped like an engorged wood tick.

Knot told me he was sorry, then dropped it onto my back, right between my shoulder blades. It wriggled about, finding the right spot, and I sensed its cold suckers caressing my flesh, exploring, adjusting to the shape and size of its new host's small body. Suddenly, it felt like glowing embers were pressing against my skin. Every muscle in my body clenched, but I didn't scream. I didn't even groan. I wasn't going to give it that satisfaction. Then I felt a new pain, much worse, a searing at the base of my skull—something burrowing in, something invading me.

"The hurt'll soon go away, Maple," murmured an old man, kneeling by my cot, as I slowly opened my eyes. I didn't say anything but raised my head slightly—wincing—and glanced around. I wasn't in the Ward anymore. I was in a small, dim room with bare, cracked walls and one high window. I could hear the wind pummelling the windowpane and felt a cold gust come through the frame. Cobwebs fluttered in the ceiling corners, making the trapped dead flies dance up and down. Despite the draft, the room smelled like dust and dried urine. I'd never been here before, but I knew where I was. My cubicle, the place where I'd spend the darkenings for the rest of my life.

My back sang with pain, and my head throbbed. I turned my eyes back to the old man beside my bed. Without saying anything, he put a cloth, wet with cool water, onto my forehead and gently rolled me from my back onto my side. The throbbing subsided slightly.

"Who are you?" I asked. My voice was low and scratchy like I'd been eating sand.

"I'm your Papa," he told me. "You're my granddaughter. You'll remember tomorrow. Getting coupled makes you forget things for a while."

I nodded uncertainly. I didn't recognize the wrinkled face that peered out from behind his grey beard, but there was something about his voice that was familiar and soothing. His eyes were kind.

Coupled. Yes, that's what had happened. One of the Headmasters—one whose host had died a few days ago—had now been attached to me. Twelve was young for that to happen. But they must have had their reasons.

Through the window, I noticed the sky tinged with red. "Is it morning?" I asked him.

He shook his head. "Almost night. The darkening will soon start, so I can't stay long." He flipped the wet cloth over on my forehead, his hands smelling like pine sap. "You've been coupled to your Headmaster, Maple, but next, it's going to start to link with you. A neural link. It won't hurt, but you're going to feel confused. You might see things that don't make sense. You might feel like you're losing your mind."

He paused as he saw my eyes widen with fear.

"I know you're scared," he continued. "Just like I was when it was done to me a long time ago. But you need to keep strong and focused."

He stroked my hair and gave me a sad smile. His furrowed brow told me he was worried.

He went on. "It helps if you can hold a good memory in your head when the linking starts. Can you remember anything yet? Anybody?"

I tried to think, but it was hard when my head was throbbing. Then something surfaced. Something furry.

"Farley," I muttered.

"The last dog?" Papa asked, his eyes lighting up ever so slightly. "That's what you remember?"

I nodded as the memory began to bloom. Soft golden fur. Brown eyes circled by rings of black. A tail quick to wag. "He stayed with me when I hurt my leg," I said. "When I fell in the forest. He kept barking."

"That's right," Papa said. "Thanks to him, I found you and carried you back." He stood. "Keep thinking about him, Maple. Keep Farley in your head when the linking starts. Hold on to him, and he'll help you hold onto yourself."

"What was your memory?" I asked him, not wanting him to leave. "What did you hold onto when they did it to you?"

He was silent, and his eyes grew distant.

"Maybe you don't know anymore," I said, "because it was so long ago."

He shook his head. "No, I remember. It was a memory of someone I hadn't known long but who I admired. That was the memory I held onto." He squeezed my hand. My palm was damp, but his felt dry and rough. "I need to hurry back to my cubicle before the darkening starts. I'll come back tomorrow when toil is over."

He smiled again, turned, and limped through the doorway. As he stepped into the dark hall and closed the door, the last thing I saw was the bulge of a Headmaster beneath his shirt.

Papa was right: not long after he left, my throbbing headache and the searing pain between my shoulder blades faded away. Instead, my back just felt numb and distant—like frostbite. Then, as Papa had said, the linking began. With its pair of sinewy coils now deeply wormed into the base of my skull, my Headmaster started to establish its link with me.

At first, it felt like I was sinking slowly into an icy stream, flowing in all directions. Then, tiny orange and blue and red fish appeared and began to bite at my skin, nipping off bits and gulping them down, their glassy eyes locked onto mine as they nibbled.

As I sank deeper, the fish turned into formless shapes, smudges of colour that slipped around my arms and legs, my face and fingers—as if they were examining me—then moved away. I released my breath, and thousands of bubbles escaped my lungs and rose around me. I could see into each one; I could see everything, so deeply, each bubble enclosing a universe of galaxies, each galaxy whirling and throbbing, individual stars brightening, dimming, vanishing, planets spinning, masses of continents drifting, colliding, piling, creatures, innumerable creatures, minds, ideas, thoughts, words, symbols, everything meaning something, none of it comprehensible.

Then it all melted away, and I was suddenly a tree. A maple tree. Alone on a rocky hill. In autumn. My red and yellow leaves began to pull loose, a rising wind tugging them free, the leaves scattering. The tree was bare, and I was nothing. Gone.

Then Farley rested his head on my lap, and I was sitting in a forest, my back against the maple tree, birds chittering and the sun just dropping out of sight. I put my hand on Farley's head, but it passed through, then swept through my own leg, then through the mossy ground I was sitting on. But that didn't matter. As long as Farley was there, I was there.

I focused my mind on his warm brown eyes, then opened my own. The pink light of dawn was beginning to make its way through the small window of my cubicle. I was drenched in cold sweat and exhausted, but I felt almost normal—except for a vague sense that something was watching, listening.

surveilling

I slowly sat up on the edge of my cot. Unsteadily, I got to my feet and made my way to the cracked mirror on the wall beside my door. Craning my neck around, I could see the Headmaster's dark, glistening shell stretching from my neck to the middle of my back. Most of the shell was as thick as my thumb, but toward what seemed to be its head—where its two coils sprouted like the feelers on a water beetle—the shell got fatter. As thick as a man's fist. The other end—its tail?—grew more narrow, tapering almost into a point. The whole thing seemed much heavier than it should. I felt weighed down and tippy.

All my life, I'd seen Headmasters lurking under the shirts of adults, clinging to their backs like leeches. Still, it was hard to imagine getting used to this one being coupled to me, directing my actions for most of the day, even shaping my feelings.

When he came back the next slackening to see me, Papa started by asking me if I remembered him. I told him I did, that I'd seen him last night and that I'd known him all my life. *You're my Papa.* Then he asked me if I remembered River and Lark. Of course, I did—my brother and sister. Could I tell him the names of the other kids still in the Aery? *Larch, Twilight, Alder, Wren.* What was our community called? *Blue Ring.* What season was it? *Spring. Knot picked me a crocus as they walked me to the Ward.*

"Good," he smiled. He seemed satisfied. "Your memories are back."

Then his face clouded, and he told me something that he knew I already knew: if I tried to remove my Headmaster, I would die.

"If you try to pull it off or cut it off, it'll kill you. Same thing if you try to burn it off. The moment you start—the instant you even think of doing that—it'll send a poison through its coils and into your brain—

neurotoxin botulinum

"—and you'll be dead before your noggin hits the ground."

"What if I slip and fall on it?" I asked, still thinking about the tumble I had in the forest when I was little.

Papa took off his spectacles and began to rub the glass lens with a flap of his shirt. He only had one lens. The other side was an empty circle of wire. "You can't hurt it. It's not possible. Headmasters aren't made of the same stuff as us. They're not from here—from this world. You can't cut them or smother them or drown them. And they never die. The Headmasters on us now are the same ones that showed up a long time ago—at the Arrival."

I was about to ask another question—about where they came from—but he abruptly stood up and spoke again. "Enough bleak talk. Let's get out of this musty air. Get dressed and put your foot wrappings on. We'll take a saunter into the forest before the slackening ends."

I nodded and kicked the nylar blanket off my legs. As I put my bare feet on the cold floor, I asked him, "Papa, who had my Headmaster before me?"

"Hurry and get dressed," he replied. "The slackening will end in a couple of hours. I'll wait for you in the hallway."

CHAPTER 2
WE SHOULDN'T TALK ABOUT HIM

The next morning, I woke up from a sudden jolt of pain, like someone was pinching me inside my head: it was my Headmaster impelling me to open my eyes. I sat up, swivelled on my cot, and stood, still a bit unsteady. Then I found myself picking up my slop jar and walking to the collection room, where I dumped it into one of the many big buckets sitting there on the floor. I left as quickly as I could—the stench in the collection room stung my eyes and burned my throat.

On my way back to my cubicle, I thought, *That's weird—I knew where to find the collection room.* Down the hallway, turn right, then down another hallway to the far end. But I'd never been to the collection room before. How did I know where it was?

Back in my cubicle, I found an older woman with a grey ponytail laying a shirt and trousers on my cot. I'd never seen her before. There were only a couple of hundred people at Blue Ring. How could I not know her?

"I take them for cleaning every fifteen days," she snapped in a shrill, crow-like voice. "Fifteen. Understand that?"

I nodded.

"You pick them up yourself from the drying room every fifteen days at the end of toil. That means at the end of the grip. Toil ends when the grip ends. Understand that?"

I nodded again.

"Same thing for foot wraps, winter wraps, and blankets."

I nodded for a third time, then asked, very quietly, "Where's the drying room?"

"What?" she snapped.

"I don't know where the drying room is."

She stared at me like I'd just asked her to help me find my elbow. "You'll know when you need to know." She paused, and her brow seemed to soften for an instant. "It's in the sub-basement." She pointed a bony finger toward the floor. "Of this building. This building is the Cube. Where people sleep. You know that?"

"Yes," I said. "What's your—"

But she interrupted me before I could finish. "People don't talk to me. You should understand that." Then she was through my door and heading down the dim hallway.

As I stood there, mulling over my brief encounter with this sour old woman, I had a sudden urge to go to the Meal House. I got dressed as fast as I could. I slipped the new nylar shirt over my head, poked my arms through the other two holes, and cinched it at my waist with a strap. It felt rough and stiff against my skin. Then I pulled on the trousers—also nylar—and looped the suspenders crossways over my chest, then up over my shoulders. The trousers were so baggy I could have fit two of me into them. My foot wraps—more nylar—took the longest. I started at my toes, then wound upward over the arches of my feet and finally around my ankles and halfway up my calf.

I left my cubicle, found the stairway, and started climbing down the three levels that led to the ground floor. The stairs looked slippery—the black slabs of the steps, glinting with small white crystals, were polished to a sheen, the middle of each one worn to a shallow hollow by decades of footsteps. I went slowly, hanging onto the remnants of a rickety metal railing that followed the staircase down. Others began to pass me as I went, moving much more surefootedly down the stairs. Most of them didn't say anything—didn't even seem to notice me—but a few greeted me with a muttered, "Here we are."

The bright spring sunlight hurt my eyes when I stepped out of the Cube onto the edge of the large, circular compound that most of the buildings at Blue Ring were arranged around. The surface of the compound was cracked and uneven. Scrubby trees and vines grew up out of its broken concrete.

A sudden twinge of pain—like a bee had stung me inside my head—got me moving again. I started heading to the Meal House. Before he'd left the night before, Papa told me to eat as much as I could at morning meal.

"It's the only food you'll get till the grip ends and the slackening starts," he'd said. "It's not like it is in the Aery."

My eyes had to adjust again as I walked out of the morning sun and into the dim Meal House. It had a high, arched ceiling, with only a few dirty windows at the back for light to trickle in. Some of the beams that held up the roof were so rusted they'd broken away and dangled over the tables. It looked like a few more layers of dust on them might bring them down.

After a moment, I spotted my Papa already at a table with a half-eaten biscuit wedge on the plate in front of him. I waved and called out: "Papa, over here!" He looked up, then jerked his head back down at his food. Puzzled, I started to run toward him but suddenly found myself coming to a halt and turning around. I needed to get my food. I had to do that. I *had* to.

Before I knew it, I was in line, waiting for a biscuit wedge to be plopped into a bowl I was now holding in my hand. I then found myself heading over to a table—but not the one that Papa was at.

It was all disorienting until I realized, *This is what my Headmaster wants. It's forcing me to do these things.*

But "forcing" isn't quite right. It doesn't exactly describe what the Headmasters do to their hosts. The coupling that my Headmaster had established with me was only a day old, still settling, so I was probably especially aware of how it wielded control.

It wasn't like someone or something was giving me an order. It wasn't like I was hearing a voice in my head. It was more like an idea would occur to me, or an impulse would emerge in my mind, one that I felt compelled to follow through on—even though another part of me knew I didn't actually want to do it.

It reminded me of when I got into poison ivy last summer. It gave me a terrible, oozing rash. Halo told me not to scratch it, but the urge was too strong. I couldn't resist. I still have scars on my left arm.

As I sat down at the table, its yellowing surface pitted and gouged from use, I saw that sitting across from me was Thorn. In the Aery, we'd often played together. And sometimes squabbled together—in fact, he was the one I'd been mad at when I threw the warming stone. It missed him but hit one of the windows, cracking it. Over the next few moon cycles, the crack got longer and longer until the Menders took it out and put a metal sheet up instead. I felt bad for doing it because it made it a lot darker inside.

I hadn't seen Thorn since he'd been harvested about a year ago. He was older than me, but I wasn't sure by how much.

"Maple!" he said, glancing up, a fleeting smile flashing across his face. "Here we are! You got harvested!"

"Here we are," I replied. "You look—" I began to say and

then stopped as I found myself staring down at my biscuit wedge.

"It's easiest," Thorn said, sensing my confusion, "if you just focus on what you're supposed to be doing. Just go along with it, and your Headmaster won't put as much grip on you. Right now, they want us to eat, so just keep looking at your food as you eat it. If you do that, we can still talk."

I kept my eyes on my biscuit wedge and watched as my fingers broke off small chunks, raised them to my mouth, and poked them in.

"You look older," I said as I began to chew. The biscuit wedge was dry and spongy like bog sod and tasted vaguely of wild meat and mushrooms and burdock root.

"I am older. So are you."

"You look a lot older."

He kept his head down and didn't reply for a minute. He picked up his dented mug of water and took a big gulp, some of it dribbling down his chin. "What cubicle are you in?"

"On the third floor. I think the numbers on my door look like this." I slowly traced their shapes with my finger on the tabletop.

"Looks like 388," Thorn said. "I'm on the same floor but on the other side. My numbers look like this." He traced them for me, saying the name of each one in turn. "Three . . . five . . . nine." I tried to memorize the shape of his numbers, imagining them as snakes curled into sleep. I knew how to count in my head, but nobody had ever taught me how to draw numbers. Or letters, like the ones I saw on the signs that still hung crooked on a few of the buildings.

"Why did my Headmaster make me sit here?" I asked him. As soon as I said this, I regretted it. I didn't want Thorn to think I didn't want to see him.

"They've made you a Picker like me. That's what all of us

are," he said, nodding his head toward the others at the table. "One of us died a few days ago. You're replacing him."

"Kestrel didn't die," growled one of the others at the table without turning toward us—a huge, hulking man with green eyes and a long, reddish beard. "They killed him."

"He was old," said a woman sitting across from him. She had a narrow face and slightly hunched shoulders. A scar ran from the right corner of her mouth toward her ear, disappearing under her long brown hair. Her face was wrinkled with age. "With knees like that, he could hardly make it to the bushes anymore. We knew they wouldn't keep him around much longer." She shrugged. "He knew that, too." She reached a finger into her mouth and pulled out a piece of bone. She dropped it onto the table.

"We shouldn't talk about him," said another woman at the table. She had dark skin, darker even than mine. Her hair was cut short.

"The Headmasters don't care if we complain," said the man with the reddish beard as he turned toward me. "They know it won't make any difference."

"Not that," the short-haired woman replied. "We shouldn't talk about . . . the dead man. You know that." She nodded her head toward me and then said, in a hushed tone, "She must've got his Headmaster."

The bearded man suddenly stopped chewing. Still looking down at his food, he nodded. "Sorry. Stupid of me. Still half asleep, I guess." Then he leaned slightly toward me as if to change the subject. "So you're one of us now," he said. "A Picker. Do you know what Pickers do?"

"Pick?"

"That's right, we pick things. Berries and fruits and certain roots. All the edible things that grow inside the perimeter."

"Mushrooms?" I asked.

"Pah!" said the red-beard man, pretending to spit on the floor. "Grubbers pick those. Not us."

"You said you pick all the edible things that grow inside the perimeter," I reminded him.

"Mushrooms don't grow," he replied. "They just pop out of rotten logs like poop from a possum. They're not a proper plant." I thought he was going to frown at me, but he didn't.

"Before long," said the woman with the scar on her cheek, "they'll switch us to raspberries. Raspberries and strawberries in spring, blueberries, chokecherries, and peaches in early summer, plums in mid-summer, and apples and pears in fall."

"Do you know which berry we don't pick?" the red-bearded man asked.

I shook my head.

"Shrubbery." He stared at me to see if I got his joke.

"And what about slobbery?" I said, pointing at the wet crumbs of biscuit that trailed down the front of his shirt.

"Good one," he snorted.

The short-haired woman smiled.

"We pick grapes, too," the red-bearded man continued. "There's vines out near the wind turbine. You know where that is?"

"Past the perimeter. My Papa took me there. It's the tower with the arms that spin."

The man nodded. "Every few years, the vines out there sprout some nice grapes."

"I've never seen them," scoffed the short-haired woman. She turned slightly toward me. "By the way, I'm Rose. This man who thinks he's seen grapes is Silex."

"Here we are," I said, nodding to them both.

Rose turned back to the table and pointed at the wrinkled woman with the scar. "She's Crest. And you know Thorn from the Aery."

"Here we are," I said to Crest, nodding again.

"When it turns cold," Thorn added, "we switch to berries that stay on the bushes all winter. Like hawberries and cranberries. Rosehips. We pick up acorns, too, and walnuts, once the snow melts."

"How do you crack the shells?" I asked him. Papa once brought me a pocketful of walnuts in the Aery. He had to go to the Mending Hall to get a squeezing thing to open them.

"We don't," Thorn replied. "The Biscuiteers do all the cracking. We just haul them back here in big nylar sacks. Then I climb up there," he nodded upward to a low wall running around the inside of the second floor of the Meal House, "and when I'm ready for Silex to toss them up to me, I shout 'Heave!' Silex figures one more year and I'll be strong enough to heave them up myself, and he can catch them."

"I tell you, I've seen them and tasted them," Silex said. It took me a moment to realize he was still talking about grapes, not walnuts.

"Then you haven't tasted them for at least thirty years," Rose said, "because that's when they made me a Picker. Anyway, you wouldn't recognize a grape if it fell into your mouth. Which might happen because it's open most of the time."

"What's a grape look like?" I asked, tilting my head toward Silex.

"And taste like?" added Thorn.

Silex paused. Even with his head bent over his food, I could see his brow furrow.

"Kind of like a blueberry," he said. "They're both of that colour. But a grape's bigger. About as big as your eyeball."

I grimaced at the comparison.

"And shaped like a chicken egg," he added.

"She won't know what that is," said Crest as she swallowed

another mouthful of biscuit. "We haven't had chickens here since you and Rose were kids." Turning to me, she added, "I don't mean they did anything bad to them. One spring, the whole brood just got scrawny and died. I think they got worms inside them."

"Shaped like a big crow egg, then," Silex continued. "An egg is an egg is an egg. And they have a big, hard seed inside."

"Sounds like a plum to me," Crest said.

Abruptly, we all stood and pushed our benches away from the table, some of us still holding lumps of biscuit wedges.

"It's the grip. They want us toiling," Rose said to me. "What's your name again?"

"Maple."

"How old?"

"Twelve. I think."

Rose pursed her lips and shook her head. "You'll be tired tonight, Maple. As soon as the slackening starts, you better head back to your cubicle and get to sleep."

CHAPTER 3
RASPBERRIES AND MINT

Tired. That was an understatement. In fact, when the grip finally ended, I was so exhausted I dropped to the ground in the middle of plucking a raspberry off its vine. Thorn told me later that Silex picked me up, carried me back to the Cube, took me up to my cubicle—Thorn had told him which one—and set me on my cot. The next morning when my Headmaster jolted me awake, I remembered none of this. Every muscle ached as I was trudged again to the Meal House for a bowl of biscuit before starting another day of picking.

That's how every day went for the next couple of weeks. Wake, eat, pick, sleep. When the grip ended, I was too tired to even stop by the Meal House to grab a biscuit wedge for second meal. Wake, eat, pick, sleep.

Well, not quite. Not all of my sleep was sleep. In fact, most of it was the darkening.

Back in the Aery, all the kids fell asleep in the evening when they got tired. And they had dreams—sometimes nice ones, but usually scary ones that Halo called nightmares. But after you got harvested and taken out of the Aery for good, your Headmaster put you into something called the darkening. It happened every night as soon as the slackening ended. And you didn't have dreams or even nightmares.

The darkening wasn't the same thing as sleep. It came over you instantly, and everything just went black. When you woke up in the morning, you were lying exactly the same as when the darkening began, and it seemed like you had just closed your eyes. Like no time had passed. And if you hadn't used your slop jar before the darkening took you, you might find yourself on a wet cot when your Headmaster jolted you awake.

After the darkening took me the first time, I wondered if that was what being dead was like. I'd seen plenty of dead things in the forest after Halo started letting me wander around there whenever I was feeling mad. Lots of dead birds—robins and sparrows and crows, including little baby ones, pink and featherless, that had tumbled out of nests. Dead squirrels and a few dead foxes, and something that had probably been a raccoon, but it was hard to tell. It was so dead there was nothing left but a few bones and scraps of furry skin. Once, I almost stepped on a garter snake that had the back end of a frog sticking out of its mouth, its long, green legs kicking and wriggling. I guess it wasn't quite dead yet.

But it wasn't until Papa and I found Farley cold and stiff on the riverbank under the bridge that I really started thinking about what it meant to be dead. It meant not moving, not thinking or feeling. It meant forgetting the people and things you left behind. There were no more memories of me in Farley's dead head.

Papa had lifted him up and carried him to the boneyard, then helped me cover him with stones. He'd been gone for three days before we found him. There were no more dogs after that.

So in those first few weeks after being harvested, when I trudged back to my cubicle right after the grip ended and we stopped our toil, I did get some actual sleep like I used to in the Aery. But then the darkening took me for the rest of the night. And left my dreams behind.

Knowing when the darkening was getting close was important. If you weren't in your own cubicle and lying on your own cot when it was about to happen, your Headmaster would zap the inside of your head with agonizing jolts until you got there. Same thing if you were slow to leave your cubicle in the morning: jolt, jolt, jolt.

Papa said there was only one person who didn't have to sleep in the Cube. That was the Keeper. She stayed in the gear cabin at the top of the wind tower. Up there, her toil was to watch the blades to make sure they didn't spin too fast. Too much speed could damage them, Papa had once told me, back before I was harvested, as we were walking through the forest during a slackening and caught sight of the distant wind tower. The turbine. It was tall, so tall—like it was trying to touch the clouds. Papa said its long blades caught the wind and turned it into current, like the river but invisible, and the current kept the Aery and the Cube warm in the winter. It kept us from turning into chunks of ice like the deer I once saw the Catchers drag back from the forest—eyes frozen open, mouth fringed with ice crystals, legs stiff as dead branches.

"The tower used to look after itself," Papa had said. "It moved its levers and turned its knobs as if it had its own mind, just like a person. But then it got hit. That was a long time ago."

"Hit by what?" I asked him.

"Lightning."

"Did it hurt the Keeper?"

He shook his head. "She wasn't up there then. Nobody was. It wasn't till after it got hit and the Headmasters sensed the turbine couldn't look after itself anymore that they made the Keeper. They harvested one of the older kids from the Aery and made her climb up to its gear cabin. She had to figure out how to use the levers and knobs all by herself. She was the first Keeper. She still is."

Papa stopped talking as if that was all he was going to say about the Keeper. We kept walking in silence over the bed of soft, brown pine needles that covered the forest floor till we got to the top of a rocky crest. From there, we had a clear view of the wind tower. It stood like an upside-down icicle, soaring above the fir trees that surrounded it.

"We all thought she'd have to climb up and down at the start and end of every grip," Papa finally continued, as if there'd been no break in his story. "The Keeper, I mean. But she didn't. That first day, the Headmasters made the Menders hoist a cot all the way up to the gear cabin. That's how she knew she was supposed to sleep up there. That suited her fine. She'd been born with a twist in her leg, and it would have been a hard slog grappling up and down that long ladder every day. So she stays up there, up in the tower's gear cabin, day after day, year after year."

shalott

"Every few days," Papa continued, "Knot climbs up with biscuit wedges for her and a bucket of water. When he comes back down, he brings the empty water bucket from the last time he climbed up."

"Where does she do her slop?" I asked. That morning I'd spilled mine, carrying it to the collection room.

"She has a jar, just like everyone else. When it's full, she climbs through the hatch in the roof of the gear cabin and throws it wherever the wind's blowing."

I made a note never to get too close to the wind tower.

"Nobody's seen the Keeper since she went up. Except

Knot, of course. He says her hair's gone grey, and one eye's turned white. Sometimes he takes chunks of white pine up to her and brings her knives back down for a Mender to sharpen. He says when there's no wind, and the blades are still, she carves little animals and trees, little people. Sometimes she sends them down for the kids in the Aery to play with."

I suddenly felt like I knew the Keeper. I'd grown up with those wooden carvings. Her hands had shaped every detail of them, and mine had touched every curve and edge of their surfaces hundreds of times. I hadn't known they'd come from her. I'd always wondered why those little wooden people had no Headmasters.

After a couple of more weeks of picking, my body began to ache less. My arms and shoulders got stronger. My legs got used to crouching to reach the berries low on the bush. I got better at spotting and reaching around the thorns that grew among the raspberry thickets and blackberry bushes. The tiny punctures in my fingers and the ragged scratches on the back of my hands started to heal. My face turned browner in the sun.

Rose and Silex showed me how to rub mint leaves into my skin to keep the blackflies away. The horseflies—which were much bigger—didn't seem to mind the mint smell, so I sometimes got bit. So did Thorn and Crest and Rose and Silex. We each had our own distinctive horsefly howl. Their fiery sting reminded me of how it felt when my Headmaster's suckers first latched on to me.

One day, after the grip had ended and we'd hauled our buckets of berries back to the Meal House for the Biscuiteers, Rose asked me if I wanted to go with her to listen to the Teller.

Rose said her sole partner—Cardinal—wasn't feeling well, so he was going to stay in his cubicle and rest.

I knew about the Teller, of course, but I hadn't ever been to Gehenna—that's what they called the building where he told his stories. Back in the Aery, I used to get mad a lot, and Halo had told me that if I needed to get away from the other kids for a while, I could go into the forest. None of the other kids got to do that. Halo said wandering around in the trees was better than skulking around the tumble-down buildings that ringed the compound. So I spent lots of time in the forest with Farley, watching him plunge his nose into beds of fallen leaves and dig holes in the black soil of the forest floor. I liked to sort pebbles into different-coloured piles and stack dead branches into little huts I could wiggle into, and put red ants onto black-ant anthills to see what would happen. That's why it never occurred to me to go see the Teller.

I wasn't as exhausted as on previous days, and I was glad Rose had invited me. But I told her I'd rather find my brother and sister and Papa. I hadn't had a chance to speak a word to them since my first day of toil.

"Okay, kid," said Rose. "I know where your grandfather will be." She held her hand out, and after a moment of hesitation, I took it. Then I turned to Thorn.

"Want to come?" I asked him.

He shook his head.

Rose led me across the compound as the sun began to arc closer to the horizon. In the warm breeze, I could smell the juice of raspberries and mint and sweat mingling on her skin.

CHAPTER 4
THE BRIDGE

Rose and I crossed the compound, stepping over cracks and broken slabs of concrete, then started down one of the footworn paths leading into the forest that surrounded the ring of tumble-down buildings. With the swaying elm trees towering above us, it was darker here, and I held on tighter to Rose's hand.

With Farley, I'd never felt frightened in the forest except for the time we came face to face with a porcupine, but maybe that was because we'd always gone in when the sun was still high in the sky. This felt different, and I wanted to turn around and see him trotting behind me. But I kept looking straight ahead as I walked beside Rose with the rustling leaves whispering all around us. The path was narrow and edged here and there with orange tiger lilies, white trilliums, and purple gypsy weed. Rose called them ephemerals because they didn't last long.

As we walked, she gently tugged me this way and that, warning me to watch out for roots and rocks that made the path hazardous.

"Why's my Papa out here?" I asked her as we pushed deeper into the forest.

"It's where the Inwards meet."

"Who?"

"The Inwards," she said. "Your grandfather hasn't mentioned them?"

I shook my head.

"Inwards," said Rose, "go into the forest during the slackenings. Like right now, after the Headmasters have let go of their grip on us. Your Papa and the other Inwards gather on the old bridge. Then they ramble off somewhere and—and look at things." She paused to point out some deer droppings to avoid. "I think it was your Papa who started the Inwards."

"What do they look at?" I asked.

Rose shrugged. "Trees. Birds and rocks. The river. The moon, if it's up before the slackening ends."

"That doesn't sound very interesting."

"I'm with you on that. I went with them a few times, including once when they sat around the stump of a tamarack and stared at the moss on it."

"Why?"

She pointed ahead. "You can ask him yourself. Hear the water moving? We're nearly at the bridge."

The path opened up into a meadow of low sweetgrass with tall stands of big bluestem and goldenrod thrusting up here and there. I heard something rustling through the grass—probably a squirrel. On the other side of the meadow, I saw one end of the bridge. In the slanting sunlight, it gleamed red from a crust of rust eating away at its iron beams. Like the roof of the Meal House, it looked ready to give up and topple down.

"Come on," said Rose as she felt my pace slowing.

"Is it safe?" I asked. With Farley, I'd sometimes wandered to the bridge but never had the courage to cross it. I'd wanted to. Papa said that on the other side of the river, there were metal tracks on the ground that stretched out in both directions as far as you could see. He said that big carts had once rolled on those tracks, and that was how the bricks for the buildings got here and even the swooping blades for the wind turbine.

"It's been like this as far back as I can remember. It's not going to fall down today." She glanced over at me and smiled. "I hope."

I stepped gingerly onto the wooden planks that served as the floor of the bridge. They, at least, looked like they'd been replaced fairly recently. By the Menders, of course. Then, looking ahead, I saw a small clutch of people clustering near the middle of the bridge. Most were standing, a few sitting cross-legged. One person sat on the planks with her legs hanging over the edge, the water rushing below.

don't jacob

"Jacob!" Rose cried out. The cluster parted into two sides, revealing my Papa in the middle. "Look what I found!"

"Maple!" Papa exclaimed, beaming with delight. "Here we are! Thank you for bringing her, Rose."

"I was planning to come anyway," Rose replied in an off-hand way. "Thought I'd try one more staring contest with a toadstool."

"Finally got enough sleep, did you?" said a familiar voice.

I looked around and saw Lark smiling at me. My sister. She was the one with her legs dangling over the edge, now turning her head toward me. I hadn't seen her since before I was harvested. That seemed a long time ago.

Lark was a Catcher. During the grips, the Headmasters sent the Catchers into the forest to catch and kill whatever animals—or critters, as the Catchers called them—they could lay their hands on. They dug deep holes in the forest floor and covered them with sheets of nylar and leaves. They hung nooses in the paths the critters trampled in the grass or snow. They stood motionless as the sun slowly traced across the sky, waiting for a critter to come close enough to spear with the sharpened metal pipes they carried. And they ran. If they spotted a deer, their Headmasters would make them chase it, make them run and run and run. Sometimes they caught the critter and killed it, but mostly not. Sometimes they fell to the ground with exhaustion, and their Headmasters gave them jolts of pain until they got back up and started running again.

The Catchers hated it when they spotted a deer.

They trapped a lot of mice, squirrels, and rabbits. Sometimes foxes, especially in the winter when it was harder for them to scamper away in soft, deep snow. Porcupines and hedgehogs. Beavers and muskrats. Once, I think, a bear they found sleeping in a snow-covered cave. Not birds—that was Knot's toil. He was a Nester. And not fish—that's what the Netters did.

Whatever the Catchers caught went to the kitchen for the Biscuiteers to add to the biscuit mix.

"River's here, too," Lark said. "Down there," pointing at the far bank of the river. I squinted and saw our brother up to his hips in an eddy, the water swirling around him, a cloud of tiny fish flies dancing around his head.

"Cooling himself off," said Papa.

"Cleaning himself up," Lark said, nodding toward two young women on the bridge. They were whispering to each other and glancing down at River. I got the feeling they weren't interested in staring at anything else.

"Go ahead without me," Papa told the Inwards. "I'm going to stay with Maple. Lark, would you lead them?"

Lark nodded. "We'll head to the silver birch by the split

rock. River, come on!" she shouted over the side of the bridge. He looked up and waved, then started clambering up the river-bank. "Here we are, everyone," Lark called out to the rest of them. "Let's get moving!"

As they traipsed off the bridge, Papa turned back toward me.

"Good to see you with your eyes open," he said. I must have looked puzzled because he added, "Every time I stopped by your cubicle, you were sound asleep."

Of course. I should have known he'd be checking in on me during the slackenings.

"I'm getting used to it," I said. "My toil, I mean. And faster. Not as fast as Thorn, but faster than Silex. His big fingers aren't as good at picking berries."

Papa nodded and smiled. "Silex is a good man," he said, gesturing me over to where Lark had been. "Let's sit." We both squatted and then swung our legs over the edge of the bridge. "It's a big change," he said after a few moments. I knew he was talking about my life in the Aery versus now.

I shrugged. "It had to happen," I replied, trying to sound mature. "Just sooner than I thought."

I looked down and studied the darkening water as I consid-ered whether I should ask my next question or not. "Papa, do you remember telling me you were scared when you got coupled to your Headmaster?"

"I do."

"Did you think about fighting back? Or running away from here?"

He fell silent, and his legs, which he'd been gently swinging back and forth over the river, grew still.

When he spoke at last, I knew he wouldn't be answering my question. "Did Rose tell you what we do out here? Why we meet on the bridge?"

"She said you were Innards."

"Inwards," he said.

"But she didn't tell me what that was. She said you would."

Papa picked up a handful of pebbles someone had piled on the edge of the bridge. He began dropping them into the river, slowly releasing them one by one. In the middle of the bridge, where we were, the water was a long way down. It took each pebble a couple of heartbeats to fall. Each splash vanished in an instant as the strong current swirled it away.

"We used to call it meditating. That's where you close your mind to what's outside of you and focus on what's inside. You let go of what you can't control and focus on what you can—on your breathing or your heartbeat. Then you watch the thoughts that dance around in your head until they get tired and lie down. I started doing it a long time ago, right here on this bridge. Eventually, a few others wanted to do it with me. Now there's about twenty of us, including your sister. Your brother comes sometimes but not so much lately."

"If you're thinking about what's inside your head, why do you need to come out here to do it?"

He dropped another pebble. "Because meditation is like a journey into a boundless forest—like this one." He waved his hand at the trees that stretched out as far as I could see from both banks of the river. "And beholding something beautiful, something in nature, helps us find ourselves."

trataka

"Like what?" I said skeptically. "Like a rock?"

"Every rock is beautiful. Every rock has a story. They were here long before us, and they'll be here long after we're gone."

I wasn't convinced. The endless red-and-grey rocks my

Headmaster made me scramble over during the grip were ugly and annoying.

"You come here in the winter, too?" I asked.

"Yes. Beautiful things are still beautiful when they're covered in snow. But if it's too cold or wet, we gather in the greenhouse."

"Where you grow the flowers. The ones you used to bring me in the Aery."

He nodded. "I have a little corner at the far end, away from the cabbage and beans. The Inwards don't spend the whole slackening meditating. We save time at the end for other things that need to be done. That's when I go to the greenhouse and tend my flowers."

We fell silent for a few moments, watching the river rush below us in the gathering darkness, until I asked, "Has Thorn ever come out to practice the meditating?"

"The young fellow who picks faster than you?" He smiled at me as he said this. I knew he knew who Thorn was. "No, he's never come with us." Papa's face suddenly darkened with concern, and he murmured, "I hope he keeps away from the Thankfuls."

I shrugged. I'd heard of the Thankfuls but didn't really know what they were and didn't ask. I was starting to get sleepy. Papa noticed my drooping eyes and said I should get back to my cubicle.

We began walking back along the narrow path. It was very dark in amongst the trees, but he was so sure-footed I got the feeling he could have walked it with his eyes closed. When we reached the Cube, he went with me up to my cubicle and waited for me to get onto my cot and under my nylar blanket.

"I love you, Maple syrup," he said before turning to leave. That was what he always used to say when he left after visiting me in the Aery.

"Wait, Papa," I mumbled sleepily before he was through the door.

"Yes?" he said, turning back toward me.

"Last night, before the darkening took me, I had a dream. You were in it, but you didn't have a beard or any wrinkles. You didn't even have a Headmaster. And I was somebody else. You called me—" I yawned and felt my eyes closing.

Papa didn't say anything for a moment; then I heard him turn and step toward the door.

"Wait, Papa," I mumbled again.

"Yes?" he said. His voice sounded far away.

I yawned once more. "I forget."

CHAPTER 5
ZIG ZAG LIKE A LIGHTNING BOLT

The next morning was hot and muggy. Spring was finally slouching into summer. As I was trudged to the Meal House, the almost windless air was thick with a stew of pungent smells. The pails of slop dumped on the corn fields. The barrels of rancid grease behind the Meal House. The carcass of a skunk rotting under the woodshed. The sharp odour of old sweat clinging to the people walking in front of me. At least out in the forest and bush, we'd be away from all that stench.

After first meal, as we were heading out to the blueberry bushes, I asked Thorn if he'd ever gone to stare at rocks and tree stumps with my Papa and the Inwards. He said no. Then I asked him what he did during the slackenings. He said sometimes he went to Gehenna and listened to the Teller, but mostly he just stayed by himself and did his own thing. And when I asked him what his own thing was, he mumbled that maybe he'd let me go with him sometime so I could see for myself. I frowned and told him I might think about going with him if I didn't have anything better to do.

Over the following days, I also learned, mostly from Rose, what others did during the slackenings. She said a lot of them—

especially the older ones—were so exhausted they stumbled straight to their cubicles and slept until the darkening took them. Like me when I was first harvested, they were too tired from their toil to even stop at the Meal House to get a biscuit wedge for second meal.

Toil. That's what the Headmasters made us do for more than half of each day, every day, spring, summer, fall, and winter. It didn't matter how tired you were. Your Headmaster would put you in its grip and keep your eyes open and your body moving and your hands working: picking, planting, weeding, watering, catching, grubbing, cooking, cleaning, mending, washing, digging, sewing, hauling, slopping, mixing, nesting, wood chopping—whatever toil the Headmasters had allotted you when you were harvested.

Same thing if you got injured or sick: you still had to toil. Once, when the two of us were unloading the sledges, Rose whispered to me about a Grubber who'd tripped on a loose chunk of concrete in the compound and fallen hard on his wrist. Something inside it got torn, maybe even broken, but his Headmaster made him keep toiling, even though he screamed every time he had to lift up an old log or claw through a pile of leaves. I asked who it was, but she wouldn't say. He wasn't alive anymore, she said.

She told me there were 218 people at Blue Ring, not including the kids in the Aery. There were always 218 because that's how many Headmasters there were. One person—one host—for every Headmaster. When somebody got terminated, the oldest kid in the Aery got harvested—and then we'd be back to 218.

Rose guessed around seventy-five people trudged straight back to their cubicles as soon as the grip ended and the slackening started. "They're exhausted," she said. "But that's not all. Some of them just don't want to think or feel."

The Jimsons were another group Rose told me about that gathered during the slackenings. They were the ones I'd seen burning jimsonweed leaves and breathing in the smoke. They grew it all summer behind the greenhouse, and they tried to dry enough to last them through the winter. Rose said the dust in the jimsonweed smoke made them feel like they were far away. Or like they were floating over Blue Ring like a tuft of dandelion fluff.

The Jimsons had a metal thing—a steam catcher, Papa called it—behind the greenhouse, deep in the forest near the bog, made out of pipes and pots they'd wired together. If you saw it from the corner of the greenhouse when the sun was going down, it looked like a grey bear with long teeth and with copper worms spiralling out of its belly.

During the slackenings, the Jimsons scraped up rotten fruit —stuff we Pickers left on the ground because it was so soft it was more like snail slime than apples or pears—then cooked it and left it in the pots of the steam catcher for a few weeks. Then they'd cook it again and catch the steam and turn it back into water. But this new water, Rose said, was like fire. It could even burn. The Jimsons drank it if they ran out of dried leaves, even though it usually made them sick. If they were still sick the next morning, their Headmasters made them regret it even more.

The steam catcher was one of the things that Papa warned me to stay away from. Sometimes it blew up, and pipes went flying every which way. Last time that happened, Bullfrog got awfully scalded. After that, the skin on one side of his face got hard and ridged like oak bark, and his right eye looked like a lump of dirty snow. Some people wanted the Jimsons to stop making the burning water, but Jenna said it was good to have some of it to use in the Ward, where she helped people who got sick or hurt. I remember her pouring it onto my leg after I fell on the stick. It burned, all right.

Once, I crept up to the steam catcher when the Jimsons were burning their leaves in the compound. I knew they were floating away into their clouds of smoke and wouldn't notice me. I held my breath and jabbed it with a stick, then ran away.

The Listeners also gathered during the slackenings. They met in Gehenna—Papa said it used to be called the gym—where they sat facing the Teller, who stood in front of them on a much higher platform, kind of like in the Meal House. Papa told me the Teller was even older than he was and that he'd been spinning his story every slackening for more than fifty years.

During the grip, when the Headmasters made us do our toil, the Teller didn't want us to call him the Teller. Then he was just Virgil the Slopper. He took the big buckets of slop from the collection room and carried them to the corn fields and turnip fields, where he emptied them. He'd been doing that for more than fifty years, too. When it was warm, he spread it around the furrows with a rake and worked it into the soil. In the winter, when the ground was like iron, he dumped it on the snow-blanketed fields until they were dotted with hundreds of black piles of frozen excrement. I wondered how much longer he'd be able to lug around the heavy buckets of human waste, but his old arms were still thick with muscles.

Papa told me Virgil had first started telling his story to himself as he carried the buckets of slop back and forth from the Cube to the fields. "He did it to keep his own mind right, but then he figured others might need stories, too. So he'd think something up while he was toiling with the slop and then tell it during the slackening to whoever showed up."

"Is it hard to tell a story?" I'd asked him. We were standing on the bridge again.

"I don't know," Papa had replied. "Not for him, I guess. He said he started the story with characters from a play he'd seen before he got here. Before the Arrival. And then he just thought of new things to have happen to them."

"What are characters?

"Characters are people who don't really exist."

This was puzzling. How could they be people, I wondered, if they don't exist? Were they dead? "And what's a play?"

Papa frowned and shook his head. "I shouldn't have even mentioned it."

"Please," I said, putting my hand on his elbow. "Please tell me, Papa. I need something to think about when I'm picking."

He took a big breath. There was nobody around, but he leaned closer and lowered his voice. "A play was where people made themselves remember words that somebody wanted them to say—a conversation, like we're having right now. Then those people—they were called actors—they all went into a special building and took turns saying those words to each other and walking around while other people watched them and listened to them."

I frowned, not fully understanding. It sounded kind of like what the Teller did in Gehenna, but there was only one of him. I'd think about it more during the next day's toil.

After a moment, I asked, "Why did you need them?"

"Need what, Maple?"

"The stories. The ones Virgil—I mean the Teller—started telling. You said people needed them."

"Because—" His face clouded, and he hesitated. But I knew

he was going to tell me. He was just putting the words together in the right way.

"Because after the Arrival, a lot of us were very sad." Then he stopped again and eyed me as if he had two things in his head, and he was trying to decide which one was heavier. He sighed. "We were beyond sad. We were broken. Like eggshells. We couldn't close our eyes without seeing what the Headmasters had taken from us—and how they'd taken it. When Virgil started telling his story, it helped keep the old world alive. It gave us hope that we might one day get it back."

He stopped and leaned wearily against the iron railing of the bridge. "But false hope, I guess. And now, all the people here—all the Originals except me and Jenna and Virgil—all of them have been born into this. They don't know what life was like before the Arrival. And we can't tell them. History doesn't exist for them. Traditions don't exist. It's just one day after another."

"But doesn't Virgil's story still show them what it was like? That old place?"

"Not really. The Teller soon learned it was dangerous for others if his stories were too—too real. Too memorable. So he started changing things and made a new world in his stories, so they wouldn't trigger old memories. His stories became no more real than the things the Jimsons see in their puffs of smoke. Or like the stories about the boy and the bear I used to tell you when you were still in the Aery."

"Were the boy and the bear characters?"

"That's right."

"Did you make up those stories?"

"No."

"Bears can't really talk," I said.

"No," he replied, "they can't."

Then there were the Thankfuls, a group Rose warned me about.

"You've seen the people who tie a strip of black nylar around their head?" Rose asked me. We were working on a mulberry bush, looking for the few berries the robins and blue jays hadn't stolen.

"The ones who walk around with their arms folded on their chests?"

"That's them," Rose replied. "Those are Thankfuls. And I'll be thankful if you stay away from them. If any of them ever try to talk to you, just nod and head in the other direction."

Of course, as soon as she said this, I wanted to find a Thankful and talk to them. But not long after, Papa warned me about them, too. And his description scared me.

"Never go to the fourth floor of the Cube," is what he'd told me. "That's where they gather during the slackenings. Keep clear of them."

"Why, Papa? Why is everyone so worried about them?"

He paused before answering. "They're different from the rest of us. They think the Headmasters are a—a blessing. That means a good thing. They hate the slackenings because, for those few hours, we don't have the Headmasters controlling us. It terrifies them, having to make their own decisions, having to think. They're like ducklings when something happens to the mother duck—they don't know what to do without their Headmaster's grip."

"What do they do up there? On the fourth floor?"

"They get into a huddle and chant. They say they're talking with their Headmasters. Communing with them, that's what they call it. But I think they're just trying to push the world away. One of the wood gatherers got lured into them last year.

His sole partner went up there to try to get him back. But the Thankfuls made a circle around him and drowned her out with their chanting."

"What's chanting?"

"Saying the same thing at the same time over and over."

That sounded pretty creepy. "What do they say?"

"Something like, 'Return to us—extend yourselves—fill your empty vessels—hear our plea.' Things like that."

"Do they?"

"What? Hear their plea? Probably not. Jenna thinks that during the slackenings, the Headmasters are busy sorting through all the sensory stuff they collect through us every day. Kind of like we do when we dream. I mean, when we used to dream."

"So, the slackenings are when the Headmasters are sleeping?"

"That's sort of what Jenna thinks."

"Then what are they doing when we're sleeping? I mean, during the darkenings?"

Papa shrugged before answering. "I think that's when they use our minds to talk to each other."

The last group I learned about was the Frolics. I'd heard others mention them, but whenever I asked Papa or Rose, they'd start talking about something else. So I went to Lark to find out, and after I'd asked her about ten times, she finally told me.

It was near the end of a slackening, but the evening was still luminous with the pale blue light that fills the sky at the end of the long days of summer. Lark and I were sitting cross-legged, facing each other in the enormous metal sign that stood near the old iron gate that led into the Blue Ring compound. The letter we were in was the one at the very end—it looked like an egg with a curling tail. I couldn't read, of course, but I knew what reading was. Papa had told me it was a way of making words so that what you said stayed after you left. I even knew what a couple of the letters were. The one Lark and I were sitting in was called "jee." The one that went up, down, up, down was called "em," and it was what my name started with. Papa told me there was even one that went zigzag like a lightning bolt, but I'd never seen it.

"The Frolics do sex things," is what Lark finally said with a sigh after I'd worn her down with my pestering.

I'd heard of sex. "With who?" I asked.

"With each other. There's about thirty of them."

I pondered this revelation for a few moments. Around us, the crickets chirped, and the grasshoppers whirred.

"Men and women?" I asked.

"Yes. And some who don't see themselves as just one or the other."

"They do this every slackening?"

"Maybe. Probably."

"For the entire slackening? Aren't they tired out from toil?"

"I don't know, Maple. This is what I've heard."

"Where do they do it?"

"In the drying room in the Cube. They spread the blankets and wraps that Fern hasn't washed yet on the floor. To make it softer."

I suddenly felt very aware of how my shirt and trousers, damp with sweat, were clinging to my skin.

"Why don't they want to be with just one person? Like Rose and Cardinal?"

"A sole partner? Some people want to have one person all their life, and some don't."

More pondering.

"Did Papa have a sole partner?"

"I think so. A long time ago."

"Why doesn't he talk about her?"

"He can't. He's not supposed to."

Still more pondering.

"How do they . . . the Frolics . . . how do they do the sex with . . . I mean, don't their Headmasters get in the way?"

Lark rolled her eyes and exhaled loudly. "Oh, for shit's sake," she said. I'd never heard her swear before. Papa didn't want us to. "Come over here." She jumped out of the egg with the curling tail, and I followed her over to the waist-high, flat surface of another shape in the Blue Ring sign. It had a thick coating of dust.

"Like this," she said as she sketched in the grime with her finger. "Or like this," as she drew three new figures.

"Okay," I said, trying to imagine what expressions might be on the round circles of the figures' faces. "I get it. You're a good drawer. They really look like people. Are they anybody in particular?"

"No." Lark sighed again. "They're just something I had to draw for my annoying little sister." She leaned forward and, with one hand, swept away her sketches.

I said the Frolics were the last group, but actually, there was one more—sort of. The Grubbers. The Grubbers were the only toil crew that was also a slackening group. During the grip, their Headmasters made them tramp out into the forest and scrabble around on their hands and knees, looking under fallen logs and wet leaves for worms and grubs. And mushrooms. Whatever they found, they dropped into their buckets and took back to the kitchen in the Meal House for the Biscuiteers, just like we Pickers did with fruits and berries.

During the slackenings, the Grubbers stuck together, and nobody else joined them. Other slackening groups—like the Jimsons, the Listeners, the Frolics, even the Thankfuls—were made of all different kinds of toilers. But the Grubbers stuck to themselves. "They're a moody bunch"—that's what Silex said— "but I would be too if I had to snort through the dirt all day like a skunk."

The Grubbers mostly sat around in the compound or the Meal House during the slackenings, muttering and making fun of whoever happened to pass by. So it wasn't a surprise that when fights broke out, a Grubber was usually involved.

But others got into scraps, too. Sometimes it was the Frolics when one of them got jealous and didn't want to share someone with someone else. And sometimes one Jimson would accuse another Jimson of breathing in too much smoke from a roll of smouldering leaves—but since they were Jimsons, most of their swings and kicks missed their targets, and it wasn't long before they forgot what they were fighting about.

When fights did happen, the brawlers were careful not to seriously hurt each other. Punches to the body were acceptable. So were slaps to the face and biting and pulling hair. The Headmasters didn't care about minor injuries like that.

But if someone got so hurt that it affected their toil—like a broken collarbone or a gouged eye—then at the beginning of the next day's grip, the Headmasters would punish both scrappers with the jolts. They might do this again the next morning and the day after that.

It was even worse if someone got killed, and it didn't matter if it was accidental or not. The killer got the jolts every day for the rest of his life. And everyone else—except the kids in the Aery—also got the jolts every day for a long time. As far as the

Headmasters were concerned, we were all guilty of not preventing the loss of one of their hosts.

That hadn't happened in a long time. Silex once told me— quietly, which was rare for him—that the killer was Fern, the old woman I'd met in my cubicle right after I was harvested. She was one of the two Washers whose toil was to collect dirty blankets and wraps and then wash and hang them to dry in the basement of the Cube. Even now, years after the killing, Fern still got a daily jolt. It always happened in the Meal House during morning meal, so everyone had to watch. That suited some people just fine. They hadn't forgiven Fern for the weeks of jolts they endured after she stabbed her sole partner to death for what he did to her during the slackenings. They liked to see her suffer.

There was one other thing that resulted in everyone getting punished with jolts—as I would soon learn.

CHAPTER 6
THE BERSERKER

Berserk. That's what we called it when someone was seized with an irresistible urge to uncouple from their Headmaster. Papa warned me about it before I saw it for myself. He'd seen it happen at least fourteen times.

He said you sometimes knew when a person was heading toward berserk. You could see it come on slowly over the course of a couple of weeks. First, they'd start to blink faster and make horrible grins as if two fishhooks were jagging back the corners of their mouth. A few days later, they'd start to rub their hands together, rub and rub till they got blisters and the skin started peeling off. After that, they'd pull out their eyelashes and clumps of hair and catch bugs and tear off their legs and wings. A few more days and something in them would snap: all of a sudden, they'd reach behind their neck, grab the coils that burrowed into the base of their skull and yank. A moment later, they'd drop dead.

Other times, they'd just go berserk out of the blue—no warning, no sign, like the way an old pine tree will sometimes just lean and fall, almost before you have time to jump out of its way. I was with Papa once, on the path to the bridge, when one of the Inwards ahead of us stopped in her tracks and grabbed at one of her Headmaster's coils. She fell like a sack of walnuts, her face mashing into a big black stone beside the trail.

No matter how it happened, slow or fast, everyone got punished if a berserker died. So, if someone started showing signs—the gradual kind—we put them in the Box during the slackenings to keep them safe. The Box was a small room in the Menders Hall with a metal door and no windows. On the outside, the Menders had fastened steel rings on both sides of the door frame, so when you slid a bar through, the door couldn't be opened from the inside. The room was bare: no table, no chair, no cot. Just a big iron hook in the middle of the ceiling.

After they were led or dragged to the Box, the berserker's hands were tied together with one end of a long rope. The other end of the rope was looped up over the ceiling hook, and they were hoisted up till their feet were almost off the floor. That way, they couldn't reach behind their head, ram themselves into the walls, or slam themselves onto the floor. No one liked treating berserkers this way. It wasn't for punishment. Locked in the Box, they howled in terror, pleading to be let out, begging someone to pull the thing off their back. Even with the door of the Box closed, you could still hear them shrieking all the way across the compound.

When the slackening was almost over, two or three men would go to the Box to get the berserker ready for the darkening. They'd lower the berserker from the hook, tie their feet together, then truss their hands to their feet with a short length of rope so they couldn't stand or straighten out. They'd carry the berserker back to their cubicle, set them down on their cot, then hurry back to their own cubicles just before the darkening descended.

The next morning, as soon as the darkening ended and the

grip began, someone would go to the berserker's cubicle and untie them. They weren't a danger to themselves during the grip. Their Headmaster kept extra strong control over them, preventing them from acting on their deadly urge, though they still howled and grimaced throughout the grip like a lynx with a broken leg.

This happened every day until the berserker's obsession started to fade. Papa said that usually happened after about one moon cycle. You could tell because their screams softened to moans, then whimpers, then weeping, then nothing but silence. At that point, they didn't have to go back into the Box.

But they were never the same as before, Papa said. Their eyes looked flat and dull, like a stunned frog's. They were like wisps of smoke from a fire that had almost burned itself out.

catatonic

That's usually what happened when someone started to go berserk. But it's not what happened to Sleet late that summer. Sleet was one of the Wipers. Their toil was to roam around the Aery, the Meal House, and all the floors of the Cube, rubbing the walls with a white stuff they cooked up from ashes and bones and animal guts the Biscuiteers threw away. The white stuff smelled awful—you'd feel a stab under your eyes if you took a close whiff—but it stopped black mould from growing on the walls or at least held it back. Black mould, Jenna said, was tiny mushrooms that got into your chest and made you very sick.

Sleet was tied up and hoisted onto the hook in the Box as soon as others saw the signs. Every slackening, his condition got worse. He screamed till his voice was ragged. He bit the end of his tongue off.

Then one day, when somebody went to untie him at the

end of the slackening, they found him hanging from the hoist—dead. One arm dangled by his side. Somehow, he'd wriggled a hand free. That's all he needed.

His Headmaster wasn't on his back. After it terminated him, it had detached and crawled over onto his face. It had burrowed its coils into his eyes.

His eyes. According to Jenna, his Headmaster likely acted so spitefully because it sensed there weren't any kids in the Aery old enough to become its new host. That meant the other Headmasters would make us store it on a shelf in the Ward until one of the kids got big enough to fit it. While it waited, Jenna said, the hostless Headmaster was likely disconnected from the others, unable to communicate with them. Isolated. And probably not happy about it. Assuming they could feel things like happiness.

Jenna had to look at the Headmaster sitting on the shelf—the one that came off Sleet—every day for ten moon cycles. She said she often thought about taking it during a slackening and chucking it into the river so that it would get carried too far away to be found. But of course, she'd never actually do that. The punishment the other Headmasters would have inflicted on us would have been unimaginable.

The morning after Sleet's body was found, news of what he'd done was muttered quickly from table to table in the Meal House. Before long, we all knew what was coming. It would probably happen that morning at the end of first meal before we were sent out to toil.

I fell to the ground when the first jolt hit. It felt like somebody had rammed their hand through my skull and made a fist in my brain. Then it hit again, even worse. And again. The pain was like nothing I'd ever felt before. It was like skinning a squirrel alive and then letting it run through the dirt and dry leaves on the forest floor.

But it wasn't just physical agony. As the fifth and sixth and seventh jolts hit, I was filled with horror. With dread. A dread of nothing—of nothingness. It was as if the layers of my very being were stripped away until only a void was left, an emptiness so absolute, so dark and bleak, that it defied thought. It was this feeling not the physical pain—that I most remembered after the jolting stopped.

I would always carry that with me: a scar in my brain.

trauma

CHAPTER 7
THE TELLER

As summer wore on, it got even hotter and more humid. We'd moved on to the blueberries and hawberries, and picking was more tiring in the sticky heat, even though I was used to climbing and scrabbling around on rocks and tree roots to reach the bushes.

Sometimes, when the grip ended, I'd head back to my cubicle like I did back when I was first harvested and fall straight to sleep. Other times, when I felt up to it or when my cubicle was stifling—its outer wall faced west and got the last of the day's sun—I'd go to the bridge, where it always seemed cooler. There I'd talk with Papa and maybe Lark and River while the rest of the Inwards melted into the forest to meditate without him.

I was planning on doing that one evening as I trudged back from toil with the other Pickers. But then Thorn asked me if I wanted to go listen to the Teller.

"Why?" I replied. "With who?"

"With me," he said. He frowned and kicked at a stone by his foot.

"You should go," Rose said. "The Teller will make you

see things you never imagined. I'm going, too." The Headmasters had terminated Rose's sole partner—Cardinal—toward the end of spring. He'd cut his foot on a scrap of rusty metal behind the Meal Hall. Not a deep cut, but he got sicker and sicker till one morning, he couldn't get off his cot, no matter how many times his Headmaster jolted him. After they terminated him, Rose began going to the Teller every slackening. A couple of moon cycles later, Silex started going with her.

"We won't crowd the two of you," Silex added, smiling. I wasn't sure what he meant. Gehenna, where the Teller told his stories, was one of the biggest buildings at Blue Ring. There was lots of room.

I turned to Thorn and nodded. "Let's go."

I'd never gone into Gehenna before. As soon as I stepped through the double doorway, I was struck by the echoing chitter of noise. The high ceiling was crisscrossed with metal struts, and on the struts perched hundreds of birds: sparrows, wrens, starlings, martins, nuthatches, robins, larks, cardinals, and pigeons—lots and lots of pigeons.

Plastered against the walls, too high to reach, were hundreds of swallow nests made of mud, grass, and bird spit. Some of the swallows were swooping from one nest to another. The din of chirping and squawking and cooing and flapping was almost overwhelming.

"We'll need one of these," Thorn announced as he picked up a sheet of nylar from a pile by the door.

I could see why. A dozen people were already sitting on the floor, facing the balcony where the Teller would soon appear. All of them were draped under nylar sheets like the one we'd just taken. You could tell who'd been there longest by the number of bird droppings on their sheets. Some of the Listeners had brought blocks of wood to sit on. Some were chewing on leftover biscuit wedges or potatoes they'd just boiled, the steam still wafting up from them.

The Teller—Virgil—had already arrived and was scraping the droppings from the floor with a sheet of metal tied to a stick. More accurately, he was spreading them around so they'd dry more quickly.

Thorn and I pulled the nylar sheet over our heads and walked to a spot Virgil had just cleared. We sat.

I leaned toward Thorn and whispered, "What was this place for? I mean, before the Arrival."

"They did running games here. With sticks and balls filled with air. See those boards?" He pointed at one end of the long room we were in and then the other. "They used to have rings on them, and dribblers ran back and forth to drop the balls through them."

"How do you know all that?"

Thorn ignored my question.

"They called it *sport*," he added. He paused. "Don't tell anyone I told you that."

"People must have been taller back then," I said as I gazed up at the boards where the sport rings used to be.

By now, the Teller had gone outside and returned through another entrance that led up to a balcony.

magda   roman

I felt a strange and sudden chill as others continued to drift in around us.

I leaned toward Thorn again. "Why does he do his Telling here with birds crapping down on everybody? Why not outside or in the Meal House?"

"He likes the echo in here—how it makes him sound. And

he doesn't care about the falling crap. You know what he does during the grip, right?"

I did. Emptying the slop buckets the rest of us filled after we woke up from the darkening.

"Anyway," Thorn continued, "he won't do his telling anywhere else. So if we want to hear his story, we have to come here."

"Let us begin!" the Teller abruptly cried out from the edge of the balcony. In an instant, the birds stopped chirping and cooing and bent their heads to eye him with interest. His bare skull gleamed with sweat, and his eyes glimmered. I wondered when the first bird would crap on him.

"I see that some of us are neophytes," he shouted, looking toward me, "so we will commence by recapitulating the most recent and salient segments of our saga." He accompanied these words with big gestures, pulling his arms into his chest and clasping his hands together as he said the word *recapitulate*. He began.

> "Lo! I sing the narrative of a nation,
> of a people who arose long ago
> from a confluence of strangers,
> a courageous community led by a man
> and a woman, a husband and wife
> who had sole-partnered for life.
> The man they called Orlando.
> His wife was known to most as Rosalind,
> though a favoured few addressed her as Roz.
>
> "Those two progenitors—Orlando and
>   Rosalind—
> have long passed from our story. They lived four
>   score

and seven years, and sired many scions,
many children and great-grandchildren, before
*   meeting*
their demise in the same instant, cradled
in one another's arms, at the hands of the
ghastly Gunther, he who had plotted against
them all their lives. Their peerless progeny
live on in the silvery syllables of our story,
seeking to eschew the continued malignant
malevolence of Gunther, who has lamentably
lengthened his loathsome lifespan by stealing
life's vital essence from infants—mere babes
in arms—whom he abducts every full moon
and then savagely slaughters."

Someone right behind us gasped, but she didn't really sound shocked—it was more like she was doing it for the Teller's sake or maybe for mine. The Teller himself was getting more animated, his face glowing with intensity, his arms waving about as he spoke.

"I don't understand a lot of his words," I whispered to Thorn. "Is he making them up?"

"They're real words," Thorn replied. "Just old ones. I bet your Papa knows them. If you don't understand them, just guess what they mean."

The Teller continued.

"As you recall from our last interlude,
Gunther has followed the new Orlando
and Rosalind—those names having been
bestowed successively on each new
generation—followed them to a new city,
a huge metropolis dubbed Freedonia,

a shining city on a heavenly hill,
perched on the peak of a precipitous
promontory.

"Woefully, their attempt to elude him,
to gain time and means to reconnoitre
with family and friends, has been to no avail.
They do not realize that some weeks prior,
Gunther, under perfidious pretense,
had cunningly contrived to be hired
as a bewhiskered barista in a busy bistro
where Orlando often betook himself
for brunch and beverage. There, Gunther
had sneakily secreted a tiny ticking tracking
device into Orlando's bean-and-barley
bisque. That device now resides in Orlando's
befuddled bowels, relaying his every move
to his nefarious nemesis like a
tattling tell-all tufted titmouse.

"Now Gunther has clambered up, up, and up
to the belfry of a cathedral kittycorner
to the fifth-floor flat where Orlando and
Rosalind have betaken themselves. There—"

The Teller pointed to the high, curving ceiling, where the
birds continued to perch and watch in silence.

"—he has fashioned a fantastic fortress
of fiendishness from flotsam found around
the floor of the belfry, a fitting lair
for the leering liar that he is.
By means of his sorcerer's spyglass,

Gunther perceives that the pair of paramours
have passed the afternoon unpacking
their oodles of attire: trousers from Dulce
Banana, sensuous silk shirts from Prawna,
shoes for their feet, dozens of them, from the
most bountiful boutiques in all of Cornucopia.
'They will be famished,' Gunther murmurs to
himself as he lays a fusty finger on his chin.
'I divine they shall soon order some
delectable funistrada, or perchance pasta
a la poutina.' He cackles quietly as a scurrilous
scheme skulks in his mendacious mind.
'I shall deceive the delivery person,' he decides,
'as he or she descends from his or her autocart.'
Gunther declares this out loud to better
savour the umami of his own evil intent.
'I shall expropriate their repast as it
is borne toward them and deliver it myself
to my unwitting victims.' He feverishly fondles
the propulsive pipe tucked within the left pocket
of his pestiferous pantaloons, the trabecular tube
through which he will puff deadly darts
of vile viper venom. Thus resolved, like a wily
weasel from a bush of brambles, he slinks
from his belfry . . ."

"Maple, wake up." Thorn was gently shaking my arm. I'd fallen asleep leaning against him. "The slackening's going to end. We need to get back to our cubicles."

I nodded, mumbled something incoherent about Gunther, and got myself up. A few minutes later, I was in my cot and sleeping. Just before the darkening came, I dreamed about eating something called a funistrada.

CHAPTER 8
THE RULE

I was dangling my legs over the edge of the bridge, Papa sitting on one side of me, Thorn on the other. We were sweating out the lingering heat of a long, windless day, too tired to do anything more than try to toss pebbles onto leaves that floated past us below. It hadn't rained in weeks, and the river had shrunk from its banks, the current slowing to a ripple so gentle the pond skaters rested on the water's smooth surface with their six thin legs, spinning in slow circles as they drifted along.

clockwise diba'igeziswaan

After we'd almost used up our handfuls of pebbles, Thorn climbed down the riverbank to gather more near the iron footing of the bridge. It was then that I finally asked Papa something I'd been wondering about since spring.

"You used to have a sole partner, Papa?"

He raised his eyebrows and hesitated before replying. "Yes. A wife. I was her husband. That's what we called each other back then."

I tossed one last pebble at Thorn as he clambered along the

water's edge below. He looked up and smiled when it splashed beside him.

I turned back to Papa. "You haven't told me about her. Not ever."

"That's true." He took a deep breath and then exhaled slowly between his parted lips. "That's because we don't talk about the ones who've gone. The ones who've died. That's part of the Rule."

"I know," I said, nodding—but I didn't. I knew there was a Rule, but I didn't know what it was. Nobody had ever told me. Nobody ever talked about it. Maybe the rule was to not talk about the Rule.

I glanced sideways at Papa, wondering if my question had troubled him. But his eyes were clear and bright. I returned my gaze to the river, following the current to where it bent around the base of the gorge and vanished from view.

"It's a natural question, Maple," he said as if he'd sensed my concern. "Everyone asks it eventually—after they're harvested."

We don't talk about the ones who've gone. I pondered this, swinging my dangling legs back and forth. My bare feet were still dusty from our walk to the bridge, all the way up to my ankles.

"What about Farley? Can we talk about him? He's dead, but he was never a person."

Papa was silent for a long time. I knew he wasn't ignoring my question. He was thinking.

"With me, you can talk about Farley," he finally replied. "But you shouldn't with anyone else."

"Not even with River or Lark? Or Thorn?" I asked, frowning. My wrists were beginning to tighten and ache.

"Best if you don't."

"Why?" I said sharply as I scrambled to my feet. "Why

can't I talk about Farley? And why can't you talk about her—your wife? Don't you remember her?"

He winced as I said this, then smiled sadly. "I remember her, Maple. I remember so much. And I wish I could tell you and Lark and River about her. But I can't. It's not safe."

My heart was thumping hard in my chest. My face felt hot, and a lump was squeezing in my throat.

"So when you're gone," I stammered, "I won't be able to talk to anyone about you? Why, Papa?"

He looked at me but didn't reply. His eyes glistened.

At that moment, I heard Thorn's footsteps pounding on the bridge. He ran up to us, out of breath, a load of pebbles carried snugly against his belly in a fold of his nylar shirt. He stopped as still as an oak stump when he saw our faces etched with sorrow.

"It's okay, Thorn," Papa said, beckoning him closer. "Sit beside us again. Let's divvy up the pebbles you've collected." I knew Papa was getting me to focus on something else for a few minutes. Thorn carefully counted them out into our open hands. They felt cool and damp. I rubbed my fingers against the fine, grey silt on their surfaces.

After a moment, Papa spoke again. "Maple, when a garter snake gets too big for its skin, what does it do?"

"It slides out of it," I said. "Sheds it."

"There's a new skin underneath," Thorn added.

Pap nodded. "Does a tree do that?"

"Of course not," I replied sulkily.

"Then how does the tree get bigger?" asked Papa.

"Every spring, a new layer grows under the bark," Thorn said. "That's why they've got rings." It annoyed me that Thorn blurted this out before I had a chance to.

"That's right," Papa said. "The oldest ring—the smallest one—is the one in the centre of the tree." He paused to drop a pebble. "Got one," he announced as it fell onto a leaf, momentarily submerging it.

"Birch leaves don't count," I snapped. "We said elm." Sometimes Papa's explanations seemed more like riddles. What did snakes and trees have to do with not talking about dead people?

"Having a Headmaster," he continued, "is kind of like being a tree. When a Headmaster attaches, it starts to seep up the memories of that person. And when that person eventually dies, those memories stay in the Headmaster even after it's coupled to the next person."

My brow furrowed. I didn't like the sound of that. "You mean the memories of the people who had my Headmaster before me," I said slowly, "are still in it? Inside it?"

"Maybe not all their memories," Papa replied. "But at least some of them. So when a new person gets coupled to a Headmaster, their new memories start to grow around those old memories. Like tree rings. Deep in the centre are the oldest memories—the ones from the Headmaster's first host. And then the memories of the next oldest host around those memories. And so on, till you get to the person who has the Headmaster now."

Thorn had been nodding while Papa was talking. I got the feeling he already knew about this.

I frowned and bit softly at my lip. "Then why can't I see those other people's memories? The ones from the people who had my Headmaster before me."

"Sometimes that happens," Thorn said, leaning toward me, before Papa could reply. "But then you go crazy."

Papa gently put his hand on Thorn's arm. "Hold on there," he said to him. "Let's not get ahead of ourselves."

Thorn blushed, then muttered, "That's what Silex told me."

Papa turned back to me and continued. "Yes, that can happen. It's called the seizures."

I nodded. I'd overheard people talking about the seizures. Not often, but when they did, they used the same hushed voice as when they mentioned the berserkers.

"The seizures happen," Papa continued, "when one of the memories from a previous host surfaces in your own memory. That's dangerous. Imagine the middle of a tree gets heart rot— you don't want the rot to spread to the outer layers."

He paused to let me process what he'd told me.

"What do the seizures do?" I asked.

"The first time it happens," Papa said, grimacing, "you get very confused, and you fall down. If no one wakes you up, you might die. If it ever happens again—if more memories from a previous host emerge—it gets worse. More confusion, more mind chaos, until eventually, your brain just breaks like an old rope. You go into what's called a coma. And nobody can wake you up."

"Then the Headmasters kill you," Thorn said. "They squirt their poison into your brain." Papa nodded but then frowned when Thorn added, "Or else they do the blood punishment."

"What's that?" I asked him.

"They make someone else kill you," Thorn replied.

"Why?" I asked.

"Probably to remind us they can make us do anything they want."

"No, I mean, why does your brain break when you get the old memories?"

I saw Thorn open his mouth to reply, but Papa raised his hand to catch his attention, and Thorn fell silent.

"The dog you were asking about—" Papa said to me.

"Farley."

"Farley. Imagine he was still alive, and he's right behind me, sitting in the middle of the bridge and scratching his ear. Then imagine you're on one end of the bridge, and Thorn's on the other, and you're both calling him at the same time. He'd find that confusing, wouldn't he?"

"No," I scoffed. "He'd come to me because he liked me more. I'm the one who brought him leftover biscuit from the Aery." Papa raised an eyebrow, and Thorn frowned. "But I understand what you mean," I added.

"If he was really confused, he might not come to either of us," Thorn said, looking to Papa before speaking further. "He might stay put, or maybe he'd even jump into the river to get away."

I shook my head. Farley wouldn't have done that.

Papa continued. "The seizures can be triggered if you hear someone say something about the past. The words can make an old memory—from one of your Headmaster's previous hosts—come into your mind. That's why we don't speak of the dead. Or the past at all, if we can help it. That's the Rule. Or part of it."

I nodded solemnly. What Papa was telling me made me feel more grown up. As if he'd decided I was ready to be told something important. Something that only adults knew.

"What's the other part of the Rule?" I asked.

"That we don't talk about the Rule unless we have to," Papa replied. "Like right now."

I was right.

"One thing I've wondered," Thorn said, rushing ahead like always, "is why you can't trigger a previous host's memory in yourself?"

Papa shrugged and pushed his broken spectacles farther up his nose. "Nobody knows. We learned a long time ago that a past host's memories can only be triggered by hearing somebody else say something. Or by reading something. That's why we got rid of all the things that still had words in them—reports, diaries, letters, books. They all got thrown into the river. To protect us from the memories they contained."

I felt Thorn flinch beside me, and when I glanced over at him, he looked uncomfortable. He gave me a weak smile, then opened his hand and let the rest of his pebbles trickle into the river.

"Have you ever had the seizures, Papa?" I asked.

"No. And there's a reason for that." He paused and looked at us both as if he wanted us to explain why.

Thorn answered first. "Nobody else has ever had your Headmaster. It doesn't have anybody else's memories in it."

"That's right," Papa replied. "Who else is like that?"

I recalled my conversation with Papa from a few days ago. "Virgil and Jenna," I said. "You were all here when the Arrival happened. The three of you are a lot older than everyone else."

"We're the last of the Originals," Papa said with a sad smile. "All the other people who were here at the Arrival—they've died. So the Headmasters that they had have all been coupled to people who were born after the Arrival."

"So you can't ever get the seizures, Papa," I said, feeling relieved.

He nodded. "But apart from me and Jenna and Virgil, it can happen to anyone. Including you. And Thorn. That's why we have the Rule."

"And that's why you said I can talk to you about Farley. It's not going to trigger anybody else's memories in you."

"Yes, but it's still not entirely safe. The person who had your Headmaster before you—"

"Kestrel," I interjected, trying to be helpful.

Papa's raised his bushy eyebrows. He looked alarmed. "How do you know his name?"

"Knot told me." It was actually Silex, but I didn't want to get him in trouble.

Papa frowned. "He shouldn't have done that."

"He probably forgot about the Rule," Thorn said. "Knot doesn't . . . think very well."

"I know that," Papa continued, "but just by saying that name, he could have made an old memory surface in Maple. It could have given her the seizures."

But it didn't, was what I was about to say. I decided not to.

"Anyway, Maple, what I was going to tell you is this. Yes, it's safe for you to tell me about Farley—there's no danger to me. And you can't trigger a previous host's memory in yourself. But I shouldn't talk to you about him because Kes—because the person who had your Headmaster before you also had memories of Farley. So if I say something about Farley, that might trigger an old memory in you."

"But you're talking about him right now. About Farley," Thorn said. "And when you had us imagine calling him on the bridge."

Papa sighed. "I know that, Thorn. According to the Rule, I shouldn't be mentioning him to either of you. I try to follow it because it's what we all decided a long time ago. But sometimes . . ."

He shrugged, and his words trailed off. But he must have sensed I was thinking again about Farley. "I know how hard it is, Maple. Believe me, I know. When the Arrival happened, there were more than two hundred people at Blue Ring. They walked on this bridge, sat right where we're sitting, ate with the same spoons we still use, drank from the same cups. But the only people who remember them now are me, Jenna, and Virgil. The three of us can talk about them among ourselves but not with anyone else. We can't tell you their names. We can't tell you about the brave things they did or the sacrifices they made. When we're gone, the last memory of them will vanish with us."

I turned toward Papa and took his hand in mine. I saw him in a way I never had before. I stared at his bowed head—wrinkled, a fringe of grey hair encircling it—and thought about all the forgotten people walking around inside it.

CHAPTER 9
THERE'S A SQUIRREL IN YOUR PANTS

The mornings were getting cooler. Often, not till the sun was high in the sky could I feel its light falling warm on my skin. But as fall came on and the days grew shorter, what I noticed most were the changing sounds of the forest. The leaves rustled more crisply. Our feet scraped over the rocks and roots more harshly, as if the air had become dry and thin. The trees grew quieter as the songbirds left, replaced by the far-off, discordant calls of geese, who passed over us in arrow-like formations. Papa said they were flying to warmer places, but I wasn't sure what he meant. Didn't fall and winter come everywhere?

We'd been picking apples for almost a full moon cycle and still weren't done with them. Yet one morning, after we left the Meal House and retrieved the sledges, the Headmasters surprised us, and we found ourselves trudging south instead of east, where the remaining apples were.

"They're moving us on to pears," Silex said. "Must be a real cold snap coming, and they want them picked before they freeze and get mushy. Hard to store mushy pears. Apples can handle the cold better." He then added, turning to me, "Sometimes the Headmasters know the coming weather better than us. Better than the crows, even."

"Thanks to my knees and hips," said Crest. "My old bones tell them when a frigid spell is on its way."

I laughed at what Crest had said.

"Girl," she replied—she often called me that, but in a kind way—"I'm not pulling your leg. The changing weather galls my joints."

Pulling my leg? My feet were steady on the ground. Sometimes the older people said peculiar things.

"Headmasters don't just use our eyes and ears," she continued, huffing hard as she tried to keep up with us. "They go piggyback on what we feel, too. Even taste and smell. Long time ago, a smoulder started in the Cube, middle of a darkening. Probably a rat gnawing a current wire from the wind tower. They jolted everyone awake and made us grab our slop jars and run like jackrabbits up to the third floor and throw whatever was in them onto the flames. After that, they made us stand there to watch it didn't flare up again. What a stink. That's when I saw Tamarack looking out a window, so I looked too. The sky was black as a raven and spangled with more stars than I'd ever seen—."

"Crest!" Rose cried as she slowed her steps and realized what Crest was telling us. "Hush!"

But it was too late. Thorn had already come to a standstill on the rocky trail, staring with dull eyes into the distance. Then he collapsed onto his knees and slumped forward, his head coming to rest on a patch of moss.

"What's wrong with him?" I cried out.

"Memory from a previous host," Silex blurted as he strode over to Thorn. His voice was tight, but he was trying to sound calm. He stretched Thorn out on the trail, face up, then pulled him by the shoulders into a sitting position.

I glanced back at Crest. Her face was twisted with horror. "I did it!" she gasped. "I triggered it! So stupid!" She pushed her fingers through her grey hair. "No, no, no," she wailed as she pounded her head with her palms.

Rose dropped the sledge she'd been dragging and sprinted toward her. "He'll be okay, Crest," she said, hugging her tightly. "It's his first time. Silex will fix him."

Silex had got down onto his knees and was peering into Thorn's open but unseeing eyes. "Look, Thorn," he shouted as he shook him like an apple branch. "There's a squirrel in your pants! A squirrel! Can you believe it, Thorn? And up there on the moon—see those two bear cubs? Dang it, they just flew away. Can you smell the thunder?" Silex shook him harder, making his head flop like a dead snake. "Thorn, is anything better than nothing? Where did you go before you were born?"

The hair on my neck was standing up, and I started to back away. I had no idea what Silex was doing, and it was making me panic.

Silex kept shouting. "How many catfish have we picked, Thorn? Why do we call a pear a pear if there's only one of them? Look at me, Thorn! Do you like my new ear lobes? Come on, Thorn, climb out of that river—it's too deep! Swim, boy! Swim!"

Rose must have noticed my wide eyes and gaping mouth because she beckoned me over. She put an arm around me, still keeping the other one on Crest.

"Don't worry, Maple," she whispered into my ear. "Silex is helping him. He's distracting him from the emerging memory so it doesn't cascade. It's best if he tells him crazy things—things that don't make sense—something to grab his attention."

Even as she was telling me this, Thorn began to blink, and his body relaxed. He shook his head like Farley used to when he got soaked in the rain, then looked straight into Silex's face—barely a handsbreadth from his own.

"What are you doing, Silex?" he muttered. "Why am I on the ground?" He looked down at Silex's big arms enfolding him. "And why are you hugging me?"

Silex burst out laughing, then wiped his berry-stained hand over his sweating brow. "You slipped on some loose acorns, Thorn, and hit your head on that rock. Your hard noggin split it right in two!" More overly hearty laughter from Silex—so loud it made the squirrels start from the branches around us. Still part of his act, I guessed, to keep Thorn's surfacing memory at bay. "But you're okay, and now we've got to get moving. Up, up, get up. Hey—that cloud looks like Rose's moustache. Let's get cracking before they give us a jolt for dawdling. Here, your turn to pull the sledge. Come on, Rose! Crest! Maple!"

And off we went, the whole episode having lasted not much longer than it takes to eat a wedge of biscuit. Thorn walked in front, pulling a sledge, while Silex followed closely behind him, still prattling on about things he saw along the path or pretended to.

"Silex, did you chew on some sassafras root this morning?" Thorn finally asked, sounding exasperated. "You're chattering even more like a magpie than usual."

"That's right, bramble boy," he laughed. "That sassafras perked me right up!"

Bramble boy?

Rose had taken the harness of the second sledge and was pulling it behind Silex and Thorn. She kept glancing over her shoulder at me and Crest.

"We'll tell Thorn in a few days what really happened," Rose whispered to me. "He needs to know about it, but not till that host memory has totally faded."

"Should have known better," Crest was muttering. I wasn't

sure if she was talking to Rose or me or neither of us. "Just slipped my mind. The Rule. Forgetting things. Couldn't find my teeth yesterday." All of Crest's lower teeth had long fallen out. Someone—maybe the Keeper in the wind tower?—had carved her a set from a chunk of walnut root. "Next, I'll be squatting in a puddle of pee, yelling at the clouds. Then what?"

I waited for Rose to say something reassuring to Crest, but she didn't. We kept a brisk pace, and before long, we were at a far meadow ringed by pear trees. I'd never been to it before. Silex and Rose let go of the sledges, and we each grabbed one of the buckets stowed within them. Thorn and I climbed to the higher branches while Rose and Crest picked the pears lower down and Silex the ones that had already fallen to the earth.

No one said anything for a long time. A lone chickadee chirped in a treetop, and the dry leaves rustled in the breeze.

CHAPTER 10
SEPTEMBER 24, 2122

That day, the sun took forever to arc across the sky. I thought the grip would never end. Usually, if I could clear my mind and give it over to my Headmaster, time would pass more quickly. It was like I was half asleep while my body kept reaching and plucking or doing whatever my Headmaster wanted me to do. But after what happened to Thorn, I couldn't get myself to settle. I kept seeing the dull stare that had quenched—if only for a few moments—the usual bright glint in his eyes.

But Thorn said he didn't feel any different than usual, apart from a headache he kept complaining about. He was puzzled he didn't have a lump on his head from smacking it on a rock after slipping on some loose acorns, as Silex had told him.

When we finally trudged back to the compound and deposited the pears at the Meal House, I left the others without saying a word and found Papa. I told him about Thorn. He could tell from the quaver in my voice that I was still upset. He wondered if instead of going to the bridge with the Inwards, the two of us might climb to the top of the Deep. We could talk and watch the fireflies rise from the grass as the sun completed its descent toward the horizon.

"But you told me not to go inside there," I reminded him.

"We won't be inside. There's a staircase on the outer wall at the back. It goes up to the roof."

I was still nervous. The Deep had three floors, and falling from the top or crashing through the roof was not how I wanted to end my day.

As we climbed the metal stairs, our steps making them ring like a bell with every footfall, I recalled how Thorn had told me the Deep used to have a much longer name. *The Deepak Chandra Interdisciplinary Research Commons.* He said it used to be packed with knowledge—knowledge about things we didn't even know had ever existed. Some of that knowledge, he said, had been in the books that were later thrown into the river, so they wouldn't trigger old memories in anyone.

But there were three books they didn't throw away. All three were big and thick, two of them blue and one of them black, and they were kept in a steel box in the Ward, and Jenna would heave them out and open one of them when someone got hurt or sick. She'd flip through the pages for a while and stare at it. Then she'd come over to the person with the broken finger or stomachache or whatever it was and help them. I'd watched her do this when Papa carried me to the Ward after I hurt my leg in the forest. Jenna was the only one still allowed to read, and only those three books.

Still, most of the knowledge in the Deep, Thorn had told me, hadn't even been in books. He said the top two floors of the Deep had been full of blue tables shaped like the crescent moon. On each, there'd been a glass box, and that was where the knowledge was. People used to read words on them. Thorn said the words flew through the air from one glass box to another. I couldn't imagine what it would be like to look up and see words flying over me like geese.

Some of the glass boxes, Thorn said, were still there, in the Deep. But they were cracked and caked with bird droppings. All the words in them had melted away.

Thorn knew that nobody was supposed to go into the Deep. And he knew that I knew that nobody was supposed to go into the Deep. And he knew that I wouldn't tell anyone that he had.

The platform at the top of the staircase wasn't quite as high as the roof, so Papa had to lift me up to it. He was old but still strong from his toil in the Menders' Hall, trying to patch whatever had broken or fallen apart.

"Let's sit on that side," he suggested. I followed, zigzagging around puddles and clumps of milkweed that had taken root on the sagging roof. I was unnerved when I saw him sit down on the ledge and swing his legs over the side.

"It's a long way down," I said, staring at the pile of jagged glass and rusting pipes dumped below.

"You sit on the edge of the bridge all the time," he replied, laughing. "Have you ever fallen off?"

No, I thought, *but water is softer than glass and metal.* Still, I didn't want Papa to think I was still just a kid, so I took a deep breath, sat down on the ledge beside him, and swung my legs over the edge. Once I was settled, it didn't seem so scary. In fact, as I leaned my head against Papa's shoulder and gazed out over the grassy sward that lay between the forest and the Deep, I felt safer than I had since I'd left the Aery.

sward?

"How did this happen, Papa?" I asked, reaching over and

touching a long scar that ran from below his elbow to the middle of his forearm.

"That?" he replied. "I don't remember. Must have bumped into something sharp. Lots of little accidents over the years."

Dusk was beginning to gather on the horizon. Shadows were already lengthening from the trees and the rocky outcroppings of the endless Shield. Everything around Blue Ring was the Shield. The rail tracks that passed by Blue Ring went in two directions, but the rock of the Shield went in all directions. Papa had once told me it was called that because it was like a huge stone shield that a giant had dropped from the sky. He said we were pretty much in the middle of it, and you'd have to walk for a hundred days before you came to any end of it. In some places, it was covered with a thin layer of soil, so thin it was hard to see how trees and plants could take root in it. But a lot of it, especially near the river, was bare rock—it looked like red muscles that had pushed out of the earth, then flexed and twisted before turning into stone.

A dozen bats whirred out of a broken window in the floor below us. I suddenly realized how tired I was. I wished I could stretch out on the warm rooftop and fall asleep.

"Are the Headmasters always watching our thoughts, Papa?" I yawned.

"Not now," he replied. "Not during the slackenings."

"During the grips?"

"During the grips, I think they're interested in our toil and intentions but not our specific thoughts. If you saw a milk snake slither by your feet while you were picking—you know the kind I mean? The ones with red and black stripes?"

I nodded. Milk snakes were the only pretty snake.

"If you saw one of those while you were picking, I don't think your Headmaster would actually see a picture of a snake in its—head. But if you decided to stop picking and chase it, your Headmaster would sense that and stop you. Most of the time, if we're toiling the way they want, I think they only keep one eye open."

"They've got eyes?" I asked, puzzled. Usually, everyone kept their Headmaster covered. Papa said it upset people to look at them. But in the summer, on really hot days, shirts sometimes come off. So I'd seen a few Headmasters close up, but I'd never taken close note of their anatomy.

"No," Papa said. "What I mean is, they're only half paying attention to us." He paused, and I knew he was thinking of a way to explain. "When I was your age," he continued, "I had a dog—"

"Like Farley?" Farley was the only dog I'd known. There'd been other dogs before I was born, but they got a disease, and all died except him. And Farley did, too, when he got old.

"Not quite. She was a different kind of dog. A beagle."

"That was her name?"

"No, her name was Dee'ohjee."

Suddenly, I felt a surge of anxiety.

"Aren't you telling me about the past?" I gasped. After what had happened to Thorn earlier that day, I didn't want to risk hearing something that would trigger a previous host's memory. I suddenly felt very aware of the black mass on my back, its cool shell against my skin, its two coils snaking into my skull.

"Yes," he replied, "I'm breaking the rule. But it's safe because what I'm going to tell you happened ten years before the Arrival—so none of the people who had your Headmaster before you would have known about it."

Reassured, I was eager to hear about Papa's dog. I wondered if she and Farley would have been friends—or maybe even sole partners. Did dogs love each other?

"On warm days," he continued, "Dee'ohjee would nap on

my parents' front step, soaking up the sun. We lived beside a busy road in—in a place—so there was constant noise from—things. Dee'ohjee was oblivious to it all. She'd lie there, snoring. But the moment another dog barked, even if it was a long way off, her ears would twitch, and she'd get up and look around."

I pondered this. "The Headmasters are like that?" I asked.

He nodded. "That's why you and Thorn can talk to each other when you're toiling. Because you're doing what the Headmasters want you to do. But if you try to do something else, their ears—not real ears—their ears twitch, and they stop you."

"Once, I tried to throw a rotten peach at Thorn," I said. "But my Headmaster wouldn't let me open my fingers."

Papa nodded. "Try again," he replied, smiling, "during a slackening."

I made a note to do that.

As I mulled over what Papa was saying, an image of three river leeches clamping onto my leg flashed into my head.

bloodsuckers

But I couldn't remember when that had happened. Or where.

"If they can't listen to us in the slackenings," I asked, "why don't we pull them off then?"

"Right after the Arrival, some people tried that. They died every time, just as if they'd done it during a grip. Jenna says it's some sort of automatic reflex."

Four pigeons fluttered down to the corner of the ledge we were sitting on and began to murmur. Their orange eyes inspected us.

"You remember when I was born, right, Papa?"

"Of course."

"When was it? I mean, what time of the year? Can you tell me?"

Papa didn't reply for a few moments. I knew he was deciding if he could risk telling me.

"It was winter," he replied finally, "but it was a warm day. Strangely warm. The snow was melting, and water was running down the ridge." He paused again. "You know the day in winter when the light is shortest, and the dark is longest? It was that day." He stopped and looked at me. I knew he was watching for signs of a previous host's memory emerging. Satisfied none was, he continued. "Back then, we would have called it December 21."

"December was one of the ten months?"

"One of twelve."

"What were the other months called?"

"I shouldn't tell you," he replied.

"But are you going to anyway?"

He shook his head. "No."

"Do you still use months?"

"In my head, yes. And with Jenna and Virgil."

"What's today called?"

He looked at me with an exasperated smile. "September 24, 2122."

Just then, a grasshopper landed beside me. How did it get up to the roof? It lifted its front legs, one by one, and began to clean its antennas.

"Do you want to know something, Papa?"

"What?"

I pointed to the small, bright disk hanging over the horizon. "That's not a star. It's a planet. Like what we're on. It's called Venus."

"Now, how do you know that?" he exclaimed, twisting toward me.

"Thorn," I replied.

"And how does he know?"

I shrugged casually. "He tells me lots of stuff nobody else tells me."

Papa paused thoughtfully. Then: "Where does Thorn go during the slackenings? When he's not with you at the bridge?"

"Sometimes, he goes with me to listen to the Teller. The rest of the time, he doesn't say."

"Might be good to find out."

I was about to tell Papa I'd ask Thorn again, but just then, I heard River calling out, "Papa! Papa! Maple!" There was panic in his voice.

We looked down and saw him standing beside the pile of jagged glass and rusted pipes. "Come down! It's Lark!"

CHAPTER 11
BREEDER

We scurried back across the roof to the metal staircase, where Papa lifted me down to its platform. As we clambered down, pivoting at each floor as it switched back and forth, his steps were fast and reckless—I was afraid he might slip.

River met us at the bottom.

"What's happened?" Papa panted. The descent had winded him.

I could see anguish in River's eyes, even in the waning light of dusk. He glanced at me, then back to Papa. "Should Maple . . .?" he asked.

"It's fine," Papa replied, laying his hand on my shoulder.

River closed his eyes and exhaled deeply as he spoke. "They've made Lark a breeder."

I knew what that meant, of course. It meant that from now on, Lark's only toil was to give birth to future hosts for the Headmasters. Her new, sole purpose was to populate the Aery with babies.

It meant that Lark would be forced to mate with a series of men—one each morning—until she showed signs of pregnancy. Every morning after first meal, a man would be sent to her in her cubicle. Like her, he'd be forced to perform, whether he wanted to or not. I couldn't help remembering the human figures Lark had drawn for me in the dust.

After becoming a Breeder, Lark would have three moon cycles to get pregnant. If she didn't, the Headmasters would terminate her. Same thing after she gave birth: she had three moon cycles to get pregnant again—otherwise, termination.

But even if she kept getting pregnant according to the Headmaster's schedule, Lark wouldn't live very long. No Breeder had ever given birth more than five times. Being a Breeder, Halo had once told me, wore them down, physically and mentally. Eventually, they just died of exhaustion, like a rabbit that's been chased and chased and chased by a fox. Even Jenna, with her three big books of knowledge, couldn't help them at that point.

Halo had told me all this when I was still in the Aery because there was a chance, she said, that after I was harvested, the Headmasters might eventually make me into a Breeder. She didn't want to frighten me, but she wanted me to be prepared.

She said the Headmasters had created Breeders a few years after the Arrival. It was then, Halo believed, that they became aware of a plan the community had devised: to stop having babies—to stop creating new hosts for the Headmasters. No one wanted to bring new life into this brutal world. So, the members of the community made a collective decision to let themselves—one by one—become extinct.

Halo said that Jenna was the one who was going to help make this happen. If a woman became pregnant, Jenna would boil bark from a red cedar into a tea. After drinking it, the woman's baby would slip out of her before it was ready.

When the Headmasters sensed what the community was plotting, the first thing they did was punish everyone: every morning after first meal, for ten days, everyone received agonizing jolts to teach them not to oppose the will of the Headmasters.

Then, the Headmasters selected two women and made them into the first Breeders.

And lastly, they suppressed the moon cycles of all the other women so they couldn't have children even if they wanted to. The Headmasters had taken control of the community's reproduction.

Halo told me that the Headmasters had eventually made my own mother into a Breeder. She hadn't always been one. For the first ten years after she was harvested, she'd been a Tree Chopper. But then one of the Breeders died, and the Headmasters selected my mother to replace her. I don't know why she did, but Halo told me her name. Sparrow.

My mother—our mother—survived giving birth to River and to Lark and to another baby that died and then another one after that that also died. But she didn't survive giving birth to me. By then, she was too worn out, too worn away, too worn down. Halo said she died before I had slid out, and Jenna had to cut her open to save me.

So Sparrow was our shared mother—me and River and Lark and the two dead babies—but because she was a Breeder, none of us knew who our fathers were. Same thing for most of the people at Blue Ring: children of dead Breeders and unknown fathers.

River closed his eyes and exhaled deeply as he spoke. "They've made Lark a Breeder. They terminated Sweetgrass."

Papa's expression didn't exactly change, but something about his face seemed to go slack. When he spoke, his voice was tight and thin. "Lark told you that herself?"

He nodded. "Just now. She told me that right after morning meal, they sent her away from the other Catchers and back to her cubicle. A man was already waiting for her there."

"Who?" Papa asked.

"Cobalt," River replied.

Papa nodded slowly. Cobalt was one of the Grubbers.

"She won't stop crying," River added.

"Let's go see her," I said, taking Papa by the hand.

Papa cast his eye toward the setting sun, estimating when the slackening would end.

"We don't have time right now. I'll go to her tomorrow, alone. You two can wait a couple of days to see her?"

River and I nodded. It didn't seem like a good time to disagree or ask questions. Without saying anything more, we headed back in the gloom of twilight to our cubicles. It bothered me that Lark was alone and upset. I was glad the Headmasters would soon put us all into the darkening so she wouldn't have to think about it.

As we walked, I wondered why the fireflies hadn't come out.

After I got back to my cot and lay there waiting for the darkening, I suddenly found it hard to breathe. It was a new moon that night, so my cubicle was in total darkness. I sat up, gasping for air. My chest felt tight, and my hands seemed to have lost their warmth. My wrists ached as if something was pressing hard against them. I was terrified—I'd never felt this way before.

But then, in the next moment, I realized that wasn't true: deep down, I'd always felt this way.

Helpless. That's what I was feeling.

I closed my eyes. It seemed like my heart was trying to pound its way out of my chest. *Farley!* I thought. *Farley, come here! Help me!*

But this time, Farley didn't come.

CHAPTER 12
HELD BY THE RIVER

No, Farley didn't come to me that night. But something else did. As I lay there, feeling helpless and afraid, something spoke words in my mind.

moksha

prana

sama

aywastan

I didn't know these words, and yet they felt familiar. I heard them over and over until they gradually blended into a soothing blur like the murmur of a lazy river.

Then, as always, the darkening suddenly took me. My thoughts slowed. Grew dimmer. Fainter. In a moment, a black void would possess my mind—followed instantly by my eyes jolting awake to the dawning light of a new morning. It was as if time, during the darkening, stopped. Or jumped ahead. Either way, the experience was always the same: the darkening flowed by without any awareness of time passing. That's what always happened.

Except this time, it didn't.

This time, after it filled my mind, the black void began to swell, rolling forward into a deeper darkness, unspooling like a ball of raven-hued string. I was still aware—aware of myself, aware of the dilating void, and aware that something was about to happen. Slowly, a thin and undulating ribbon of white emerged in the darkness. It seemed distant. I felt myself drawn toward it. It grew wider. I was pulled closer. Black shapes emerged in the white ribbon. Rocks. Green edges became distinct. Trees. Closer. The ribbon itself gradually revealed a textured surface, rough with hints of icy blue. A river, frozen solid, in midwinter.

But not our river. Not the river Papa and I dangled our legs over when we sat on the bridge. This river was wider—far too wide to cast a stone across. Its breadth gave the impression that when it wasn't frozen, it was slow and lazy, moving so languorously it would be hard to tell on a summer day which way it was flowing. Unlike the river that curved around Blue Ring, this one had grassy banks sloping gently to the edge of the rolling water, not sheer walls of rock. A river like this, I'd never seen before.

Then I was upon it, on its icy surface. I was still disembodied, with no legs or arms that I could see, yet I somehow sensed I was kneeling—I could feel my knees pressing against the frigid, rippled ice. An unseen hand—mine?—began to brush away snow until the glassy surface of the ice appeared. The ice was thick, too thick to discern any water moving beneath it. But I could see, encased in its frozen grasp, bits of twigs and maple leaves.

I began to hear a voice, a slow stream of words, not my own. Like a distant echo piercing the fog, like a seed of memory pressing upward through the soil, blossoming, the words grew louder, more distinct. I listened. The words tumbled forth, rising and falling like a birdsong. They were conjuring a beauty I'd never before known, eluding recognition or identification.

Then, suddenly, the ice began to melt. I was sinking. I was under. The water turned from silver-blue to blue-black. I could feel its gentle push, its flow. Slowly, it pulled me along. Now and then, I felt a dull bump from other things carried by the river. But I wasn't worried. I was held safe by a pair of loving hands.

Always held by loving hands. That's what I thought when I opened my eyes to a new day.

CHAPTER 13
SOMETHING TO BE DONE

The three of us, Papa, River, and me, were in my cubicle with Lark. Lark didn't want to be outside where others might see her. And she didn't want us to be in her own cubicle.

Papa was sitting in my only chair, a wobbly thing stained with decades of sweat and sorrow.

"Be careful, Papa," River murmured, nodding toward one of the chair's front legs, which jutted to the side like a broken bone.

greenstick

Lark and River perched on the edge of my sagging cot. I sat cross-legged on the bare floor. I'd been hoping to tell Papa about the strange things I'd seen during last night's darkening, but it didn't seem like the right time.

A heavy silence hung in the air.

I glanced up at Lark. Her eyes were swollen and red, but her face was blank as if she had wept away all her feelings. She seemed to be staring through the wall of my cubicle. On top of everything, Fawn had just told her that she didn't want to spend the slackenings with her anymore. They hadn't been sole partners, but they'd been heading in that direction. Fawn told Lark she just couldn't bring herself to partner with a Breeder. She couldn't love someone who likely wouldn't live another five years.

"Fawn's a fool," River said. Lark winced, but River didn't notice. "Any of us might die next year or tomorrow," he added.

"She's just scared," Lark murmured. I could barely hear her. "I don't blame her. I wouldn't want to be with me either."

I looked at Papa, hoping he would say something to make things seem better. But he sat in the chair silent and still like a stone in a frozen river. I wondered what he was feeling, first having a daughter and now a granddaughter turned into a Breeder.

"Anyway," Lark added, "there's nothing to be done. I'm a Breeder now. If it wasn't me, it'd be somebody else."

River began to twist a sprig of cedar he'd torn off a branch on the way to my cubicle. Its sharp scent cut through the stale air. "Nothing to be done," he muttered.

"It wasn't always like this, was it, Papa?" I asked. There had to be something else to talk about.

"No," Papa replied softly, "it wasn't always like this."

"What was it like? When you were young?"

River looked down at me and frowned. "He can't tell you that, Maple. It's in the past."

"But what if he smoothed it out?" I replied, persistent.

"What do you mean, Maple?" Papa asked, his brow furrowing.

I paused to figure out how to explain what I meant. "You know that stone I found? I gave it to you a while back."

"The black one with a white stripe running through it?"

I nodded. "You told me it wasn't always that smooth. You

said it started off rough and jagged, but the edges got worn down."

"That's right," he said, reaching into his pocket. "It probably got tumbled around in the river for a thousand years"—he leaned forward, put his closed hand behind my left ear, and then drew it back in front of me—"until it was smooth as an egg." He opened his hand, and there was the stone I'd given him.

I smiled. So did River and Lark, a bit less sadly. Papa had done that trick to each of us dozens of times before. Our ears had produced a variety of small items—pebbles, acorns, snail shells, crickets. Once, he pulled a tiny goldfinch from my ear, and it flew away in front of my eyes.

"Can't you tell us something so that it's like that stone?" I continued. "Something with all the edges smoothed off?"

"You mean, leave out the details?" River asked skeptically.

I nodded to him, then turned back to Papa. "Wouldn't that make it safe?"

Papa was silent as he considered this. His eyes flickered to Lark, her slumped shoulders, her blank stare. The Headmasters had sent a different man to her every day since making her a Breeder. I'd seen her each time, being trudged back to her cot after she finished first meal.

Papa's silence continued. I knew he was weighing two things: the hazard of triggering a memory in one of us versus the comfort—or at least distraction—that his words might provide.

He straightened himself in the chair. He'd made his decision.

"No, it wasn't always like this. When I was young—I mean, before the Arrival—people could make choices. Real choices. They went where they wanted, did what they wanted, ate what they wanted—they ate a lot more things than just biscuit wedges. They talked about whatever they wanted—including the past. And about people who'd died. They had traditions. They did work they enjoyed—"

"No toil?" I interrupted. "No grips?"

"That's right," Papa replied. "Work instead of toil. Meaningful work. And they didn't work till they were exhausted, and there were days when they didn't work at all. Weekends. Holidays. Free time. Time when they could choose to do nothing, or play games, travel, read books—"

"Games like ring sport?" I asked, trying to encourage him. I wanted his words to blossom.

"Ring sport?" Papa replied, looking at me with a puzzled expression.

"Like what the dribblers did in Gehenna. Where the Teller tells his story."

"Oh," Papa replied, smiling slightly, "yes, ring sport. And dribblers. Even I was a dribbler. Can you imagine me running around bouncing a ball?"

His smile suddenly melted away.

"So many things we've managed to forget," he said wistfully. When he spoke again, he was gazing up through the one window of my cubicle. He seemed to be talking more to himself than to us. "Like stars winking out one by one."

Thorn had told me that in the middle of the night, the sky was covered with thousands of stars. He said there was a wide ribbon of them called the Milky Way. I'd never seen that, but in the winter, when nights came earlier, you could sometimes see hundreds of stars in the evening before the slackening began. But it was hard to imagine the entire sky being speckled with them.

"Music was my favourite thing," Papa said. "The world throbbed with it, made out of sound and silence. Notes were ordered into melodies like leaves on a honeysuckle vine.

Harmonies were draped over the melodies like weeping willows. Beautiful structures that moved through time."

the fresh streams ran by her
and murmured her moans,
sing willow, willow, willow

He paused and looked down at me. "A meadow full of flowers waving in the breeze—turn that sight into something you can hear, and that's what music was. Like thunder rolling, birds singing, and frogs croaking. But made by human art instead of Mother Nature."

The three of us stared at him in silence. Papa was in a place we'd never seen him in before.

"The beauty of music," he continued, his eyes gleaming, "is what made it so dangerous after the Arrival. Music gets embedded deep in the mind. Once, when I was Lark's age, I visited my grandfather. He had dementia—his mind had softened. He didn't recognize me or even my mom, his own daughter. But when she played music for him—the music he'd grown up with—he started singing. Such a powerful trigger for memories."

"Do you remember music like he did?" I asked.

"Oh, yes," Papa said. "I've still got hundreds of songs in my head. Sometimes, they come to me when I start to meditate. I'd so much like to sing them—to teach you and others—but, of course, I can't. It would be an awful risk. Most of the songs would be ones my dead friends at Blue Ring also knew—which means they were carried over with other memories when their Headmasters were transferred."

No one spoke.

"Papa, I'm sorry you can't tell us those songs," Lark finally said, looking up for the first time.

Papa smiled at her.

"Where were the Headmasters back then?" I asked.

"There weren't any," Papa replied. "The sol—" He caught himself before he could finish the word. "They hadn't arrived yet."

"And there were lots of other people?" I already knew the answer to the question, but I wanted to hear it from Papa again. It made it seem more real.

He nodded. "Ten billion."

"How many is that?" River asked.

"A billion is more than all of the heartbeats I've had in my life," Papa replied. "There were people on every continent. Continents are like huge islands surrounded by salty water. There were even a few hundred people living on—on another place away from Earth."

utopia

"I wish I was alive then," I said. "It sounds like utopia."

"Like what?" River asked, a puzzled look on his face.

Papa turned to me and smiled. "Another new word from Thorn? You better tell your brother and sister what it means."

I turned to River and Lark, who were still sitting on the edge of my cot. "Utopia was a perfect place," I said to them. "Sort of like in the Aery, except you're not little anymore." They continued to stare at me. "Utopia didn't really exist. It was just a story. Like a character." More staring. "Thorn knows words like that and tells them to me." Except I was pretty sure I hadn't learned that word from Thorn.

River and Lark nodded but still looked bewildered. It was probably the first time I knew something they didn't.

"It wasn't perfect," Papa said. "Many people didn't have enough to eat. Millions had to leave their homes when the oceans rose, and the storms got too fierce and frequent. People died in terrible wars. They killed each other. It was a long way from perfect."

"But it was better than this?" I asked.

Papa nodded. "It was better than this because most people were trying to make things better. For everyone."

"There was something to be done," River said.

"That's right," Papa replied, his head slowly nodding. "Something to be done."

CHAPTER 14
WE WILL MISS YOUR BRIGHT EYES

"I think I know what music is, Papa." It was the next day, nearing the end of the slackening, and Papa and I were in the greenhouse, watering the three boxes of flowers he kept at the back—purple violets, blue forget-me-nots, white saxifrage. After that, we'd move his mint plants into bigger pots. Papa sometimes boiled the leaves and drank the liquid.

"Yes," Papa replied quietly. "I told you about it last night."

"That's not what I mean. I mean I know some music. I can hear it in my head." I thought sharing this with him might get his mind off Lark. His eyes seemed to have grown sunken overnight, his movements slower and more uncertain. The news about Lark had devastated him.

"Oh," he said, but it didn't seem like he was really hearing what I was saying.

Then, I did something that made the plant pot drop from Papa's hands. I said the words from my dream and even made my voice go up and down just like I'd heard it—like a bird song:

> From this valley they say you are going,
> We will miss your bright eyes and sweet smile,

For they say you are taking the sunshine
Which has brightened our—

I could have gone on longer, but I stopped when the pot crashed onto the floor of the greenhouse. Papa was staring at me, his mouth gaping.

"That's music, Papa?" I asked.

"Yes," he stammered. "But you—you shouldn't know it. How? From Thorn?" He seemed almost angry.

I shook my head. Maybe I shouldn't have told him.

"No, no, not Thorn. He doesn't know music. I heard it a couple of nights ago during the darkening. But instead of the darkening, something came into my head. It was like I was somewhere else. And looking at someone else. Or looking at myself. I'm not sure. It's like it was both."

"Where were you?" Papa asked.

"In my cubicle. On my cot."

"I mean, in your head, where did you seem to be?"

"At first, I was up above a river covered with ice. It was a lot wider than ours. Then I was kneeling on it, and I heard the music. Then it melted, and I was in it, and it carried me away."

Papa glanced around, saw an overturned water pail, and slid it over to sit down on heavily. He still seemed bewildered.

"Did you feel okay after it happened? When you woke up? Did you have a headache or feel confused?"

"No."

"And this definitely happened after the darkening began?"

I nodded.

"Nobody dreams during the darkening," he murmured as if to himself.

"But it didn't feel like a dream, Papa. I used to have dreams all the time before I was harvested. This was—different. And when I was still in the Aery, I always forgot my dreams. This I can still remember like I was actually there."

Papa stared at the spilled dirt and pot shards at his feet. I knew what he was worried about. He knelt and took the slumping mint plant in his hand.

"Could it have been a memory, Papa? From somebody who had my Headmaster before me?"

"I've never heard of a memory surfacing during a darkening." He lifted his gaze from the floor to me. "Did anyone tell you something right before the darkening started? Something that could have triggered it?"

I shook my head. "I was with you and River, Papa. Remember? We all walked back to the Cube. We didn't talk to anyone else before we got to my cubicle."

He stood up slowly as if his knees and hips were suddenly very tired. He took a few steps over to the side wall and lifted down a flat square of metal from a nail. He walked back to the broken pot, bent onto one knee, and began to brush the dirt and shards onto the metal surface with his hand.

"It was a memory, wasn't it, Papa?" I asked. "You recognized it. That's why it startled you."

Still without replying, he rose again to his feet and tipped the contents of the metal square onto the potting counter.

"Papa?" I said again. "Papa, it didn't hurt me. See?" I began to repeat the words. "I wish I had—"

I stopped. Papa's eyes were filling with tears.

"Papa, what's wrong?" I stepped to the counter and put my hand on his arm. "Papa—whose memory is it?"

Still looking at the broken shards and scattered dirt, he answered. "Your grandmother's. My wife, Zara. Her name was Zara."

CHAPTER 15
CREST AND WREN

One morning, Crest didn't show up at the Meal House.

We were very sad but not surprised. It was midwinter, a few moon cycles after she'd accidentally triggered the memory in Thorn. She'd felt so bad about it and was so worried she might do it again that she'd entirely stopped talking during our toil. She'd give a small smile and nod when one of us spoke to her, but I never heard her say another word. Sometimes, when we were walking back to Blue Ring after the grip had ended, she'd wander off the path into the forest. Rose would follow her and guide her back.

The day after Crest was terminated, while we were eating morning meal in silence, a new Picker sat down beside us, freshly harvested from the Aery. I remembered her, of course. Her name was Wren, and she looked about eleven years old, but it was hard to tell. She didn't seem to have grown since I last saw her. Her face was gaunt, and her eyes had dark moons beneath them. She had a cough that sounded like she had rain in her chest.

She didn't say much that morning—just followed us through the fresh, deep snow to the hawberry bushes and started pulling the berries off, one by one. I don't think she managed to fill more than two buckets all day. When the grip ended, Silex had to carry her back to the Cube, just like he'd once done with me.

The next day's toil was just as gruelling for Wren as the first one. Maybe worse because it was even colder, and a bitter wind was throwing hard sleet into our faces. Silex's beard grew white with frost, and I envied him for having that extra protection from the cold. When the interval ended, Silex carried Wren back again as she slept in his arms.

When we got back to the compound, I began heading to the greenhouse where Papa and the other Inwards were meeting. Halfway there, I started thinking about Wren again and how tired and scared I'd been when I was first harvested. I decided to go to the Meal House to find some leftover biscuit and take it to her. Maybe I could also show her how to wind her foot wrappings better to keep out the wet. I ran into Thorn on the way, and he came with me.

We got to the open door of Wren's cubicle and saw that Silex was already sitting beside her. It looked like she was asleep. He'd brought a biscuit wedge, too, but it hadn't been touched. He was hunched over in the chair with his head in his hands. Thorn and I looked at them for a moment and then left without making ourselves known.

No one showed up to replace Wren the next day or for a long time after. Rose said it was because everyone in the Aery was still too young to be harvested. The Headmasters would have to wait for one of them to ripen.

CHAPTER 16
THIS PAIN IS MINE

Day after day, we slipped deeper into the unyielding jaws of winter. Silex said it was colder than any time he could recall. The wind turbine near the edge of the perimeter sent its invisible current into the Cube and Aery, but it could barely keep things from turning to ice. Some mornings, when I was jolted awake, there was a skiff of frost where the nylar blanket covered my mouth.

After the darkening ended, we didn't have much time to get ready to face the wind and snow. I had to work fast. The floors were like ice, so I'd start with my feet. They were already wrapped in one layer of nylar, but I'd add a couple more. Then I'd put finger-thick pieces of hickory on the bottom of each foot and wrap around more nylar to hold them in place. The Menders had cut and shaped them for us to protect our feet from sharp rocks hidden beneath the snow.

Next, I'd take off my shirt and trousers so I could wrap my body—legs, hips, waist, chest, arms—round and round, layer after layer, till it was almost hard to bend. Then I'd put my shirt and trousers back on. After that, I'd put my head through a big square of nylar with a hole in its centre and let it drape down.

These nylar squares helped keep us dry. We called them slit blankets, but I knew they had once been called ponchos. It wasn't Thorn who'd told me that name. I knew it from one of Zara's memories. I was beginning to realize that quite a few of the things I knew—things nobody else seemed to know—were from her memories.

After that, I'd head outside and cross the compound to the Meal House, where I'd meet up with Silex, Rose, and Thorn for first meal. I'd take more nylar strips with me to wrap around my fingers and head once I'd finished my biscuit and before our Headmasters impelled us out to our toil.

The winter nights were long, so it would still be dark when we left. If the moon was out—even a sliver of it—the snow would glow under its pale light, so it was easy to follow the trails into the forest. If not, we'd follow Silex through the darkness, trusting him to feel his way to wherever they wanted us to forage that day.

As we were trudged around in the snow, picking whatever stayed on the bushes in the winter—mostly hawberries, cranberries, and rosehips—I'd often think about how warm it had been in the Aery, even in winter. But yearning for my old days in the Aery didn't help me stay warm. If anything, it seemed to make the cold more cruel, creeping deeper into my layers of nylar.

It was then I decided to take a different tack: to claim the cold as my own. This wasn't entirely my idea. I borrowed it from one of Zara's memories that had surfaced during the darkening just a few days before.

In the memory, Zara has a terrible pain in her head—in her thoughts, she calls it a

migraine.

Whatever it was, it was awful, because I could feel it too, though maybe not as keenly as she did. For me, it felt, somehow, like an echo of pain.

She's sitting in a dim room, leaning forward, resting her head in her hands. She closes her eyes. Through the throbbing pain, I can hear her breathing and feel the rising and falling of her chest.

Inhale. Exhale.

Then, more slowly.

Inhale. Exhale.

Then even slower, deeper.

The murmur of her thoughts begins to diminish, like ripples on a pond as a rain shower comes to an end, until only this thought remains:

this pain is mine I claim it as my own this pain is mine to do with as I wish I own this pain it does not own me this pain is mine I claim it as my own this pain is mine to do with as I wish I own this pain it does not own me this pain is mine I claim it as

my own

Then, as if I'm gazing through a window etched with frost, I see what Zara is envisioning: a dark red sheet billowing angrily in a formless black void. Then, something unseen folds the sheet in half. Then folds it again. And again. And again, each time shrinking it in size. Once more. Once more. And then, it's gone, having been somehow folded out of existence. And with it, most of Zara's pain has also melted away.

The way Zara dispelled her pain wasn't completely new to me: it reminded me of some of the meditation practices I'd learned over the past few moon cycles from Papa and the other Inwards during the slackenings. One particularly cold morning, I decided to try it after we'd made our way out to the rosehip bushes. Plunging through the knee-deep snow was tiring, but at least the exertion helped us stay warm. Once we got to the bushes, we mostly stood in one place, reaching here and there into the twigs and branches. That's when we really started to feel the cold, especially our feet. Stamping them or running on the spot could only help so much.

Thorn had told me pain was a warning signal. I told him it was a stupid warning if you couldn't do anything about whatever was causing the pain. So, I decided, the best thing I could do was to stop minding the pain. To claim it as my own. To do with as I wished.

It didn't work the first time, maybe because I was focusing on the pain instead of on what was causing the pain: the cold. So the next day, as my numb fingers clumsily pulled berries from the bushes and dropped them into a bucket rimmed with frost, I told myself over and over that the cold was mine. I told myself the cold wasn't a thing—it was just a lack of a thing, of heat. Cold was a nothing, less than a nothing, but I was *something*. I was in charge.

Slowly, almost imperceptibly, the cold began to ebb away. First, the shivering stopped. Then my feet and hands started to feel a warm glow, almost as if my veins had discovered new channels for distributing heat. For a moment, I wondered if the weather had suddenly changed—but when I glanced over at Thorn, I saw he was still shivering.

Thorn must have felt me looking at him because he turned toward me and nodded. Then, suddenly, his brow crinkled with bewilderment.

"What's happened to your breath?" he asked.

"What do you mean?" I replied.

"Your breath—I can't see it."

I realized he was right. As Thorn inhaled and exhaled, his breath came out in huge plumes of frosty, white vapour. On cold days, this happened to us all, of course, and sometimes it was so thick it shrouded the berries on the branches in front of our faces. But that wasn't happening to me—not now. I was breathing, slow and regular, but my breath wasn't turning to vapour as I exhaled.

"Are you okay?" he asked, still looking puzzled.

I nodded.

"You can feel your toes?"

"I feel fine," I told him.

"Okay," he said as his Headmaster jerked him back to the bush he'd been working on. "Very strange."

Days later, I tried to explain to Thorn and Rose and Silex how to think away the cold, but it never worked for them. I had them repeat the words—*the cold is mine, the cold isn't a thing*—over and over, but nothing happened.

Maybe they didn't believe it would work. Or maybe they had to have Zara's actual memory of doing it—which I couldn't even tell them about. So, they had to shiver and stomp through a couple of more moon cycles of winter till spring and the birds began to return.

In the late summer, Lark gave birth to her first child. After consulting with Jenna and Virgil, Papa suggested he be called "Birch." Newborns had to be given new names—unique ones that had never been used before. Names were powerful triggers and could cause memories to surface in anyone with a Headmaster whose previous host—or hosts—had once known someone with that name. Papa said when the community realized that names could trigger memories, they even decided that newborns should be given totally made-up names—clumps of sounds that nobody had ever heard before.

"That's how Sprunk got his," Papa said. "He was the first child born after that decision."

Sprunk was a middle-aged man, one of the Biscuiteers. During the grip, the Biscuiteers chopped up the potatoes, apples, worms, squirrels, mushrooms, eggs, or whatever else had been brought to the kitchen the previous day. They dumped it into a long row of pots, added water, and boiled it over wood fires till it became a thick, grey sludge. After that, they plopped it by the handful onto metal sheets, set the sheets over the dying embers of the fire, covered them with more metal sheets, and let it bake till it was dry and hard. The result—different each day— was biscuit, ready for the next day's morning meal.

Sprunk had one thumb. The other one, Silex had told me, had gotten nipped off a long time ago when another mixer's blade slipped. The wayward thumb ended up in that day's biscuit mix.

"Garzina, too," Papa continued. Garzina was one of the five grubbers.

"So when you were a kid," I asked Papa, "*Sprunk* and *Garzina* weren't names?"

Papa shook his head and laughed. "They weren't even words. Just sounds we spliced together."

I found that odd. To me, *Sprunk* and *Garzina* seemed as ordinary as *Lark* or *Thorn*.

Papa continued. "But after Garzina, we stopped making up names for the newborns. It just felt like one more step toward turning us into things. So instead, we started taking names from the things we saw all around us in nature." He smiled. "Like maple leaves."

PART TWO

CHAPTER 17
THE BLUE SKY
BEHIND US

Alder and Raindrop got terminated. Larch and Thistle got harvested.

Papa lost most of his hearing in one ear and started using a walking stick.

Thorn got tall.

And handsome.

Silex and Rose stayed pretty much the same.

Lark had more kids. After Birch, a girl—Prairie. Then, another girl—she was born lifeless, so she never got a name. Then, two boys born on the same day—Lynx and Fox. Identical. I got to name them.

That's what happened over the next four years.

As for me, more of Zara's memories kept emerging during the darkenings. Not many, at first—one every moon cycle or so. Then they started coming more often—about every ten days. I think I was fifteen then, but it was hard to know your age when we were supposed to let the past drift away like a puff of Jimson smoke.

By the time I was about seventeen, it was happening every night. Sometimes, several memories came in a single darkening.

I knew all these memories belonged to Zara, not to the people between us who'd also been hosts for our mutual Headmaster: there was something about the memories that marked them as uniquely hers—like the smell of rain. Nothing else has that fragrance. Like summer showers, each memory was different, and yet they were all coloured with her distinct sense of self.

imbued

I hadn't told Papa I was getting more of Zara's memories. For a while, I wondered if I should. I thought maybe it would make him happy. Like part of her was still here. In my head.

But I also sensed he'd fret if he knew more memories were coming to me.

None of them caused me harm, though. I never experienced the confusion that seized Thorn back when Crest talked about the fire in the Cube. I wasn't sure why. Maybe because the memories were coming to me while I was sleeping. Or maybe because they were my own grandmother's memories, they somehow fit better into my head.

Something else made me reluctant to tell Papa. The memories were more than what Zara had just seen or heard or thought. They also held feelings connected to the experiences. Many of the memories were about Papa—or Jacob, as Zara had called him. And some of those memories were suffused with so much emotion—such a deep tenderness—that I would have felt awkward telling him about them. They were too intimate.

I don't mean physical intimacy. A couple of Zara's memories did involve that—from both before and after she met Papa —but I tried not to think about those ones. I mean memories where Zara and Jacob were just spending time together during the slackenings,

doing simple things like
clambering through

snowbanks she can feel the runoff soaking through her shoes and
she knows she'll have to
throw them away soon and start wearing foot wraps like the
others
and she doesn't want to but she laughs because jacob shakes
a pine branch and snow is tumbling down on us
and we're getting near the sugar bush
and i can see the three trees we tapped yesterday
black maples
and now we're peering into the cans we hung from spiles
we made the spiles from a sheet of tin we took
from a broken window frame
and yes there's sap in the cans a knuckle deep
and two of the cans pour into the third
and we scoop snow onto bare palms
and drizzle sap and bite it from each other's open hands
and it's the most delicious thing I've tasted
and jacob grins at me and says
i love you

I was shocked the first time one of Zara's memories of Jacob came to me. He looked like Papa, but not in the way I imagined he'd have looked fifty years ago. His hair and beard were black, not the grey and white I was used to. His eyebrows weren't a crazy pair of caterpillars. No wrinkles around his eyes. Perched on his nose was a metal frame that held two—not one—round lenses. He wore a kind of blue wrap around his upper body that looked puffy and warm, so unlike the nylar strips and slit blanket I'm used to.

But after a few more of Zara's memories of Papa emerged,

the young version of him settled comfortably into my mind. So much so that sometimes, when I came around the bend on the forest pathway and saw him waiting for me at the bridge, I was shocked that he seemed to have suddenly grown old.

I felt almost ashamed that Papa was unaware I was slowly getting to know his much younger self. Like I was watching him through a window. But I couldn't help it. Zara's memories surfaced, whether I wanted them to or not.

I also had a sad realization: in all of the memories that came to me, Papa was a young man. It seemed that Zara never had the opportunity to see him grow older.

Other kinds of memories had also emerged over the past four years. Many of them didn't seem especially memorable—which was strange, considering that Zara had remembered them.

washing my hands in a gleaming white sink and turning
a silver tap to make the water cooler
feeling anxious

clasping my hands around a warm mug that rests
in front of me
on the grainy surface
of a wooden table
a woman's voice more coffee zed
feeling content

pulling off a sock
and poking my finger through a huge hole in it
feeling hopeless

In fact, it was Zara's hands—her long fingers, narrow wrists, light-brown skin, short but neatly trimmed nails—that I grew most familiar with. They were literally front and centre in most of her memories. Sometimes, on the little finger of her right hand, she's wearing a silver ring with a green stone. The stone was—Zara often tries to remember its name. It's always on the tip of her tongue. *Ammolite?*

I glimpsed her face only twice in her memories. The first was on her birthday. She's ten, and she's watching her father pry a wooden cover off a well. Once it's free, he shoves the cover to the side, and they kneel, peering down the shaft. A grey pipe stretches down into an abyss.

At the bottom, our reflections gaze back up, small and shimmering, with the blue sky behind us.

CHAPTER 18
WHAT DOES "ARBITER" MEAN?

I hadn't told Thorn about the memories that surfaced during the darkenings, either—not yet. I wanted to. It would have been something else to talk about during our long grips. It didn't take long to get tired of sharing our observations about berries, birds, clouds, and various kinds of animal droppings.

But as much as I wanted to, I'd decided that telling Thorn about Zara's memories would be too dangerous. His Headmaster's first host—whoever it had been—must surely have been coupled with someone who had known Zara. There was a good chance that some of Zara's memories might trigger ones from that previous host in Thorn. Having seen that happen once, I wasn't eager to repeat it—especially when Papa said the effect of surfacing memories got worse each time.

Maybe I could have told Thorn only the memories from Zara that didn't involve anyone else. Or only memories of experiences that had to have taken place before the Arrival, like when she was a child, and she went to a place where the land met the water, and the water stretched out and out until it met the sky, and Zara went into the water, and the old people told her to be careful, not to go too deep because there were hidden currents that can pull you under. I could maybe tell Thorn about that—but then, what if the original host of Thorn's Headmaster had once gone to a place where the water stretched out forever? I couldn't risk it.

When I looked over at Thorn during our toil, staring blankly at the bush in front of him, I felt so sorry for him. He liked thinking about things, but being a Picker required zero thought. It was one of the most monotonous toils the Headmasters allotted, and it was for life. I think only the Keeper, up in the gear cabin at the top of the wind tower watching the blades of the turbine turn and turn and turn, had toil more boring than ours. Or maybe the Nurser. During the grips, she sat on a stool in the Aery, doing nothing but waiting for the two or three kids who were still nursing to cry out for her ponderous breasts.

Whether we were sweating in the sun or shivering in the rain, I felt grateful that, by now, I'd accumulated hundreds of memories from Zara to think about. Some of the most interesting were those I couldn't make sense of. In one, Zara is sitting at the end of a row of narrow chairs. Something around her hips is preventing her—me—from getting up. There are three strangers on one side of me and a small window on the other. My ears feel clogged with an awful noise, a relentless roar like when the river surges into a spring torrent. Through the window, clouds of fog roll by, while down below, huge outcroppings of black rocks with white peaks whirl slowly along. What kind of world had Zara once lived in?

I also discovered that I could recall Zara's memories and then linger over them, turning them this way and that until their details became more distinct and vivid: in one, what was at first just a blur of orange and purple on the edge of memory emerged as a beautiful glass jar of flowers, unlike any I'd ever seen around Blue Ring.

In another, Zara's fingers pulled strips off a curved yellow thing, then broke off the end of a white substance inside and popped it into her mouth. If I closed my eyes and turned my full attention to the moment after the bite, I could discern a sweet, mild flavour—or imagined I could. It felt soft and satisfying in my mouth.

Thanks to Zara's memories, I had another life, a better and more interesting one, one I could travel to whenever I wanted. I wished I could share it with Thorn. No one would have appreciated it more.

After Lark's son Birch was born, I'd started spending most of the slackenings at the Aery. I loved holding him. I loved it when his tiny hands reached up to me. I loved his smile and his tuft of brown hair. Most of all, I loved how he was still his own self. No Headmaster had claimed him. Not yet.

By the time Fox and Lynx were born, there was another reason for me to go to the Aery after the grips: Halo's health was starting to fail. For more than forty years, Halo had been the Minder of the Aery, looking after children, including me, from birth till harvest. Her heart and mind weren't worn out, but her body was.

Of course, Mallow was also in the Aery during the grips—Mallow was the Nurser—but the Headmasters didn't let her help Halo with the kids, and as soon as the slackenings started, she left and went back to her cubicle to sleep and rub grease on her nipples. The Headmasters had made Mallow get pregnant about twenty years before—just once, not over and over like the Breeders. Ever since then, her toil was to sit there and let the kids drink her milk until they were old enough to switch to milk and biscuit and then finally to just biscuit. As long as there were babies to suckle, her breasts kept producing.

After I'd arrive at the Aery, Halo would ignore my pleas for her to go to her cubicle to rest, but she'd agree to just sit and watch as I tended the kids. Often, she'd nod off in her chair, and I wouldn't wake her till the darkening was near. I'd help her get to her feet and then hold her arm as she staggered groggily to the Cube, asking how each of the children had been during the slackening.

Because I was spending so many slackenings at the Aery, I saw Papa less often. Sometimes, on his way to the bridge, he'd stop in to visit his great-grandchildren, but he usually didn't stay long. He said the Inwards needed him. If he was away for too long, they might start to drift away. One of them—Daisy—had already been approached by a Thankful to join their group —their coven, as Jenna called it. Papa didn't want more of that to happen.

When I told Thorn about what I did during the slackenings, he wasn't interested in the kids themselves, only in what he called the "mechanics" of the babies. How often and how much they ate, pooped, threw up, burped, cried, slept, and so on. I'd update him about these things during the grips because he still spent most of the slackenings off on his own, doing his own thing. Even by then, I didn't know what that was—his own thing. I'd invited him several times to come to the Aery, but he told me it was better if he didn't, so I'd have more to tell him during the next grip.

"How do you tell Lynx and Fox apart?" he asked me one day. "Do they have different poop smells?" It was early fall, and a furious wind the previous night had shaken thousands of walnuts from their branches. We were on our hands and knees, scrabbling to collect them. So were Silex and Rose, but under different trees. I could hear Silex quietly mutter and curse as the walnuts dug into his knees.

I wasn't sure if Thorn was being serious. "They wear different coloured nypers. Lynx is red, and Fox is white."

Thorn nodded and looked thoughtful.

After a few moments, he said, "But what if Halo accidentally puts them in the wrong nypers? Would Lynx become Fox, and Fox become Lynx?"

"Maybe that would be a good thing," I replied. "It would make more sense for Fox to wear the red nypers."

Thorn looked puzzled.

"Because," I explained, "foxes are red."

"Some are silver," he said.

"Only when their mother puts the wrong fur on them."

Now, he wasn't sure if *I* was being serious.

"Anyway," I continued, "if Lynx and Fox got mixed up once, they'd likely get mixed up again, which would undo the confusion. And besides," I added, "if they're identical, then what difference would it make if they got mixed up?" I didn't really believe what I was saying, but it felt good to be getting the best of Thorn. For once.

turn the tables

"Interesting point," he replied. "In other words, if I can't tell two things apart, like these"—he held out his palm with a pair of walnuts on it—"then they're the same. The same walnut."

"No," I said, not understanding where my next thought was coming from, "they're not the same walnut because they exist in different locations on your hand. And they have different pasts—one of them must have fallen off before the other." I paused to let Thorn mull this over. "And just because you can't tell them apart," I continued, "doesn't mean that someone else can't. You're not the only arbiter. Maybe a crow or a squirrel can see how they're different from each other."

Thorn's eyes widened, and his jaw dropped ever so slightly. For the first time, I'd beaten him in an argument. He fell silent and focused on his berry plucking till the sun was high in the sky.

"Maple," he said, finally breaking the silence. He almost sounded apologetic. "What does *arbiter* mean?"

Another first.

CHAPTER 19
THANKFULS

You've been wondering: What happened to Lark?

I've put off telling it till now because what happened to her in those four years was the worst thing I'd ever had to deal with.

She became a Thankful. That didn't change anything about her being a breeder. Breeding was her toil.

When she wasn't pregnant, the Headmasters sent a different man to Lark every morning to make that happen. After he left, they'd make her lie on her cot for the rest of the grip, her hips slightly raised on a ragged pillow. Most of the people at Blue Ring had been conceived on that pillow—it was transferred from Breeder to Breeder whenever one replaced another.

When Lark's Headmaster sensed that her bladder or bowels were full, it impelled her to get off her cot, use her slop jar, and get back onto her cot. Tundra, one of the Biscuiteers in the Meal House, was sent to her three times a day with water and biscuit wedges. Tundra's greasy fingers would then poke the wedges into Lark's mouth, which Lark's mouth would then chew and swallow. It didn't matter whether she was hungry or not. The Headmasters assumed that fertility needed plenty of fuel.

Once she did get pregnant, Lark's toil was to keep the child growing within her till it was ready to be born. That meant continuing to lie on her cot, continuing to be force-fed, and continuing to use the slop jar when the need arose.

That was the extent of the Headmasters' understanding of reproductive care: lie in bed, eat biscuit, use the jar.

Of course, once the grip ended, Lark could do what she wanted during the slackening. But that's where being a Thankful came in. She never went to the Aery: she had no interest in her children. By the time Prairie, Lynx, and Fox were born, she didn't even want to hold them before they were taken over to be nursed by Mallow in the Aery. She didn't spend time with me, River, or Papa either. She didn't go for walks or listen to the Teller. Instead, she trudged up to the fourth floor of the Cube and sat or stood in a huddle with the other Thankfuls until the slackening was almost over.

Getting drawn into the Thankfuls had happened gradually, then suddenly. Looking back, I realize it began during the two moon cycles it took for Lark to get pregnant with Birch. That meant more than fifty morning visits from more than a dozen different men.

In the first of those moon cycles, Papa, River, and I had urged her to pass the slackenings going for walks with us through the forest. She did, but not with any enthusiasm: she didn't want to talk and mostly kept her eyes downcast on the path. Not once did I see her look at the trees or up at the sky. She wouldn't meet our eyes. Then, after that first moon cycle, she'd stopped going with us. She said she was always tired and needed to spend the slackenings alone, which made me angry because it hurt Papa so much. And Fawn, who'd broken her heart, had refused Papa's plea to just go and see her.

As fall approached, and Lark's belly began to swell, she passed the slackenings sitting on the shoulder of the huge rock that pushed through the earth beside the Meal House. Not long before, that rock had been a meeting place for us, the spot where we'd wait for each other when we were planning to go to the bridge to be with Papa and the Inwards. From a distance, the rock looked almost pink.

gneiss

Close up, you could see the rock held flecks of black and red, with freckles of quartz that sparkled when the sun slanted low. It felt good to sit on, feeling the release of gentle warmth it had borrowed from the sun throughout the day.

As she'd requested, we left Lark alone during the slackenings, though for a while, Papa settled himself on a fallen tree trunk at the edge of the forest, where he could keep a concerned eye on her without intruding. One evening, as he told me later, he saw someone approach her as she sat on the rock. Even in the dim light of dusk, he could tell it was a Thankful, with a narrow strip of black nylar around her head and her arms folded across her chest. It was Ivy, the leader of the Thankfuls. When she started speaking to Lark, Papa got up and walked toward them, but Lark waved him away.

After that, we didn't see Lark during the slackenings. Papa's voice broke when he told me where she was: huddling with the Thankfuls.

That's when Papa started going back to the bridge to be with the Inwards, something he hadn't done for almost two moon cycles. He said they needed him, but I knew he also needed them, especially now. I sometimes went with him, but more often went by myself to listen to the Teller. And once, about one moon cycle after we'd lost Lark to the Thankfuls, and even though I knew Papa wouldn't want me to, I climbed up to the fourth floor of the Cube, opened the door, and peeked in.

I saw them in the dim light, the Thankfuls, standing in a tight circle. They faced inward, their arms draped over the shoulders of those on either side of them. They were quietly murmuring something, but I couldn't make it out—the room was large and empty, and the echo blurred their overlapping voices. Through the gloom, I could see Lark on the far side of the circle, leaning forward with her head bent low. Like the others, she had a strip of black nylar tied around her forehead. I was working up the courage to call out to her when one of them left the circle and walked toward me. It was Ivy.

"Here we are, Maple," she said through the crack in the door. She was smiling, but her eyes were grim. "I know you have questions." I didn't have questions; I had accusations. "Let me answer them for you," she continued.

I felt like ramming the door open and shoving her to the floor. *"Answer this!"* I imagined snarling. But I didn't.

I slowly opened the door and let her into the stairway. As she slipped past me, the other Thankfuls began to step sideways in unison, their circle beginning a slow rotation. Their murmuring grew louder.

"Please sit," Ivy said, pointing to the top step of the stairwell. I sat down, and she did the same beside me. She was closer than I wanted, so I edged toward the wall.

"Why did you take her?" I spat. I fought back tears. I didn't want her to see me cry.

"We didn't take her, Maple. She found us. She found our better way of being."

"Shuffling in the dark with a bunch of croaking magpies?" I said, my words dripping with sarcasm.

"You think what we're doing is pernicious, Maple. Did you hear what we were chanting when you were spying?"

"I wasn't spying."

"Did you hear us when you were staring at us without permission as we said our private and sacred invocations?"

I shook my head angrily. *Sacred.* I could feel the weight of that word in Zara's memories.

"Would you want me to spy on your grandfather and his followers when they undertake their practice in the forest?" she asked.

I shook my head again. I felt the stirrings of shame beginning to displace my anger.

"Then we're not so different, are we?" Her voice was low and even, her measured words almost comforting. She reached out and gently put her hand on my shoulder. I don't know why, but I didn't push it away. Through the fabric of my shirt, I could feel the moist heat of her palm.

"That's right," she breathed. "You see, my child, your mind has been chaotic; your heart has been angry since the day you were harvested. But it doesn't have to be that way. Your mother died of blood loss as you were being born. You were cut from her belly as she took her last breaths. And yet, her loss does not now cloud your thoughts. Her death does not breed anger or sorrow in your heart."

"I was just a baby," I replied, surprised she was talking about the past. "I don't remember her."

"That's right," she murmured. "To you, it is as if she never was. What a blessing! Can you imagine how wonderful you would feel if all your hopes and expectations—all your pent-up desires—were as dead as your mother? The people on the other side of that door—hear their chants? Hear their chants? They have no hopes, no expectations, no desires but one: that our Headmasters extend, expand, and deepen their loving grip on us—their mastery of us. When that happens—and it will happen, Maple, in good time—we will all become our destiny.

We will be beautiful and constant vessels for the creatures providentially sent to us long ago when your grandfather had scarcely entered manhood. That will be our final incarnation. We will no longer be afflicted with the selfish desires and confusing choices that are resurrected every evening when our Headmasters give us over to the slackenings because there will *be* no more slackenings. Already, Maple, we have moved closer to our sole desire. The slackenings are becoming shorter. That is because of our service to our Headmasters—our daily invocations to our lords. It has made them stronger, more efficient, less needful of slackening time to consolidate and share the disjointed sensory input they accumulate through our primitive perceptions during our grips."

I nodded weakly to Ivy. While she'd been speaking, my eyes had become heavy, the stairwell hot and stuffy. I realized my head was resting on her shoulder. She smelled like wood smoke and moss. *Come with me, Maple, into our invocation chamber. The windows are open, and you'll feel a nice breeze.* Had she said that to me, or had I imagined it?

Now I was in the room, and the circle of Thankfuls stopped moving and chanting as they turned their faces toward me. In unison, they smiled—huge, warm, welcoming smiles that made their eyes crinkle and shine in the red light of dusk. Then they all raised one hand and wordlessly beckoned me to join them, to join their circle.

All but one: Lark. She had dropped her hands to her sides, where they continued to hang motionless. Our eyes locked across the room, and I saw her shake her head, so slightly it was barely perceptible.

Suddenly, I felt as if I'd been pushed into a cold river. Gasping, I tried to turn toward the doorway but found my hand tightly clasped by Ivy's. I shook it free, stepped to the door, yanked it open, and twisted back toward Ivy with a fierce glare.

"This is not a better way of being," I bellowed, my chest heaving as I gulped in breaths of stale air. "And you're not a messiah," I added, even as I wondered where that word had come from. "Choice is what makes us human, and even when we're slaves, we can still choose to hate our masters, and we can still choose to hope for something better to come." I looked past her shoulder at the circle of Thankfuls. "All of you are cowards, collaborators with our enemy."

Ivy continued to smile as she listened with calm assurance to my rant, her arms crossed over her chest, even when bits of spit flew from my lips and onto her cheek.

When I stopped, she nodded and began to gently close the door, pushing me back into the stairwell.

"So happy you stopped by, Maple," she said. "I'm certain we'll see you again."

CHAPTER 20
LOVE AND RAIN

I think it was the moment when Thorn asked me the meaning of the word "arbiter"—as we were scrabbling for walnuts, side by side, on our hands and knees—that I began to fall in love with him.

I'd known Thorn all my life. Apart from the year between his harvesting from the Aery and mine, there'd never been a time when he wasn't in my world. I knew him better than I knew anyone else, including Papa, River, Lark, and Halo. But until that moment, I'd always felt like I was playing catch-up with him. As if he saw me as a little sister, someone he had to teach and protect. But just knowing one thing he didn't—just that one word, "arbiter"—suddenly made him reconsider who I was.

I could sense it was hard for him to adjust: it must have been like hearing a crow sing like a robin or waking up on a summer morning and finding everything blanketed in snow. I'd be telling him about something Lark's kids had done the previous slackening—like Birch learning the word "butterfly"—and he'd start to interrupt me to share his idea about how butterflies were able to fly without feathers. But then he'd catch himself and stop.

"Sorry," he'd say. "Keep going." It was a confusing time for him.

And for me. I almost didn't know what to do with the newfound respect he had for me. Or the new way he seemed to look at me. We'd be deep in the blueberry bushes, and I'd see him, out of the corner of my eye, glancing at me through the leaves as I reached up for the highest berries.

When the grip ended, I could feel his gaze upon me as he walked behind me on the path back to the compound. I wondered, too, if he could feel my gaze when I walked behind him. I wondered if the broad strip of grey nylar that I some- times wrapped around my hips instead of trousers was attrac- tive. And I wondered if Thorn would prefer the colourful, complicated garments that I saw in Zara's memories, the ones from before the Arrival. I felt silly for wondering all this.

But I still wondered.

Once, the four of us were picking crab apples in an early summer shower—Thorn, Silex, Rose, and me. The trees were giving us a bit of protection. Instead of falling as a constant drizzle, the rain accumulated into shimmering domes on the leaves, which intermittently tipped big, lazy drops onto us. We stayed mostly dry: the water couldn't penetrate the nylar of our slit blankets or foot wraps.

But our bare faces were a different story. Water rolled steadily down my forehead and cheeks, then dribbled off my chin. Squinting to keep it out of my eyes, I reached through the leaves and found myself grasping Thorn's fingers as they cupped around a crab apple. Despite the cold rain, his hand was warm. He turned toward me and smiled. I could feel a pulse throbbing—mine or his. Our eyes locked for what seemed like a very long time. I returned his smile, then watched as my

Headmaster intensified its grip, and my hand was impelled to release his and resume its toil.

I realized Silex had been watching us and smiling—one of the few times I'd seen him look happy since Wren. But when he saw me gazing back, he suddenly spotted a crab apple on the other side of the tree and hurried over to it. Later that day, after the rain had stopped and I was helping put the pails of crab apples onto the sledges, Silex nodded toward Thorn and then gave me a wink.

When the grip ended, Thorn and I each grabbed one of the sledge ropes and began to haul it back to Blue Ring. We were shoulder to shoulder as we dragged the heavy load, but Thorn was silent for a long time. I began to wonder if I'd misunderstood that moment in the rain.

Then, he suddenly spoke. "Maple, could I come to the Aery this slackening?"

I smiled. I hadn't been wrong after all.

"Sure, but why?" I asked, pretending not to know what he was up to. "You never wanted to go there before."

Thorn's brow furrowed slightly, causing raindrops to drip from his forehead. "I guess I want to see these kids you're always telling me about. Birch and Prairie. And Fox and Mink."

"Lynx, not Mink."

"Right, Lynx. And maybe I can help out."

"You mean, you'll stay with them so I can go see my Papa at the bridge? Or to Gehenna to listen to the Teller? I'd love that."

He frowned and exhaled loudly. "No, that's not what I mean. I mean, sure, I could do that for you sometime. After you show me how to hold them and put food into them and stuff. But this slackening, I just mean with you. To be in the Aery. With you."

"Oh. Like before we were harvested?" I asked. "When we were kids?"

"No, not like that exactly." He was sounding a bit exasperated. Then he glanced over at me for the first time since we'd started hauling and saw me trying to suppress a laugh. As it dawned on him what I'd been doing, his face lit up.

"Actually," he continued, in a mock-serious tone, "that would be fun. We could push each other on the swing like we used to. And play hide the pebble—or you could throw a warming stone at me. And then we could have a nap together. Just like we used to."

"Maybe," I replied. "We'll have to see if we can get Lark's kids to sleep earlier than usual."

He smiled again, then began to pull harder on the sledge.

CHAPTER 21
HALO

Over the following moon cycles, Thorn and I grew a lot closer. It wasn't easy. We could talk during the grip, but our Headmasters would snap us back to attention if we started to focus too much on one another and not enough on our picking. I appreciated that Silex and Rose, to the extent their Headmasters would let them, sometimes tried to give us privacy by picking from a tree or bush out of earshot. It was during one such time that Thorn said:

"Maple—I think it's time I told you something. I love . . ." He paused and gave me a serious look. ". . . picking hawberries." Then the grin that had become so endearing to me burst onto his face.

"Thanks for sharing that with me, Thorn. And I want to say that when the two of us are under a tree, I adore looking over at you—and seeing a sparrow crap on your head."

Thorn laughed. Then, he was abruptly jerked back to his toil.

Even during the slackenings, it was hard for us to connect as much as we wanted to. With Halo getting more frail, there was more to do when Thorn and I got to the Aery. Sometimes, she'd forgotten to give the kids a third meal, so they were hungry and crying when we got there. Dirty nypers the younger ones had been wearing since the afternoon needed to be changed. Fox and Lynx were getting their first teeth and would scream for hours. Jenna came by with a tea of boiled willow bark, but there was only so much we could do for their pain.

If we got all of them settled and asleep half an hour before the slackening ended, we felt lucky. But after spending more than half the day picking fruit and another three hours of tending kids in the Aery . . .

"I'm tired out," Thorn said as he sank down to the floor where I had just finished picking up stray crumbs of biscuit.

"Me, too," I replied as I slumped down beside him. "My feet hurt."

Thorn leaned over and began to unwind my foot wrappings so he could massage them.

"Still," I added, "we're not as tired as Halo." She was sleeping in a chair across from us, her head leaning on a stack of clean nypers that Thorn had tucked in beside her.

"True," Thorn replied. He paused, then began to ask in a hushed tone, "I wonder how much longer she has until—"

"Don't even think that," I said, cutting him off. "If we help out here during the slackenings, catching up on what she can't get to, she'll have a lot more time. They won't sense she's failing."

"I hope so," Thorn replied. "She raised us."

"She raised most of the people at Blue Ring."

Halo snored gently.

"The slackening's going to end soon," I said. I sighed and leaned over to give Thorn a kiss on his lips.

"Too soon," Thorn replied, sounding as disappointed as I was. "The slackening, I mean."

"We should wake Halo and take her to her cubicle."

"Sounds good," he said. We got up and walked over to her. Thorn gently shook her shoulder.

"Halo," he said. "Halo. Time to go."

But Halo didn't wake up, and for a moment, my heart dropped into my stomach, thinking she'd been terminated right in front of us. Then I remembered what others had told me: being terminated wasn't peaceful or quiet.

The Headmasters had terminated two people since I'd been harvested. One was Cardinal, Rose's sole partner, after he got sick from getting cut. The other was one of the Grubbers who'd been mauled by a black bear in the forest. Jenna said she probably could have survived the attack but wouldn't have been able to walk anymore.

I wasn't there when either of them was terminated, but I'd heard enough from others that I knew it didn't look like sleep.

I lay my ear against Halo's chest and heard its slow beat. Thorn suggested the best plan might be to let her keep sleeping while we carried her back to her cubicle. We tried and got a little way out of the Aery, but it was slow going, and I was afraid we might drop her, so Thorn ran over to the Meal House to get one of the wheelbarrows—actually, *the* wheelbarrow, the only one that hadn't yet fallen to pieces.

While I was waiting for him, a few others who weren't yet in their cubicles hurried by, heading for the Cube. They slowed and looked concerned when they saw me sitting on the ground with Halo slumped against me but didn't stop. I didn't blame them: getting to your cubicle late resulted in ever-worsening jolts of pain.

It didn't take Thorn long to get back with the wheelbarrow. He'd even been able to throw in some castoff nylar to soften its bottom. We carefully lifted Halo into it, and Thorn began pushing it over the cracked and craggy surface of the compound. She snorted when its metal wheel hit a hole—it was getting hard to see in the gathering darkness—but she kept sleeping.

We were almost at the door of the Cube when we got hit with the first jolt. The wheelbarrow thudded to the ground as its handles slipped out of Thorn's grip, and we both fell to our knees, our hands clasping our heads in agony. After a moment, the pain subsided.

"Hurry," I said to Thorn, still wincing. "We've only got a couple of minutes till the next jolt, and it'll be worse."

Thorn picked up Halo—still sleeping, despite getting knocked about in the wheelbarrow when Thorn dropped it— and draped her over his shoulder. I pulled open the door to the Cube, and Thorn began to race up the stairwell, Halo's limp arms flapping against his back. I followed, knowing that if the Headmasters gave us another jolt on the stairs, we'd all go tumbling down.

We made it to the Halo's floor, and I ran ahead to open the door to her cubicle. Thorn went in, dropped her onto her cot, and threw a sheet over her. We looked at each other, nodded once, and then ran in different directions down the hallway, Thorn heading for his cubicle and me for mine. I made it into my cot without getting a second jolt—which meant that Thorn had made it, too, since his was closer to Halo's.

A moment later, the darkening began, and—as usual— another memory from Zara began to surface.

CHAPTER 22
A BOLT ON THE WALL

"How's your head?" Thorn asked when I sat down beside him in the Meal House the next morning.

"Hurts. Like a badger's trying to claw its way out."

"Willow bark," he said, laying a few pieces on the table. "Give it a chew when you're done eating."

My mouth was full of biscuit—more dry and meaty than usual—so I just nodded and reached for the water jug. After a couple of gulps, I said to him, "I don't think Halo got jolted last night."

"That's good."

"But isn't it odd?" I continued. "Why didn't she get jolted like us?"

Thorn shrugged. "Maybe because she was already asleep."

"Even when you're asleep, they jolt you if you're not in your own cot when the darkening starts. River said it happened to him once when he dozed off in —" I smiled—"someone else's cot."

"Right," Thorn said. "I knew that. Not the part about River being in somebody else's cot—though that doesn't surprise me. I mean, the part about getting jolted even if you're already sleeping." He paused and looked thoughtful. "But what if Halo was in a really deep sleep?"

"What do you mean?"

Thorn glanced around. Silex and Rose were at the table but didn't seem to be paying any attention to us. He lowered his voice. "You know the drops Halo gives the kids when they have —what's it called—colic?"

I nodded. "To settle their stomachs," I said. "Jenna makes it for Halo. From some kind of root. We probably all had it when we were in the Aery. Why are you talking so quietly?"

Thorn kept his voice low. "The drops don't actually settle the kids' stomachs. It just numbs the pain so they can fall asleep. Jenna doesn't want others to know that."

"Why? What does it matter as long as it helps them?"

"She thinks if others find out, they'll want to start using it. The drops can make you feel sort of happy and careless."

"Like jimsonweed."

"But more dangerous. After a while, you can't stop using it. And if you use too much, you fall asleep and don't wake up."

"Does Halo know that?" I asked.

"She must. Jenna would have told her why she has to be careful with it."

What Thorn was suggesting suddenly dawned on me. "You think Halo gave herself a bunch of drops after we got there? And that's why we couldn't wake her?"

"Just wondering. Maybe that's why she didn't feel the jolt."

"Why would she do that? She doesn't have any trouble falling asleep."

Thorn looked at me steadily. He paused for a moment before replying. "Maybe she didn't want to wake up."

I felt like he'd dropped a sack of walnuts on me.

"That can't be true," I gasped. "She'd never do that! She wouldn't leave the kids—she loves them too much." My Headmaster jerked my head down to my bowl of biscuit. I was getting too agitated.

Thorn was silent. My head spun as I thought through what he'd suggested. Halo was old, yes. But not as old as Papa. She hadn't been herself for a while but didn't seem to be in pain. But maybe she was and just wasn't telling anyone.

Rose said there'd been people in the past who'd killed themselves, but she didn't know how many. She said they didn't act like berserkers. They didn't try to tear off their Headmaster. They just found a quiet way to make themselves die—always during a slackening. No one told me details, of course, but I think the last one, before I was harvested, took nylar strips and made a rope. They found him—or her, I'm not certain—hanging from an elm tree behind one of the buildings.

What was certain was that the next day, the Headmasters punished someone else for what the person had done. They didn't terminate anyone because they'd already lost one host and couldn't afford to lose another. So they did the blood punishment instead. When I first heard about it, I thought of Crest and the scars she had on the right side of her face. But there were others, too, whose faces had been cut or snipped or somehow marred.

Halo wouldn't do anything that would get someone else punished. Would she?

I forced up my head for a moment and looked at Thorn again. "Who else knows about this—about what the drops do?"

"Your Papa, probably," he said. "And Jenna, of course. And Virgil."

I fell silent again as I considered what Thorn was telling me.

"Which one of them told you this?" I asked as bits of biscuit fell out of my mouth. It was awful to be this upset and still be forced to eat.

Thorn suddenly looked uneasy. He glanced over at Silex and Rose.

"The grip's going to start any second," he said, pushing a last piece of biscuit wedge into his mouth.

"Thorn? Who told you this? Who told you what the drops can do?" I could sense something wasn't right, and he wasn't telling me. It was chilly in the Meal House, but a sheen of sweat was gathering on his brow.

"Thorn! Who?"

He suddenly looked straight at me. "No one," he said in a low and even voice. "No one told me." Then, even more hushed, "I read about it in Jenna's writing book."

For the second time that morning, I felt dumbfounded, like the floor was sinking beneath me.

"Thorn!" I gasped. "You can read?"

I'd always known what reading was. Papa could do it. Virgil and Jenna, too. The three people who were born before the Arrival. But Jenna was the only one who was still allowed to. She kept her black and blue tattered books on a shelf in the Ward.

Once, when Silex skidded down the side of a ravine into a thicket of stinging nettles, he got a rash that pretty much drove him crazy. I learned some new curse words that day. I went with him to see Jenna, and before she did anything, she opened her book and flipped through its pages. Then I watched her make a salve for him out of ground-up pumpkin and three pigeon eggs.

All of the other books at Blue Ring had, of course, been thrown into the river a long time ago when people realized reading could make a previous host's memories surface. But as

Thorn had once told me, there'd never been many books to get rid of. The Originals had mostly read on glass rectangles, and those stopped working after the Arrival. Papa said they eventually burned all the writing sticks, too. But I once found one stuck behind the mirror in my cubicle and showed it to him. He'd called it a pencil and used it to draw a zigzag lightning bolt on the wall beside my cot. Later, he gave the pencil to Jenna and asked me not to tell anyone about it.

"Thorn! You can read?" My words were still hanging in the air as he stared at me without responding. I'd spoken louder than I meant to, which caught the attention of Silex and Rose. They were staring at us with puzzled looks. Silex opened his mouth to say something to Thorn, but then we found ourselves standing up and heading for the door.

The grip.

CHAPTER 23
IN THE DEEP

Thorn kept his distance from me that day as we stripped hawberries from their thorny bushes. Every time I edged closer to him to ask about what he'd said at the table, he'd step around to the other side. Finally, I gave up.

"Fine," I called out through the twigs and leaves. "I'll leave you alone for now, but you better talk to me once the slackening begins."

He looked at me, still without saying anything, but gave me a quick nod. Silex and Rose, who'd been watching us dance around the bushes all morning, looked concerned but stayed silent.

Throughout the rest of the grip, questions raced around my head. Had I heard Thorn correctly? Had he actually said what I thought I'd heard? Did he really know how to read? If he did, when had he learned? Who'd taught him? What was there for him to read, anyway? What was a writing book, and why did Jenna have one? Why hadn't Thorn ever told me about any of this?

When the slackening began, we loaded the sledges and

started hauling them back to Blue Ring. Silex and I dragged one, Thorn and Rose the other. As we walked, big, white clouds took turns passing in front of the sun, throwing us into shadow, then sunlight, then shadow again. Once we got to the kitchen, Thorn slipped away before I could talk to him. That made me mad. And he didn't show up at the Aery either, which made me madder. I was relieved, though, to see that Halo was there and seemed to be her normal but exhausted self.

She dropped into her big, tattered chair and watched as I started to put a nyper onto Fox. He'd been running around the Aery naked when I arrived. He'd pooped twice on the floor, but luckily, he was over the diarrhea he'd had the previous two days.

"I couldn't catch him," Halo said with a sad smile. "His little legs have gotten too fast. That's why he doesn't have a nyper on."

"I'll have it on him in a minute," I replied. "Besides, it looked like he was having fun—maybe we should all run around naked."

Halo chuckled. "There were days last summer when I wanted to do just that. But I didn't want to give the children a scare."

I laughed and finished tying on Fox's nyper. "Halo," I then asked casually, "do you remember us helping you back to your cubicle last night?"

Her brow furrowed in thought. "You and Thorn? No, I don't think I do. That's strange, isn't it?"

"You were really sleeping. We couldn't even wake you up. But we got you back to your cot."

Halo's eyes narrowed, and she frowned with concern. "I must have taken more than I meant," she muttered, more to herself than me.

"The drops?" I asked.

She looked up and nodded.

I felt my shoulders relax with relief—Thorn was right about the drops, but it had been an accident.

"Why do you take the drops, Halo?"

Her head lowered as she replied. She almost seemed ashamed. "I know I shouldn't. It could mix me up when I'm tending the children. But Maple, my hip's been hurting so much. More than a year. It grinds when I walk." She paused and looked back up at me. "Can you hear it grinding?"

I shook my head.

"It's no fun getting old, Maple," she added sadly. Then, with a small smile, "But I hope you and Thorn do."

I lifted Fox back down to the floor, and he scampered away on all fours to where Birch was playing with some new wooden figures—hand-sized animals and people. The Keeper had carved them and sent them down from the wind tower with Knot.

"We'll set up a system for you," I said. "How many times a day is it safe for you to use the drops?"

"No more than three."

"Okay, I'll get three pebbles and put them on the shelf beside the bottle. Every time you have a drop, put one of the pebbles into that jar. That way, you'll know if you've already taken it."

"Good idea," she said, seeming relieved. "Just like your grandmother—a problem-solver." Then she leaned back, closed her eyes, and sighed. "Poor Zara," she murmured. "She came so close."

She relaxed into the chair, not realizing she'd just spoken about the past. That she'd broken the rule. She began to snore.

I spent the next hour feeding the kids, washing them, changing nypers yet again, and trying to get them to fall asleep. When they finally did, I went outside, found three pebbles, all about the same size, and took them back in to set beside the drops. I hoped the next day, Halo would remember what they were for.

Just then, I heard the outside door of the Aery creak open and closed. A moment later, Thorn appeared. River was with him, not looking pleased.

"Maple," Thorn announced, "River—River is going to look after the kids till they fall asleep."

I turned away from him without meeting his eyes. "They already did," I replied icily. "So you can both go."

River turned to leave. Thorn put his hand on his shoulder to stop him.

"Then River can stay and get things set for tomorrow. So you can leave."

"But I don't have to clean that up, do I?" River whined, pointing to a pile of poop in the corner.

"Yes, you do," I said, my anger at Thorn spilling onto him. "And over there, too. And you'll need to scrape the nypers in the compost yard."

River sighed. "Okay, okay. I thought you liked doing this stuff, but Thorn says my sister needs a break."

I gazed at Thorn while I stood, considering. Then I handed the scraper to River and walked to the door. I pushed it open, and then Thorn followed me outside onto the crumbling steps.

"Maple," he said, turning to me, "I want to show you something."

"What is it?" I asked, my voice still as cold as the chilly autumn air.

"It'll help explain things. Please."

I didn't move.

"It's in the Deep."

In the Deep? What could he want to show me in that wreck of a building?

"Fine," I said. "Let's go. We don't have much time till the darkening."

CHAPTER 24
B IS FOR BEAR

I'd been on the roof of the Deep a few times with Papa but never inside. It wasn't one of the buildings the Menders maintained, so it had long fallen into ruin. When you walked by, looking through the broken windows, you could see dark shapes that seemed askew or tipped over. Papa had told me long ago the Deep was dangerous: the floors of the upper levels, he said, were made of transparent acrylic, and the cycle of scorching summers and freezing winters had weakened them. As we approached the building, I told this to Thorn.

"We won't be on any of those levels," he said. "We'll stay on the main floor. It's safe."

"Unless the floor above it collapses," I said.

"It won't," he replied. "I've done this a thousand times."

A thousand times?

Thorn led me around to the side of the Deep, through thick shrubs and weeds. Vines hung on its outside walls, insinuating curious tendrils into widening cracks.

"Watch out," he said as we approached a spot where the wall had crumbled, and the bricks and adjoining soil had tumbled into the basement. He jumped over the gap. He held out his hand, but I ignored it and leaped over by myself.

We were now near the back corner of the building, and I saw a set of crumbling steps leading up to a door. It was partly open.

"It's jammed," Thorn said. "You have to go in sideways." He went in first.

The gap was narrow, so I took a deep breath and squeezed between the door and its frame.

Inside, it was almost completely dark. But that's not what got my attention. It was the sudden stench. It rose into my nostrils as if it were trying to assault me. It smelled like a dank mixture of animal urine and rotting meat. With Silex and Rose, we'd once passed a dead fawn in the forest on our way to pick apples. Its stomach had been torn open, and maggots wriggled inside. It smelled awful. This was worse.

"Sorry," Thorn said when he noticed me covering my nose with my hand. "I should have warned you." I felt him reach past me and put his hand into a dark hole in the wall. A moment later, he pulled out a dull green cylinder.

"What's that?" I asked.

"Watch," he said. Then he pressed something on the cylinder, and a faint light came out of one end. "I found this in here —in the Deep. You leave it in the sun to store up light, and then you press this to make it come out."

I stared at him.

"I haven't had it in the sun for a long time," he said as if he were apologizing, "not since I started helping you at the Aery. So some of its light has leaked out. It's not very bright."

"Good," I replied. "I don't think I want to see what else might be in here anyway."

Thorn smiled, the light casting strange shadows on his face.

"Why didn't you show this light thing to anyone?"

He shrugged. "I needed it here." We stood in silence for a few moments. I was processing the fact that Thorn had kept secrets from me. And from everyone else.

"It doesn't smell where we're going," he finally said. "Not as bad, anyway."

He pointed the cylinder toward the floor and started walking deeper into the building. There was a path of sorts through the broken furniture, fragments of glass, and twisted metal rods that littered the floor. I assumed it was Thorn who'd cleared the way. As we walked farther, the light from Thorn's cylinder jostled up and down, making the looming shadows around us rise and dip as if they were alive. I looked up and realized I could see dimly through the ceiling above us. Like Papa had said, the upper floors were made of transparent acrylic.

"This is it," Thorn said, stopping in front of a massive grey rectangle that seemed to be built into the side wall of the building. He took a deep breath as if he were readying himself for something. "Can you take this?" he said, holding out the cylinder. Then he reached forward and put both hands on a plate-sized, shiny wheel that protruded at waist height from the grey rectangle.

"Wait," I said. "What are you doing?" I hoped I didn't sound frightened. "What is this?"

He stopped and turned back toward me. "It's what the Originals used to call a vault," he said. "Its walls and door are made of titanium—a really strong metal. They locked things inside it to keep them safe."

"So then, why did they leave it unlocked?"

"They didn't," Thorn replied. "It was locked when I found it."

I gazed at him, waiting for more explanation.

"It was six years ago," he continued, "not long after I was

harvested. I wasn't interested in what everybody else did during the slackenings, so I started exploring. I hiked out to different parts of the Coil. A few times, I followed the metal rails for as far as I could and still get back before the darkening. Both directions. Once, I even climbed all the way up the ladder in the wind tower. After that, I started exploring all the buildings in Blue Ring—including the ones we're supposed to stay out of." He lowered his voice, even though we were alone. "Did you know that in the boarded-up shed, there are six bodies with nothing but the bones left? People bodies."

"Obviously not," I replied, both frightened and annoyed. "How could I have known that?" I stared at him, but he didn't reply. "So you were exploring," I said, getting back to his story so I'd stop thinking about what he'd said was in the shed.

He nodded.

"Or more like sneaking," I added.

"I guess so," he replied. "It didn't hurt anyone."

"It could have. What if you'd got stuck in here and others got hurt trying to help you?"

He shrugged. "I was careful."

I was getting a little tired of all those shrugs.

"Anyway, after I found this vault, I pretty much stopped going anywhere else during the slackenings."

I was silent for a moment, imagining a little Thorn—probably no more than twelve—creeping for the first time into this carcass of a building. I almost smiled at his boldness. Or stupidity. "You said this thing was locked when you found it. So how did you get it open?"

"Thanks to that," he said, pointing at a table with drawers that loomed out of the dark. It was tipping on an angle as if it had only three legs. "I took its drawers out and carried them outside to see what was in them. When I flipped the last one over, I saw some numbers drawn on its back. And then I remembered I'd also seen numbers on this dial." He put his finger on a knob beneath the metal ring that protruded from the grey door. "I didn't know how to read numbers then, but when I brought the drawer over to the door of the vault, I matched the number shapes on the drawer to the ones on the dial. See—" he said, twirling the knob—"you can move this so the little arrow lines up with the numbers."

I grasped the knob with my free hand and gave it a twist. It spun easily.

"I didn't expect anything to happen," he continued. "But after I tried a few different ways of spinning it to the numbers, I heard a click. Then I turned this big ring—and the door swung open."

I could feel my anger at Thorn melt away as I marvelled that he'd thought of connecting the numbers drawn on the bottom of the drawer to the tiny numbers on the knob. And now I was curious: what had he found inside?

He must have sensed my sudden interest because he turned back to the door, spun the metal ring, and gave it a pull. The door swung open without a sound, its movement gusting the cobwebs all around us.

Thorn pointed the light cylinder downward and held out his hand. "Come inside," he said, smiling. I took his hand as we stepped gingerly into the room—into the vault. Then he lifted up the cylinder and began to play its circle of light over the walls. They were lined with dozens of long, grey shelves, and on each shelf, from one end to the other, were—

"Books!"

Thorn nodded. "That's right. More than a thousand of them. One thousand, three hundred forty-seven, to be exact."

I stood motionless, taking in the colours I saw before me— reds and blues, greens and yellows—each book a different hue. I moved closer to a shelf, lifted my hand, and warily touched the top of one. It felt warm, warmer than the metal the shelves were made of.

I looked back at Thorn. "Can I pull it out?"

He nodded. "Just open it slowly. The pages are brittle. Like old leaves."

I opened the book and peered into it. It was full of words—they ran like rows of potatoes over the pages. I put my finger on one of the letters I recognized: *em*.

"Are these healing books?" I asked Thorn. "Like the ones Jenna has?"

He shook his head. "Most of them are story books. They're about people doing things. Getting into trouble. Or out of it. Or animals. Some have a bunch of small stories in them."

"Stories like Virgil's?"

"Sort of. I think they're better than his. They have the advantage of actually having endings."

"What are the ones that aren't storybooks?"

"These ones," Thorn said, moving toward the back wall and putting his hand up on the highest shelf. A dozen books were arranged there, all of them the same size and all the same grey colour.

"What are they?" I asked.

"They're called en-cy-clo-pe-dia." He pronounced the word carefully. "See?" He pulled one down. "On the front of each one, it says *Book of Knowledge*." He paused and then added in a hushed tone, "Everything we used to know is in these books."

"And you've read them? Is that what you were doing during the slackenings all those years? Coming here?"

Thorn nodded. "But I haven't read all of them. Not nearly. So far, only 168 of the story books and most of the Books of Knowledge."

"But how—how did you—"

"Look," he said, guessing my question before I asked it. He drew me over to another one of the shelves. "These books were for little kids." He pulled one of them out. On its front was a young girl holding an apple. She was smiling, and her brown eyes were looking straight at me. The apple was red, more red and shiny than any I'd ever picked.

"Each page," Thorn continued as he slowly opened the book, "has a word written over a picture. See—here's a bear, and the letter on it is called *bee*—that's the sound that 'bear' starts with. That's what it looks like. B is for 'bear.' He flipped through a few more of the pages—dog, egg, frog . . . ladybug, robin, snake, wolf.

"This is how I learned to read," Thorn said, looking at me almost sheepishly. "Or at least, how I learned what most of the letters look like and sound like. Some I couldn't figure out right away. Like this one." He turned to the last page of the book. On it was a strange-looking animal—kind of like a deer but with black and white stripes and a bushy tail like Farley's. On top of it was the shape that Papa had drawn with the pencil beside my cot—the lightning bolt.

"After I'd memorized most of the letters, I started looking at the other books on this shelf. They were for older kids." He pulled out another book. On its front was a crow dropping a pebble into a jar. The crow was black, the jar was red, and the pebble was white. You could even see blue water in the jar. "I used all of these—" he pointed at the shelf in front of us—"to learn how to read words."

I was dumbstruck by what Thorn was telling me. He'd taught himself how to do something that nobody else at Blue Ring—except Papa, Jenna, and Virgil—knew how to do. He'd taught himself to read.

"How long did it take you?" I asked him. "To learn the reading, I mean."

"Longer than I expected. Putting letters together to make words is called spelling, and with a lot of words, the spelling seems kind of broken. Or maybe how we're saying them now is broken. Like this—" he opened the crow book and put his finger under a word. "See that one? That word is 'night.' The beginning and the end make sense—that makes the *en* sound and that makes the *tee* sound—but look what's in the middle—a *gee*, which makes a *guh* sound. But when we read that word, we don't say the gee. It took me a while to figure out those kinds of words. I started in the spring, and it wasn't until there was snow on the ground that I got better at it." He frowned as if this was an embarrassingly long time. "Sometimes, when I got frustrated with the spellings, I looked at the arithmetic books instead. Numbers make more sense."

I gazed at him, trying to let everything he'd told me settle in my mind.

"We need to head back," he said abruptly. "I don't want to get another jolt like a couple of nights ago."

I didn't reply but nodded. We stepped out of the vault, and Thorn quietly swung the door shut. "To keep the bats out," he said.

Thorn's cylinder was almost out of light, so we carefully picked our way back to where we came in. Thorn put the cylinder back in the hole, and then we squeezed through the narrow gap. Without exchanging a word, we hurried back to the Cube and climbed up to the third floor. Thorn walked with me to my cubicle, where we stopped before I opened the door.

I turned to him. "Why didn't you ever tell me?"

Thorn must have known that question was coming.

"If I'd told you back then, what would you have wanted to do?"

As I pondered his question, the crow with the pebble and jug came into my mind. "I'd have wanted to learn to read, too."

"I knew you would. And eventually, you'd have started to read the books in the vault. And that might have harmed you—memories surfacing and all that."

"You did it," I said. "You took that risk."

"But that was my own choice," he said.

"Can't I make my own choice, too?" I replied.

Thorn smiled and nodded. "It took me a long time to realize that." Then he leaned forward to give me a kiss before turning and walking down the hallway toward his own cubicle. I watched him as he slipped into the darkness.

"Thorn," I shouted before he turned the corner.

"Yes?" I heard him reply.

"Why did you stop going there? To the vault."

There was a long pause before he spoke. "I found something even better to do."

I couldn't see him, but I could feel his beautiful grin.

CHAPTER 25
SIX TOES

River didn't know he was going to spend the next two slackenings in the Aery, feeding the kids, putting them to bed, and scraping their nypers. But that's what he ended up doing. Because the morning after Thorn took me into the Deep, as we walked to the Meal House, I told River that's what he had to do. I needed time to talk to Thorn. River complained, but less than I thought he would, and soon agreed.

"It'll give me and Birch another chance to practice," he said.

"Practice what?" I asked.

"Making fart sounds."

Yes. The kids were in good hands.

I was worried that when we were at the table the day before, Silex and Rose might have heard me blurt out something about Thorn being able to read. Thorn must have been thinking the same thing.

"We need to act normal around Silex and Rose," he whispered as we stood in line to get our morning biscuit. "What should we say when we sit down?"

"I don't know," I replied. "Just talk about something else."

"Like what?" I'd never seen him this nervous. His hands trembled as he held his biscuit bowl.

"Something ordinary," I said. "I'll think of something. Just follow along and avoid the elephant in the room."

Thorn's brow furrowed, but he nodded. Hawk plopped two biscuit wedges into our bowls, and we headed to our table, where Silex and Rose were already sitting. Thorn and I sat down beside them and across from each other.

"I think I need to ask Fern for a new waist wrap," I announced as I picked up a knife and hacked away at a wedge of biscuit. It was harder than usual—more like a lump of dried clay.

"Oh?" Thorn replied. "How come?"

"It's starting to fray."

"Oh."

"The fibres are weakening."

"That's not good."

"This is only my second waist wrap since I was harvested."

"Hmmm. So the next one will be your third."

"We're fortunate to have so many rolls of nylar to make clothing."

"Nylar is very durable."

"Very."

"I like the word nylar."

"Yes. That's its name."

I glanced over at Silex and Rose and saw they were staring at us again. Or trying to. The Headmasters kept forcing their attention back to their bowls.

"I swear by the black snout of my Headmaster," Silex roared, slightly turning his head toward us, "that is the stupidest conversation I've ever heard. And I should know— I've had many with Rose."

Rose lifted her face to glare at him.

"Listen, you two," he continued, loud and grinning, "some advice: if you want to keep something a secret, don't try so hard to hide it. Take Rose here. Did you know that she has six toes on each foot? Of course not! Because she's not always trying to talk about non-toe topics."

"I do not!" Rose yelled.

Silex went on. "I assume you two are trying not to talk about that thing you let slip yesterday morning."

Thorn and I looked at each other, wondering how to respond. Thorn's forehead was glistening with sweat.

"See, that too," Silex quickly added, pointing his fork at us. "As soon as I said that, your eyes bugged out, and you looked like I'd peed in your biscuit. Which, I might say, would probably improve its flavour. But anyway, whatever it is, don't let your faces tattle on your thoughts."

"And as for Thorn being able to weed," he continued, turning to Thorn, "like you announced yesterday," turning to me, "I'm not surprised. Thorn has many talents, and being able to weed is no doubt among them. He's probably an excellent weeder. If he enjoys spending the slackenings in the forest, pulling out thistles and foxtails to keep it tidy, that's his choice."

Thorn and I were speechless, staring at Silex with our mouths agape.

A faint grin seemed to play around his face under his giant red beard.

"Silex," Rose scolded. "Let them be. I could tell them some of the things you did when you were their age."

Silex laughed. "Actually, Rose, you can't. All my youthful foolishness is hidden in that forbidden slop bucket of the past."

Thorn and I passed the rest of the meal interval in awkward silence. Out of the corner of my eye, I noticed Rose smiling at Silex as she shook her head.

Later, during the grip, all I could think about were the

books of stories that Thorn had read. Did he remember them all? Could he ever read so many that his head would get full? When he read, did he hear a voice in his head, like when someone talks in Zara's memories? Would he ever get tired of me and Lark's kids and go back to reading the books in the vault?

Our day of toil limped slowly along.

CHAPTER 26
THE ELEPHANT IN
THE ROOM

That evening, after the four of us had hauled the sledges back to the kitchen, Thorn and I walked together toward the bridge. Unsure of what to say to each other, we stayed silent. When we got there, we said, "Here we are," to Papa, who then asked about Lark's kids. Then he asked if I wanted the Inwards to go ahead without him so I could talk with him. I told him Thorn and I just wanted to rest and let our feet dangle over the water.

"Thorn," I said after Papa and the others had slipped into the forest, and we'd settled onto the bridge's wooden platform, "have the books ever triggered a memory in you?"

"Never," he replied.

"But you still think they might be dangerous for me?"

"Maybe. Like I said, that's why I didn't tell you about them. But I don't know if I actually believe they can trigger memories. Maybe people back then were just being extra careful. Your Papa would know if it ever actually happened."

I considered this. Could I ask Papa whether reading had ever triggered a memory without telling him why I wanted to know? Would he even care that Thorn had taught himself how to read? What would happen if everyone else found out about the vault full of books?

"I do know one thing," Thorn said, pulling me out of my thoughts.

"Just one?" I gave him a playful shove with my shoulder.

He smiled. "I know the books in the vault are really old. I mean, they were already old at the Arrival. Maybe that's why they've never triggered memories in me."

"What do you mean?"

"If they were already old when the Arrival happened, maybe no one here had ever read them. So they wouldn't have any memory of the stories in them."

I wasn't convinced, but I nodded. "How do you know they're so old?" I asked.

"They have numbers on the bottom of their first page—like one eight three six. That tells the year the book was made."

"I guess that's old," I agreed. "Papa told me it's now year 2122."

"I wonder why we stopped counting the years?"

"Easier to forget the past if you don't keep track of it," I said, thinking about how they'd got rid of all the writing sticks.

Thorn nodded. "The numbers in the books go from one eight zero two to one nine three seven. So they were at least a hundred years old at the Arrival, and some over two hundred. The Books of Knowledge all say one nine two one."

"Maybe they stopped making new books after—what did you say?—the one nine three seven year?"

"I don't think so. Jenna's medicine books aren't nearly that old. I think the books were put into the vault by someone who collected old things. They called them antiques. You probably couldn't see it in the dark, but above the vault's door, there are four words in gold letters—'Carscallen Rare Book Repository.'"

"What's a carscallen?" I asked.

"I'm not sure," Thorn replied.

We fell silent for a few moments and gazed down at the water flowing below us.

"I'm glad you told me," I said, turning toward him. "And I do want you to teach me."

"I will. But where? In the Aery after the kids are asleep?"

I shook my head. "No. I want them to learn, too. You can start with me and Birch. Then, we can teach the others when they're older."

Thorn looked surprised. "Teach the kids? They'll end up telling others for sure!"

I gave Thorn one of the shrugs he often gave me. "Maybe. But it's not fair to keep it from them. If Halo knew how to read, would you have wanted her to teach you?"

"Instead of playing with carved animals and squabbling with you for ten years? Yes, of course." He paused, and I knew he was trying to think of another objection.

He couldn't. "Okay, okay," he finally said. "But it's a big risk."

"It is. And now, I'm going to take another risk."

He smiled at me and waited.

"First off, I shouldn't have got so mad at you for not telling me you could read. You were just trying to keep me safe—"

"Is that all?" Thorn said before I could finish. "Don't worry about it. I would've been mad, too, if it was the other way around."

Ugh. I winced as he said this. Why did he have to be so understanding? I took a deep breath and continued. "That's not the thing I want to tell you."

Thorn's brow furrowed. "Sounds serious," he said, uncertain if it was. He was probably hoping it was one of the jokes we played on one another. He drew his legs back up onto the bridge, spun on his bottom, and then sat cross-legged, facing me. I did the same, then leaned forward to put one hand on each of his knees.

"Thorn," I said, looking straight into his eyes, "I've been having—I've been having—" I stopped, wondering if I was making a mistake—but what else could I tell him at this point?

"Trouble keeping your eyes off me?" Thorn said, laughing. "That's what you've been having?" I knew he was trying to reassure me, and loved him for it.

I smiled and shook my head. Then, I squeezed his knees, closed my eyes, and let it rush out. "I've been having memories from a past host emerge."

When I opened my eyes, I saw that Thorn was staring at me, his eyebrows raised and his head tilted slightly toward me. He still wasn't sure if I was joking.

"The memories belong to my grandmother. They surface during the darkenings, but I remember them when I wake up. It's been happening for eight years."

Thorn still didn't say anything. Now, he was gazing past me, deep in thought. I sat quietly, supposing he needed time for what I'd told him to settle.

"Thorn?" I said after a few moments.

"Now it makes sense," he replied, nodding and returning his gaze to me.

This wasn't the response I'd been expecting.

"What makes sense?" I asked, totally puzzled.

"Some of the things you've said over the years. They were . . . strange. I mean, it was strange that you said them."

"Like what?"

"Well—once we were wondering how far the forest went, and you called it a 'boreal' forest."

"So?"

"Then there was the time we were collecting walnuts, and I

found a rock with a spiral shell in it. You said it was an 'ammonite.'"

"It was."

"And just this morning, you said we should ignore 'the elephant in the room.'"

"Which we totally failed at."

"But I've never heard anyone else ever say that—'boreal' or 'ammonite' or 'elephant in the room.' They wouldn't even know what an elephant is."

"It's an animal," I replied. "Bigger than a moose, but it doesn't have fur, and its nose is a long tube."

"How do you know that? Have you ever seen an elephant around here?"

"Of course not, they—" I stopped. I could remember seeing an elephant—no, four elephants—standing in a grassy meadow —no, it's called a savannah. Three of them are pulling up clumps of grass and stuffing it into their mouths. The fourth— the biggest—stands there staring at me. Mountains are behind them, peaks covered with snow. Then I realized this was Zara's memory, not mine. Or maybe it had become mine.

"I always figured," Thorn continued, "that it was your Papa who told you about things like that—words like 'boreal' and 'ammonite' and what elephants are—things you wouldn't have known. But it surprised me because I didn't think he'd risk triggering a memory in you. And I didn't want to ask you about it because I was afraid even that might trigger one. But if what you say is true, then it's these memories—the ones coming to you during the darkening—that you've been drawing on."

I knew what Thorn was saying was true, but the way he said it made me feel a bit ashamed as if I'd gained my knowledge by cheating. He didn't seem to notice. He was still talking away, but I was preoccupied with a realization: the memory of the four elephants hadn't surfaced during a darkening. It had emerged the moment Thorn asked me about elephants. That hadn't ever happened before.

I turned my attention back to him.

". . . felt confused afterward?" Thorn was asking, but I responded with a question of my own.

"Thorn, how do you know I'm right? How do you know what elephants are?"

Thorn smiled. "One of the books has stories about animals in Acrifa —"

"Africa," I corrected.

"Right," he replied slowly, looking slightly abashed. "Africa. And one of those stories tells how the elephant got its long nose." He paused and frowned slightly. "I don't think it's completely accurate."

"I'm sorry I didn't tell you till now, Thorn. About the memories surfacing."

"It makes sense. I would've wanted you to tell me about them, and you were afraid of what might happen. I totally understand."

"But a few minutes ago, you said you'd be mad if it was the other way around!" I couldn't believe he was handling my big revelation so well. It was kind of annoying.

"Yeah," he agreed. "I guess I did say that. But I don't actually feel that way. I think I'm just too eager for you to tell me about some of the memories. And for me to tell you about things in the books. We can do that while we toil, as long as Silex and Rose don't hear."

"Hold on," I said, stretching out my hand to touch him gently on the arm. "I think telling you my grandmother's memories could be more dangerous than me learning to read some really old books. Just because reading doesn't trigger a past host's memories in you doesn't mean something else won't."

Thorn looked stunned. "But—" he stammered.

"And there's one more thing," I added. "Even if it's safe, I'm not sure it would be right to share my grandmother's memories with you. Her memories aren't like storybooks. I mean, I don't know if I'd want my memories handed over to a stranger to pluck through like a raspberry bush."

Thorn looked both hurt and crestfallen.

"I'm sorry—I shouldn't have said it like that, Thorn. I just mean we need time to think this through."

Thorn considered my words, then gave a slight nod. "You're very wise," he said.

"Beyond my years," I replied.

CHAPTER 27
LA JEUNE FEMME

The next evening, Thorn and I went back to the Deep. We weren't planning on staying there for the whole slackening—there were too many spiders for my liking, even in the vault. Thorn was going to get the book that showed the animals and the letters, and then we were going to climb up on the roof, where he'd start to teach me. I'd decided I didn't want Birch to start learning just yet. We needed to go slow.

As we made our way through the dry, waist-high weeds beside the Deep, I thought about a memory that had come to me during last night's darkening. Zara was sitting, holding a book in her lap, flipping through its pages. There were words on the left-hand pages, and there were pictures—called photographs, I remembered—on the right-hand side. They were of places I couldn't believe had ever existed. Or did they still exist?

In one picture, tall grass covered an endless meadow where animals with impossibly long necks and legs seemed to be eating leaves from trees. In another, mounds of dry sand stretched toward the horizon like banks of burning snow—one of them had a trail of footprints leading to its top as if someone had walked up and over its crest. Even if I did tell Thorn these memories, how could I find the words to fully describe them?

I stepped into the vault with Thorn and held the light cylinder while he pulled a book from its shelf. He folded it into a scrap of nylar that he'd brought, then turned to leave. I stopped him.

"Thorn," I said, my voice quiet but urgent.

"What is it?" he asked, his eyes wide with alarm. "Did you hear someone?"

I shook my head. Without a word, I stepped into the middle of the vault, tipped my head to the left, and began to spin slowly around, tracing the beam from the light cylinder over the shelves.

"Thorn—I can read the words on the books," I whispered.

"What?" he exclaimed, louder than he probably meant to. Some of the pigeons outside the vault flapped away from their roosts.

"The words on the sides of the books—I can read them." I moved closer to a shelf and put my finger on one of them.

"This one says *Pinocchio*." I said it slowly, letting each syllable of the peculiar word slip from my mind and through my lips. "And this one, *Frankenstein*." I slipped my finger to another book, then another, and another.

"*The War of the Worlds, The Adventures of Huckleberry Finn, The Time Machine, Uncle Tom's Cabin, White Fang, The Sky Pilot, The Jungle Book*—"

I stopped and glanced over at Thorn. His jaw was slack, his mouth gaping. I'd never seen him look so surprised—not even when Silex once draped a garter snake over his shoulders as he knelt to tighten his foot wrappings.

He stepped over beside me and pulled out the one that said *The War of the Worlds*. He snapped the book open to its first page, then winced when it made a sharp crack. The paper was brittle with age. He put his finger below the first line of words.

"What's this say?" he asked.

I lifted the light cylinder higher till it shone fully on the page. Then I read out loud, "No one would have believed in the last years of the nineteenth century that this world was being watched keenly and closely by intelligences greater than man's and yet as mortal as his own."

Thorn smiled and nodded, then carefully closed the book and slipped it back into the gap on the shelf.

"I think you know what's happened," he said.

"I think I do, too," I replied. "Zara's memories of reading— of how to read—they've emerged. It must have happened last night. I thought it was just a memory of her looking at a book."

"Amazing," Thorn said. "You said all the memories are about things she saw or did."

I nodded. "Experiences."

"But what you've remembered now is like a—a knowing. Like how Jenna knows how to make the drops for the kids in the Aery. A skill."

He paused and looked thoughtful. "I wonder . . ." he began before trailing off. He walked over to the other side of the vault, where the shelves held thicker books. He pulled one out, opened it, and then walked back to me.

"What about this?" he asked. "Can you read it?"

I looked into the book. The cylinder had lost even more of its light, so it was getting hard to see. I leaned forward and squinted.

"*La jeune femme ne répondit que par de nouveaux sanglots*," I said. It took me a moment to realize the words seemed strange and familiar at the same time.

"What does it mean?" Thorn asked.

"The young woman answered only with new sobs," I said without thinking, without effort. I simply knew.

"I guess your grandmother could read French," Thorn said. I noticed a rueful smile playing on his lips even as I realized I'd never before heard the word "rueful."

I could tell that Thorn was awash with a mix of feelings. He was pleased we'd discovered my new abilities and pleased we'd done it together. But he was still a bit bewildered by the wonder of it. And he was likely worried: would this change anything?

I wondered that, too.

And he felt—I think—some envy, maybe even some resentment. It had taken him most of a year to learn to read, hunkered down all alone in a cold vault, teaching himself, sounding words out letter by letter. And me? I'd gone to sleep and woken up with that ability—and probably, I guessed, I was a lot better at it than he was. Plus, an entire other language. It had never occurred to me before that there had once been other ways of talking.

"I wonder what else you have in there?" Thorn said, gently putting his hand on my head.

CHAPTER 28
SHARE THE BOUNTY

Would Zara want me to share her memories with Thorn? For days, I'd puzzled over that question. That's what I was doing now, in one of the storerooms in the Aery where I'd gone to think—to get away from the noise while Thorn and River got the kids ready for bed.

For the past three slackenings, River had shown up at the Aery even though I hadn't asked him to. He said he wanted to help. He spoke to the kids as if they were a huge inconvenience —"Again? You just pooped yesterday! Try to space it out!"—but I could tell he was enjoying them, especially Birch, who looked the most like him, with the same wide eyes. The kids, too, were always happy to see him, this man who called himself "Uncle Amazing."

I sat down on a pile of nylar blankets in the storeroom and tried to discern—another word I'm sure I got from Zara—the best thing to do. The memories came from Zara, but they were in my head now—did that make them mine? She'd been dead for more than fifty years. But her memories weren't. They were alive and well. Should I ask Papa what he thought? But I still didn't want him to know I was getting her memories. He already had Lark to worry about.

Slowly, my mind began to drift toward Halo, who was out in the main room sleeping, oblivious to the laughing, crying, and crashing that was happening all around her. My eyes were heavy—how had Halo managed to do this all day for so many years? I closed my eyes, and Papa flitted through my mind. But which Papa? Mine or Zara's husband, Jacob? I couldn't tell. He was more of an idea than an image. I hadn't spoken with him in more than a week, and I was missing him. It felt like I was being pulled in too many directions: Papa, Thorn, Lark's kids. I didn't have enough time for all of them. I was exhausted, but my mind was racing, and my chest felt ready to explode.

To ground myself, I decided to try something I hadn't done in years. I would meditate, like I used to when I spent the slackenings with Papa and the Inwards. I crossed my legs, leaned forward, and began to focus on my breathing, letting it grow deeper and slower, then on my heartbeat, settling into its steady presence. After a few minutes, I began to hear Papa's voice, distant, as if he were calling to me from across the forest:

Keep thinking about Farley. Keep that old rascal in your mind when the linking starts. He'll help you keep hold of yourself.

I smiled at the memory and then released it, making space in my mind for another memory of Farley to emerge. A moment passed, and there he was, lying on his side, panting happily as a litter of tiny puppies eagerly nursed from him.

But that didn't make sense. Nursing?

I drew the memory closer and realized it wasn't Farley—it was another dog, another kind of dog—female and a lot bigger than Farley. Zara's dog. Bella.

As the puppies continue to feed, I hear a woman speaking and Zara answering.

look they're latching right on to her

yes they're very hungry
they haven't fed since last night

what happened to their mom

hemorrhage

i'm sorry

i'm so glad the vet connected us

me too

it's kind of you to lend her to me

*no problem
her pups are weaned but
she's still got plenty of milk*

share the bounty

that's right share the bounty

"Maple, they're all in bed." I opened my eyes and saw Thorn, his hair a mess and a dribble of vomit on his shirt—not his, I assumed—standing in the doorway to the storeroom. "River's cleaning things up," he added.

"Come here," I said, smiling and beckoning him to the pile of nylar blankets I was sitting on. "I've got something to tell you."

We did it during the next slackening. There was no way of eliminating the risk, but we took precautions. Silex had mentioned he was going to go listen to the Teller with Rose, so we went into one of the small rooms on the second floor of Gehenna. We wanted Silex nearby in case something went wrong.

The room was dank and smelled like someone had been drying fish in it, but we had to keep the door closed. We didn't want anyone to hear us by accident. There was no window, so it was completely dark except for a slit of pale light at the bottom of the door.

I began.

"I'll start with this one. It seems like I'm high up in a building because I'm looking down at things through a window. There's a long, straight path that looks like the concrete in our compound, but it doesn't have any cracks or roots pushing through it."

I paused and peered at Thorn's face to make sure he was all right. I continued.

"There are buildings on both sides of the concrete path, dozens of them, but they're much taller than anything here. Most of them have big signs—Fairmont, one says. Scotia Plaza. Manulife. ZelonTech. On both sides of the concrete path, people are walking. Some are sitting on chairs behind little fences. They're drinking from little cups. Everyone's wearing nylar clothing that fits their shape, all different colours." I paused again. "Still okay?"

Thorn nodded.

"On the concrete path—"

"Probably what they called a boulevard," Thorn said.

"Right," I nodded. "Actually, I think I knew that. So, on the boulevard, there are dozens of big boxes on wheels. There are people inside them. I can see them through the part that's made of glass. They're all rolling in the same direction."

"Are they buggies?" Thorn asked, his eyes closed. "Are there animals pulling them? Horses?"

"I don't see any animals," I replied. "I don't know what's making them move. Maybe the boulevard is on a hill."

"Okay, I know what you mean now. I read about them in some of the storybooks. They're called motorcars. Petrol made them move. You controlled them with a chauffeur, and they took people to the beach on holidays."

I nodded. I didn't understand a lot of what Thorn was saying, but it was still helping me draw on more of Zara's memories. "My grandmother had a motorcar, too," I said, "but she didn't call it that. She called it a Honda. I don't think she owned a chauffeur."

I continued describing some of Zara's memories to Thorn for the rest of the slackening. I focused mostly on the things she'd seen and stayed away from memories that seemed more personal. That was fine with Thorn because it was Zara's world —the world before the Arrival—that he was most interested in, not Zara herself.

Nothing I told Thorn triggered any memories from a previous host. Eventually, I stopped asking him if he was doing okay and just closed my eyes and described the things that Zara and I recollected. We didn't stop until we heard the Listeners getting up to leave Gehenna. The telling had finished for the night.

CHAPTER 29
ZARA

"I can't read this," Thorn said, handing me a small book with a shiny blue ribbon tied around it.

"Why not?" I replied.

"It's handwriting. I can't read handwriting."

I took the book from him. It was a few days after we'd met in the storeroom, where I'd shared some of Zara's memories with him. Now we were in the Aery, and we'd just finished washing the kids and putting them to bed.

"You probably can," he added. "Can read it, I mean. I'm curious about what it is."

I untied the ribbon and opened the book. The first page was filled with elegant, undulating lines of faded blue that ran from one side to the other. The loops and curves of the letters reminded me of the swoops of barn swallows.

"February 16, 2065. I think I was one of the first to come to," I read. I looked up at Thorn and nodded. "I can read it."

Thorn looked both pleased and crestfallen. "Okay. Can we read it right now? I mean, can you read it to me?"

"Who did it belong to?" I replied as I flipped through the pages.

He shrugged. "No idea. It was in the vault, tucked behind the Books of Knowledge. I found it years ago, but I put it back there till now."

"When River gets back," I said, "let's ask if he'll do the rest himself." My brother was outside. He'd washed the nypers and was now hanging them up in the drying room in the Cube.

When River returned, he agreed to finish cleaning up if we found Twig and asked her to join him. We ran into her on the snow-covered compound. She was already heading to the Aery to see him.

Thorn and I went back to my cubicle. After plunging around in knee-deep snow for the entire grip, we wanted someplace warm. My cot was narrow, but we managed to lie side by side and pulled the nylar blankets up to our chins. Then Thorn closed his eyes, and I started reading.

February 16, 2065

I think I was one of the first to wake up. I was on my back in the middle of the compound. Snowflakes drifting down on me. No idea what happened. Went outside with everybody else. Celebrating. Hugging and cheering. The coil had worked! Enough energy to light up North America for two decades. Everyone jumping up and down, laughing, throwing snow into the air, at each other.

Next thing I knew, I was on my back, on the frozen concrete. It had to be the same day, or my fingers would have been frozen, even with my gloves. I pushed myself up onto my knees and looked around. A few others on their feet, wandering around the compound like they were lost. Everyone else still lying on the ground. Some stirring, most not. I saw Zara getting up from her knees—

"Zara!" I yelped, turning to Thorn. "Thorn, that's my grandmother!"

Before he could say anything, I got back to reading.

—getting up from her knees and tried to call out to her, but my voice was ragged from the frigid air. I put a bit of snow in my mouth, let it melt, and tried again. She heard me. We stumbled toward each other. I wanted to ask if she knew what had happened, but before I could, she said we needed to get everybody out of the cold. Judging from the angle of the sun, it was past mid-afternoon, and it would soon get colder. She said she'd tried contacting the provincial EMS, but no response. She called over the few others who were now standing and told them to drag the ones on the ground into the gym.

I paused to ask Thorn: "The gym—that's what Gehenna used to be, right?"

He nodded.

Each of us ran to someone lying in the snow. I knew it would take a while. There must have been nearly 200 still unconscious. Somebody yelled we should start with the ones without mitts or toques. And the kids.

I grabbed the boots of a nearby man. He was face down, no coat on. I knew it was Aaron Duggan. When I started pulling him to the gym, his shirt rolled up—it was frozen to the ground. That's when I saw the thing on his bare back. Like a water beetle, but fifty times bigger.

"The Arrival," Thorn murmured. "This must be when the Headmasters appeared." I could sense his breathing quickening.

I yelled and fell backward. Zara ran over, and I showed her the thing on Aaron's back. It had legs along its sides, wriggling against his skin. Zara told me to get it off him before I pulled him into the gym. Then she went to drag others in.

I kneeled beside Aaron and grabbed the sides of the thing with my gloves. It had some sort of hard shell. I pulled. It was either heavier than it looked or was somehow stuck. I thought it might be frozen to him. I pulled harder, and his torso began to lift off the ground. That freaked me out. I panicked and yanked as hard as I could on the right side, then the left, rocking it back and forth. Something ripped, and the thing suddenly came off. It was only then I noticed it had these two tentacles—no, more like black coils—stuck into the back of his head, just above his neck. Those slid out last, each one about fifteen centimetres long.

I threw the black, wriggling thing to the side and looked down at Aaron's back. It was a mess. Like someone had pinched off hundreds of small circles of flesh. The punctures where the coils had gone into his skull were oozing purple blood.

Aaron's whole body started to clench and spasm. Maybe I shouldn't have, but I rolled him over. His eyes were closed, but his face was twisted like he was in terrible pain. Then his knees pulled up toward his chest, and he started shaking. When it stopped, every part of him seemed to slump. I couldn't see his breath in the cold air.

I knew he was dead.

I shouted to the others. They let go of whoever they were dragging and ran back over, Zara too. I explained what happened. I must have been babbling because they kept asking me to slow down and repeat it. Zara rolled Aaron back onto his stomach. Everyone got quiet when they saw his wounds.

"That thing was stuck to him," I shouted, pointing to where I'd thrown it in the snow. But it wasn't there.

Kumiko Lee asked if that was it. She was pointing at a black shape, slowly crawling across the compound. It was heading toward several people still lying unconscious on the compound. Gus Gissing ran over and kicked it to the edge of the forest.

By then, it was nearly dark, and the temperature was dropping fast. Zara told us to get back to dragging people into the gym. Kumiko asked what if we found the black things on others. She was so scared she could barely speak. Zara said to pull them into the gym, and we'd figure out what to do later.

February 17, 2065

We got everybody in. Some have really bad frostbite. The young guy who got here just a couple of days ago was only wearing Birkenstocks. Keshti says he'll lose some toes. We're all exhausted and hungry. But right now, I need sleep more than anything. I'm going to stop writing and lie down here in the gym.

Zara just woke me. Says all the people that don't have the black things on them—95 of us—have woken up. The rest— 104, she says—have the macro-parasites. That's what Dr. Keshti is calling them. They're still out cold. She hopes they won't wake up till she figures out how to detach them.

One hundred four people with parasites bigger than a dinner plate. Can't fall back to sleep, so I'll go see what Zara needs.

February 18, 2065

Dr. Keshti didn't get her wish. The ones with the macro-parasites are waking up. The first ones freaked out when they saw what was stuck to them. The girl from Physical Plant

(Krista?) tried slamming herself backward against a wall. Virgil stopped her. Avi Besner took a swing at Dr. Keshti when she wouldn't let him try to drown it by lying in the hot tub. Then she sedated him.

February 19, 2065

Some good news: everybody's conscious, and nobody's panicking. As they woke up, we explained bit by bit what had happened to them. Zara told them Dr. Keshti has finally got through to the CDC. Communications were down for a while. She says a medical team with parasitologists is on the way.

Most of the people in the gym are too anxious to eat or sleep, but they're coping. Zara keeps circling around, reassuring them. She's amazing. I don't think she's slept for two days. She's only in her early twenties, but everyone seems glad she's taken charge. A few people have gone back to their cubicles, but most are staying in the gym. It's comforting to be with others.

February 20, 2065

This is going to be my last entry. I can't keep writing after today. After what I saw. And what I did. I need to go help the wounded. And deal with the dead. Goodbye.

"Something else is written right underneath," I told Thorn, "but it's scratched out. I can't read it."

February 22, 2065

Zara has asked me to keep writing. Says we need to record what's happened. Just in case. "In case what?" I asked her. "In case none of us survive," she said. So I will. But who's going to read it? Turns out the CDC isn't on its way. In fact, Zara and Keshti haven't been able to contact anyone beyond the coil.

Our comms are working, but no one's answering. Anywhere. Zara and Dr. Keshti told us help was coming to keep us calm.

Keep writing, Zara says. So. Here goes.

Two days ago, around 4 p.m., I was helping Dr. Keshti put fresh bandages on Sylvio's toes. I mean, where his toes used to be. He's the guy who got here just a few days ago. All of a sudden, a commotion. I turned around. Everybody with a macro-parasite was getting up. Then, they walked to a corner of the gym in a huddle. They didn't say a word.

Then, they got into two rows. By then, everybody else had noticed, and some of us were getting a little freaked out. Creepy to see them lined up, staring at us. Zara asked what the hell they were doing, but nobody replied. She asked them to go back to their bed spots on the gym floor. They didn't move.

Then Roman Ziegler, in the middle of the front row, called out. He was yelling but sounded calm. He said something like, "We don't want to hurt you, but if we have to, we will."

There are two exits in the gym. One line of them walked toward the east-side door and the other line (the one with Roman) toward the north-side door. Then, two of them opened the north-side door and left. Zara asked Roman what was going on.

This is what he said to her, word for word: "We need more of you."

Zara started walking over to him. I haven't known her long, but she looked fed up and fierce. She told him we didn't have time for this and the parasites were making them delusional. But before she could finish, three of them ran forward and tackled her. Then, they dragged her to the group by the north door.

Several of us started to run to help her, but Roman shouted, "Stop, or we'll hurt her!" He stepped beside Zara and raised his foot like he was about to stomp, then put it down gently on the side of her head, right on her temple. The ones who were running to her stopped in their tracks.

Zara shouted something like, "Stop this, Roman! Get Dr. Keshti. She can help you!" But Roman kept his foot on her head while others held her down.

Then the north door opened again, and the two who'd left (Craig Sanders, Gill Ellis) came back in. I know Craig really well—we're doing the same VRx course in Precambrian geology. Gill had a nylar sack over his shoulder. It clattered when he dropped it. Then, the people with the parasites went over and started pulling knives out of it. They must have taken them from the cafeteria. The rest of us just watched. We were too stunned to act. Then Craig and Gill left again. Roman said, "We want six of you to come over here." He said "we," not "I." That's exactly what he said.

None of us moved or spoke. It didn't seem real. Roman took his boot off Zara's head, moved down to her feet, and stomped on her left ankle. I think I could hear it break.

"No!" I cried out. I dropped the book onto my chest and closed my eyes. Thorn put his arm around me and pulled me toward him but didn't say anything. I could hear his heart racing and feel his body trembling.

CHAPTER 30
JACOB

It was a few moments before I was able to start reading again.

> Roman took his boot off Zara's head, moved down to her feet, and stomped on her left ankle. I think I could hear it break. Zara screamed. He moved to her other side and put his boot over her other ankle. Several of us shouted, "No!" before he could stomp again. They broke away from our group (Donna O'Dell, Ocksana Bablanian, and one of the cafeteria workers from Australia—I don't know him) and ran over to the pack of infected. That's how I'm thinking of them now—infected. They were grabbed and held. Roman shouted that three more needed to come over, and after a moment, Em Penner, Zbig Polat, and Malika Shay-Abboud went. Their heads were down, defeated.
>
> Roman said something like, "Now, the rest of you stay there and keep calm." Then we watched as he told the six who'd gone over to lie on the floor and wait. In a few minutes, Craig and Gill returned. They were each pulling one of the carts I'd seen beside the tool shed.
>
> Roman yanked up the shirts of the people on the floor. He undid the bras of the women who were wearing them. Roman

reached into a cart and lifted out a parasite. He handed it to Gill. Someone behind me started to vomit. Others were begging Roman to stop.

Then he pulled out five more parasites and gave them to the people standing closest. They kneeled down and laid them on the backs of the six people (not Zara—by then, they'd dragged her over closer to the north wall).

I could see the parasites start to gnaw into their flesh. Threads of blood trickled down their sides. They were clenching their jaws. Some moaned. Then, the two tentacles at the top of the parasites began pushing into the base of their skulls. All six passed out. Roman had them dragged over to a wall behind the pack.

Roman turned back toward us. He told us they'd be fine. Then he said that six more had to come over. He moved beside Zara again and stared down at her unbroken ankle. Before I knew what I was doing, I shouted, "Give us a minute, and we'll decide who to send!" Roman paused, then nodded and said we had two minutes.

I turned toward our group and whispered, "We need to fight back."

Jordan Billson said we shouldn't because they have knives.

Kelly Glenn said we had to fight back, or we'd all end up with those things on us. He said he'd rather have a knife in his gut.

Then Jordan suggested we go along with them until help arrives.

That's when I told them all that help wasn't coming. Or if it was, not for a long time.

Penny McKee asked how we could even think of fighting them because they're our friends. Mehta said that her husband (Salman) was over with them, too. Kelly pointed out that Mehta's husband had put one of the parasites on Jenna's back *about five minutes before. He said they were no longer the people they used to be.*

Roman shouted, "One minute left!"

That's when Jamie pointed at some bins behind us and said they were full of things like hockey sticks and ski poles. And ice skates with blades. We could use those to fight back, he said.

Roman shouted, "Thirty more seconds!"

Without really thinking, I nodded and said, "Let's go!" and just like that, we all started racing to the bins. We threw them open and pulled out whatever was closest, anything that we could use to hit or cut.

I looked up and saw Roman and the others approaching us. They were walking fast but not running. They looked calm. They all had kitchen knives in their hands—even the three or four kids among them.

Roman shouted, "This is not what we asked you to do!" Or something like that.

And then, we started fighting. I'd never hit anyone before. Almost 200 of us. Trying to hurt, damage, even kill each other. Less than a week ago, most of us had been in the same gym watching a basketball game between the physicists and the engineers. Team Quark versus Team Alloy.

Everything was a blur. I remember Julius Almedo lunging at me with his blade. I lifted my stick over my head and slashed him across the face. He fell backward, blood streaming from his forehead and cheek. I must have hit his eye, too, because he covered it with his hand. I froze in front of him, wondering if I should hit him again, then felt a sharp pain in my left calf. It was Gabriel (Kate and Niki's ten-year-old) latching onto my leg and jabbing me with a knife. I shook him off and kicked him away. Somebody tripped and fell on him.

I felt someone grab onto my hockey stick. I turned and saw it was Roman. He held the shaft so I couldn't swing, and then he stepped closer and jabbed in the air with his knife, and he shouted that he didn't want to kill us ("We don't want you dead," is what I think he said). Then he slashed me just below my elbow, dragging the blade down to my wrist. The pain made me drop my stick. Somebody must have picked it up and hit me with it because all of a sudden, I was on the floor, and my head was ringing. My vision was going black. The floor was slippery. I rolled over to the wall and used it to push myself back up. My head was still ringing, and my leg and arm throbbing.

The noise was awful. Screaming and grunts and the sound of wood and metal hitting bones. I was looking around on the floor for a knife, but all of a sudden, Roman shouted, "Enough! Enough! Stop now!"

Everybody in his group stepped back. Everybody on our side stopped, too, but we were all confused—panting and dripping sweat and blood. Roman shouted something like, "That's enough persuasion for now," and told us to look after our injured.

But Jamie yelled at us that they were backing down and motioned at us to keep fighting. He lunged toward them, but none of us followed. Then I heard another voice from across the gym and knew it was Zara. She was still lying on the floor and was telling us—our people—to move back to the wall.

So we started to limp and hobble to the north wall. The ones in Roman's group were moving the other way. Then Roman shouted again: "Help your injured!" I shook myself out of a daze and saw I'd been limping past people who were too hurt to get up. I stopped and helped drag them back. Some of them weren't just wounded. When we got them all back, I looked over and realized Roman's group had taken a few more of our people during the fight.

For the next couple of hours, each side looked after its own. We kept an eye on their group, expecting them to run at us at any moment. Roman sent two of his people to get bandages and medical things from the infirmary. When they got back, they dropped it all onto the floor in the middle of the gym and walked away. Roman told us to use it because we needed it more than they did.

Keshti and a couple of others retrieved it, and then she and a few with first-aid or medical training started stitching wounds and bandaging. She had us break some hockey sticks for splints. She made people with possible concussions lie still on the floor. She had some of the least wounded (including me) drag the dead to the west wall.

Then Roman shouted at her. I mean at Dr. Keshti. He told her to come over to them and help their injured. Jamie tried to hold her back, but she pushed past him and went over. She took a quick look at their injured and then called some of us over (including me again). We spent the next couple of hours doing the same with them as we had with us. When we were mostly done, Roman told us to go back to our side.

That's when I asked him if we could leave. He said, "Of course not. We haven't finished." Then he shouted that six more of us had to come over to them, starting with the least injured.

I heard Jamie, behind me, croak, "No." His voice was hoarse. He'd got hit in the throat in the fight. He said we had some of their knives now, so we had a better chance.

But Dr. Keshti pointed out that six on our side had been killed, and two more were too badly hurt to move. Only two on Roman's side were dead. Our injuries were worse, and they still had more knives, and there were more of them.

Then Jamie pleaded something like this: "But they don't

want us dead. They were trying to hurt us but not kill us. That's an advantage we can use. Let's try. Please."

Dr. Keshti shook her head and started walking over to Roman. One by one, five others dropped their sticks or knives and followed her. Bloody footprints trailed after them.

At that point, a lot of us just sank to the floor, some with their heads in their hands, others lying on their sides in fetal positions, others on their backs, staring at the ceiling.

With the adrenalin from the fight drained from my body, it was awful to watch what happened next. Roman told the ones who'd gone over to him to pull up their shirts and lie face down. Then, they pulled six more of those things out of the carts.

And then, all of a sudden, they dropped the black things back into the carts, and all the rest of them dropped their knives to the floor in one big clatter.

"The slackening!" Thorn cried out. He jumped off my cot and started pacing around my cubicle in circles, pulling at his hair. "Keep going!"

Roman dropped to his knees beside Zara. He kept saying things like, "I'm sorry, I'm sorry," and, "It wasn't me, it wasn't me." He was sobbing.

Then the most incredible thing I've ever seen happened. Zara sat up. It made her wince with pain. She picked up a bloodied knife that had tumbled down beside her.

And then she slid it across the floor to the wall.

She said, "I know, Roman," and she reached up and took his hand in hers.

Nobody moved. Jamie told me later on that when he saw them drop the knives, his first thought was to charge into them and stab Roman in the heart. But when he looked at their faces *and saw their anguish, their torment, he knew they'd become themselves again. Our friends. Our family members.*

Zara took charge again, even with her broken ankle. She told everyone we had work to do and we'd have to process what had happened later. She told Jordan and Jamie to see if there were stretchers in the infirmary. She had Niki help Dr. Keshti triage the wounded (Niki said she'd finished the first year of veterinarian school).

Zara had us carry the worst injured to the ward in the infirmary. By "us," I mean those without the macro-parasites. She told the others (the infected) that she wanted them to sit on the far side of the gym. They were so stunned by what had happened—by what they'd done—that they walked over like zombies. There were three children with them. Two of them cried and cried. The other one (Magda) was just staring into space, so someone had to lead her to a spot to lie down.

Zara called me over to the bench where she was sitting. She said to me, "Jacob—"

"Thorn!" I yelled, suddenly sitting bolt upright. "Zara called him *Jacob*—she calls him *Jacob*—it was my Papa who wrote this!"

CHAPTER 31
MAGDA

Thorn stopped pacing and looked where I was pointing to Papa's name on the page. "It must be him," he said, "unless maybe there was another Jacob here." He paused. "If it is him, they hadn't partnered yet, had they? Zara and your Papa?"

I shook my head. "Not for a few more years. He wasn't even twenty yet."

Thorn took a deep breath and then sat down beside me again. "Keep going."

> She said to me: Jacob, gather up all the knives and sticks. She wanted me to hide them in the Quonset along with anything else that could be used as a weapon, like hammers and screwdrivers.
>
> She asked Gail and Carlos to get mops and wipe up all the blood. But Gail was feeling dizzy, so Carlos and Virgil did it. And she asked some others (I was picking up the knives by then) to carry the six dead to the garden shed (it's not heated, so we could leave their bodies there till later).
>
> This went on for a few more hours, Zara telling us what to do (I think I said earlier that people seemed grateful for her to

take charge—almost everybody else was still in shock—but I guess she probably was, too). Then, she finally let Dr. Keshti put her ankle into a splint. After that, she asked Niki and me to get everyone who could walk to gather where she was (except the kids—Jenna stayed with them).

Niki and I weren't sure if she wanted Roman and the others to come over, but she did.

Fifteen minutes later, almost everybody (with parasites and without) crowded around her as she sat on a bench—some standing, some sitting on the floor. They were on one side of her, and we were on the other. It still felt like us and them—I mean *us* versus *them*—even though most of them looked hollowed up with guilt and anguish.

Here's what Zara said. By then, I'd found some scraps of paper, so I wrote it all down as she said it, word for word.

"Listen, everyone. What happened today—or yesterday, whenever it was—I've lost track. What happened was something none of us could have ever imagined. It was horrific. Right now, we're all traumatized and in shock. We all have friends or family who are dead. Or dying. But no one here is to blame. Whatever those things are that showed up after the EMP, they're the cause of this. Not us. If one of them had latched onto me while I was passed out in the compound, I'd be under their control, too. Just like Roman. Just like all of you." (She was looking at the people around Roman). "And if any of you had been in a different spot when it happened or if any of you had fallen on your back instead of face down, then you wouldn't have—have—"

She couldn't seem to find the right words, so Roman said, "We wouldn't have done what we did."

Zara: "Yes. No one is to blame. So. I want you all, right now, to lift up your heads. Look each other in the eye."

Then she reached out toward Roman, and he stepped toward her. She took his hand in hers again.

Slowly, people in both groups did what she asked and met each other's gaze. I looked at Niki (her son was the one who stabbed me in the leg). And I looked at Julius Almedo (he was the one I hit in the face—it was gashed and turning purple). I looked at Andrea Coppolino (I'd seen her stab Langdon in the neck, and Dr. Keshti doesn't expect him to live). We looked at them, and they looked at us, and I think we all tried hard to accept that what Zara said was true. Or, at least, we had to make ourselves believe it.

Zara went on. "No one is to blame. But we don't know what we're dealing with. Not yet. What these things are, or how to get rid of them. And it seems something is very wrong in the rest of the world. Maybe Dr. Keshti and I shouldn't have kept this from you, but we haven't been able to contact anyone. Not just the EMS in Sudbury. No one. Anywhere."

She paused to let it sink in. Some of us began to weep.

Zara: "All of you with the parasites—we're going to help you. We'll find a way. But until then, we need to be cautious. We don't know if you, if your minds, will be taken over again. And we can't take that chance when you're right next to the rest of us. So, here's what's going to happen."

Then she explained she wanted the people with macro-parasites to stay in the gym. Isolated. Everyone else would leave. The doors to the gym would be barred from the outside. A team of four (ones without parasites) would stay in the gym on the balcony and keep watch. There's no way to get up to the balcony from the floor of the gym. Every six hours, she said, the team of guards—actually, she called them caretakers—would get spelled off by another shift. The people on the gym floor would still have access to two washrooms, and as of now, the *toilets are still flushing. And Zara promised them they'd have plenty of food and water.*

Roman said he could see the sense in Zara's plan. But some of the others looked alarmed. Milo Kaspar asked how long they'd have to stay locked in the gym, and Zara didn't know. "Maybe until Dr. Keshti finds a way to remove the macro-parasites," she told him. Milo shouted it could take years. He said Keshti is a family doctor, not a specialist in giant woodticks (that's what he called them).

Zara reminded him that Dr. Keshti still had access to local databases on every medical specialization, including parasitology.

Matthew Roy, trying to be helpful, said that just because we hadn't reached anyone beyond Blue Ring didn't mean they were gone. Maybe their equipment had been damaged, even though ours hadn't. ("At least, not yet," Shadi murmured behind me.) "There could be other specialists working on a solution," Matthew said. "They're not stuck like us in the middle of the Canadian Shield."

Finally, Zara said that unless anyone had a better idea, they'd proceed with her plan to isolate the infected in the gym. Milo and some others didn't look happy, but nobody pushed back. Then she said that tomorrow, a couple of us would take one of the eVans to Sudbury—

"That must have been a city," Thorn said. "Where other people lived."

I nodded.

—take one of the eVans to Sudbury. She said they'd get a better sense of what was happening and maybe even come back with good news. But then, Roman put his hands on his head and cried out, "I'm sorry, I'm sorry." He said the eVans

weren't operable. None of the vehicles were. Craig and Gill had wrecked all their fuel cells while they were under the control of the parasites—dumped them in the river. Gill said (and this is word for word—I think it's important), "I didn't want to, but it was like my mind was hijacked. I couldn't do anything but watch my hands take out the fuel cells. I couldn't stop myself from taking them to the river. I couldn't resist."

When Roman said this about the fuel cells, I thought Zara might finally crack. She started to stand up, then remembered her ankle. So she just sat there, closed her eyes, clenched her jaw, and took some deep breaths for almost a minute.

When she finally opened her eyes, she asked, "Who has winter trekking experience?" A dozen of us put up our hands. She asked us to choose a team of three and then see if we could find the gear they'd need to hike to Sudbury (at least fifteen days by road—somebody was supposed to figure out if it would be shorter to follow the train tracks).

Then she told the infected to get comfortable in the gym and asked me to choose four people for the first team of caretakers. She asked everyone else to head back to their cubicles and rest. "We can't think straight if we're exhausted," she said.

Before I left, she asked me to find some soothing music and play it softly through the gym's speakers. And then, could Jagmeet and I take the carts with the parasites and lock them in the cage in the Quonset, the one where the acetylene tanks were stored?

"Music," I said, pausing to look at Thorn. "Papa told me about it. And I've heard it."

"Keep going," he said, pointing at the book.

February 23, 2065

I've got one on me now. On my back—a parasite. So does Zara. Everyone does. Please let me be dreaming.

February ~~25~~ 26. 2065

Not sure of the date. I'll ask somebody later and fill it in. Woke up a couple of hours ago on soaking sheets. Sweat and urine. Threw up, washed myself, threw up again. My back feels on fire. It must be fully attached by now. Had strange dreams. I'm guessing that before long, the parasite will take control of me. So I'm going to record what happened.

The morning after we quarantined the infected in the gymnasium, I was in the dining hall getting a plate of food for Zara. Somebody had found some crutches for her, but I told her to rest at the table. But just as I was pouring some orange juice, there was a loud bang. I knew what it was and where it came from. There was only one long gun at Blue Ring (for bears), and we'd left it with the four caretakers.

I started running and yelled at others to carry Zara to the gym. As I got close, I began to hear a pounding from inside. A rhythm. It got louder as I ran in the back door, up the stairs, and then onto the balcony. Here's what I saw: all the infected were lined up in five rows on the floor of the gym, and they were stomping their feet in unison. Lying in front of them was Roman. He was face up in a pool of blood that was getting bigger as I watched. Sitting cross-legged beside him was one of the kids, smeared with blood. The four caretakers were still on the balcony, frozen in shock. One of them (Senna Asselbergs) had the long gun in her hands.

I shouted, "What happened?" and Senna's lips started moving, but I couldn't hear her over the stomping. So I went to her and took the rifle and got her to sit down. She said (I'm paraphrasing), "Roman shouted he was going to hurt the girl if we didn't come down to him. Then he took her finger and bent *it backward till it snapped. He said he'd keep breaking them. I had to stop him. So I shot him. I was aiming for his leg. I've never used a gun before." Senna's eyes were glassy, and her whole body was trembling.*

When I looked down at Roman's body, it was obvious she hadn't hit his leg. But then I saw him move. I shouted at Jenna, who was closest to him, to stop the bleeding. Then he moved again, and I saw a black shape push out from under his shoulder. It was his parasite. It had detached from him, and it was wriggling free. Once it was clear of his body, he stopped moving.

Then Cecil and Jagmeet opened the door that led from the staircase to the balcony and helped Zara limp in. As soon as she took in what had happened, she shouted down to the child sitting in Roman's blood, "Magda, are you—are you all right?"

It was only then that I recognized the child as Magda— Roman's own daughter.

Magda nodded and stood up. She said (word for word): "Yes, but we want you to open the doors."

For a moment, Zara didn't say anything. Nobody did. We were in shock (the ones on the balcony, I mean—the ones on the floor just stared up at us). Magda's voice was a high-pitched squeak, but she spoke calmly and carefully like she was telling someone what kind of pie was her favourite.

Zara said, "I can't do that, Magda. I'm sorry about what happened to your dad. He didn't mean to hurt you. He couldn't help it."

What Magda replied sent me reeling. I slumped to a bench. She said, "Yes, he did mean to. He needed to. And you need to open the doors and send people in. Six at a time. If you don't, you're going to see more hurting and killing."

Before Zara or anyone could reply, one of the other kids (Rozin) crossed in front of Magda and lay down on his side in the pool of blood. Magda set her tiny foot on Rozin's temple. Then the two of them yelled (but it almost sounded like singing as it echoed off the walls), "More hurting and killing."

Magda raised her foot over his temple, and a moment passed as she stared up at Zara. Then Zara cried out, "Stop, Magda, stop, please. We give up." She was sobbing. She leaned forward and put her head in her hands.

"That's all," I said. "It ends there." I closed the book with trembling hands, and we sat in silence. My stomach felt like it was full of hot sand. "My Papa . . ." I began, then trailed off. I didn't know what to say.

"It's awful," Thorn said, shaking his head. "What they went through. Awful." He looked at me. "I'll take it back to the vault tomorrow."

I nodded blankly. The book could go back into the vault, but not the story it told. It was in my head. And as much as I might want to, I'd never forget it.

After that, I forever looked at Papa differently, and Jenna and Virgil, too, knowing what they'd witnessed, what they'd experienced.

I never spoke to any of them about it. But now I knew.

PART THREE

CHAPTER 32
FIVE TURTLE EGGS

Chance. That was a word I learned to appreciate as Zara's memories continued to emerge over the next two years, revealing more and more about her life and her world. In my own life, chance didn't have much sway, at least not till Canker found the five turtle eggs. But it wove its way through so many of Zara's experiences. That's what it seemed when I stepped back and reflected on the slices of her existence that had come to me.

Strangely, Zara hadn't seen things that way. In her mind, her life had mostly been a series of deliberate choices within a larger, overall plan. She chose to go to university for Museum Studies. She chose to go to the University of Toronto. She chose to apply for a job at Blue Ring. Those were choices, not chance.

But some of her memories told me another story. When she was a child, her grandfather was going to take her to the symphony—but he got the time wrong. It started before they got there. So, instead, they went to an exhibit of Indigenous artifacts at the Royal Ontario Museum. Arrowheads. Stone hammers. Small figures carved out of antlers and bone. Zara was fascinated. She decided then and there—age ten—that she was going to study old things when she grew up. She'd protect them. Care for them. All because her grandfather thought that Antonin Dvorak's "New World Symphony" started at 7:30 instead of 7 p.m.

She chose the University of Toronto. But only because her first choice—a university in a place called Arizona—lost her application when their data centre was hit by the double whammy of cyber sabotage and wildfires.

Whammy. That was a good word to have learned from Zara.

And she chose to apply for a job at Blue Ring. But that was only because she'd met Jenna at university, and Jenna eventually got hired at Blue Ring as a data analyst and happened to mention there was a collection of rare books being moved to a new research institute in Northern Ontario, and they were looking for a curator. What if Zara and Jenna hadn't met in that stats course? Then Zara wouldn't have come to Blue Ring. She wouldn't have met Papa. And she wouldn't have died trying to defeat the Headmasters.

But in my life—actually, in the lives of everyone at Blue Ring—there wasn't much room for either choice or chance. At least, it seemed that way until, like I said, Canker found those five turtle eggs.

He happened upon them by accident at the end of a grip. He told us later he'd spotted the nest on the edge of the bog when he kneeled down to tighten his foot wrap. There were twelve eggs. He left seven of them to hatch. The others, he tucked into a fold of his shirt.

He should have put them into his bucket along with the worms and newts and mushrooms the grubbers collected every day for the kitchen. That's what he was supposed to do. Sort of.

But not really. What he was actually supposed to do, as far

as the other Grubbers were concerned, was tell only them about his lucky find: turtle eggs were a rare treat. When the grip ended, the Grubbers would gather around and take turns sucking out whatever was inside the leathery shell of the eggs— sometimes yellow yolk, sometimes a pink and grey mass that wasn't quite yet a turtle. It was a right the Grubbers claimed. Turtle eggs. Others complained, but what could we do? I didn't begrudge them—was it any different than me eating a few of the apples we'd picked when we were dragging the sledges back to the kitchen?

But instead of sharing those five eggs with the other Grubbers, Canker hid them in a fold of his shirt until the grip ended. Then he trudged back to the Cube, found Knot in his cubicle— red-eyed and sobbing—and gave him all five. Knot had been heartsick for days because his raven had disappeared.

Knot had found the bird as a lone, forsaken hatchling in one of the trees he climbed while looking for eggs—bird eggs, not turtle eggs. Knot was a Filcher. Or, rather, *the* Filcher—he was the only one. In the spring and summer, his toil was to climb trees and steal eggs from nests. In the fall and winter, he coated branches with a paste of tar and pine resin and plucked off the birds that perched and got stuck to it: sparrows, chickadees, nuthatches—little birds that stayed all winter. Whatever he got—eggs or birds—he brought back to the kitchen.

For some reason, Knot got attached to this particular raven hatchling, kind of like Canker had gotten attached to Knot. Maybe they each saw their wards as smaller, more vulnerable versions of themselves or perhaps as

talismans

or perhaps as talismans. Whatever the reason, for two weeks, Knot climbed to the treetop at the start of each slackening and fed worms and grubs to his growing bird. After it was fully fledged and left the nest, it followed Knot wherever he went, often perching on his shoulder or head—all summer, even during the grips when Knot was filching the eggs of other birds. He taught it to shriek a few words: *biscuit* and *here* and *pretty*.

Until, one morning in early fall, the bird didn't show up when Knot came tumbling out of the Cube. And Stump—the leader of the Grubbers—sat down in the Meal House with a long black feather tucked behind his ear.

Knot told me, when I saw him slumped against the west wall of the Aery that evening, that he should have let the baby raven starve in its nest. That would have been better than whatever Stump had done to it.

So the next day, when Canker found the five turtle eggs, he gave them to Knot. He thought they might cheer him up. A gift. An offering. An atonement for another's misdeed.

No one knows how the other Grubbers found out about what Canker did. It's possible Knot might have told them without meaning to. He wasn't good at keeping secrets. The other Grubbers were furious. They claimed this wasn't the first time Canker had given a windfall to Knot instead of to them.

Keep out of it. That's what everyone said whenever a squabble arose among the Grubbers. *They have their own way.* So when the other Grubbers punished Canker for his kindness by hanging a dead squirrel around his neck, nobody protested. Nobody liked it—especially as the days passed, and the squirrel got more and more rank, and they especially didn't like it during morning meal—but nobody intervened. Not even when Knot went around asking for someone to help him help Canker.

He went to Papa and Virgil and Jenna, and they listened and sympathized, but they said that if they told the Grubbers to take the squirrel off Canker, they'd just find a sneakier, worse way to hurt him. *Just let it blow over*. He asked me and Thorn. He stopped us on our way to help Halo in the Aery, and I told him we'd find him again before the slackening ended—but we forgot. And he asked others. Silex and Rose. Twig and River. Perch and Juniper. Their advice was the same: *Just let it blow over*.

Knot knew he couldn't fight Stump. Stump was the Grubbers' leader because he was both big and cruel. Being their leader seemed to mean he could order them around during slackenings and make them do things like rub his feet with moss and fetch him biscuit from the kitchen. Knot was muscled from climbing trees, but he was small—the top of his head barely reached Stump's chin.

So, Knot did the one thing he knew would get our attention. One breezeless slackening, he took a hammer from the Menders Hall, walked out to the wind turbine, and climbed up the three long sections of ladder inside its tower till he reached the gear cabin at the top. There, he had a short conversation with the Keeper, who showed him a miniature replica of Blue Ring she'd carved out of wood—the Meal House, the Deep, the Ward, the Mending Hall, the Cube, and all the other buildings, all meticulously rendered in carved pine. Knot told her it was very good and apologized for what he was about to do. Then he climbed up the short ladder that led to the hatch in the wind tower's cabin, pushed it open, and squeezed through. He ignored the Keeper's cries to come back. From there, he clambered down to the turbine's hub and then edged himself along one of the motionless blades until he reached the tip.

Then he started pounding with the hammer.

In the still evening air, the clanging carried over the treetops and was easily heard back at the compound. People ran out to see what was making the racket. By the time they got to the wind tower, Knot had smashed off the narrow tip of the blade. They shouted at him to stop. He did but warned them he'd start hammering again unless they took the dead squirrel off Canker.

Somebody sprinted back and got Canker. Somebody else found Stump and brought him. They took the stinking carcass off Canker as Knot watched from high above, holding tight to the end of the turbine's blade with his strong Filcher arms. They shouted into the evening sky, asking Knot if he wanted them to hang it around Stump's neck, but Knot said no. He told them to make a cairn for the squirrel then and there, so they did, everyone gathering the rocks and pebbles strewn around them. Then he made Stump promise not to hurt people or special ravens anymore and made everyone else promise to make sure that Stump kept his promise.

By then, the sun had nearly set, and the slackening was nearing its end, so they urged Knot to climb back down. He dropped his hammer, edged himself back up the blade, and disappeared into the turbine's gear cabin. He once more told the Keeper that her carvings were really good, and then he scrambled down the three long stretches of ladder to the ground. He and everyone else made it back to their cubicles just before the darkening came over them.

The next day, when the Keeper unlocked the blades and pitched them to catch the morning wind, the turbine didn't work right. As the blades picked up speed, they started to shake. The whole tower started to tremble. The Keeper unpitched the blades as fast as she could before anything worse happened.

So now, the wind turbine is broken, the thing that sends the invisible current into the Cube and the Aery in the winter to make just enough heat to keep us from freezing to death. All because a turtle laid some eggs, and Canker chanced upon them.

These are the thoughts whirling through my head while Birch sits on my knee and sounds his way through the first page of a book. About a year after I'd discovered I could read, I decided we needed to teach the kids how. It made them so much happier. You could see it in their eyes—they seemed brighter, more alert. Apart from Thorn, only River and Twig knew about this. We told them about the vault, too. But I didn't tell them about Zara's memories.

"'The—Cat—only—grinned . . .' Maple, what's 'grinned'?"

"Grinning is when you do this with your mouth."

"That's smiling."

"Grinning is for funny things. Smiling is for when you see someone you love."

We both look up as we hear footsteps coming down the hall. It's River. He strides over and lifts Birch into his arms. "Here we are, Birchbark," he says, smiling and lifting him into the air.

Birch laughs. "Uncle Amazing!"

River lowers Birch to his chest, then turns to me with a sombre look. "There's going to be a big gathering during tomorrow's slackening." I'm not surprised by the news. He's just come from meeting with Papa, Virgil, and Jenna, the ones who make those decisions.

A big gathering. Those don't happen often—only when something serious arises. The last time was two years ago after a skunk lumbered into the potato field in the middle of toil. Mite, who was weeding and looked up when he caught its smell on the wind, said it was acting strangely. It lumbered toward him, teeth bared and snarling, but he knocked it away with a hoe.

No one thought much of it until Jenna heard about it. She and Papa and Virgil called a big gathering and told us the skunk likely had a disease, and we'd get sick if it bit us, and other animals like raccoons might also have it. If anyone got the disease, they'd die for sure. "There's nothing in my books to fix it," she said. If we saw it again, we had to kill it—but we couldn't touch it. The Menders gathered up old pipes, pounded their ends sharp, and handed them around. But we never saw the ailing skunk again.

"You and Thorn go to the big gathering," I tell River. "I'll stay here with the kids."

River nods and starts to turn. Then he stops and looks back at me. "She's not going to be there," he says, looking me in the eye. He's talking about Lark. He knows my real reason for avoiding the big gathering is that I don't want to take the chance of seeing her. I haven't talked to Lark since she joined the Thankfuls—seven years ago. As a breeder, her biscuit wedges are brought to her cubicle, so there's never been an opportunity to see her in the Meal House.

There was one time, not long after she became a Thankful, when I waited outside her cubicle's door near the start of a slackening, knowing she'd be leaving to join the other Thankfuls on the fourth floor. When she opened the door and saw me, our eyes locked for a moment, then she shook her head and closed the door. After that, I stopped trying to connect with her. It was too painful.

"Halo needs someone to help her," I say. "So that's what I'm going to do." River shrugs, knowing he can't change my mind. After a moment, I add, "Make sure Knot doesn't go to the big gathering."

Everyone had an opinion about Knot. A few people were so angry about the wrecked wind tower they threatened to yank off his Headmaster. But they didn't dare. Killing him would just lead to punishment from their own Headmasters the following day.

Others said that none of it was Knot's fault. It was Stump and the other Grubbers who killed his raven and then hung a dead squirrel around Canker's neck. They were the ones responsible. How did they think Knot—with his childish brain —was going to react?

Some didn't blame Knot but said he shouldn't be allowed to roam around during the slackenings—he needed to be tied up like a berserker so he wouldn't wreck anything else. But what was the point of that? Apart from the wind turbine, there wasn't anything else that mattered.

River nods at me. "Canker's going to walk Knot out to the Coil. They won't get back till the big gathering's over."

CHAPTER 33
WHEN ARE YOU MOST UNHAPPY?

The next day, Halo insists that I go to the big gathering in the compound. "Be there for your Papa," she says. "It might get unruly." I protest, but she nudges me out the door of the Aery. "Maple, I've done this for almost fifty years. I can handle the kids all by myself for one evening." She closes the door behind me. I sigh and walk toward the crowd near the middle of the compound.

Almost everyone has shown up. It's a warm fall evening, and they're waiting for the sun to sink behind the treetops so no one has to stare into its brilliance. I push through the crowd that's made a ragged circle around Papa, Jenna, and Virgil—the three elders of the community. I can sense—smell, even—the anxiety of those I slip past. Apart from a few whispered conversations, no one is saying much.

In contrast, Papa, Jenna, and Virgil look composed, almost aloof—as if they're patiently waiting for a drizzling rain to end. Papa's hands rest on the head of the walking stick he started using about a year ago. It's a single piece of strong cherry wood that River cut and shaped for him. Virgil has his hands clasped behind his back, his chin tilted ever so slightly upward, his eyelids almost closed as if he's preparing to tell his story. Jenna is limping a slow circle around them both, her eyes fixed on the cracked concrete she's traversing, her long grey hair pulled back into a ponytail.

Thorn is beside me, and we've moved close to the inner ring of the crowd. I reach to the side and take his hand. River isn't far off, standing between two women about his age: Twig, one of the five Biscuiteers, and Lily, one of the two Bee Seekers. Lily is offering River a bite of honeycomb she must have pilfered after the grip ended. As I gaze at them, I realize my brother is a handsome man.

"Friends!" Virgil suddenly calls out, opening his eyes and raising both hands toward the sky as the last edge of the sun slips below the tops of the pines. "Here we are! Let us commence our discussion!"

"What's to discuss?" one of the Grubbers shouts back. "Knot-brain smashed the blade, and now we're screwed." Stump, who's standing beside him, stares down at his own feet, trying to look inconspicuous. He knows many in the crowd blame him for the mess we're in.

Virgil nods twice, slowly. Somehow, he makes even that small motion look impressive. "It is true," he replies, "that the motive force captured by the aeolian turbine is presently exanimated. Consequently, our continuance, as you say, is indeed in jeopardy."

Around me, I see brows furrowing in confusion, especially people who've never gone to one of Virgil's tellings.

"What's jeopardy?" someone calls out. "Where is it?"

"Can you talk normal?" someone else yells from the outer edge of the circle.

"Yes, friends," Virgil replies, bowing slightly. "I apologize for my proclivity toward ornate locutions. I fear it is my own coping mechanism. But I will aspire to lower my register. As I was asseverating—"

Jenna leans toward Virgil and puts a hand on his shoulder. I can hear her whisper, "Maybe Jacob should take it from here."

Virgil makes another slight bow and steps back.

Papa takes a deep breath before speaking. He glances around at the people in the crowd, making eye contact with many of them.

"Friends," he begins, "for almost sixty years, the turbine's blades have taken the power of the wind and turned it into an invisible current that's warmed two of our buildings in the frigid winters. I know that those who built it before the Arrival expected it to last thirty years—not sixty. We're lucky it's helped us for as long as it did. But now it's broken. We always knew this time would come—though perhaps not for the reasons it did." Papa pauses and narrows his eyes at Stump. Stump scratches nervously at a scab on his neck, his fingers calloused and scarred like those of all the Grubbers.

A voice cries out. "No invisible current means no heat—we'll freeze to death!" The crowd begins to murmur.

"No," Papa shouts, raising his hand. "The turbine also stores the current. That's what it does all summer when we don't need the power—stores it for later, in big cubes under the tower, just like we store summer's potatoes for the winter. The three of us—" he gestures toward Jenna and Virgil—"believe that if we make a few changes to our . . . to how we live, we'll get through the coming winter."

"And then what?" Lichen shouts.

"That will give the Menders time to find a way to fix the broken blade," Papa replies. All around me, shoulders sag with dismay.

"The Menders can barely fix a broken door," Lichen retorts. "How can you fix something like the turbine? We don't even know how it works!" Others in the crowd mutter and grumble.

Papa is silent. I release Thorn's hand and push my way to the front of the crowd, ready to step in if I need to, ready to do something.

"What kind of changes?" Mist asks. "You said we have to change how we live."

Papa speaks again. "We'll need to move everyone to a single floor of the Cube. Four people in each cubicle. We'll turn off the invisible current to the other floors. And we'll move the children from the Aery in with us and turn off the current to that building, too. That will make the stored current last much longer."

"They won't let us do that!" someone shouts.

I was thinking the same thing. The Headmasters always impelled us to sleep only and always in the cubicle we'd first been allotted. We could move all the cots to the same floor during a slackening and bring the children over from the Aery, but the Headmasters would likely make us undo it all the next morning, jolting us till we did so. As Jenna once said to me, they were not fond of change.

litotes

"Yes," Papa replies. "You're right. They might stop us from doing that. It depends on whether they can understand why we're doing it."

"There might be another way." The voice calling out is as familiar as my own—it's Thorn's. He squeezes through the crowd till he's at the front, where Papa, Virgil, and Jenna can see him.

"Another way, Thorn?" Papa asks. "What do you mean?"

"First of all, I don't think—I don't think the Menders can

fix the blade. I mean, they might be able to hammer some metal into a new tip, and with ropes and pulleys, they might be able to get up there to attach it—but it's not going to stay on."

"We can use rivets to secure it," Papa says.

"But —" Thorn says, then hesitates. He looks around till he finds my eyes. I have no idea what he wants to say, but I nod encouragingly. "You see, I did some figuring," he continues, talking quickly. "Each blade is about eighty-seven feet long. So, the circumference of the circle made by the spinning blades is 546 feet. In a strong wind, the blades rotate about once every two seconds. That means the tip of a blade is travelling at 273 feet per second, which is 982,800 feet per hour, which is the same as 186 miles an hour."

"That's fast," Papa says, nodding.

Thorn presses on, words pouring out of him. "Very fast. If something were moving that quickly in a straight line, it could get from here to the perimeter in about fifteen seconds. Now, imagine the tip the Menders make weighs sixty pounds. A sixty-pound thing, moving 186 miles an hour, would create a force—I think it's called centrifugal force—of 24,000 pounds. About the same as the weight of everyone at Blue Ring combined."

Thorn stops to catch his breath and looks around. He notices for the first time that people have edged away from him. They're eyeing him with concern as if he's showing signs of becoming berserk or—and I'm drawing on Zara's memories here—as if he's been speaking in tongues or summoning demons. They have no idea what he's talking about. But I sense that Papa and Virgil and Jenna do.

He looks over at me again, this time with fear in his eyes.

Papa speaks, his words calm and deliberate, drawing attention away from Thorn. "You're saying there's no way we can attach a new tip to withstand that much outward pull. It would shear off no matter how we secured it."

Thorn nods. Then he adds, "But I think I've thought of another way to get the current flowing again."

Now it's Jenna who speaks. "Then tell us, Thorn. I think our lives depend on it." She beckons him forward with her hand.

Thorn takes a deep breath and moves closer to her. She turns him around so he's facing the crowd.

"Before the Arrival," he begins, "the people who lived here must have used a lot more of the invisible current than we do. They heated more buildings, and they had other things that needed current, like lights and ovens and—and other things. One wind turbine couldn't have made enough current for them. So there must have been other turbines that also sent current here. And there are. At least one more. On a clear evening, you can see it from the top of our wind turbine. To the west, on the horizon—just before the sun goes down."

There's a murmur in the crowd.

"I think the Menders should try to get to that other turbine," Thorn says, looking at Papa, "to see if they can get it spinning and start sending its invisible current here."

"It could be as broken as this one," someone shouts. "Or worse."

Others murmur their agreement.

Thorn scowls. "Maybe. But shouldn't we try? Or should we just use up the stored current and then burrow under the snow-banks like voles?"

"Thorn," Jenna says, reaching out and touching his arm, "if this other wind turbine is as far away as you say, how could the Menders get there and back in a single slackening?"

"They couldn't," Thorn replies. "They'd have to go there and stay until they got it working—which might take days."

"Or entire moon cycles," Jenna adds.

Everyone falls silent. The same problem as with moving the cots, only much worse. The Headmasters aren't going to let the Menders leave Blue Ring. Not unless they sense that keeping their hosts alive depends on it—because without us as hosts, they wouldn't be much more than a colony of wood ticks. But the Headmasters are slow learners. They might never understand our need to go to the other wind turbine.

"Perhaps we can help." A loud, clear voice rings through the darkening evening air—a woman's voice. It's Ivy. I see the crowd parting like reeds as she makes her way to the front. Then she steps forward until she's standing between Papa and Virgil. Her lips purse as she prepares to speak again—but River interjects.

"Why don't you just slither back into your hole?" he sneers through gritted teeth. "Thankfuls don't help. They only take, like magpies."

Ivy turns and locks eyes with him. I see a flicker of doubt cross River's face as she gazes impassively at him. "This one doesn't want you to hear what I have to say," she says to the crowd.

"Because there's already enough crap in the potato fields," River snaps back. "We don't need more of yours."

Ivy frowns slightly but holds her gaze.

"Let her speak," Papa says, raising his hand. "All are welcome to speak."

Virgil nods in agreement.

River looks at Papa in disbelief. Then he shakes his head and melts back into the crowd. Twig and Lily each put an arm around his waist.

"Yes, perhaps we can help," Ivy repeats. "You see, the Thankfuls could commune with the Headmasters. We could convey to them the need to travel to the other wind tower. We could get them to understand. And yet . . ." she trails off.

"And yet what?" shouts someone in the crowd.

"Why begin to build a bridge if you have only half the number of needed pieces?" she replies.

"What do you mean?" someone else yells.

River calls out from within the crowd. "Ignore her. She's a rusty hinge screeching in the wind."

"We are each a metal beam," Ivy continues, as she slowly saunters around Papa and Virgil, Jenna and Thorn, "and all of us together could build a bridge that would surely stretch across the entire river of darkness and reach the Headmasters. If we act together as one, they will surely hear our plea. They will surely hear our plea—if you all become Thankfuls. Join us on the fourth floor of the Cube. Commune with us. Then they will let us travel to that distant wind tower—if it does exist."

People around me groan and snort with derision. This is nothing but a ploy to get more Thankfuls.

"I assure you of the truth of what I am saying. But there is more."

The crowd grows silent again.

"When we all—as one body—commune with the Headmasters, they will unlock the doors to the knowledge residing within us. Including—" she pauses—"the knowledge of how to turn on or even repair a wind turbine that has been stilled for sixty years."

A rumble of confused voices erupts from the crowd. Ivy smirks as if she's dangling a worm over a baby robin. After the murmur dies down, Star is the first to speak.

"You mean, we'd know things like—like the Originals did? All the things they understood? Their memories?"

I hear gasps in the crowd as if just mentioning the existence of those memories threatens to shatter the lock on a sealed door.

"Yes," Ivy replies. "And we'll be able to access those memories safely because, at last, we'll all be working as one. We will all be Thankfuls. You will all be so happy—no longer plagued with worries, with sorrow, with futile yearning. You will have no need to make choices, choices that lead to error and suffering." She stops and suddenly points a finger at Chokecherry. "When are you most unhappy? During the slackenings, of course. But I promise the slackenings—those dreadful stretches of loose time—will come to an end when you fully accept the loving grip of our Headmasters."

She stops, her piercing gaze challenging the faces in the crowd.

"And who would we then be?" Another voice rings out, as loud and clear as Ivy's. It's Jenna's. She's taken Papa's walking stick and has lifted it into the air.

"Who would each of you be? Or perhaps the question is, *what* would you then be? Our lives now are hard and narrow and brutal. Jacob and Virgil and I know that better than any of you because we remember when it wasn't that way."

She turns and stares at Ivy, her eyes steady. "I don't know," Jenna continues, "if there is any truth in what Ivy has just told you. I don't know if we could get the Headmasters to let us travel to the other wind turbine if we all became Thankfuls. And I don't know how Ivy could know that. But even if it's true, is that what you want? To give up the small sliver of humanity that you have during the slackenings?"

"Better than freezing to death!" someone calls out.

Jenna pauses and looks into the crowd. I see her gaze settle on one person, and realize it's Lark. Until this moment, I hadn't seen her. I study her intently, as if she might vanish if I look away. Her face seems smaller, flatter, like it's fallen back into itself. Her hair is thin, her eyes watery and expressionless.

"If you have no freedom," Jenna replies, her gaze unwavering, "you're not really alive."

The crowd is silenced by the weight of her words. A gust of wind rises and rustles the leaves of the nearby maple trees. A flock of blackbirds flies over us, heading for Gehenna, their wings beating the air like soft whispers.

"Freedom," Ivy replies. "Yes, freedom. Your Headmasters can give you a new kind of freedom that you don't yet understand—freedom from having to choose. But perhaps you, Jenna, are willing to accept extinction because you have already lived your life. You're soon going to die anyway."

Ivy and Jenna continue to eye one another. Then Ivy abruptly turns on her heel and strides back toward the crowd. They scatter aside as she passes through them. "Make your decision carefully!" she cries out as she heads toward the Cube, the other Thankfuls wordlessly shuffling after her, arms crossed over their chests. Lark trails behind them all.

Those in the crowd turn back toward Papa, Jenna, and Virgil. Expectation hangs in the air.

Finally, Papa speaks. "We've heard a lot this evening." His voice is tight. He suddenly seems unsure of himself. "Let's take time to consider. We'll have another big gathering in five days."

Behind him, Jenna and Virgil nod. But no one in the crowd moves. We stand, staring and blinking. Uncertain. We need something more.

Virgil takes a grand step forward. "Friends!" he cries out as he once again lifts his hands toward the darkening sky. "Depart with this thought in mind! It belongs not to me but to one of the forgotten ancients." He pauses and closes his eyes. "'Time is a river of passing events, and strong is its current; no sooner is a thing brought to sight than it is swept by and another takes its place, and this too will be swept away.'" He opens his eyes and lowers his hands.

With this, the crowd seems to release a collective breath. They begin to drift away, their faces sombre but resolute.

"And remember," Virgil calls out after them, "half the slackening is still left. In a few moments, the Teller will mount his dais in Gehenna and begin to weave his tale. Our heroes, Rosalind and Orlando, have begun to doubt their new friends, Ginger and Fred. Might they be minions of the glowering Gunther?"

As the last stragglers disperse, I move closer to Papa, Jenna, and Virgil. So does Thorn. So do River and Twig. Lily seems to have vanished.

Jenna hands the walking stick back to Papa, then turns to Thorn. "Your idea is a good one. Better than what we proposed."

"But by no means certain," Papa says. "And not without risks."

"If what Ivy says is true,"—it's me asking this question—"couldn't we just go along with the Thankfuls until it's done? Then leave them?"

I see River grimace.

"Become temporary Thankfuls?" Jenna says, shaking her head. "It would be difficult. There's something about their community that's like spiderweb—once you make contact, it's hard to detach. I fear that most people would stay with them whether we got the other wind turbine working or not."

"Thorn," Papa says, turning toward him, eyebrows raised, "I don't doubt your calculations are correct. And I won't ask how you learned to do them. But your measurements—pounds and feet? No one's used those for a hundred years—long before even I was born."

Thorn's eyes dart around nervously. "Maybe I should have used cubits and furlongs."

Papa throws his head back and laughs.

CHAPTER 34
THE BONE YARD

River is running toward us as we haul our sledges, heavy with the day's harvest of walnuts, through the gate at the edge of the Blue Ring compound. Twig is with him. As he gets nearer, I see his face is heavy with sorrow. My grip on the sledge rope loosens. It slides back over my shoulder and drops to my feet like a limp snake.

I brace myself. "Is it Papa?"

He shakes his head. "Halo," he blurts. "Terminated."

In an instant, relief and grief alike seize my heart. Papa is alive. But Halo isn't. My legs tremble, but I stay standing.

I should have known. Halo had insisted I go to the big gathering last night. She told me she could get the kids to bed on her own. I stupidly let her. If only I'd stayed and helped her like we'd done every slackening for the past two years . . . but I didn't. So today, she must have been too tired to look after the kids properly—or had so much pain in her hip that she took too many of the drops—and the Headmasters had finally terminated her for it.

"When?" I ask, not knowing what else to say, tears brimming in my eyes.

"Sometime before midday. That's when Twig caught sight of Birch wandering around the compound. He'd got himself out of the Aery. He was crying out for you. All Twig could do was point him to the Mending Hall and tell him that's where Papa was. So he went there and told Papa that Halo had fallen down. And that she wasn't moving anymore."

His voice breaks, and I can feel his grief giving way to anger. I know what he's thinking—that Papa had to keep toiling in the Mending Hall, knowing that Halo was lying on the floor.

Knowing she wasn't moving and the kids were around her.

Twig speaks up, her voice a small quaver. "The Biscuiteers said they heard the kids in the Aery crying and crying and crying. Until all of a sudden, they stopped." She buries her face in her hands. "When they told me that, I was afraid something awful had happened to them."

My knees start to wobble, and River grabs my arm to steady me. "They're safe," he says, gesturing for Twig to stop talking. "I just came from there. Crying tired them out, and they fell asleep, that's all. Papa's still there. He went as soon as the grip ended." It tears at my heart, the thought of our grandfather trying to hobble as fast as he could across the compound.

Six people had been terminated since I'd been harvested. Of course, the details of their deaths weren't discussed—at least not after their Headmaster had been transferred—but I'd heard enough to know that each one was its own horror. One of the older Tree Choppers was terminated when her eyes turned white, and she couldn't see well enough to wield her axe. The Headmasters did it to her in the middle of a grip. The other Tree Choppers could only watch as she tumbled onto a bed of pine needles in agonizing convulsions. They had to step around her as they continued to chop a tree into smaller chunks. When the slackening came, they lifted her onto the pile of wood on their sledge and brought her back so they could take her to the Bone Yard.

Awful. But this hit even harder. This was Halo. Almost everyone at Blue Ring had once been in her care.

"I want to see her," I say to River.

"And me," Thorn adds.

"I'm not sure you'll—" River begins to say, but I cut him off.

"I need to."

River nods.

Silex and Rose have been standing to the side. "Rose and I will take the sledges to the kitchen," Silex murmurs. "And I can heave the sacks up myself." I turn toward him and see that his face is also etched with grief. Rose's, too.

"Thank you," I say to them.

We head to the Aery, Thorn on one side of me and River on the other. As we approach, I notice someone leave the Aery by the side door and then slip around the back of the building— it looks like Lark, but I must be mistaken.

A few moments later, we're stepping into the Aery, the door held open by a rusty chunk of metal someone's set on the top step. Instantly, the smell of urine, feces, and—already—bodily decay assails us. It grows more intense as we pass through the hallway to the central room. There we find Papa, Jenna, and Virgil on their knees, trying to lift Halo's stiff body onto a sheet of nylar they've spread on the floor beside her. They look up as we come in.

Papa pulls at the sheet and drapes it over Halo, but not before I glimpse her swollen face, her mouth open and twisted, as if her last moments were in agony. One eye is fully closed, the other halfway. A puddle of dark urine has pooled beneath her.

No one speaks for several moments. I stare at the motionless lump beneath the sheet.

"Her hip is broken," Jenna finally says, breaking the heavy silence. "She probably stumbled over something and broke it when she fell."

"Where's everyone else?" River asks.

"We asked them to depart," Virgil murmurs, "as this is not how we wish Halo to reside in their memories. They have gone to gather rocks for the cairn."

"And the kids?" I ask.

"Lily took them to the Ward," Jenna replies, "until we move Halo."

"Let us help," I say as I kneel beside her body. River and Thorn do the same. Then, the six of us gently lift her from the floor and move her onto the nylar sheet. She lies flat: her Headmaster has uncoupled from her body. *She's free*, I say to myself. I glance around, half expecting to see her Headmaster lurking in some corner, but of course, they've already impelled someone to retrieve it to transfer to a new host—one of the kids. It'll probably be Wing. He must be twelve now. He'll become the new Minder of the Aery.

We fold the sides of the sheet over Halo's body. Then we lift her again and clasp hands with the person on the other side of her body. This is how it is done. We carry her in silence away from the Aery where she passed her life, across the compound, past a copse of willows, over the bridge, and finally to the Bone Yard. We wind through the stone piles—the cairns, more than two hundred of them—that are scattered over this wide and rocky plain.

A crowd is waiting at the far end of the Bone Yard. Each person holds a stone. They part as we approach, and we make our way slowly to the centre. We set her down with care on a small space cleared of debris. We pause for a moment. Then, six people step forward and hand us each a fist-sized stone. Papa kneels and places it gently against the shrouded body.

Jenna and Virgil do the same, then River and Thorn. Then me. Others begin to file past, each laying two or three stones around or on the body. When they have finished, only a mound of loose rocks is visible.

Then, as he's done so many times before, decade after decade, Virgil steps forward to say the Cairn Words. His voice is loud and echoes off the high walls of rock on either side of us. "This person is gone. Yet our memories of him or her persist. Cherish those memories in your heart if you wish. But they must not be shared. This person will not be spoken of again. That is our rule. Are we in agreement?"

With one voice, everyone responds, "We are in agreement."

Everyone but me and Thorn.

CHAPTER 35
UNBREEDER

The next morning, as I'm jolted out of the insensible oblivion of the darkening, I awake in the grip of two awful passions. The grief I feel for Halo presses like a heavy stone hard upon my heart. But the anxiety I feel for the kids in the Aery—now being tended by a twelve-year-old Minder who only yesterday was himself a kid in the Aery—feels like walking on the surface of a barely frozen pond.

As I go through the motions of the day with the others—eating, trudging, picking, trudging—the sun traces its arc through the sky, the clouds sweep past in silence, and the birds hop branch to branch, just as they did yesterday, and the day before, and the day before that—all ignorant of what I'm feeling, all insensible to Halo's death. Sometimes, my sorrow and dread surge in unison like two waves converging on a lake, overwhelming me—but when that happens, my Headmaster gives me a jolt to snap me back to my toil: filling a juice-stained bucket with bitter gooseberries.

The moment the grip ends, Thorn and I drop our buckets and abandon Silex and Rose, leaving them to haul the berries to the kitchen as we rush back to the Aery. Released from the grip of my Headmaster, my grief and anxiety deepen as I run, imagining the mistakes that Wing is certain to have made, the accidents and injuries that have befallen the kids.

We burst through the outer door and stumble down the hallway to the main room, panting and sweating, where we pause to survey the damage. What I see shocks me.

It's not a disaster. Nothing is on fire. No one is screaming. No chairs are overturned. No small fingers lie severed on the floor. There aren't even dirty diapers smeared against the walls.

Instead, Wing is in the middle of the room, sitting at a table where he's mashing biscuit and water into a bowl. Encircling him on the floor are the four kids, sleeping, each with a tattered nylar blanket and pillow. Mallow the Nurser is squatting on a stool in the corner, gazing at them with her usual complacent indifference.

All is calm. It's so quiet I can hear the kids' gentle breathing.

Wing glances up at us, looking puzzled by the commotion we made rushing in. "Here we are, Maple," he says. "Here we are, Thorn." His voice—still high and thin like a chickadee's call —sounds tired but steady. His eyes are bloodshot but calm.

"Here we are, Wing," I say, my anxiety ebbing away.

He nods toward the kids on the floor. "They didn't want to go to their cots," he says. "So I let them nap in here. They're really tired. From yesterday. Because of what happened to— because of what happened."

His eyes begin to glisten, and I know he's yearning to talk about Halo—to say her name—to tell me he misses her—but he knows he can't. He shouldn't. Her lifetime of memories is tucked away in the Headmaster that's now been transferred to his back.

"You must be tired out, too," Thorn says.

He nods. "My head is pounding. And underneath—" he

nods over his shoulder to the lump under his shirt—"it's burning. Like the worst sunburn ever. And it's heavy. How can it be so heavy?"

"It's not made out of the same stuff as you and me," I say, remembering what Papa told me when I was harvested. "And you can't ever—"

"I know," he says, interrupting me and seeming almost annoyed. "I can't ever try to pull it off. I know that already."

I change the subject. "The kids have eaten and had nypers changed? How'd you manage that?"

He shrugs. "They know what to do. When to eat. When to nap. What to play with. How to tell me they need changing. The bigger ones help the littler ones, and I help the bigger ones."

"Good," I say, nodding, but also thinking that it might not always be so easy—they won't always be this tired out. But his first day is over, and that's a good thing. "You should go back to your cubicle and sleep," I say to him.

"I don't mind staying for the rest of the slackening," he says. A look of concern flashes over his face. I can tell he's reluctant to leave the building where—up until yesterday—he's slept every night of his life.

"You need to rest," I insist. "In a few days, after you settle into things, you can stay during the slackenings if you want."

He puts down the short stick he's been using to mash the biscuit. "This is pretty much ready for when they wake up," he says. He stands up, then steps carefully around the kids on the floor.

As he walks toward the hallway to leave, I call out, "You know about the darkening, right?"

"Yes," he calls back, sounding more like a weary old man than a twelve-year-old. "It happened to me last night. And I know I can't ever try to take my Headmaster off, and I know if I don't do what it wants, I'll get jolts, and I know it's always going to be like this." His words trail off as he steps through the outer door.

I look at Thorn. "The day before yesterday, he was playing with the wooden animals along with the rest of the kids."

Before Thorn can reply, we hear the outer door open again. "Maybe he forgot to tell us something," I say.

But a moment later, the last person I ever expected to see is standing in the doorway—Ivy. I saw her yesterday, of course, at the big gathering, and heard her speak—but I haven't actually said a word to her since I went up to the fourth floor of the Cube to accuse her of taking Lark. Occasionally we cross paths, early in the slackenings, as she hurries across the compound to gather with the other Thankfuls and as I'm heading to the Aery. Whenever that happens, she locks her eyes on me as she passes by.

Once, I turned around to look after her and saw that she had twisted around, stepping almost sideways so she could still gaze after me. She smiled flatly and waved—then pointed up at the fourth floor as if she were inviting me there. I scowled and turned back around. Not a good way to start a slackening.

Now I feel her piercing gaze on me again and shiver. There's something about her—I don't have the word, but Zara did—something *ghoulish* about her, that's what Zara would have said. For a moment, I almost feel sorry for Ivy's Headmaster. What would it be like to be coupled to a mind as rigid and narrow as hers?

Ivy offers no greeting. Instead, she simply announces, "Your sister will be dead soon."

I stare at her, speechless.

"I thought you would want to know," she adds.

I still find no words to speak.

"Share this news with your grandfather," she continues.

"Unlike most, he has often treated me with respect." She suddenly pivots and begins to stride away.

"Wait!" I cry out. "What do you mean? What's wrong with Lark?"

Ivy pauses and turns back toward us. "Three moon cycles have passed without her conceiving. As you know, the one requirement of Breeders is they must breed. Be fertile. If a breeder becomes barren—an unbreeder—then the Headmasters will replace her with a woman who can perform that toil."

"I—I want—I want to see her," I stammer. I need to hear if this is true from Lark herself.

Ivy shakes her head. "I suggested to your sister," she says, "that accepting a visit from you or any of your kin would not be in the interests of the Thankfuls. It would disturb our communing and, therefore, undermine our efforts to close the circle. When she is terminated, we will deposit her in the Bone Yard."

Thorn must know me better than myself because his hand is already on my shoulder, holding me back before I can pounce on her. Still, Ivy takes a step backward and momentarily looks alarmed.

"You what?" I shriek. "She might be killed soon, and you told her not to see us? We're her family, not you!" Spit dribbles down my chin from the force of my words.

"She has not used that word—'family'—about you for a long time. You and she may have sprung from the same womb, but you are as different as a yolk from its shell."

I struggle to break free from Thorn. "Let me go!" I cry. "I'm going to find Lark right now!" But Thorn holds me tight.

Ivy twirls through the doorway and is gone. Suddenly, my legs melt beneath me, and I fall onto Thorn's shoulder. He holds me up as I sob uncontrollably.

"Maple," he murmurs, "Maple. I'm sorry. I don't know what to say—what to do."

"There's nothing to do," I cry. "Nothing." I lean against him, trembling with rage and despair. An image flashes through my mind of Zara in the gym, sobbing: *We give up.*

My shouts have awakened the kids. They're staring at me with wide eyes, wondering what's going on. I straighten up, wipe away my tears, and make myself say, "Oh, Birch, Prairie, Fox, Lynx—here we are! Wing made some wet biscuit for you. Let's add a little honey to it." They slowly get up and climb onto the benches arranged around the table. They don't say much as they eat. Fox asks Thorn to bring them some water. Birch asks who Lark is, but I pretend not to hear him.

After they're finished, they still seem tired, so we have them use their slop jar and then take them into the other room to get them into their cots. As they settle in, Birch asks me to tell them a story.

"How about if you tell the rest of us a story instead?" I ask, afraid that I'll start crying again if I keep talking. "I bet you'll be good at it."

"One of your stories?" he asks.

"That'd be fine," I say. "Or maybe you can just make one up. Something about a fish. Or a squirrel and a raven. How one time they helped each other."

And so he does.

CHAPTER 36
BIRCH'S STORY

There was a squirrel who left his tree and ran into the forest. He ran and ran and ran. Finally, he stopped. He turned around to go home. But he hadn't paid attention to where he came from. And the wind had blown away the trail he'd left in the leaves. I mean, it had blown away the leaves, so he couldn't see the trail. It was getting dark, and he was scared. Because he was lost. And he knew that a bad badger lived in the forest, and it ate squirrels. He climbed up a tree to sleep, but he couldn't remember if badgers could climb trees. So he didn't sleep.

Finally, the sun comes up. The squirrel sees a raven standing on a branch of the tree. Sitting on the branch, I mean. It's looking at him with one eye.

Then, it turns its head and looks at him with the other eye. It can't look at him with both eyes at the same time. That's just how ravens are. The raven looks at the squirrel and asks him if he is lost. The squirrel says yes, and the raven says that she had a raven baby that flew away and never came back. So she will help the squirrel get home. She tells the squirrel—his name is Bluebird—to follow her. Then, she flies to another tree.

Bluebird jumps from branch to branch and follows her.

Then she flies to another tree, and Bluebird follows. He can get from one tree to the next one by jumping. He's glad he doesn't have to go on the ground because he's still afraid of the bad badger. Finally, after lots of flying and jumping, the squirrel finds his home. His brothers and sister are so happy to see him. They had been afraid.

The raven's name is Blackie.

CHAPTER 37
HOPING TO FIND A SISTER

Thorn usually sits across the table from me during morning meal. This morning, he's beside me, one arm doing what his Headmaster wants—lifting food to his mouth—and the other wrapped around my waist, gently hugging me.

He's already told Silex and Rose about the visit from Ivy and what she said about Lark. Rose's eyes glisten with tears. Silex's face is clouded with anger. He's fiercely clenching his spoon, his knuckles white with squeezing. All three of them are silent. What is there to say? Yet I feel their presence with me—their furious love for me.

I have no appetite, but I obediently chew and swallow the pieces of biscuit wedge. It strikes me how dehumanized that makes me feel right now: to have fuel forced into me while my heart is so heavy.

"I'm going to go see Lark this slackening," I announce, trying to still the quaver in my voice.

Rose and Silex nod and murmur their support.

"I'll come with you," Thorn says. "River can take over for Wing with the kids."

"Rose and I can help Thorn with them, too," Silex quickly

adds, eager to do something for me. Despite my anguish, I almost smile. The thought of Silex trying to change Lynx and Fox's diapers with his enormous hands, looming over them with his huge frame and ruddy face, as the kids howl at his wild red beard and furry eyebrows, seems wonderfully ridiculous.

"Thank you, Silex. But Thorn and River can handle them." I turn to Thorn. "I want to go alone," I tell him. "I'm not sure if she'll even see me. And if anyone is with me, I'm sure she won't."

Thorn doesn't argue.

The Headmasters impel us to finish the remaining crumbs of biscuit and then push us onward to our toil. The trudge to the pear orchard seems longer and more stubborn than usual. Several times, the sledges get jammed against upthrust rocks, and we have to stop and lift them over. Once we reach the orchard, we pick in silence until the sun is high in the sky. Then, my thoughts about Lark are interrupted when Thorn pauses—holding a pear in mid-air—and speaks. His voice is low. I don't think he wants Silex and Rose to hear.

"I'm getting an idea," he says. There's a distant look in his eye as if he's speaking as much to himself as to me.

"What do you mean?" I ask. "About what?"

"I think it could work," he says, still distracted.

I can tell he's drifting back into his thoughts, so I don't say anything more. Before long, he's become almost oblivious to his toil. He's still reaching out and pulling off pears, but every third or fourth one he's dropping absentmindedly onto the ground instead of his bucket. When Silex and Rose notice what he's doing, they glance over at me with raised eyebrows. I shake my head and shrug.

We let Thorn continue like this for the rest of the grip, occasionally taking turns to walk behind him and collect the fruit he's letting fall to the ground. By doing so, we're hoping his Headmaster won't sense his diminished performance and jolt him.

When the grip ends, Thorn lags behind us as we make our way back to the compound. We have to keep turning around to tell him to hurry up. He catches up, then a few minutes later is lagging again. As soon as we get to the kitchen, Thorn drops his sledge rope and begins to walk away—and he's not heading toward the Aery.

"Thorn," I cry out. "Where are you going?"

He stops and turns, then almost seems surprised to see me. "Maple," he says. "I'm going to—" he pauses and looks around —"I'm going to walk to the Coil. I need to think something through."

"And I'm going to try to talk to Lark, remember?" I say. "So what about the kids?"

I'm half expecting him to reply, "What kids?" but he doesn't. He just looks blankly at me. I decide if he's acting like this, he'll be useless at the Aery. "Never mind," I sigh. "I'll go and help River with them for a little while. Then I'll find Lark." I'm not angry with him. He's never let me down before.

He nods and starts walking toward the Gate. That's what we call the entrance to the Blue Ring compound. But if there was ever a gate there, it's long gone. It leads out to what Zara's memories tell me was once a smooth, black road, but now is nothing more than a long stretch of rubble that heat and cold and roots have heaved out of place like a mouthful of smashed teeth.

In a way, I'm glad for the delay in looking for Lark. As the day's grip wore on, I'd started to lose my resolve. What if what Ivy said is true? That Lark no longer thinks of me as her sister— as family?

Then I begin to feel guilty: maybe I shouldn't have given up when Lark first rejected me outside her cubicle. Maybe I should have gone to her again. And again, till she agreed to see me. But there was no guarantee she ever would have. And it had been easier to try to push her out of my mind, to forget her and bury my heart in the kids and Thorn and Papa and River. Maybe my chance to reconnect with Lark has long passed.

I walk through the doorway of the Aery and find River already here, watching Wing mash up biscuit for the kids while they play with a few wooden animals on the floor.

"A bit more water," he advises Wing. "Too dry for them. Might as well feed them dust."

"I know what I'm doing," Wing says.

I haven't told River what Ivy said. Or Papa. I haven't had a chance yet. I'm wondering if they already know. Ivy would never speak to River, but she might have told others who might have told him. But as I listen to River's gentle banter with Wing, I can tell he hasn't heard. There's no anguish in his voice.

I decide in that moment not to tell River. Or Papa. Not yet. Not till I speak with Lark and find out if it's true.

"Here we are, River," I say.

He doesn't turn around but gives me a quick backward glance over his shoulder.

"Here we are, sister. Wing is doing great. The kids love him. They're already washed and almost ready for bed. Birch wants to tell Wing a story. That's why he hasn't left yet."

"Already washed?" I ask. "Fast work."

"We only did them from their waists up today," he replies. He's joking, of course. "You can wash them from the waist down tomorrow. Saves a lot of time."

"My favourite part, the bottom half—thanks for that."

He smiles at me. "There you go, kids," he says. They look up at him from the floor. "Wing has made some more delicious biscuit paste. I think he even added some beaver tails to make your teeth strong."

"He didn't," Birch says, groaning.

Lynx reaches his arms toward me.

"I can't play with you tonight, Lynx," I tell him. "I have to go see someone." As I look into his eyes, it strikes me—as it often has before—how much they resemble Lark's.

"Wing and I are more fun than Maple anyway," River says to him. "Isn't that right, Weasel?"

Lynx laughs and throws his hand up in exasperation. "I'm Lynx!" he burbles.

"Are you meeting up with Thorn?" River asks me.

I shake my head. "Not tonight. He's on a walk. Says he's thinking."

River nods and doesn't ask me who I'm going to go see. Something I've always liked about him is his ability to sense when someone doesn't want to talk.

"I'll see you tomorrow," I say. Then I turn and head for the doorway, leaving a brother and hoping to find a sister.

CHAPTER 38
WE ARE THANKFUL

After I leave the Aery, my mind becomes a hail of thoughts as I try to figure out what I'll say to Lark when I see her—*if* I see her. I'm so preoccupied I don't even remember crossing the compound. But here I am, standing in front of the door into the Cube. Now, my hand is on the doorknob, pulling hard to get it open.

The swoosh of my bare feet on the stairs seems loud as I ascend. The steps are cold. Fall is almost here. Tomorrow, I'll start keeping my foot wraps on after the grips end.

I'm standing in front of the same door where Ivy found me lurking three years ago. It opens, and there she stands again as if she's been expecting me.

"Maple, so nice you returned. I knew you would." The sides of her mouth seem pulled up by invisible threads. Not a smile—it's called a smirk, Zara's memory tells me. "Are you here to join us? Our numbers have grown since the big gathering."

I can see the ring of Thankfuls in the dim light behind her, sitting cross-legged on the floor. Motes of dust drift through the shafts of sunlight slanting through the windows. I stand on my toes to peer over Ivy's shoulder—she's very tall—and try to spot Lark. There she is—she's not sitting among them—she's lying on the floor in the middle of their ring. My heart drops. Has she been terminated already? Is this their body ceremony?

"Lark," I scream, somehow grappling Ivy out of my way. I run into the room, jump through the circle of Thankfuls, and in a moment, I'm kneeling beside her, staring at her closed eyes, grabbing her hand. "Lark!"

She doesn't respond—but her body isn't cold, her muscles aren't stiff. I put my ear to her chest and hear a steady heartbeat.

Ivy has stepped back into the room. "She is very not dead, Maple. Apart from a small bed sore on her left shoulder blade, she is in fair health. The Headmasters have continued to spare her. For now."

"What are you doing to her?" I cry.

"We are not doing anything to her," Ivy replies. "We are doing something for her. We have decided to beseech our Headmasters to extend her time—to give her just one more moon cycle to conceive a child."

I look up at Ivy, bewildered by what she's said.

"We support one another, Maple. We are Thankfuls because we have received the gift of Headmasters. But we are also thankful for one another. I am thankful for Lark. I do not want to lose her if it can be helped."

The ones surrounding me murmur in unison: "We are thankful." I hear it murmured beside me, too, and look back down at Lark. Her eyes are now open but without expression—like the eyes of a trout pulled from a river.

I look back at Ivy. I want to tell her their effort—their beseeching—is futile. They're deluding themselves. The Headmasters can't hear them, won't hear them. But instead, I find myself saying through tears, "Will it work?"

Ivy gazes coolly at me. "That is why we are here," she says. "We are trying."

I look back down at Lark. For a moment, I think I see a flash of my sister in her eyes—a connection. Then it's gone, and the trout eyes return.

"Would you like to help us in our beseeching, Maple?" Ivy asks in a low, soft voice. "More bodies will make our connection to the Headmasters stronger. They will be more likely to heed our plea."

My gaze returns to Lark. Her eyes are closed again. I rise to my feet, step toward the edge of the circle, and then sit down cross-legged between two of Ivy's Thankfuls.

CHAPTER 39
THE MANXOME FOE

I drop onto the bench at the meal table with Thorn, Silex, and Rose. Thorn looks up at me and flashes a faint smile, then returns his attention to his bowl. Somehow, given his odd behaviour yesterday, I'm not surprised. I mutter a greeting to Silex and Rose, then also turn to my bowl of biscuit.

I don't feel like talking. My emotions are at odds with one another. Part of me feels ashamed for what I did with the Thankfuls last night—as if I've made fun of Papa or lied to Thorn. Part of me feels hopeful—as if Lark might now be in less danger. Part of me feels like a coward for not just grabbing Lark and hauling her off the fourth floor. And part of me feels drawn to return to the fourth floor during tonight's slackening, to sit again with the Thankfuls and share their chants.

My thoughts are interrupted by Rose.

"Maple? Maple?"

I look up at her.

"Thorn told me something when he sat down," she continues hesitantly, "and he asked me to repeat it to you. He doesn't want to risk explaining it twice. He told me he has an idea to help Lark. He told me he can't tell anyone what it is because he doesn't want his Headmaster to sense it and stop him. He told me that if you hear him saying something over and over, not to worry about it. He said he has to keep his mind like a blizzard—that's what he said—like a blizzard—to keep it from them."

Thorn glances up, nods quickly, then lowers his gaze back to his bowl.

"Is he okay, Maple?" Silex asks, his eyes dark with concern. "Even for him, this is odd behaviour."

"He didn't have a memory surface in the last few days, did he?" Rose asks.

"No," I reply, though I'm beginning to wonder if something did happen to him during his walk to the coil last night.

As if in response, Thorn shakes his head and mutters quietly into his bowl, "He took his vorpal sword in hand; long time the manxome foe he sought—so rested he by the Tumtum tree and stood awhile in thought." Then he repeats it, word for word.

Silex blinks twice and shakes his head. "I wonder if the Grubbers have the pleasure of such conversations?" he asks.

"We'll leave him be," Rose says. "Thorn," she says, turning toward him, "do what you need to do." Then she says to me, "Maple, did you find Lark?"

I close my eyes and nod.

"You don't have to tell us anything, honey," she adds. "But you can if you want. Anytime. Sometimes, you can lighten a burden by sharing it."

"Also," Silex growls, "this slackening, I'd be pleased to go to the fourth floor and take her away from them." He leans toward me with a grave look on his face and adds, "Just say the word."

I manage a small smile and shake my head.

"Ivy has a cunning way with words," Rose says to me.

"They slide around and get under your skin, and before you know it, you're half-believing what she's saying."

Now, she's the one giving me a searching look. Does she know I sat with the Thankfuls last night?

"I should know," Rose adds after a moment, more quietly. "I was the first one she convinced to join."

"And the only one to ever leave," Silex says. His voice is dark and low.

"You were a Thankful?" I ask Rose, my eyes widening.

Rose frowns and nods. "Back then, Ivy didn't call us that. She called us the Insightfuls. She promised our lives would get better if we gathered and thought good things about the Headmasters."

Silex snorts. "Insightfuls—pah! Everyone else called them the Assholes."

"Until Maple's Papa asked them not to," Rose reminds him. "He said people should be allowed to call themselves what they want." She turns back to me. "Fear is what motivated us, at least at first. We'd all been punished so many times for—for falling short. We lived in dread of getting more jolts. We thought if we could do exactly what the Headmasters wanted— if we could be extra-obedient—we could avoid future punishments."

"Then what made you leave?" I ask.

"When others started to join, I could see my own fear reflected in them. And I began to see how Ivy fed off that fear and used it to control them. Then Ivy began to devise her own punishments for Thankfuls who didn't meet her expectations. It was hard, but I decided I didn't need two Headmasters."

As I ponder Ivy's words, I realize that Thorn has been continuing to mutter quietly beside me: ". . . vorpal sword . . . manxome foe . . ." I sigh and decide I'm looking forward to losing myself for a while in the mindless toil of berry picking.

A few moments later, we find ourselves pushing away our bowls of biscuit and rising to our feet. We trudge through the doorway of the Meal House and turn toward the kitchen side to fetch our sledges.

Except, not all of us do. As Silex, Rose, and I turn to the left, Thorn veers to the right. He's not heading to the sledges. He's walking across the compound toward the Cube. For a moment, I'm puzzled by this deviation from our ritual. Then I stop in my tracks as I realize what's happening.

Thorn is being sent to Lark. The Headmasters are giving her one more moon cycle to conceive.

They're going to make him mate with her.

I twist around and watch in horror as he begins to resist what his Headmaster is impelling him to do. He's walking as if his feet are stuck in pine sap, each step an awkward jerk. He falls to the ground, then instantly rises again like he's being drawn up by strings. His Headmaster is undoubtedly intensifying its grip, making it harder and more dangerous for Thorn to resist. And if he doesn't stop resisting—

He drops to his knees, his hands clasped around his head, and his jaw clenched tight as he releases an animal-like howl of physical anguish. Against my will, I'm turning away from him and back toward the sledges. I try to stop but can't—the impulse is too strong. Rose half-turns and holds out her hand to me as she continues to walk. "Come, Maple. Just come with us. I'm sorry, honey, I'm so sorry. There's nothing you can do."

My vision dims as if a black cloud has passed over the face of the sun. Everything seems to be a shadow. I look down and see my feet moving steadily over the broken concrete of the compound, but can't feel them. Someone is saying my name, but it's like I'm hearing it from underwater. I remember being upset, but I'm not sure why, and the feeling is fading away. I'm feeling . . . nothing . . . like a leaf slowly drifting down to the surface of a river.

Now I'm grasping an apple, twisting it from its branch, and pulling it back through the trembling leaves. The sun is high in the sky. Silex and Rose are toiling on the other side of the tree. Every few moments, they glance toward me, their faces etched with concern. Thorn is nowhere to be seen. I wonder when he'll arrive.

But he doesn't. The grip comes to an end. We load the pails of apples onto the sledges, fewer than usual because of Thorn's absence. Then, Silex picks me up without a word and sets me down on one of the sledges where Thorn's buckets of apples would usually be.

"No arguing," he says, looking straight at me. "You rest, we haul."

"Listen to the man," Rose says, smiling sadly. Too tired to protest, I nod and lean back against the buckets. They each pick up the ropes of a sledge and begin to pull.

As I drift into a dreamless sleep, I hear Silex's booming voice stretching back to me. "It's all good," he's saying. "I need the exercise." I imagine Rose shaking her head and still smiling sadly.

CHAPTER 40
KISAKIHITIN

I'm jostled awake as we approach the compound. I open my eyes and see the red and yellow leaves of overhanging elm trees sliding past against the fading light of the evening sky. Silex glances over his shoulder and sees that I'm awake.

"Sorry about that last bump," he says as he and Rose bring the sledges to a stop.

Rose says, "As soon as we empty the sledges, I'll walk you to your cubicle. You need rest."

I shake my head. "He might go there. I don't want to talk to him. Not yet. I want to be alone to think."

Rose nods. Then, after a moment, she asks, "Do you want me to tell your Papa and River about this morning?"

I close my eyes and try to push away Rose's question. I don't want to think about my grandfather and brother right now. But I know someone will tell them eventually about Thorn and Lark, and I'd rather it be Rose.

"Yes," I reply. "If you can tell them together." Wearily, I stand up and step off the sledge.

Rose nods, then adds, "Silex and I will stop by the Aery, too, and see if River and Wing need any help."

Lark's kids. I hadn't even given them a thought.

Rose is about to turn away, then hesitates before saying, "Maple—at least it means the Headmasters have decided not to terminate her."

"Not for another moon cycle, at least," I reply flatly.

Rose nods once, then she and Silex start dragging the sledges the last stretch to the Kitchen. I stand motionless for a few moments, not knowing where to go, then start walking toward the Deep. A gentle breeze sends fallen leaves scurrying after me.

Thorn and I had always known that he might one day get sent to a Breeder. But we thought that day would be a long way off. The men who were sent to breeders were always a lot older —in their thirties or forties, sometimes even fifties.

Papa said it hadn't always been that way. Originally, the Headmasters had sent only young males to the Breeder. As young as thirteen. The women selected as Breeders were just as young—girls, really, straight from being harvested. But when four of those Breeders in a row died in childbirth, without a single newborn surviving, things changed. The Headmasters started using women closer to twenty and much older men. It was as if they'd decided that too young was too risky.

That's why we thought that if Thorn was going to get sent to a breeder, it wouldn't happen for at least another ten years.

But it had. And with my sister.

But perhaps it could have been worse. It could have been River they sent to Lark. Maybe they still would.

I pause in front of the Deep and stare at its ruined face. Its empty windows are like pockmarks. A white column that once helped support a little roof—Zara's memory tells me it was called a portico—has fallen and smashed into fragments in front of the entrance. The chunks of broken marble look like crooked teeth. The milkweed peeking over the ledge of the roof is a fringe of greasy hair.

I decide to go around to the back and climb the staircase to the roof where Papa and I used to go. Up there, looking down at whoever happened to be crossing the compound, I could be alone without feeling alone. But when I push my way through the weeds toward the back of the building, my eye catches sight of the rear entrance that leads to the vault. I change my mind about going to the roof and squeeze past the jammed door, waiting for a few moments until my eyes adjust to the gloom.

I haven't been in here for a long time. Whenever Thorn and I have needed a new book to read to each other or for Lark's kids, he's been the one to come here to get one. The pungent smell that overwhelmed me when Thorn first took me here isn't as intense, and the air feels drier. Pigeons have settled on some of the still upright shelves and are gently cooing. They don't seem troubled by my intrusion.

I take the light cylinder from its spot in the wall, flick it on, and step gingerly along the cluttered path that winds through the cavernous room until I'm in front of the vault. The door is almost shut, but not quite: Thorn didn't trust the old locking mechanism. We'd never get in again if the door closed and the lock jammed.

I give the door a tug, and it swings open without a sound. I step inside and cast the light into the corners and over the metal panels of the ceiling—I don't want to be in here with any rats or bats. Then I settle myself cross-legged on the floor and lean sideways so my left shoulder presses against the wall. I don't want to feel my Headmaster pressing into my back. I switch the light cylinder to its dimmest setting and close my eyes. It's quiet. Even the pigeons must have left.

There's a rotting tree stump that we pass every time we get sent out to the blueberry bushes. For years, the only thing on the stump was a small, speckled rock that Thorn once set there as we trudged by. Then, one morning, I glanced over and saw dozens of orange mushrooms with long, skinny stems growing out of the stump. They hadn't been there the day before. They'd simply appeared overnight and all at once.

Those mushrooms come to mind as I think about the past few days. Like them, so much has emerged so quickly—the wind turbine failing, the threat of Lark being terminated, Thorn's strange behaviour, Thorn being sent to mate with Lark —all of it seems to be pressing down on me and yet as distant as the moon.

I remember, too, how the mushrooms on the stump were gone the next day. Or seemed to be gone. When we got closer, I could see they'd simply collapsed and shrivelled and were dissolving into a brown sludge. Thorn's rock was still there.

I hear a loud and metallic noise outside the vault. It sounds like someone or something has crashed into one of the broken chairs strewn along the path. My breath catches in my chest: it must be Thorn. Suddenly, I want to see him, to hold him, but I still don't know what I'll say to him. I grab the light cylinder, switch it to its brightest setting, and stand up just as the door to the vault is pulled wide.

Standing before me, squinting at the light, is Papa.

"I haven't seen one of those in a long time," he says, gesturing toward the light cylinder. Then he adds, casually, as if he's just bumped into me in the compound, "Rose tells me you've had a hard day."

"How did you find me?" I ask, still shocked to see him.

"You weren't in your cubicle, so I thought you might have climbed up onto the Deep. I was almost at the fire escape stairs when I saw a glow through one of the windows. I thought it had to be you or Thorn. Or both."

He steps into the vault and walks over to one of the shelves.

He gently runs a finger along the spines of the books. "And it's been a long time since I was in here, too," he says. "A lifetime ago. A world ago."

"Before the Arrival?" I ask. It's a relief to talk about something in the past, something that isn't now.

"Yes," he replies. "A few months before the Arrival. It was your grandmother who showed me. We weren't married yet, of course. That didn't happen until years later. I was just a kid. Seventeen. My parents were researchers, and we moved here six months before. They weren't here when the Arrival happened—they'd gone to a conference for a week. Your grandmother—"

"Zara," I say. I want to hear Papa say her name—to make her real.

"Yes, that's right—Zara. She'd arrived just a couple of weeks before. She'd been hired to catalogue these old books and decide which ones needed to be sent off for repair. They belonged to the man who paid for this building."

"Deepak Chandra," I say.

"That's right," Papa says, looking less surprised than I might have expected. "I never met him."

"She was older than you," I say. "Zara."

"Seven years," he says. "When I met her that day, in this very building, I never dreamed that she and I would one day . . ." His words trail off. He smiles and looks at me intently. "Or that I would be standing here more than sixty years later telling our granddaughter about her."

"Why are you telling me now, Papa? After all this time? We're not supposed to talk about the past."

He sighs and looks around for something to sit on.

"There're chairs out there," I tell him. "I can get you one."

"No, no," he says, waving his hand. "If we cut ourselves on

one of those things, we'll get tetanus for sure." I've never heard of tetanus before, but I suddenly know what it is.

He slowly bends his knees—I hear them crack—and sits on the floor, leaning back against one of the bookcases.

"Your grandmother was willing to take risks," he says after he's settled. "That's part of what made her a natural leader. The last risk she took ended up getting her killed, but I know she'd still say it was worth the attempt. But after she was gone, people here pretty much lost hope. Resisting the Headmasters had led to nothing but suffering and death. So, we gave up trying and made ourselves small. We let go of so many things that made us human—reading, music, the past, taking risks—to cling to the little scrap of living we still had left. We thought it was the right thing to do."

He pauses and shifts his legs around.

"But now I'm beginning to regret that approach. Partly because of you and Thorn. I figured the two of you had found this place"—he smiles fondly and gestures at the walls of the vault—"and had taught yourselves to read. You and he know things—not just words, but facts, ideas—that no one else here knows except for me and Jenna and Virgil."

"You've known all along that we came here?" I exclaim.

"For a while. And Jenna and Virgil," he replies.

"Why didn't you say something to us?"

"The three of us talked about it. The prudent thing would have been to tell the community about the books so we could destroy them. But we couldn't bring ourselves to do that. This vault is a time capsule. So is every book in it. Do you know what that is—a time capsule?"

I nod. I do now.

"Who knows if there's anything left of the rest of the world? We need to keep these books. Not throw them away."

Papa pauses to stretch out his legs.

"You and Thorn took a risk in teaching yourselves how to read. And it's turned out for the best. So I think it's time for us —or for me, at least—to start talking about the past. It's a risk I'm ready to take—now that I'm nearly eighty."

I mull over what Papa has told me. It seems strange that someone so old is still learning, still rethinking life, still willing to change.

"Papa—" I say. "Papa, I didn't teach myself to read."

"You mean Thorn taught you? Is he also the one who figured out how to open the vault?"

I shake my head. "He didn't teach me. He was going to. But we came here once—about two years ago—and I discovered I could already read."

"I don't follow you," he says, his brow furrowing with puzzlement.

I sigh. The time has come. "Do you remember a long time ago when I was helping you in the greenhouse? When I told you that I knew some music?"

"Of course. You sang something that—that was important to Zara. You said one of her memories had surfaced in you the night before."

"And they kept surfacing, Papa. More and more every year."

His eyes widen with surprise. "More of them? And they never harmed you?"

"No. They're in my head with my own memories. I can tell which ones are hers and which ones are mine. Mostly. But I remember hers just like I can remember my own. That's why I can read—because she could."

Papa runs his hand through his thinning hair as what I've told him sinks in. He seems overwhelmed. "How—how many?" he asks. "How many memories?"

"I don't know how to answer that, Papa. Some of them

overlap. Some are just faint flashes of something she saw or did. Or thought. Some are intense and cover a lot of time. Some are memories of things she learned how to do—like reading."

Papa nods. "The darkening—that's when they come to you?"

"It was. But lately, even when I'm awake, if I need to know something or if somebody says something unfamiliar, all of a sudden, I'll understand it. Like when you asked me a minute ago about time capsules."

A look both sad and hopeful falls over his face. "*Kisaki-hitin*," he says to me.

"I love you, too, Papa," I reply.

He slowly shakes his head in disbelief. "You'd never heard that word up until just now? But as soon as I said it, you understood it?"

"I guess so," I reply. "It's another language, isn't it?"

"It's called Cree. The language of one of the peoples who lived here centuries ago. The first people. One side of your grandmother was descended from them. Her mother's father taught her how to speak it. She'd be so glad to know it's been passed on to you—though she could never have imagined it happening this way. She spoke a lot of different languages."

"*Ich kenne*," I reply, smiling. Then I add, more gravely, "I'm sorry, Papa—maybe I should have told you years ago that her memories were still coming to me."

"Zara used to say that things have a way of revealing themselves at the right time," he says.

"Maybe," I say. "But that doesn't mean things will work out."

"Yes," he sighs. "That's very true." Then, after a pause, he adds, "There's something I've never told you, too, Maple." He pauses again. "I should really talk to Jenna and Virgil first, but I think they'll understand. I hope so."

I look at him expectantly. His eyes lock onto mine. "My Headmaster," he says, "is impotent."

I can't help it. I burst out laughing. It seems so ridiculous. "Impotent?" I exclaim. "What do you mean?"

Papa looks at me almost sheepishly. "I mean, it doesn't have any grip on me. It's alive, or as alive as it ever was, but it's stuck in a kind of mental loop. It's experiencing over and over the same few minutes from sixty years ago. It has no awareness of what I'm doing or not doing, of what I'm thinking or feeling. Same for Jenna and Virgil."

"Who else knows this?"

"Just the three of us—me, Jenna, and Virgil. If we told others, then they'd think about it—they wouldn't be able to help thinking about it—and then, during the grip, their Headmasters might sense their thoughts and find out. So, to stay under the radar—" He pauses and gives me a questioning look.

"I know what you mean," I tell him.

"—to stay under the radar, the three of us have acted like our Headmasters still have a grip on us. We do our toil, we go to bed like everyone else when the slackening ends, we get up when we hear others getting jolted awake. Except sometimes, the three of us get up in the night—if it's a full moon—and go for little walks into the forest. Sometimes, I go by myself. The silence is remarkable."

"Sometimes you'd come into the cubicle, too? To look in on me? And River and Lark?"

"Yes. But I couldn't tell you that then."

"So you and Jenna and Virgil have been faking it. For sixty years."

Papa nods.

"But how? How did it happen?"

"It was Zara," he says sadly. "She broke the link to our Headmasters. It was the last thing she did before we killed her."

CHAPTER 41
RUN

Suddenly, it hits me. "You could have left Blue Ring!" I cry out. "The three of you could have just walked away and found somewhere else to live—maybe even other people."

Papa shakes his head. "We could have," he says, "but if we'd decided to leave, we wouldn't have walked. There was a small boat on the riverbank from before the Arrival. During a darkening, the three of us could have pushed it into the river and been carried far away. By the time the Headmasters would have realized we were gone, we'd have been too far away for them to make the others catch us." He pauses, and a faraway look comes into his eyes. "But a few things held us back."

"What, Papa?" I ask gently.

He heaves a sigh before replying. "After Zara was killed, I was a wreck. Like this building," he says, waving his hand toward the ruins outside the vault door. "There were days when I wished my Headmaster was still in control—then I'd at least have a bit of relief from my anguish during the grip and the darkening. I was a mess, Maple. I couldn't have managed an escape, not even with Jenna's and Virgil's help.

"There was our little daughter, too," he continues. "Your

mother. Her name was Sparrow. I couldn't abandon her here. But she was too young to take with me. We didn't know what we would find down the river. I didn't think I could take that chance. Though, given that she was eventually made into a Breeder, maybe it would have been better to take that chance. Anyway, we also felt we couldn't leave because of what the Headmasters would have done to those we left behind. Punish them all? Terminate someone? Too steep a price for our escape. So we stayed."

Suddenly, there's a crashing outside the vault. Someone's in a hurry to find us.

Another loud crash. "Goddammit!" someone yells. It's River's voice. In another moment, he's standing in the doorway of the vault, breathing hard. His left leg is bleeding from a fresh cut. "Maple," he pants. "I need to tell you something. I just found out about it. I'm so sorry—they—they sent Thorn to Lark this morning."

"I know, River," I reply, closing my eyes. "Who told you?"

"Twig. She saw them together on the bridge. Right after first meal."

What? My eyes fly open. "The bridge? That can't be right, River." Twig had to be mistaken. They would have made Thorn go to Lark in her cubicle. That's where the daily matings always happened.

"It's true," River says. "Twig was at the river getting water for the Biscuiteers. She saw Lark walk onto the bridge, to the very middle. She was crying and dragging a rope. Then, a few moments later, Twig saw Thorn stagger onto the bridge—he was trying to resist his Headmaster. Twig said he—Maple, I'm so sorry—she said he was screaming from the jolts they were giving him."

My heart seems to stop beating. I start to hear ringing in my ears and have to grab onto River's arm to steady myself.

The bridge. The rope.

So Thorn wasn't sent to mate with her. He was sent to kill her. He was sent to tie her up and push her into the river. The blood punishment. So my sister is dead. Drowned. And the man I love did it. They made him do it.

Papa says nothing. His eyes have turned to blanks.

River must suddenly realize the impact of his words because he whirls me toward him and hurriedly adds, "No, Maple, Thorn didn't do it. They were trying to make him kill her, but they couldn't. Twig said he hooked his arm through the railing and held on, getting jolt after jolt from his Headmaster. His body was convulsing, but he wouldn't let go. Even when he passed out, they kept jolting him. He was lying on the bridge for the whole grip, unconscious and twitching. Then finally, the slackening started, and the Inwards found him and helped wake him up."

"How much of the slackening is left?" I cry out.

"Not much," River says. "It took me a while to find you."

"I have to go find him before the darkening. And Lark, too. I need to see them."

"We will," Papa says quietly. "But Maple and River, remember: nothing has really changed. The Headmasters will make Thorn do the same thing tomorrow. He'll eventually break down and kill her. Or they'll terminate him."

I'm barely taking in Papa's words. I drop the light cylinder, push between them, race through the clutter of broken chairs and desks, squeeze through the door to get outside. I have to find them. But where? Will they still be on the bridge? The slackening is going to end soon—I don't have much time.

Run!

CHAPTER 42
A LILY BLOOMS IN WINTER SNOW

I'm nearly there. At the bridge. I can see them. They're both there—Thorn and Lark. And Ivy. What's she doing there? It must be very near the end of the slackening because all the Inwards have left. I sprint toward the three of them but get a stabbing cramp in my side that makes me stop and catch my breath. I look up and see Thorn and Lark climb over the railing of the bridge—and then down onto the edge of the platform that hangs over the raging river below.

I struggle to run, drop to my knees when the cramp splits my side again, worse this time, and call out to them—"River! Lark! Wait! What are you doing? Ivy, stop them!"—but they can't hear me. The roar of the river is too loud.

I stumble forward onto the wooden platform of the bridge and grab the railing to steady myself. The slackening will end any moment. I watch in horror as Lark presses herself against Thorn's back and wraps her arms around him. Ivy steps forward, her brow furrowed with fear and uncertainty, then passes a short piece of rope around them and ties it together at their hips.

Ivy stoops to the platform, picks up a longer coil of rope,

and hands it to Thorn. He loops it around one of the struts of the railing, then drops the two ends so they unfurl toward the water surging below. He grabs one side of the rope with one hand and one with the other and then begins to slowly slide down, lowering himself and Lark till they're hanging well below the level of the platform, suspended over the river.

He's holding tight, but I can see his arms quivering with the strain—he'll never be able to pull the two of them back up. I push away the pain in my gut and run till I'm beside Ivy, heaving for breath, then look over the railing at Thorn and Lark dangling below.

"What are they doing?" I scream at Ivy. "We need to pull them up! Hurry, the slackening is going to end!"

Ivy stares at me blankly and says nothing. I peer down at Thorn and shout. This time, he hears me and turns his face upward. He looks fearful and in pain from the strain of holding the weight of them both, but he manages a faint smile at me. "I had an idea!" he shouts up to me.

Suddenly, I feel it: the slackening is over. The Headmasters will punish us any second for not being in our cubicles, but that's hardly my concern at the moment.

I hear Thorn shouting again. Not to me—to Lark. "Open your eyes," he's yelling at her. "Let it see where we are!"

Lark's eyes open wide and lock onto my own. Her lips move silently: *Maple.*

Then something happens that I didn't dream possible. The lump that is Thorn's Headmaster begins to move beneath his shirt. Its pair of coils retract from the base of his skull—he winces in pain but keeps his grip on the ends of the rope. Now, it's Lark's Headmaster that's retracting its coils. Her face contorts with agony, and her arms release their hold on Thorn. She slumps down along his body till her arms snag over the loop Ivy tied around their waists. Her head lolls to one side, and her eyes close as she presses against him.

Thorn's fingers are sliding down the last bit of rope. Then I freeze with astonishment: their Headmasters have fully detached; they're climbing up toward me, over Thorn's and Lark's torsos, up their necks and onto their heads, then up Thorn's trembling arms, trying to reach the rope with their beetle-like legs. Beside me, Ivy has dropped to the platform and is reaching under the railing of the bridge, extending her hand to the Headmasters that have just climbed over Thorn's knuckles—

I'm suddenly hit with a jolt of punishment that knocks me to the platform. A moment later, I'm back on my feet, Ivy struggling beside me to get up. I lean over the railing to call out again to Thorn and Lark.

But they are gone. Even the rope has vanished.

I guess I'm sitting at our table in the Meal House.

"Incredible!" Silex is saying again. "Incredible! In two days, the lad came up with a scheme to make them detach. Without getting terminated! Something no one else did in sixty years. Ha!" He slaps the table with his big palm, and it shudders. "They had to detach! As soon as the slackening ended, the ugly buggers realized they were hanging over the river and knew the lad's arms were going to give out. But they couldn't terminate him! Because then they'd have fallen into the river and been swept away on Thorn and Lark's corpses! Never to be found!"

"Silex," Rose says sharply, nodding toward me.

"What?" Silex replies, looking puzzled. "Oh—corpses. I'm sorry, Maple. I just mean that's what their Headmasters were afraid would happen. But it didn't. Thorn and Lark didn't drown. I just know it. They got away in the river. And one of these days—during a slackening, of course—they're going to show up. They'll be back, and when they do, I'm going to give that lad such a hug! Brilliant!"

I muster a small smile for Silex. But I don't think he's right. They won't be coming back.

"Best of all," Silex continues, his eyes gleaming with admiration, "is that he didn't tie the rope to the bridge. He knew that as soon as he let go, it would slip off the strut and take the two Headmasters with it. I wish I'd been there—to see the miserable faces of those two bugs as they dropped into the torrent and got washed away. If they had faces, I mean."

I swallow a lump of biscuit and nod. Rose reaches across the table, puts her hand on my shoulder, and gives it a squeeze. It occurs to me for the first time that they'll need a new breeder. I vaguely wonder if it might be me. But I don't really care.

"I understand why Lark went along with his plan," Silex says to me. "You said Ivy told her to, and the Thankfuls do whatever she tells them. But why did Ivy help? If the Headmasters ever find out what she did, there'll be wicked punishment—either for her or for everyone."

I knew why Ivy had done it. She'd told me as we stumbled back to our cubicles, saying a few rushed sentences between the jolts of agonizing pain the Headmasters were inflicting on us.

She said Thorn had barged onto the fourth floor of the Cube about halfway through the slackening, looking for Lark. When he didn't see her, he grabbed Ivy, shook her, and asked her where she was. Ivy pushed him away and told him to leave, but he wouldn't. Finally, she told him that she hadn't seen Lark since yesterday—Lark had asked to stay in her cubicle during the slackening to rest. That's when Thorn told Ivy that the Headmasters had tried make him kill Lark that morning—the blood punishment. At first, Ivy didn't believe him. She said the Thankfuls had communed with the Headmasters just last night, beseeching them to give Lark one more moon cycle to conceive. Why wouldn't they have listened?

Then it occurred to her: I'd been there with them. I'd communed with them. She thought maybe my doubt or my anger had upset them. Tainted their communion. That had got her worried. She pushed past Thorn and started down the stairs to Lark's cubicle, Thorn trailing behind. They found her, and Lark told Ivy it was true: the Headmasters had tried to make Thorn kill her that morning.

But then, Thorn told them he had a plan to save her—to stop it from happening tomorrow. He tried explaining, but by then, he was so frantic he wasn't making any sense. He gave up trying and just said that if Ivy didn't help, Lark was sure to die tomorrow morning.

Ivy didn't know what to do. She didn't want to resist what the Headmasters wanted. But she didn't want a Thankful to die. She didn't want Lark to die. Maybe she and the Thankfuls could get the Headmasters to see things differently—to realize they were making a mistake. They just needed one more opportunity to try again, one more slackening, without me there muddling things. So, she decided then and there to help Thorn: she told Lark—who was still stunned by what had almost happened to her that morning—to do whatever Thorn asked. That's when the three of them went back to the bridge.

That's what happened. But I don't feel like explaining all that to Silex right now. So, I stay silent. Rose gives my shoulder another gentle squeeze.

By the time Ivy and I had made it back to the main door to the Cube, she'd concluded she'd made a terrible mistake. "I failed them," she moaned. She seemed to be talking to herself now. "They were testing me, testing my thankfulness, and I fell far short. I need to be punished to purify my faith."

Her usual bravado was gone. I'd never seen her—or anyone, except perhaps Lark—look so broken, so vulnerable. Her face was contorted with shame and regret and pain. And then, in another moment, it all vanished, and rage rose in its place. She turned to me, her face hard and angular, thrust her finger at me, and cried out.

"This is all because of your man! First, he resisted them. Then, he tempted me into helping him break the bond between host and Headmaster. And now, both of them have been lost!" It took me a moment to realize she meant the loss of the two Headmasters, not Thorn and Lark.

"I yearn," she'd snarled at me, "for his head to split on the ragged rocks, for his lungs to churn with water, for river snakes to crawl into his dead and gaping mouth—"

Then we were both hit with another jolt, stronger than ever. When I regained my senses, she was gone. I climbed up to my cubicle, and my Headmaster immediately pulled me into the darkening.

No punishment comes, not the next day or the day after that. Not for Ivy or for any of us. It's as if the Headmasters haven't realized that two of their kind have been lost and swept away by the river. Maybe it's because they detached before they could alert the others. Or maybe they need a human host to communicate with one another. Surely, they'll eventually sense that two of their own and two of their hosts have vanished.

But not yet.

For the next few slackenings, the only thing anyone talks about is what Thorn did. Some don't believe it. They can't accept that two Headmasters were forced to detach—it's like seeing a river flow uphill or a lily bloom in winter snow. It's bewildering, impossible. But others do believe it happened, and for them, it's like a miracle, and Thorn has become like a hero in one of the vault's storybooks—a legend.

But to me, he remains Thorn—the man I paired with—and my heart aches from his absence.

The following slackening—four nights after they vanished into the river—everyone except the Thankfuls gathers in the Bone Yard to build empty cairns for Thorn and Lark. As always, Virgil speaks. But his words are not the usual ones.

"These two humans—Lark and Thorn—are gone. Or not. We can hope—yes, hope, that rare word—hope they survived their harrowing plunge into the torrent, and we can hope they will somehow return to us in good time. But if not, or until then, we build these cairns for them. Cherish in your heart your memories of Lark and Thorn if you wish. But also share them with one another if you wish. Speak of them. Remember them. There is no need to avoid talking of them because their Headmasters are, by now, at the bottom of the great lake into which our river flows. They will not be coupled to anyone else. No one will ever again have those Headmasters. There is no danger of their memories surfacing in new hosts because they will never have new hosts."

He pauses, and the crowd is still and silent. Then someone shouts out, "Remember them!" Someone else repeats it even louder. "Remember them!" And then others, until everyone is shouting, "Remember them!" and it's echoing off the cliff face on the far side of the Bone Yard.

CHAPTER 43
PUNISHMENT

River and Ivy are straddling a bench in the Meal House, facing each other, close enough to kiss. Their eyes are locked on one another. Knot lurches toward them with a knife in each hand, his face twisted, reluctant to do the task his Headmaster is impelling but fearful of provoking punishment by trying to resist.

Knot halts beside them. "I picked . . . the sharpest," he says to them, his voice slurring as his Headmaster exerts its powerful influence over his will. "The cuts . . . will be . . . less raggedy."

"I appreciate it, Knot," River replies, still looking at Ivy.

Knot holds out one knife for River and one for Ivy. They each lift a hand and accept what is offered. I can see that neither of them is attempting to resist—River because he knows it's futile and could draw down more punishment on others, Ivy because she craves to receive the gift of correction from the Headmasters.

I'm standing with everyone else in a circle around River and Ivy. We were impelled to gather like this right after morning meal. I knew it was coming. The blood punishment. We'd been joined at the table that very morning by Twilight, a new Picker. That meant the Headmasters had finally sensed that Thorn and Lark were gone and needed to be replaced—and that we needed to be punished for letting it happen. Twilight got the Headmaster that had been waiting in the Ward for nearly a year, ever since Sapling died, while she grew big enough to be harvested.

The Headmasters likely chose Ivy for the blood punishment because she'd been thinking hard about how she'd helped Thorn and Lark at the bridge. She wanted to expose her thoughts to the Headmasters, have them sense her guilt—wanted to make her confession.

As for River, they might have selected him at random. A scapegoat—that's what Zara would have called him. Or maybe it wasn't random. Maybe they chose him because he was friends with Thorn. Either way, it amounts to the same: River and Ivy are about to receive a blood punishment, and our punishment is being forced to watch.

Everyone in the circle is strangely still, held motionless and in place by the collective will of the Headmasters. Everyone except Papa, Jenna, and Virgil. I can see Papa on the other side of the circle, trembling, the anguish on his face contrasting with the numb expressions of those around him.

Papa warned me long ago that if I were ever forced to watch a blood punishment—and he knew it was just a matter of time—I'd feel numb while it was happening, like I was watching it through someone else's eyes. That was the effect of the Headmasters collectively impelling us to participate. He said the numbing would linger through the grip, and then, when the evening's slackening began, it would fall away in an instant, and all the emotions provoked by witnessing the punishment would roar back like an ice jam breaking in the spring.

I know Papa wants to rush forward, knock the knife out of

River's hand, and yank him away. And he could. His Head-master is inactive. Impotent. Papa, Jenna, and Virgil are standing among us not because they're being forced to by their Headmasters but because they have to pretend to be under their grip. If they do anything that shows otherwise, the Head-masters will impel us all to seize them, to kill them, and then River will get punished anyway.

Papa must be in torment knowing he's free to act and yet doesn't dare. I know this, too, but his distress doesn't bother me. Not yet. I'm too numb.

River and Ivy continue to stare at one another, each holding a knife in their right hand. No one knows yet what the Headmasters will make them do for the blood punishment. They won't make them kill each other. That would be a waste of healthy toilers. It won't be their eyes. They need those to toil. It could be their noses. Or ears or tongue. It could be a slash across the face—like Crest had. The Headmasters will make it something conspicuous, something to remind us of the cost of disobedience every time we look at River or Ivy.

memento doloris

Into the gathered silence, River suddenly speaks, haltingly. "If this is . . . the cost of Thorn . . . and Lark's escape . . . even if they died doing it . . . then I'm glad to pay it." He pauses, then adds a phrase Virgil sometimes says at his tellings. "Now let's cut . . . to the chase." A joke? At this very moment? If I could shake my head in wonder, I would. Later on, my heart will swell with pride and admiration for my brother.

I half expect Ivy to say something, but she remains silent. I suddenly experience a tightening of my Headmaster's grip, as does everyone else, judging from their widening eyes. A moment later, Thorn and Ivy raise their knives to each other's left ear and begin.

It doesn't take long. When they have finished, River reaches down to the floor where Ivy has dropped his ear and picks it up. Then, he lifts it high above his head in a gesture of silent defiance. Blood streams down his neck, then onto his shoulder.

Ivy murmurs something too quiet to hear. Later on, River will tell me she said, "I am justly rebuked. I will amend."

Knot approaches them, this time with narrow strips of nylar. He bunches one strip into a wad, then secures it against Ivy's ear by wrapping another strip around her head. He does the same for Thorn.

We find ourselves turning away and being impelled outside. As we head to our toils, I wonder what Twilight—our new Picker—will think about this start to her first day of toil.

CHAPTER 44
ORION

I'm lifting the last bucket of crab apples onto the sledge when the grip ends. Suddenly, my eyes fill with tears, and a wild howl of white-hot fury escapes my throat. The feelings provoked by Thorn's and Ivy's punishment—pent up till now—flood through me. My chest heaving, I glance around at the others. Rose and Silex have both fallen back against the trunk of the tree, faces newly contorted with pain and sorrow. Twilight has tumbled to the ground and is staring blankly into the canopy of branches above her, overwhelmed with exhaustion and trauma.

I want to smash my bucket, tear branches from the tree, tip the loaded sledge onto its side, but I hold myself back. Any of those things will just delay our return to the compound, and I need to get back there as soon as possible. I force myself to stop sobbing, heave the last bucket of crab apples onto the sledge, and begin to haul it back by myself.

this pain is mine

Silex and Rose call out to me, but I don't need their help and don't want to wait for them, especially since Twilight will likely need to be carried back by Silex. I'm glad for the pain of the sledge ropes as they tighten around my hands and dig into my shoulders. I welcome the strain on my legs as I charge forward. The physical effort brings some order to my mind, makes it easier for me to decide what I'm going to do.

I drag the sledge to the concrete pad behind the kitchen, throw down the rope, and head off to find Papa, my fists still balled with rage. He'll be with River, and they must be in the Ward with Jenna, getting his ear patched up. As I cross the compound, a few people see me and either nod to me wordlessly or murmur a sombre, "Here we are, Maple." They can tell I'm in no mood to stop and talk.

I reach the Ward and push fiercely on the door, slamming it against the wall harder than I intend. River is sitting in a chair, Jenna and Papa standing beside him, examining his wound.

"Can you please be quiet, sister?" River says, grinning even as he winces in pain. "You're hurting my ear."

This is my brother, I think with pride.

Knowing that he won't want me to feel sorry for him, I search for a smart-ass reply. "Okay, I'll cut it out," I tell him. I reach out to take his hand, intending to give it a squeeze, but he beats me to it and takes mine. Then I turn to Papa. "I need to talk with you, Papa."

He hesitates for a moment, unsure what to do.

"Go ahead," River says, casually waving us off. "Jenna's not Virgil—she doesn't need an audience."

Papa puts his hand on River's shoulder for a moment before following me outside. We head to a nearby opening in the forest, where we settle onto a brown layer of dry and brittle pine needles.

"Are you okay, Papa?" I blurt out. "It must have been awful for you to be—to be feeling things when it was actually happening."

"And just as awful for you," he replies sadly, "when the grip ended." He sighs and looks out over the compound. "I'm fine. The worst part was not knowing how badly they would hurt him—whether they might even make them kill each other. I knew it wasn't likely—now that they've taken Twilight, there's no one else in the Aery old enough to harvest. Compared to that, an ear isn't so bad." He manages a grim smile.

"River will be okay," I say.

"As long as the wound doesn't get infected," he replies. "I hope the best for Ivy, too."

I say nothing in reply. Ivy. The person who lured Lark to the Thankfuls. Who helped Thorn when he was trying to save Lark's life. Who hates Thorn for what he did and me for loving him. Who lost her ear this morning to a knife wielded by my brother. My feelings toward her are in turmoil. I try to push her out of my mind.

"Papa," I say abruptly, putting my hand on his, "I want to learn what Zara did. Before they killed her. I want to learn how to do what she did to your Headmaster."

I'm expecting him to look shocked, to cry out, to insist that I can't, that he won't—but he doesn't. Instead, he nods and quietly says, "A lot has happened in a short time. One terrible thing after another. You want to do something."

"Yes," I exclaim. "I need to."

"I'm not surprised," he sighs. "Fifty years ago, I had a similar conversation with Zara. I couldn't have stopped her if I'd wanted to. No doubt, the same is true of you."

"You told me the last thing she did before she died was break the link—the neural link—between you and your Head-master. She was going to do that for everyone—is that right?"

"Yes, but—she ran out of time."

"How did she do it?"

Papa doesn't reply right away. He tips his head back and

closes his eyes as if he's bracing himself, like he's getting ready to jump from the edge of the gorge into the river. I wonder: given what happened to Thorn this morning, maybe I'm asking too much of him. I'm about to suggest we talk in a few days, when—

"Your grandmother was just a child," he says, "when her mother began teaching her a form of meditation called Kinikatos.

kinikatos   pointed arrow

"Zara's mother had learned it from her own mother, and that mother from hers, and on and on, going back many generations. It was always the daughters who were taught. Tradition said that men, if they learned it, would try to use it to gain power instead of to heal."

"But she taught you?"

"No. Zara taught me another kind of meditation—the one I've shared with the Inwards—but not *Kinikatos. Kinikatos* is a special way of discovering and exploring the hidden depths of your own mind—the nooks and crannies that are a part of who you are, even though you're not usually aware of them. When people do *Kinikatos*, sometimes they uncover strengths they didn't know they had. Sometimes, they also discover traumas inflicted on their ancestors and passed down to them—

genetic memory

—traumas that continue to harm them. But once they recognize them, they can start to heal. Are you understanding what I'm saying?"

I nod. "It's coming to me as you speak—her memories about that."

"The coils that go into the base of our skulls are how they control us. Back when we were still trying to find a way to remove them, Dr. Keshti did autopsies on two people they terminated. She told us the coils wrap over our brains—

over the dural membrane

"—and then onto our frontal lobes. Zara's plan was simple: use those same pathways to get into her Headmaster's brain or mind or whatever they have. And then either get them to uncouple or learn how to control them.

a two-way street   reverse the flow   I'll turn the arrow

"I was with her the first time she tried. We went to the bridge, her favourite spot. I hadn't started the Inwards yet—not till after she died—so nobody else was there."

"Were you worried? About her plan?"

"Not really. I didn't think anything would come of it. And at first, nothing did. But she tried again the next slackening, and that time, something did happen—

waking

into
a flat place a desert place   light without sun   a twilight
place without shadows   darkness visible   noise   from nowhere
like many hundred hands   rubbing palm to palm
a black shape looms   far away   on the horizon (i am afraid)
but now Bear is here
thank you Bear   i will follow you
Bear-that-guides
Bear-that-won't-back-down
let me hold your ear

"—and that time, something did happen. Her breathing slowed, and when I asked how she felt, she didn't respond. Before she'd started, she'd told me I wouldn't be able to wake her—to pull her out—so I didn't try to. I just waited—

> *nearing the black shape   a jagged mass as tall as me*
> *a jumble of black stones   a heap   a pile   no order   no structure*
> *i approach   i hear: a hiss*
> *eyes gleam in the dark   in the crack between two stones   a*
> *snake*
> *its head darts out   a tongue   fangs*
> *Bear swings his paw*
> *pushes me toward the snake   no choice   fall or grasp*
> *i seize the snake beneath its head*
> *draw it from the stones   its body coils round my arm   i turn*
> *and walk and walk with Bear until the heap of stones*
> *is far away   sinks below the horizon*
> *and then i drop the snake*
> *and watch it*
> *slither away*
> *thank you Bear   take me home*

"—and I just waited. Then, when the slackening was almost over, Zara let out a gasp, opened her eyes, and jumped to her feet. She was so excited. She said she'd done it, said she'd entered some place with a pile of rocks, that she'd been led by an animal special to her grandmother—a bear. She told me she'd found the neural link—she called it a snake—and carried it far away. I didn't know what to think. She said these were images her mind created to understand this other strange reality but that didn't mean they weren't real. I wondered if she'd just had a dream."

"But?" I ask, knowing it wasn't just a dream.

"But the next morning, when I got jolted awake, my head was at the bottom of my cot."

still awake and sitting in my cubicle
the darkening has come
but not to me
i walk to jacob's cubicle and there
he is lying on his cot
i sit beside him, shake him, try to wake him but
of course he can't   i slide my arms under him and turn him
in his cot till his head is at the other end and
i put the blanket on him   and then down the staircase
and to the aery where
i see our daughter   sparrow   sleeping with the other children
and I'm careful not to wake her
now standing on the steps outside
gazing up
at orion   his bel   his knife

back to my cubicle   get some sleep
jacob will know when he wakes that
I did it

CHAPTER 45
OUROBOROS

"What?" I exclaim, totally puzzled.

Papa smiles. "She'd turned me around on my cot. It was her playful way of showing me that her Headmaster hadn't been able to force her into the darkening. She'd broken its grip." He pauses, then frowns. "But it only lasted till the next morning."

> *jolted awake*
> *i was free for a while jacob*
> *but now it has control again*

"Did it punish her?" I ask.

Papa shakes his head. "No. Her Headmaster didn't sense what she'd done. Hadn't felt her poking around in its mind while it was dormant. So she tried the *Kinikatos* again that evening—

> *bear takes me in   leads me to the*
> *heap of stones*
> *there it is   hissing again   its head*
> *shadowed in the dark among the*

> stones   eyes glinting
> i do what bear expects   plunge my
> hand into the crack   hot fangs pierce
> my flesh   i seize the snake   yank it
> out   begin to dig one-handed in the
> dry hard clay of the desert place   dig
> till my fingertips can only graze the
> bottom   then drop the snake   push
> the clay   fill the hole   roll a stone on
> top   the largest i can move

"—so she tried again that evening, and the evening after that, and the one after that. She said she tried doing different things to the snake each time—and each time, the grip stayed broken for most of the night but was restored by early morning. But she kept trying."

Papa sighs and closes his eyes. "Here, it gets hard to talk about, Maple. You see, Zara started acting strangely. Going into her Headmaster's mind over and over must have taken a toll on her. On her mind. One morning, when I saw her across the Meal House like usual, she seemed different. She wouldn't look at me, and there was panic on her face—

> I feel a presence in my mind
> it's listening to me now   right now as I eat
> sensing something   sensing
> my thoughts about the desert place
> about the stone pile   the snake
> sensing what i'm doing
> in the slackenings   trying to break the link
> it's going to find out
> it will punish me   will stop me
> i need to not think about it   not

remember it   but i can't not think
think
think
what about   camouflage
white noise
mental static
the roar of the river

7 times seven is 49
49 times 94 is   4616   no 4606
my id number was 8426255
hydrogen
helium
lithium
beryllium
boron
carbon

"—and there was panic on her face. She was at the table with the other Tree Choppers, staring at her bowl, and her lips were moving, but she wasn't talking to anyone. My friend Olaf was a Tree Chopper, too. He told me later that for the entire Grip all she did as she chopped and gathered wood—"

Papa stops and takes a deep breath.

no no
I can't keep that up for the entire grip
i need something that sustains itself
something to fill my mind for hours
a pattern   a rhythm
what about   singing
keep a song in my head

Papa stops and takes a deep breath. "All she did was sing the same song over and over."

"It was the same song," I say to Papa, "that I told you about a long time ago, wasn't it? The one I said I knew?"

Papa nods. I think he knows I can hear Zara singing in my head at this very moment.

> From this valley they say you are going,
> We will miss your bright eyes and sweet smile,
> For they say you are taking the sunshine
> Which has brightened our pathways a while.

The song keeps flowing in my head as Papa continues. "I tried asking her what she was doing, why she wouldn't stop singing, but she wouldn't talk to me. Wouldn't let me know what was—

> i can't tell him
> i can't tell jacob   they're suspicious
> they'll be watching everyone   sensing our thoughts
> jacob can't know   no one can know
> can't take that chance
> not till i figure out how to make the severing last

—what was happening. This went on for days. The singing. And the *Kinikatos*. As soon as another slackening began, she'd run to the bridge and go straight into it to try again. She was consumed by it."

> Bear takes me in again   to the heap   and it's back again
> the hissing   the head   the eyes   the fangs
> i bring one hand toward the crack to lure it out
> its head darts out   i seize it with my other hand   draw it forth

with two hands now I squeeze its throat   to crush it   crush
its life
its eyes blink at me without concern   darts its tongue and tastes
the air
i grip it harder   arms quivering   won't give up
unrelenting   waiting for it to struggle   to flail   to gasp for air
and die
but it doesn't
Bear waits and watches me   yawns   waits
bands of red begin to stain the yellow sky   Bear sniffs the air:
the slackening is ending
i've stayed too long   all around me the desert place begins to
crack   split   fissure
a rumble like thunder   then heap after heap of stones
dozens   hundreds   thrust upward
through the clay then stop   silence   clouds of dust hang in
the air
slowly settle   i wait   i watch   then from each heap a snake
crawls forth
they slither down the stones to the surface
of the desert place   they slink to the middle
converge in a writhing mass
this is their collective mind
their network
how they share information perceptions make decisions
commune
time to leave   i tug Bear's ear   we try to slip away nnoticed
but the snakes   the writhing mass   surge suddenly toward me
they've sensed me   know i'm here
i break into a run with Bear
feet pounding the dusty clay
but the snakes sweep after me   reach my heels
wrap around my ankles

i trip and they swell over me   enveloping   entangling
my hands weighed down   they push into my mouth   my
nostrils   i can't breathe
i'm going to die
then suddenly the knot of snakes is wrenched apart
Bear pulling them away stripping them off   getting me clear
now back on my feet standing gasping for air
still holding the first snake in my hand
the others already regrouping around me
then once more they surge toward me
i look to Bear for help for guidance   he lifts one paw high
then swipes it down against me   massive claws slashing my
shoulder
through my flesh through the bone   my arm severs
flies through the air and strikes a heap of stones
i scream in rage   in horror   in disbelief
Bear has betrayed me
i fall to my knees   close my eyes   i can't escape
in a moment the snakes will overwhelm me
but they don't   i open my eyes
they're slithering away   back to their heaps of stone
i smell their sour fear   i rise to my feet and they slither faster
impeding
each other in their haste to get away

i look down at the snake in my hand   it's become a rigid ring
its tail drawn into its mouth
its eyes open   unblinking   staring inwardly
not dead   but stiff   paralyzed   trapped in perpetual flight
ouroboros

i understand   thank you Bear i murmur
Bear grunts   drops low

i climb onto his back   he carries me home
i carry my arm

"She was consumed by it." Sorrow lines Papa's face. "Then things got even worse."

He sighs deeply. He looks down at his hands clasped in his lap, the wrinkled skin, the calloused fingers. "Early one slackening, I went to her at the bridge, like always. But she wasn't in *Kinikatos* yet. This time, she was waiting for me. I could tell as I approached that something was horribly wrong. She was glaring at me like I'd never seen before. Her eyes seemed like ice, but her face was flushed. Her whole body was taut, almost quivering, and her breathing was fast and shallow. I moved close to touch her, to hold her, but she struck my arms away. Then she finally spoke to me." Papa closes his eyes. "No, that's not right. She screamed at me."

i've never loved you   there's nothing in you to love   i paired
with you
only to have a child   but when I see her i hate her because
she looks like you   get away from me   never come toward me
never speak to me   if you do   if you try
i will harm myself   i will harm your daughter
i will break her fingers   if you dare approach
you are dead to me

CHAPTER 46
ANGUISH

"She screamed she hated me. Hated our daughter. That she'd hurt Sparrow if I didn't stay away. I was in shock, paralyzed, so she shoved me. I staggered back, and she shoved me again. I turned and stumbled away from the bridge."

I'm speechless. Papa's words—and Zara's memory—have knocked me senseless. Why did she do that? Why had she said it to him? What went wrong?

> it's morning   still in control of myself
> the coupling hasn't returned   its grip is gone   but i can't show
> that yet
> still can't tell jacob
> i know i can defeat them   the headmasters
> Bear has shown me how
> shown me what they cannot withstand
> what they cannot comprehend: anguish
> i need to go in again when the slackening ends
> need to be there when their minds coalesce
> when all of them are there
> i can break the couplings one by one   or maybe all at once

but I need anguish
i need to fill my heart with crippling mind-crushing soul-tearing
anguish
Bear can't give me that again   not if i know why he's doing it
i need to break the thing i love   break jacob's heart
because that will break mine too

"I don't remember going back to my cubicle," Papa says. "But that's where I was—sitting on the edge of my cot, staring at the floor. Stunned by what had just happened. By what she'd said. I was heartbroken. So full of anguish. But I wasn't angry. Not at her. She'd tried to find a way to free us from the Headmasters. And the price she paid was her mind. Her sanity. I knew that's what had happened because of what she said about our daughter. She loved Sparrow more than anything. More than herself." Papa pauses to take off his broken spectacles and wipe tears from his eyes. "I knew she'd never recover. She was lost to me forever."

I want to tell Papa, to cry out to him, that Zara never stopped loving him; that she told him those things only to gain what she needed to defeat the Headmasters; that she did it for him, and for Sparrow, and for everyone at Blue Ring, and there was no other way. And that, if she had succeeded, she would have come to him and explained it all, and then he'd know that everything was all right and that she loved him, of course she loved him, as much as ever.

But I know Papa's story isn't over. Not yet. I stay silent.

"I didn't want that slackening to end," he says. "You might think that I'd welcome the darkening, the hours of oblivion it brought. But I dreaded it because I knew that in the morning, I'd wake up, and there'd be a moment before I'd remember what had happened, a moment of stillness, and then all that pain would come crashing back like a tidal wave."

tsunami

"But that's not what happened. The slackening ended, but the darkening didn't come. Instead, I found myself swinging my legs over the edge of the cot, rising to my feet, and being pushed toward the door of my cubicle, where I was brought to a stop. My Headmaster was impelling me, but it was far more intense than usual—as if its grip on me was being echoed by all the other Headmasters. I stood there, paralyzed, in front of the door. My eyes started to burn—they were getting dry because my blinking, even my breathing, was in their grip. That hadn't happened before.

"I yanked the door open and stepped into the hallway. I couldn't turn my head, but I could see out of the corner of my eye that everyone else on the floor had also just stepped into the hallway. Then I was turned, and the others were turned, and we started to walk to the stairwell, everyone stepping in unison. No one said anything as we descended—no one could—and as we left the building and streamed onto the dark compound, we were pulled and tugged into three lines. I had a glimmer of what was happening—of what they were going to force us to do —but it was like trying to hear a sparrow in a hurricane, drowned out by the noise of their insistent demand.

"After the last person came out of the Cube, they made us start to run. It was havoc. The Headmasters were sending us all in the same direction, but not everyone could keep up. Some of the children and older people stumbled and fell, and others tripped over them. They'd get to their feet, start running again, fall again, get stepped on. The Headmasters didn't seem to care. Something far more urgent was making them drive us forward.

"It was the bridge we were running toward. I was near the front of the mob, and when we came around the bend in the path, I saw her in the fading summer light: Zara, still on the bridge, sitting cross-legged, deep in *Kinikatos*. When we reached the wooden platform, our footsteps shook the bridge, but of course, she couldn't hear us, wasn't aware of us. Half of us ran past her to the other end of the bridge, then turned and stopped. It suddenly grew still except for the sound of people panting for breath. Even the frogs had stopped their singing.

"After a few moments, the stillness was broken by new footsteps on the bridge. Benjamin Weber was running toward us. In one hand, he held a loop of nylar cable that slapped against his thigh with every step. I watched—we all watched—as he approached Zara, then came to a halt beside her. He knelt and pulled at her arms and legs until she was stretched out and lying flat on the bridge. He tied her feet together. Then he tied her hands.

"Maple, I knew what was happening was horrifying. I knew we were killing my wife. But the thought of it was like a spider web in shadow—you think you see it when it trembles in a breeze, but you're not sure—it's faint, almost non-existent, like it belongs to another world."

The rumbling stops and the dust begins to settle around the
heaps of rocks
the snakes do not come out
they cower in the cracks
I smell their fear   their terror   their panic
they feel my anguish   they shrink from it
my anguish for jacob's broken heart
if i fail   if i don't return to tell him   his heart won't heal

Bear and i wander among the heaps   looking for the one to
begin with
looking for the one that is jacob

this is it   i reach into the darkness between the stones
the snake cowers inside its hole
it trembles as i grasp its neck   pull it out   look into its fearful
eyes
and think of what i did to jacob   his suffering
the snake's tail curls up and slides into its mouth
it stiffens   its eyes freeze into a cold unblinking endless stare
i cast it on the ground beside the heap and move toward another
then another

"David Ackerman rolled her onto her stomach. There was a stirring beneath her shirt as her Headmaster pushed itself up to draw its coils from the base of her skull. Then it released the suckers that adhered to her back. I thought I heard her softly moan. The Headmaster crept out from under her shirt and onto the bridge.

what's wrong Bear   why are you suddenly sad
i'm doing it Bear   we're doing it
Bear—

"Then, everyone watched as I lurched forward, picked her up in my arms, and threw her over the railing of the bridge. I saw her head hit a rock, and the water turned crimson. Then she went under, and the black current carried her away."

CHAPTER 47
THANK YOU, BEAR

It wasn't till two days later that I told Papa the truth: that Zara's repeated descents into her Headmaster's mind hadn't made her unstable—hadn't made her hate him or hate their daughter. I explained to him her plan, her need to charge her mind with an emotion the Headmasters couldn't fathom or endure—with anguish—so she could use it to overcome the Headmasters. Spurning Papa filled her with that anguish.

Maybe I should have told him this right away, right after he told me how Zara had died. But at the time, it seemed better to wait. What he'd shared with me was his version of the truth, one that had held a place in his memory for almost sixty years. As Virgil once said to me, someone's story, after it's been shared, should be honoured. It needs time to settle and resonate. A person's story, Virgil said, is their identity in motion, so it needs to be handled with care.

If I hadn't heard those words from Virgil, I might have expected Papa to be overjoyed when I told him the truth about Zara. His wife hadn't become psychotic! She hadn't lost her love for him! Instead, as I tell him, he listens with a grave look on his face and then, when I finish, begins nodding ever so slightly as he stares into a dark cave that isn't there.

Finally, after a long spell of silence, he speaks.

"I'm glad you told me this, Maple. But in a way, it doesn't change the essence of how I remember your grandmother. I did believe, for all these years, that toward the end, she'd become unstable—but I also knew that deep inside, in her core, she hadn't stopped loving me. I always knew that in her final moments, she was thinking of me—because she freed me from the grip of my Headmaster. What you've told me doesn't change that—except, perhaps, to know that she was herself until the very end. And I'm glad of that."

He pauses and gazes at me. "You have her memories, Maple."

"A lot of them," I reply, unsure why he's saying what he knows to be true.

"Then maybe you can tell me something I've wondered about since the moment she was gone."

"I'll try," I say.

Papa reaches up and grasps a branch of the yew tree we're standing beneath. The golden sunlight dapples through the leaves and onto his face.

"Did she know it was me who—who dropped her into the river?"

> *what's wrong Bear   why are you suddenly sad*
> *i'm doing it Bear   we're doing it*
> *Bear—*

"No," I say without hesitation. "No. She was still fully immersed in the *Kinikatos*. She sensed that something had gone wrong, but nothing more."

Papa closes his eyes and nods. He exhales slowly, quietly, as if a weight, sixty years in the making, has been lifted from him.

"And she wasn't alone, Papa," I add. "She had Bear. Bear was still with her. And Bear was real."

"That's comforting to know," Papa says. "Thank you, Maple." Then, more quietly, almost a whisper, "Thank you, Bear."

CHAPTER 48
JARS OF TEETH

I find the door I'm looking for. It's the door with a small hook at eye level, one end of a string tied to it. To the other end, a tooth is tied. A molar. I knock, and after a moment, the door creaks open, making the tooth swing back and forth like a pendulum.

"Maple," Jenna says, squinting at me in the dim hallway. "Here we are!"

"Can I come in?" I ask.

She steps aside, and I slip past her.

"Sit down," she says, gesturing to a knee-high block of wood someone hauled in and set beside her cot. "I have mint water."

"I'll have some."

I look around Jenna's cubicle as she takes two chipped mugs from a small table beside her cot and fills them from a blue jug. A crack running from its spout to its handle has been patched with pine sap.

I haven't been in her space before. It looks pretty much like every other cubicle except for a high, narrow shelf that stretches across one wall of the room.

"That's a lot of teeth," I say, gesturing toward the twenty or so glass jars that line the shelf. Each jar is filled with teeth, some of them white, most yellowed with age.

"Over seven hundred," she replies as she hands me a cup and sits wearily down on the other side of the table. "A few of them are your Papa's. But I don't have any of yours yet." She gives me a crinkled smile.

"Do you remember everyone whose teeth you've pulled?" I ask.

"Well," she replies, "yes, because I remember everyone who's ever lived here. But if you mean do I remember each and every tooth-pulling—" She pauses and looks thoughtful for a moment. "I think I do. But, of course, if there are any I don't remember, then I can't know that because I don't remember them."

"You stitched me up once," I tell her.

"I do remember that clearly," she says. "You fell on something sharp. A tree root, I think. I had to pull splinters out."

"Farley was with me, and he barked till someone found me."

"I don't remember that. But I do remember the dog. Last of his kind, poor pooch. Your Papa ran up here with you in his arms and set you on this very table. Now I do remember—the dog followed you in. Anyway, I guess Halo let you out of the Aery, or maybe you sneaked out and you wandered away. Lucky it happened during a slackening, or who knows how long you'd have been out there? I fixed you up here on this very table. It was your left leg above your knee."

I nod and smile. No need to tell her it was my right leg, and they had taken me back to the Ward to patch me up. "Were you always the dentist here? And the doctor?"

"Dentist?" she laughs. "I haven't heard that word in a long time. I don't know if I'd call myself that. All I do is pull teeth when they go rotten." She points to three pairs of pliers of varying sizes hanging on the wall. "And as for doctoring, about the only thing I can do is stitch up cuts like yours."

I frown, puzzled. "But you have those books. The ones you open when somebody's sick. Don't they tell you what to do?"

"Knowing what to do and doing it are two different things. I might know how to diagnose an infected appendix, but there's nothing I can do about it. I don't know how to do surgery on the inside organs. I don't have the right tools or medicines. If I tried, I'd only make things worse.

"Besides," she continues. "Only two of those books have anything to do with medicine. The other one is a very old volume of the Oxford English Dictionary—*Volume 6, Follow to Hogweed*. Not much help unless I want to look up the history of the word 'gingivitis.' Which I have."

"Then why do you look in them when somebody gets sick?"

"Did I look in them when you hurt your leg?" she asks.

"Yes, you sent Papa to—" I begin to say, then break off as I realize that Jenna was right, after all. I stayed with Jenna in her cubicle while Papa ran to the Ward to get the things Jenna asked for. "Yes," I continue. "Papa brought back one of the books. And some nylar bandages and Jimson firewater."

"How did that make you feel?"

"It hurt."

"No, I don't mean the Jimson water. My looking in the book."

I consider her question. "Like you were making sure."

"There you go," Jenna replies. "Those books were like a placebo—

placeo placere placui placitus placebo i will please

"—they inspire confidence, and confidence can help somebody get better. Not always, but sometimes."

"But you know how to make the sleeping drops for the Aery."

"That's easy. I learned that sixty years ago from Rukhsana Keshti. She was a real doctor. She's also the one who told people about jimsonweed. I wish she hadn't."

"You're not afraid of telling me about the past."

She shrugs. "Your grandfather told me last night about the memories surfacing—Zara's memories. So it doesn't seem like there's any need for concern."

"And he told me that you and Virgil are like him—your Headmasters don't have a grip on you."

"That's right," she says, reaching over her shoulder and giving her Headmaster a pat. "Thanks to Zara, it's just for decoration."

"Zara's the reason I'm here. I want to learn how she did that to your Headmaster. And to Papa's and Virgil's. Papa said you might be able to help."

Jenna nods. "Your Papa told me your plan. But the *Kinikatos?* I don't know anything about that. She didn't teach me."

I shake my head. "I don't need you to teach me that. I just need you to help me get more of her memories. Memories of how she got into the *Kinikatos*. I already know what to do once I'm in—how to beat them. Those memories already came to me."

Jenna listens intently and pauses before replying. Her brow furrows. "Your Papa also shared with me what you told him about why Zara was so—so cruel to him. So hurtful. That she needed to fill her mind with anguish to defeat them."

"Grief is like poison to them," I reply.

infects them like a virus traps them in a loop

"Or maybe more like a virus," I add.

Jenna begins to look uncertain. She puts her hand over mine, then speaks slowly, choosing her words with care. "Yes. But if you really intend to try what she did—do you think you— I mean, Maple, I know you've been through a lot—but will it be enough—?"

I interrupt her. "I know what you're asking, Jenna. My heart is broken, yes. It was only a few weeks ago I lost Thorn and Lark. My partner and my sister, both at once. Two days ago, my brother had his ear cut off. I can push down that anguish when I need to, but it's never far from the surface. I'm trusting it will be enough. I can't imagine having more. So, yes, luckily, I have lots of anguish to use against the Headmasters." Tears begin to fill my eyes.

"Of course, Maple. I'm sorry. I thought I should ask. We don't want to lose you."

We sit in silence for a few moments as she strokes my hand.

"I'd like to ask you one more question, Maple. Something I've been thinking about since your Papa's visit."

I nod.

"Zara told your Papa that the things she saw when she was in *Kinikatos* were metaphors, symbols her mind draped over the mental landscape of the Headmasters so she could under-stand it. Interact with it. How do you know that what you'll find there will be the same as what she saw?"

Jenna's question takes me aback. Zara's memories of the desert place—the stone piles, the snakes, the searing fangs piercing my hand—are so vivid, so real, it doesn't seem possible they could be anything other than what they were for her. It would be like walking to the bridge and finding the river gone.

"I guess I'm worried," Jenna continues, "that your mind might make a different reality. So maybe her memories won't help you in there."

I ponder this while Jenna fills my cup with more mint water. It's cold in her cubicle, but that's not why a chill runs down my spine.

"I don't know," I tell her. "All I know is that Zara figured it out. If I have to, I'll do the same."

Jenna nods. She can see my determination. Or stubborn foolishness.

"And maybe you'll find a bear waiting for you there to help," she says with a small, encouraging smile.

I shake my head. "Not a bear."

CHAPTER 49
THE AMBER NECKLACE

Before I left Jenna's cubicle that night, I told her more about how she could help me. I needed her to give me prompts to make specific memories surface. She'd known Zara longer than anyone—they'd met in university—and they were friends when Zara was still learning the *Kinikatos* from her mom. If Jenna told me about that part of Zara's life, it could trigger memories about how she entered into *Kinikatos*.

At least, I hoped that would happen. Those memories might emerge on their own, but that could take years. Jenna's prompts were a potential shortcut, and now that I'd made my decision, I wanted to act. Maybe I was afraid if I didn't, I'd lose my nerve.

Jenna told me to come back the next slackening.

"When I was little," she says as we sit down again at her table, "my Grade 4 teacher asked us to bring something to class that would show people in a hundred years what our lives were like. She had a big aluminum cylinder with a screw-on lid, and we put everything the students brought into it. Well, not everything. Brandon Cameron brought a pumpkin—it was nearly Halloween—so she had him draw one instead. Katherine

Lithgow put in a letter she'd written, Bahattin Altay a newspaper, Eliot Angus a recipe for chocolate procarb cookies. Those kinds of things. Madame Ellis told us it was called—

a time capsule

"—a time capsule and that they'd been popular at the end of the previous century."

"Then, you and the others buried it," I say. Jenna looks surprised, so I explain. "You once told this story—or part of it— to Zara, and I remember it."

Now Jenna looks unsure about whether she should continue, so I encourage her with a question. "What did *you* put into the cylinder?"

"A little round mirror. Like this." She puts an index finger and thumb together to make a circle.

"Why?"

"Because I wanted the person who dug it up, whenever that would be, to wonder why I included it."

"That's not much of a reason," I say.

"It's the best reason." She smiles. "Anyway, I was thinking that you, Maple, are a kind of time capsule."

"That's what Papa said about the books in the vault."

Jenna nods, then continues. "From what your Papa's told me, when Zara's memories surface in you, they're fresh—as if the experience you're remembering has just happened."

"I guess that's true," I reply. "I hadn't really thought about it."

"Most of my memories aren't like that. I suspect the same is true of your Papa and Virgil. By the time you get old like us, you've replayed your memories over and over. That changes them. Distorts them. When I remember the day I first rode a horse, or when I remember the day of the Arrival, am I really remembering it, or am I remembering myself remembering it? Or remembering someone else talking about it? My memories have become bent and wrinkled like me. The memories you get from Zara are like newborns. I envy that."

She sighs and looks up at the window.

I nod and try to look interested in what Jenna is saying. I wish Thorn was still alive. He'd love to hear Jenna's reflections. But I'm eager to move on to what I came for. I notice my fingers are quietly thrumming on the table. I think Jenna notices, too.

"Let's get down to brass tacks," she says. "But first, I want you to tell me about the amber necklace."

"What?" I reply. "What amber neck—"

two hands folded on a tabletop
i look up from them to the warm and smiling eyes
of a young woman—jenna
her skin smooth her hair chestnut brown her cheeks with a
rosy glow
her lips move but I hear no words
only a chorus of birds robins blackbirds sparrows chittering
a blanket of song and clamour
jenna reaches down into a bag at her side
and pulls out a small leather pouch
she gazes at me
then draws from it a stone   glowing like a dollop
of dark maple syrup
as the setting sun slants across it from an open window: amber
she lifts her hand higher and gently dangles the stone
from a leather cord   a necklace
she reaches across the table and cups the stone into my palm
i feel warmth as we clasp the stone between us
her lips move but it's not until a moment later
as if her speech is passing through the languorous amber itself

that I hear her say one word: maple

"You gave it to her," I say to Jenna. "The necklace—it was a piece of amber on a leather cord. You were sitting across from her, and there were birds all around, and you put it in her hand."

"That's right," Jenna says, looking impressed. "It was her birthday."

October 11

"And then," I add, "you said my name."

"Your name?" Jenna looks puzzled. "Oh, yes, I did—sort of. It wasn't your name yet, of course. Zara hadn't even given birth to your mother, so you were still a long way off."

"Then why did you say 'maple'?"

Jenna slowly rises to her feet—her legs seem stiff—and hobbles over to the window, where yet another jar full of teeth rests on the sill. She brings it back to the table and pours out the contents. There, among the fifty or sixty scattered teeth, lies the amber necklace from Zara's memory.

She picks it up, hands it to me, and says, "Hold it up to the window."

I do so and realize the stone is translucent. I can see through it dimly and notice something suspended in its warm glow.

"Do you know how amber is formed?" Jenna asks.

"It's tree sap that turns into stone after a long time."

"Tree resin, actually, but that's the basic idea. And often, other things get trapped inside it because resin is sticky. Things like insects and—

inclusions

"—bits of leaves. Look closely—inside the stone you're holding is a piece of a 150-million-year-old leaf. Give or take a week or two."

"A maple leaf," I say, feeling a bit embarrassed. Of course, she hadn't been saying my name.

Jenna must sense my disappointment because she adds, "But in a way, it really was your name I was saying, or at least it's why you ended up with the name you have. Kind of like a future memory." She pauses. "Do you know why Zara came here? To Blue Ring?"

"Papa said she was looking after the books in the vault."

"That's what they were paying her to do—in the Deepak Centre, I mean. But she had another reason, too. She wanted to be here to keep an eye on the digging. The Blue Ring Group was building an airstrip farther out in the forest, and there were rumours that when they were digging and levelling, they found some things. Stone tools. Even some human bones. But they hadn't told the authorities because then they'd have to stop the project. When Zara heard that, she decided to get hired here. Some of your mother's ancestors—on her mother's side—once lived around here.

Anishinaabe   Ojibwe   Dokis

—once lived around here. If Zara saw any evidence they were bulldozing an ancient settlement, she was going to tell the Dokis council. Then they could step in and make sure the artifacts were protected."

you'll lose your job

i'll get another

not if blue ring wants to make it difficult for you

i can make things difficult for them too

"I'm telling you this, Maple, because I want you to know—and maybe you already do—that protecting the past was very important to your grandmother. That's why I gave her the amber: it's kept this little bit of leaf intact for millions of years. I thought it was the perfect metaphor for her."

Jenna turns her gaze to the window and looks out as the dying rays of sunlight cast a dulcet glow over the trees in the compound. "Your Papa was thinking of this piece of amber when he suggested to your mother—Sparrow—that you be called 'Maple.'"

"Why not 'Amber'?"

Jenna grins broadly, and I see she's missing two molars. I wonder if she pulled them out herself. "Your Papa had a girlfriend named Amber when he was fourteen. He's never liked that name since."

I nod and squeeze the amber in my hand one more time before holding it out to Jenna.

"It's yours now," she says. Then she adds, "But I'll keep the teeth." She sweeps them into the jar and sets it back on the windowsill. I reach over my head to put on the necklace, then hesitate: if I do, part of the leather cord will be touching the black coils of my Headmaster. *Good*, I decide after a moment. *Just like it did sixty years ago.*

"Now," Jenna continues, "how should we do this?"

"Zara was still learning the *Kinikatos* when you met her. Tell me what was going on in her life then. Anything you can think of. Big things, little things. I'm hoping you'll hit on something that triggers the right memories."

"I'll do my best, Maple. And it will be a pleasure to finally tell you about her. But remember, we're talking about more than sixty years ago. Lots of things have stayed with me, but I'm sure lots haven't."

"I understand," I say.

"And I'd like to do this outside, where I can hear the trees rustling. Zara loved the green world."

The evening air is chilly, so I bring Jenna's nylar blanket with us. We leave the Cube and step into the crisp fall breeze. I take Jenna's arm as we walk to a log that someone long ago peeled the bark off of and rolled to the edge of the compound, propping it in place with a few rocks on either side. We sit, and I drape the blanket over her knees. Then she begins.

"I met Zara when I happened to sit beside her in a classroom at the University of Toronto. We were in different graduate programs, but we had that one course in common: Human Gross Anatomy. That fall, she started dating a guy who worked at a procarb store—

mikah silverberg

"—but that ended after a few months when he became a—what do you call it—a Jain. He stopped eating anything that wasn't made in a biospdome and wanted her to do the same. Good luck with that . . . that winter, she almost got hit by a streetcar—

dundas and bathhurst
falling on the tracks   push off   roll roll
I'm okay I'm okay   just some cuts
so stupid   wearing my ear pods

"—she was fine, but her bicycle was bent like a pretzel.

Took her a while to get the nerve to get back on one. She loved the winter—driving to Algonquin to snowshoe. I couldn't keep up with her, so she'd tramp way ahead and then double back to me. I used to have a wonderful picture of her with her eyebrows all frosted up . . . She loved strawberry-rhubarb pie and would make it in the summer. No, sorry, that was my friend Marguerite Love. Zara didn't like rhubarb . . . She'd go berry picking on Manitoulin Island with her mom . . .

blackberries and hawberries
chi-cheemaun debajehmujig m'chigeeng

"She was allergic to cats, but she had one anyway—

mr katabisis

"—that she'd found in an alley—

head stuck in a pipe

"—in an alley with its head pushed into a can. She figured somebody had purposely done it to the poor thing, so the next day, she put up postings saying she had VRx of the person doing it, and if he didn't turn himself in, she'd publish it on LookHear."

it worked

Jenna turns and looks at me. "Is any of this helping, Maple? Anything happening?"

"It's triggering lots of memories," I reply, my eyes closed, "but nothing about the *Kinikatos*. Not yet."

"On we go, then. Your grandmother's favourite VRx that summer was called *The Winter Dogs* . . .

the dogs of winter

"I never saw it, but I know it starred an old actor she admired—William Bradley Pitt. It was his first VRx after being in cryostasis for more than three decades. They cured him and brought him back. She was glad he got to make one more before he died for good in a wildfire . . . She was afraid of heights and snakes . . . She had a younger sister named—

lilith

"—Lily, who died when she was just a toddler. I guess that doesn't have anything to do with when she was learning *Kinikatos* . . . that February, she mixed up two churches—

st. benedict　st. bernard

"—and ended up going to the wrong wedding—

where's liam's family
why is the priest speaking russian
oh no

"—wrong wedding, but she didn't want to disturb anyone, so she stayed for the whole thing—even got invited to dinner afterward by the best man . . . She once called me in the middle of the night to let me know her second toe was longer than her big toe, and there was a name for that. I called her back the next night and told her that one of my nipples was bigger than the other one, and there was no name for that." Jenna grins and the creases in her face crinkle, like the shell of a walnut. She looks at me hopefully. "Anything?"

I shake my head and smile. "But it's entertaining."

She half-closes her eyes and tips back her head. "She told me she had no middle name—

eleanore

"—because her parents couldn't agree on one . . . She talked about wanting to visit Baffin Island after she finished her degree . . . She could never remember how to spell the word 'misspell' . . .

mispell   misspell   misspel

—the word 'misspell' . . . She said the sound of running water always made her have to pee—

> *sound*
>> *of running*
>>> *water*
> *a murmur   a rush   a roar*
> *follow the current   immerse yourself*
> *let it carry you   take you*
> *lose yourself in the white*
> *of the river*
> *let your body   disperse*
> *into the flow of time and space*
> *imagine a cavern in the landscape of your mind*
> *make the river surge toward it*
> *make it plunge into the chasm*
> *go in go under and wait*
> *breathless*

wait
until your guide appears

"—have to pee, even if she heard it in a VRx—"

"Wait, Jenna. It's coming." I close my eyes and open myself to the memory, letting it surface, letting it deepen and extend into all my senses, until I can hear the white roar that Zara imagined, taste its purity, feel the river's cold cascade envelop me and carry me along . . .

. . . feel myself plunging . . .

down

Jenna's hand is on my shoulder, shaking me. She's out of focus, leaning toward me, her lips moving, but I can't make out her words. Then, slowly, they reach me. "Maple! What's happening? Are you okay?" Her brow is furrowed with concern.

"I'm fine," I reply, getting to my feet, though I'm still feeling like I just stepped off a tilt-a-whirl. "I think you hit on the right trigger."

"What," she asks, "having to pee?"

I shake my head, but before I can answer, I double over and throw up a well-digested biscuit wedge.

"Whatever it was, it seems to have given you a hangover," Jenna observes.

tequila   southern comfort

I spit onto the ground and wipe my mouth. "Hopefully, that's a good sign," I say.

CHAPTER 50
PERPETUAL GYRATION

I used to like snakes. I felt sorry for them when the Grubbers came across them during their foraging. They'd step on them, pin them to the ground, and shear off their heads with a grubbing blade. Then they'd either bring them back to the kitchen, where the scaly carcasses would be thrown into the biscuit mix, or they'd gobble down the raw ropes of snake meat themselves.

My fondness for snakes cooled after I recovered Zara's memory of them swarming over her in the desert place. But they still didn't frighten me—not out in the bush, anyway, where they slithered away the moment you disturbed them. Maybe that's why it wasn't a snake I encountered when I finally got into the *Kinikatos* the day after Jenna helped me.

At first, I thought it hadn't worked. As I sat down on the bank of the river to meditate, I drew on the memory Zara had given me: I envisioned a fast river, let myself hear its roar, felt myself carried along by it, plunging into a cavern, being dispersed—and yet no snake appeared, no pile of black stones.

But when I opened my eyes and let things come into focus, I saw that I really was . . . elsewhere. I certainly wasn't beside the river, where I'd settled down to try the *Kinikatos*. Slowly, as

I got my bearings, I noticed a few things in common with the landscape Zara had entered so many times: the yellow sky, the hard, cracked clay beneath my feet, a sound like a hundred palms rubbing together. I was in the desert place. But it was my own desert place, not Zara's.

I heard a thumping behind me and knew even before I turned around what it was—what it had to be. My own version of Zara's Bear—Farley, looking up at me and thumping his tail against the cold clay. If my mind was going to give me a guide, what else could it possibly be? A chipmunk? A cricket? I bent down to pat his head and scratch behind his ear.

"It's good to see you again, Farley. It's been a while." His tail thumped faster, and his warm brown eyes seemed to smile. Then, he turned his head toward something sitting by itself on the flat waste of the desert place, a couple of hundred steps away. I raised my hand over my eyes to blunt the glare of the yellow sky and squinted. It was a bucket—a Grubber's dented bucket. It was overflowing—something was oozing over its rim, but it was too far away to tell what it was.

Farley nudged my knee, and we began to walk toward it. We should have quickly reached it, but I soon realized that with every step I took, it receded. It wasn't that it moved away—it was more like the space between me and the bucket kept expanding. I tried a few other tactics. I sprinted toward it. I casually ambled in its direction without looking at it. I walked toward it backward. Each time, the bucket got farther away. I sighed and looked down at Farley.

"Okay," I said to him, "is this where you show me what to do? Can you give me a hint? I'm out of ideas."

Farley panted happily and began walking perpendicular to the bucket—or almost perpendicular. As he went farther, I realized he was circling it. I followed him, caught up to him, and we kept walking. We rounded the bucket several times before I understood the path he was taking was actually a spiral—and with each lap, we were getting closer to the bucket. Or maybe it was getting closer to us as if we were winding it in on an invisible string. It was hard to tell.

As the distance diminished, our orbits got smaller, and we completed them faster and faster. Finally, we were standing beside the bucket. I could have reached down and picked it up if I'd wanted. But I didn't want to because it was full—overflowing—with hundreds, maybe thousands, of white, glistening, writhing, eyeless maggots. Maybe these maggots were just a metaphor my mind created, but here in the desert place, they were as real as stepping on a nail. Even their smell—moist and sickly sweet—was as pungent as any animal carcass I'd ever encountered on a hot day in the forest.

"I guess I'm supposed to empty it, right?" I said to Farley. He gave me an inscrutable look. I lifted one foot, set it against the rim of the bucket—a spot where no maggots were spilling over—and gave it a push. The only thing that moved was me: the bucket was fixed in place as if it were frozen to the clay. I reeled back several steps from the force of my push, then regained my balance. Without thinking, I stepped toward the bucket, and it once more receded from me.

"Oh, for shit's sake," I yelled, cursing out loud for the first time in my life. *Well*, I told myself, *at least I said it in here, not out in the real world.* Scowling with frustration, I began walking in small, fast circles around the bucket until I was back beside it. Farley continued to gaze at me placidly.

"So, there's something at the bottom, is there?" I said to him. "I'm supposed to reach in and get it?" There was an audible plop as a large clump of maggots slipped over the edge of the bucket and fell onto the clay. "And what's the prize waiting for me at the bottom? A porcupine? A handful of broken glass?"

Farley chose not to reply.

There's no other option, I told myself. *Get it over with.* Before I could reconsider, I thrust my hand into the bucket, down through the layers of wriggling maggots, until I was in up to my elbow. I felt around but found nothing except more slippery maggots, not even the bottom of the bucket. I reached farther, till I was in up to my shoulder, and my cheek was almost pressing against the reeking surface of the writhing mass. How could it possibly be this deep?

Suddenly, I felt something clamp down hard on my submerged middle finger. The pain was immediate and intense. It was like my finger was being squeezed in a Mender's vice. I struggled to withdraw my hand, but if anything, I was pulled down deeper. Now, my left cheek, ear, and one nostril were in the slurry of maggots.

"Farley!" I tried to yell through the side of my mouth that was still above the maggots. "I don't know what to do!"

Farley wagged his tail, turned, lifted his leg, and began to pee on the side of the bucket.

As I watched him blithely relieve himself, everything suddenly became hilarious—the bucket, the maggots, the maggots in my nostril, the sturgeon or raccoon or whatever it was that was biting my finger, Farley's look of nonchalance as he continued to aim his yellow stream—it was all absurd. *Ludicrous.* What if I'd been born a hundred years ago? What would I now be doing, at age nineteen? Probably not this. Probably not up to my nose in maggots in a shadowless desert I was co-imagining with giant wood ticks. As these antic thoughts danced around my mind, the pull on my hand seemed to dwindle, and I was able to draw my arm up and out of the bucket.

Something was still clamped onto my finger, though: a medium-sized snapping turtle.

I shook off the maggots that were still glomming to my arm,

then set about to get the turtle to release my finger. Without a stick or knife, there was no way I could force its jaws open. Instead, I rolled up a corner of my shirt until it was about the width of my finger. Then I waggled it in front of the turtle's eyes, brushing it against its nose, teasing it.

Without warning, the turtle released my finger and snapped its jaws closed on the roll of nylar. I quickly grabbed it by the shell, one hand on either side, and waited. In another moment, the turtle spat out my shirt, perhaps realizing what it held in its jaws was not flesh and bone. It thrust its neck forward, then craned its head around, snapping again and again at my hands.

Now what?

I remembered Zara's attempts to neutralize her snake. Carrying it away from the stone pile hadn't worked. Neither had burying it. It was only when Bear had pretended to betray her—had attacked her—that a surge of rage and grief had paralyzed the creature.

Still gripping the turtle's shell, I closed my eyes, released a deep breath, and let the memory I'd been pushing away for weeks fill my mind: Thorn and Lark dangling over the raging white water of the river—then, Thorn and Lark suddenly not there. White-hot rage and anguish erupted in my belly, shot up through my chest, and exploded into my brain. I felt my legs trembling, heard myself screaming, and felt my grip around the creature in my hands grow tighter. The sound of the hundred palms rubbing together grew louder, higher pitched, more frantic—and then abruptly stopped.

I opened my eyes and saw the turtle that I still held in front of me. But only its shell. Its head, its tail, its legs—all had withdrawn beneath its carapace. And it was motionless. Its wriggling and thrashing had stopped. I crouched and set it onto the clay of the desert place. I stood back up, considered it, and then had a better idea. I kneeled down and flipped the turtle onto its back, then gave it a spin. Around and around like a top it went, neither stopping nor slowing—caught in perpetual gyration.

Farley nudged my knee, then began leading me around the turtle in ever-widening circles. Soon, it and the seething bucket of maggots had vanished over the horizon. Then, I opened my eyes, and I was once more on the bank of the river.

CHAPTER 51
IT WAS MOSTLY TRUE

Anyway, that's the story I tell Papa the next day, and it's mostly true. Of course, I change some parts and leave out others—like how the maggots actually had teeth, how the bucket was as wide and deep as a barrel, how I had to entirely immerse myself into it, and how the turtle was a big as Silex and had a head on both ends instead of a head and a tail. I want to give Papa a sense of what happened so he knows I'm ready for the challenge—

she girdeth her loins with strength

—but I don't want to alarm him with awful details. I don't want him to worry.

"So it worked!" Papa says. I've already told him it did, but he wants to hear it again. "You neutralized your Headmaster?"

I nod. "The darkening didn't take me last night," I tell him. "I was able to stay awake. I left the Cube, walked around, and looked at the stars. I even saw Orion—Zara's memory told me which constellation it was. After a few hours, I got too tired and went back to my cubicle to sleep. I half-expected that my Head-master's grip would be back when I woke up, but no—the coupling was still broken—*is* still broken. I've put my Head-master into some sort of perpetual loop. I went to the Meal House to keep things looking normal—just like you do. And then, I toiled with the other Pickers like nothing had changed."

"You haven't told anyone else?" he asks.

"No."

"Not Silex or Rose?"

"No."

"River?"

"I haven't even seen him yet."

"Make sure you don't. If they know what you've done, their Headmasters might sense it in their thoughts."

"I know, Papa."

He nods and looks out at the compound below. It's gotten hard for him to climb stairs, but he insisted we talk on the roof of the Deep so no one could possibly hear us. After a moment, he reaches over and takes my hand in his.

"Zara would be so proud of you, Maple. Not just for what you've done but for who you are. The person you've become. I am, too."

I nod and squeeze his hand but don't reply. I know I wouldn't have become who I am without Zara's memories. And maybe it's more true to say that Zara has become me—*is* becoming me. What will happen if her memories continue to surface for the rest of my life? Who will I be then?

who will i be then?

I shake my head to get these thoughts out of my mind. I've got more pressing things to worry about.

Sitting in silence, we watch the sun slip toward the horizon.

After a few moments, Papa says, "You could stop now, Maple. Live the rest of your life like I have. Like Jenna and Virgil have—with the link to your Headmaster broken. It's a bit of freedom."

I shake my head. "I can't stop now, Papa. There's no point breaking the link with my Headmaster if I still have to pretend I'm under its grip. And anyway, it's not really freedom if others don't have it. There's no turning back. I need to enter the Headmasters' collective mind so I can neutralize them all."

in for a penny in for a pound

He sighs. "I guess I know that. When will you do it?"

"Tomorrow. I'll go into *Kinikatos* at the start of the slackening and then wait for the darkening. That's when they'll all emerge in—in that desert place. When they merge into a collective mind."

Papa doesn't say anything, but I can sense his misgivings.

"It's going to be okay, Papa. When Zara went into their collective mind the first time, it was by accident—she stayed longer than she meant to, and they all emerged. But she didn't know how to defeat them all yet. So, she had to go in a second time after she'd pretended to reject you. Which meant they were ready for her. They're not expecting me. They can't even sense I've neutralized my Headmaster. I'll have the advantage of surprise. I'm not worried."

Papa gives me a weak smile and tries to look reassured. We spend the rest of the slackening talking about Lark's kids. How talkative Birch has become. How Prairie adores River and cries when he can't come to the Aery. How Lynx seems shy, but Fox is becoming outgoing and curious. How they keep asking when Thorn is coming back.

Eventually, I walk Papa back to the Cube. I don't tell him

that as we were descending the metal staircase, I noticed Ivy peering at us from the shadowy edge of the forest.

CHAPTER 52
HEAVE!

It was when the others got up and began to surround our table that we knew something bad was about to happen. Silex and Rose and Twilight and me.

We were in the Meal House for morning meal. I was supposed to be eating my biscuit wedge, but I wasn't. Without my Headmaster impelling me, I couldn't bring myself to swallow it. It was an especially awful concoction that morning. It smelled like pond scum and looked like something that came out of a Grubber's nose. I made a show of poking it piece by piece into my mouth, but then I inconspicuously dropped it onto the floor under our bench. It didn't matter if the Biscuiteers found it later—if things went as I planned, before tomorrow morning, the Headmasters would be little more than mindless back scabs.

Or else I'd be dead. That was the other possibility.

I hadn't fooled Silex, though. Every time I dropped a bit of biscuit, he stretched out one of his long legs and batted it closer to the wall where it was less visible. He must have been wondering what was going on with me, but he didn't ask. He just kept telling Twilight that today our Headmasters would probably make us switch to picking dingleberries. He'd told me the same thing when I was Twilight's age.

"Silex!" Rose had scolded him. "Stop teasing the girl."

"What?" Silex had replied in mock indignation. "Dingleberries are part of nature's bounty, Rose, just like apples and grapes. They might not taste as good, but at least we don't have to go far to pick them."

Rose had smiled and shaken her head. Silex winked at Twilight. And then I heard benches scraping the floor and saw the others standing and quietly shuffling toward our table. That's when I knew something bad was going to happen.

They've now formed a semi-circle around us, hemming us in against the west wall of the Meal House. All of them look confused—they don't know what's going on any more than we do. Neither does Papa. When he saw everyone else getting up, he did the same and followed them. I see him off to the side, his eyes darting around the crowd, trying to anticipate what's going to happen.

"What's the trouble, friends?" Silex asks warily. "What are they making you do?" He starts to get up from the table but stops halfway through the motion and sits down again. His Headmaster wants him to stay put. Rose and Twilight also appear to be frozen in place, their palms firmly pressed against the tabletop. It's best if I do the same.

"Perhaps I can shed some light," says a voice from within the crowd. It's Ivy. She pushes her way to the front as others awkwardly try to make way for her, their bodies stiffened and held in check by their Headmasters. She then takes a few lurching steps to the side until she's standing behind Twilight and looking across the table at me. She drops her hands to Twilight's narrow shoulders as if to support herself. Twilight jerks as she feels Ivy's touch and begins to tremble.

Silex glares up at Ivy. "Get your hands off her," he growls.

"Yesterday morning," Ivy says, ignoring him, "our gracious Headmasters selected a new Breeder for our community. One to replace Lark, who was lured away by an apostate. Lark's death was regrettable. I am sure you miss her as I do. Yet, her death is a small thing compared to the loss of two Headmasters. I was complicit in that loss—tricked by an evil man—and for that, I was given necessary and righteous correction." She reaches up and places her fingers on the red wound where her ear once was. "But I've vowed not to fail our lords again.

"I learned yesterday," she continues, "that the first man sent to the new Breeder was Stump. Is that not correct, Stump?"

"Yeah, it was me," a ragged voice replies from within the crowd. Then I hear him quietly laugh.

"But Stump says things did not go as expected," Ivy continues, "because when he arrived at the new Breeder's cubicle—the new Breeder wasn't there." Ivy now locks her gaze on me. "Which means that one of two things must have happened. Either the new Breeder was somehow able to resist her Headmaster's impulse to return to her cubicle, or the new Breeder didn't even know her Headmaster was attempting to impel her. Either way, it's a problem. A problem for the Headmasters, a problem for us—and a problem for Maple."

In unison, everyone in the crowd takes one clumsy step forward, tightening the knot around our table—around me.

"Fortunately," Ivy continues, "I was able to inform my fellow Thankfuls of this fact last night, just before the slackening ended. And together, we communed briefly with our Headmasters to warn them." Ivy beams with pride. "They heeded us, and here we are," she says, looking again at me, "ready to deal with this problem as the Headmasters direct us."

My eyes break away from Ivy's and lock onto Papa. I can see him desperately looking around, wide-eyed, trying to think of something to do, find something to help me. I stare at him and shake my head. *No, Papa,* I think. *Don't even try.* I see him shift his grip on his walking stick and begin to raise it into the air. But before he can act, Rose cries out, "Silex! Heave!"

Silex doesn't move for a moment, then suddenly pushes himself to his feet with a thunderous roar and clasps his hands together at his waist. Unable to speak from the agony of resisting his Headmaster, he stares at me, willing me to act—but I don't know what he wants me to do.

"Maple!" Rose cries out, her face twisted with the effort to get just one more word out, "Heave!"

Suddenly understanding, I scramble onto the bench, jump onto the table, and charge toward Silex. I lock my knees as I step onto his clasped hands, and already he's lifting me, heaving me up in a smooth arc over the half wall of the second floor that runs around the Meal House. I land hard on the sacks of walnuts and chestnuts stored there for winter, knocking the wind out of me.

As I gasp and roll to my feet, I hear Silex release another roar of pain—then the thud of something large and heavy falling to the floor. I resist the urge to look over the half wall to see what's happened to him. Instead, I leap to the clear path beside the sacks and begin running around the perimeter of the Meal House, heading toward a second-floor window at the back. It's open. The sheet of plexibar that covers it in the winter hasn't yet been nailed on.

I know the drop from the window to the ground isn't as far here as at the front—the back of the Meal House is partly built into a hill. I leap through the window without slowing, sail through the air, and land on a thick layer of ashes the Biscuiteers have dumped there for years. My head grazes a rocky outcrop, but I'm unharmed.

I'm certain the others will now be pouring through the

front doors of the Meal House, impelled into a frenzied chase by the Headmasters. My head start is slim, and some of them are faster runners than I am. *Your only chance*, I tell myself, *is to get into the river. You'll never outrun them all.*

I can't run to the front of the Meal House and then cross the compound to take the usual route to the river—they'll see me for sure. My only option is to keep climbing up the slope I'm already on: I can follow the top of the ridge north until it reaches the river. From there, the slope to the water is steep, but I think I'll be able to scramble down it.

I'm halfway to the crest when I hear the first wave of the others. I glance over my shoulder and see them standing in clusters behind the Meal House. They haven't seen me yet—I stop my climb in mid-step and hug the ground. The branches are low here, and the slope is in shadow, so they might not notice me. Then my foot slips, and a stone goes tumbling down toward them. I don't wait for them to look up and spot me. I start climbing again, digging my nails into the loam and moss to keep myself from sliding back down.

I've reached the top of the ridge. I haven't fully recovered my breath, but I don't stop. Running along the crest is easier, especially for a Picker like me, who's used to moving through the bush over rough ground. I weave and duck to dodge the face-high branches, but one of them still scrapes across my cheek and forehead, scratching my left eye.

I know I'm getting close to the river—the air is moist with its spray. Suddenly, I reach the crest of the ridge and have to drop into a slide to keep from tumbling down the other side. It's much steeper than I expected. As I start to make my descent, I hear the others crashing through the trees behind me. If I slip and fall, I'll almost certainly hit one of the rocky outcrops and split my head open.

Suddenly, a fist-sized rock sails past my head and thuds on

the riverbank below. Then another one, this one even bigger, lands behind me with a dull *whump* and then bounces over my shoulder. I glance back at the others. They're not following me down—their Headmasters have calculated they can't catch up to me before I reach the river. Instead, they're making them pull up stones and lob them down at me.

I hear someone—Twig, I think—struggle to cry out, just before a jagged rock lands behind me and careens between my ankles, "I'm—sorry—Maple!" I'm almost at the river's edge, but the hail of rocks has increased. Others must have caught up with the first wave of pursuers and are joining the barrage.

Just as I step into the river, I hear a rumble from the slope behind me, louder than anything before. I twist around in time to see a massive log hurtling toward me, bouncing end over end as it approaches. I crouch but can't get out of its way, and it clips my hip, sending me spinning into the river. I'm dazed by the impact and sink below the water, but fight my way to the surface, where I wrap an arm around the log before it floats out of reach. I duck my head behind it as rocks and stones continue to pelt down. Then, the current catches the log and begins to pull me downstream, away from my pursuers.

The log is old and heavy but buoyant enough to keep me afloat. As the current takes me around a bend in the river, I look back and see them all standing on the crest of the ridge. Some of them—probably the Thankfuls—continue to throw rocks, but by now, I'm well out of reach. A few others manage to give me a stilted wave, though I'm sure the effort of that small show of encouragement costs them dearly in pain.

The sun climbs high into the sky as I continue to hug the log, letting the river carry me away. It's hard to tell how far it's taken me. Where it widens, the current slows to almost nothing, and I have to get behind the log and churn my legs to keep moving. Where it narrows, it's all I can do to hang on while the white water surges around me, sweeping me over rocks that bruise and scrape my belly and legs.

I need to get out soon. I'm exhausted from clasping the log and fighting the rapids, and I'm shivering with cold. The problem is getting to the riverbank: I don't know how to swim. Years ago, Rose offered to teach me, but the prospect of more exertion after toiling all day wasn't very appealing. I was content, when the evenings refused to cool down, to wade into a gentle eddy where the river slowed as it went around a bend.

I know Zara could swim. I have a memory from her of diving into a huge rectangle of blue water and swimming from one end to the other. But a memory of swimming isn't the same as knowing how. I close my eyes for a moment and try to get more swimming memories to surface—but I get nothing.

I look ahead and see another bend coming up. As it approaches, I flail my legs, trying to propel myself close enough that I'll be able to grab onto a rock or root and haul myself to shore. But the riverbank here is smooth granite, and there's nothing to grab. The current speeds up again as it comes around the bend, and I fear I've lost my chance. But just ahead, I see the thick limb of an elm tree dipping low over the water. I manage to pull myself up onto the log so that I'm straddling it, riding it like the horses in Zara's memories.

As I pass under the limb, I stretch up and grab some of its smaller branches, barely twigs. They hold, but my hands begin to slip off them, stripping them of leaves as the river pulls me back. I twist sideways till the supple branches wrap around my left wrist, then grab another branch, a thicker one, with my right hand. I do this several times, right hand then left, until I'm close enough to crook my arm around the main limb. I hang there for a few moments, catching my breath, then scissor my legs over the limb and pull myself free of the river.

I drop onto the narrow stretch of flat shore beneath me and

collapse. I lie face down on the damp clay till the next morning, too exhausted to do anything else.

CHAPTER 53
JUST ME AND THE TURTLE

I wake up shivering and take inventory of my injuries. Most of my body is blotted with scrapes or bruises or scrapes on bruises. My left eye, scratched by the branch as I fled the Meal House, is still blurry. There's a sandy crust around it. My hip throbs with a deep ache from getting clipped by the tumbling log. I feel around in my mouth with a finger. At least I still have all my teeth.

I venture up the riverbank to find some cedars. My joints ache from lying on cold clay. I spot a long shaft of driftwood and pick it up to lean on as I walk. I find a copse of spruce—just as good as cedar—and strip off the branches. I bring them back to my little spot and spread them out on the ground. Much better. I lie down and sleep again.

On the third day, I wake up thinking how strange it is not to be jolted awake and sent out to toil. Then I start wondering what I'll do if a bear comes along. But so far, I haven't seen anything larger than a deer taking a drink from the bank on the other side of the river and a few curious squirrels checking me out upside-down from some overhanging honeysuckle vines. I begin to let my mind wander back to Blue Ring—I've been pushing those thoughts away.

I wonder about Silex. Did they terminate him? There still isn't anyone old enough in the Aery to be harvested, so maybe they only punished him. A couple of days of agonizing pain. Or maybe, like River, blood punishment. Who would they get to do that to him? Rose? Maybe they'd force him to do it to himself.

What's Papa thinking, and River? That I'm gone for good? That I'm lost to the river like Lark and Thorn? What have they told Birch and Prairie and the twins about why I'm not coming to see them?

I suddenly feel sick as it hits me that the river might have taken me past Lark's and Thorn's bodies, tangled in roots and weeds along the bank or spinning around in an eddy. But the river was higher when it took them and faster. They were likely swept much farther downstream.

That's what I hope, anyway. I try to imagine them being carried along forever, that the river is endless and will take them farther and farther away from the Headmasters at Blue Ring.

But then I freeze, as I think: their Headmasters also fell into the water and were carried away by the current. They're somewhere in the river I've been sleeping beside.

I take a breath and give my head a shake. *Relax*, I tell myself. *The chance of them being anywhere near me is slim.* And what can they do to me, anyway? I still have my own Headmaster coupled to me. My poor, impotent Headmaster. I smile as I remember Papa using that word to describe his.

Fourth day. My muscles ache less, and my scrapes are beginning to heal. The nights, luckily, have been warm for autumn. My hip still hurts, and I'm covered with bites from black flies and mosquitoes, but my main problem is I need food.

My ribs have become easy to count. I think the pain of my bruises and cuts has blunted my hunger till now. I don't want to venture away from the river to look for berries or nuts—too much chance of getting lost in the unfamiliar bush.

Instead, I get up and follow the shore downstream. I limp along, still leaning on my driftwood staff. Before long, I find a shallow eddy, take off my shirt, and use it like a sieve to catch some of the thousands of tiny, silver minnows that dart beneath the surface. Slow work, but after doing it a few dozen times, I've harvested almost a handful of them.

I swallow them without chewing—most of them still alive and squiggling as they slip down my throat. I manage to catch a few small frogs basking on rocks in the sun. I smash their heads with a rock, then bite their legs off. I've eaten frogs many times before, but only when they were ground up and cooked in the biscuit mixture. Eating their cold green limbs with their little webbed toes is different. I feel bad for them and wonder what the other frogs are thinking, the ones still watching me from the rocks.

Day five. I feel strong enough to resume my original plan: to enter the collective mind of the Headmasters and neutralize them. But I'm worried. Because of Ivy and the other Thankfuls, the Headmasters now know what I've done to my own Head-master. They'll be expecting me—just like they were expecting Zara. And that didn't turn out well.

Still, what choice do I have? I can't just go back to the Blue Ring. If I show up during a slackening, everyone—well, almost everyone—will be overjoyed to see me, to know I'm still alive. But once the slackening ends, their Headmasters will make them turn against me once again.

On the other hand, there's no point following the river farther downstream. I won't find anything there that isn't here. As for staying put, I could last for a few more weeks, but eventually, it will get too cold. I can't survive a winter outside.

But so what? None of those things matter anyway. I have a job to do. Not a job—a mission. That's how Zara had thought about it. And now it's mine. Whether Zara intended it or not, it was handed to me. I have a chance—a smaller chance than a few days ago—to do something. Actually, to *undo* something. That's the better way to put it. To undo what was inflicted on us sixty years ago. The Headmasters didn't just enslave the people at Blue Ring. They also took our past. And our future.

"Screw them!" I shout. It echoes along the rocky walls of the gorge. It's only the second time I've ever cursed out loud. Assuming that "screw" is a curse word. If it is, I think the situation warrants it.

I wait till I'm sure the slackening must have begun. It's hard to judge time because the sun slips behind the high walls of the gorge, making it darker sooner. My plan is to use the *Kinikatos* to enter the neutralized mind of my Headmaster. Then, I'll wait until the sleeping interval begins and the other Headmasters emerge. Then, I'll—I'll play it by ear. Or something.

I enter my own Headmaster's mind space without difficulty. The turtle is how I left it: on its back, its four legs and two heads all tucked in, spinning. The huge tub is still there, but it's empty. The toothy maggots are gone. So is their awful smell.

I stand beside the turtle and wait. And then I wait some more. Then I sit down and wait. *Why couldn't my mind have given me a book to read while I'm waiting?* I wonder. Maybe I should use the time to brood about Lark and Thorn—their bodies being smashed around in the river—so I'll be primed with maximum rage and anguish when the other Headmasters emerge. Or maybe I should distract myself by focusing on other things, happier things like Lark's kids, so that when the Headmasters show up, I can suddenly release a torrent of pent-up pain and wrath.

It turns out it doesn't matter. The other Headmasters don't emerge. It's just me and the turtle and the tub under a yellow sky on the cracked clay.

Time to leave. When I open my eyes, it's morning. A bear hasn't eaten me while I was in *Kinikatos*, and more frogs are sunning themselves on the rocks where I harvested their kin yesterday.

What went wrong? Why didn't the Headmasters emerge in their collective mind? Or did they, and I just wasn't able to join in? What was different this time?

Distance. That's the only thing I can think of. I don't know how the Headmasters connect, but maybe they need to be near one another to make it happen. Maybe that's why they kept us in Blue Ring all these years, close to one another.

It looks like I've got to head all the way back after all.

CHAPTER 54
FROG LEGS

The next day, I wake up tired. It was too cold and damp to sleep well. My shivering kept me awake most of the night.

But tired or not, I need to start tracing the river upstream. I leave in the late morning after scooping up as many minnows as I can and spreading them out on a flat rock in the sun. They're so small it doesn't take them long to dry. I end up with about four handfuls. Along the way, it won't be hard to find snails to eat, too. I'm planning to avoid frogs if possible.

I don't travel very fast. The scrub bush that grows along the top of the riverbank is too thick to walk through easily. The shore is alternately wet sand that slurps over my feet or fist-sized stones that are easy to turn an ankle on. Tiny fish flies swarm around my head and flit into my eyes, making them sting and water. So I content myself with a slow but steady pace beside the river.

After walking for a while, I come to an abrupt halt just before a bend in the river. A sickly sweet smell is on the wind. Rotting flesh. Maggots. The smell of death.

Please, I think, *don't let it be them.* I'm not sure who I'm pleading to. I'm familiar with the idea of an all-powerful god. Zara has memories of going to a cathedral with her grandfather when she was very young. The main thing she remembered was a painting of a man coming out of a cave with a big round rock beside it. He was showing people outside the cave that he had holes in his hands. Zara's grandfather said he was the god's son. She asked him how the god could be good if he let them do that to his son. I'm not sure what he told her. That part of the memory is hazy.

But in my head, I plead anyway. Maybe to a god, maybe to hope or expectation. Maybe to time, the river that carries all things to their conclusion. *Please, don't let it be them.*

I begin moving again, wondering what I'll do if I see their bodies. What would Lark and Thorn want me to do? Pass on by? Drag whatever is left of them into the bush and bury them? Zara's mother once told her you can't unsee what you see. I know that all too well.

As I come around the bend in the river, I spot two turkey vultures crouching over something at the edge of the river.

It's a dead deer—a bloated buck. It must have run off the edge of the gorge that looms above the river. Easy to do in the dark. One of his antlers is missing, probably smashed off from the impact. Where his eyes were, there are holes. And maggots. I speed up my pace, eager to get beyond him. The turkey vultures watch me warily as I pass, jealously guarding their feast.

Thank you, I think. Again, I'm not sure who I'm thanking. Maybe the deer for not being them.

For the next three days, not much happens. I get up at dawn, walk, stop to eat minnows or snails when I'm hungry, walk some more, eat some more, lie down when I need to, and shiver through the nights. I feel tired and yet more powerful each day. It's a new kind of strength, a strength that comes from doing something meaningful, from having a goal and moving steadily toward it.

On the following day—the ninth, I think, since I escaped—I find a chokecherry bush leaning out over the riverbank and stop to swallow a few dry berries the squirrels and birds haven't plucked. I eat as quickly as I can: there are bear prints in the clay, a set of big ones and a set—maybe two—of smaller ones. I wonder if there's a way I could cross to the other side of the river—but no, I don't want to risk being swept away again.

Later that afternoon, I find a relic—that's what Papa would call it. A piece of the past. I know from one of Zara's university memories it's called a motorcycle. It's wedged between two large rocks that jut through the surface of the water. Only its skeleton is left, of course—two wheels held together by a rusty frame, with handles like antlers on one end to steer it. If it ever had nylar on it, that's long gone. I wonder if a high spring runoff carried it here before the Arrival. Or maybe it fell from the top of the gorge like the deer—along with whoever was on it.

That evening, after eating a couple of dozen snails, I wade into the river up to my thighs, then crouch so the water flows over my shoulders. It's cold, but it feels good to wash off days of dust and sweat. As I'm gazing upstream, wondering how much longer I'll have to walk, I notice something coming down the river, bobbing up and down as the current carries it. It's blue and white, about as long as my forearm, and it's glinting in the last rays of the day's sun. Suddenly, I recognize it: it's Papa's water bottle, the container he fills every slackening so it's at hand the next day when he's in the Mender's Hall.

Without thinking, I stand up and scramble farther into the river to grab it as it passes. The tug of the water gets stronger as it gets deeper—I stop when I can feel it almost lifting me off my toes. I can't risk going in farther. The bottle dips and bobs straight toward me, but then, when it's almost within reach, the current nudges it sideways, and it slips past me, my fingers just grazing its metal surface. I turn and try to grab it again, but it's already beyond me, tumbling downstream. I stare after it till it's receded out of sight.

Papa has had that water bottle since before the Arrival, I think. *How did it get in the river?* Various possibilities flash through my mind. He went to the spot where I got into the river, stumbled on the steep bank, and tumbled in. Or he was pushed in. Or he dropped it in by accident. Or he was trying to send me a message. Or I'm wrong, and it wasn't his water bottle at all—just something my tired brain imagined.

I focus on the possibility that's most hopeful: he was sending me a message. He must have written something and put it inside. But was it a message for a Maple he hoped was still alive—some encouragement or news about something else that's happened—or was it a message for a Maple he assumed was dead—a sad farewell to another granddaughter?

Hopefully, within a few days, I'll be able to ask him myself.

The next morning, a chilly fall rain begins and doesn't let up all day. I find a spot where the wall of the gorge leans out over the river and hunker under it. I don't want to be hiking over the treacherous ground of the rocky shore with water streaming into my eyes, making it hard to see the best footing.

It stops late in the day, but now it's too late to get moving. The rain has washed all the snails away, but the frogs come out with the sun. I don't want to, but I catch a half-dozen of them—big ones with sad eyes that seem to say, *Why me?*—and make a meal of their legs, along with a few wild carrots I found the day before. I consider tossing the frogs' legless bodies into the river but think better of it and bury them in the clay.

CHAPTER 55
GRIFFIN ECCLESTON

I almost swear for the third time in my life when I see them. But I don't. Cursing wouldn't begin to express my astonishment.

Footprints. I'm looking down at human footprints in the wet clay by the river. Whoever they belong to, they can't be from Blue Ring. Some of the prints have hard edges, like shoes —like the ones I've seen in Zara's memories. I stare at them, trying to figure out how many people there were. Four, I think, but the prints crisscross one another, so it's hard to be certain. It looks like they came out of the bush, scrambled down the riverbank, walked up to the river's edge, and then went back into the bush.

Not from Blue Ring. That's the thought careening around my mind. *Others exist who aren't from Blue Ring. Other people.*

But the magnitude of that revelation quickly gets pushed aside by some practical considerations. Do I want to find them or hide from them? Can they help me, or will they hurt me? Do I worry about them now or after I finish with the Headmasters? Or ever? For that matter, do they have Headmasters?

They must have been here fairly recently, or the rain would

have washed away their footprints. Then it occurs to me they might still be close—very close. Maybe even watching me from within the trees as I stand here. I feel goosebumps rise on my arms, but I try not to show my sudden alarm. I casually clasp my hands together, lift my arms into the air, and then twist at my waist as if I'm simply stretching—but my eyes are scanning the bush that runs along the riverbank behind me. It's pointless —the bush is so dense, every last person from Blue Ring could be hiding there, and I wouldn't see a single one of them.

Oh, to hell with it, I suddenly decide. *I'm not going to walk the rest of the way to Blue Ring looking over my shoulder, wondering if I'm being spied on.*

"Hey!" I yell. "Are you there?" I can shout louder than that. "Hey," I yell again, this time my voice echoing down the gorge. "Hey, I'd like to see you."

I pause and listen. Nothing.

I try again. "I'm beside the water! I've got . . . I've got something to show you!" I'm not sure why I say that, especially when I have absolutely nothing to show anyone unless you count my ability to cross my eyes one at a time. I stop and listen again. It's hard to hear much with the river babbling around me. Finally, I give up—they must be gone—and start walking upstream again. I realize I'm relieved that no one answered.

Then I hear it, distant but unmistakable. "Yes! We hear you. Stay where you are till I comes where you're at."

"Okay!" I try to shout back, but it barely comes out as a whimper. No turning back now.

I stand over the footprints while I wait. I consider wading back into the river, ready to plunge into the current if I feel threatened. I still have my walking stick. I twist it in my hands nervously.

I hear a rustling coming from the trees and bush on the riverbank, over to the left. I pivot and see movement in the foliage—branches trembling and leaves fluttering as someone pushes steadily through them. The shaking of the branches and leaves gets closer, the rustling louder, and then the greenery suddenly parts, and someone steps out.

A man. Taller than River but not as tall as Silex. Older than River but not as old as Silex. His black hair is short and curly. He doesn't have a beard. Most of the men at Blue Ring have beards. His skin is much darker than mine—like Rose's. He's wearing what looks like a grey blanket with holes cut into it for his head and arms. A piece of rope pulls the garment tight around his waist. He's wearing black boots that go up over his ankles.

He doesn't look dangerous, I think. That's because his hands are open, and he's holding them outward. He wants to show me that he doesn't have anything to hurt me with. He's smiling, but there's a look of uncertainty in his eyes as if he's waiting to see how I'll react to him.

"Name's Griffin Eccleston," he says. "But my mates call me Eccles. You can call me that, too. If you like." He pauses as if he's waiting for me to tell him my name. I don't. He slowly lowers his hands. "Fair game to step closer?" He smiles again and raises his eyebrows as if he's looking for my approval. His speech is clear, and his voice is strong, but there's a strange quality to it, as if his words are being bent around a corner.

I don't say anything for a moment. I'm still looking him over, examining his face. His eyes look kind and honest.

"Not too much closer," I reply, being sure to keep a firm grasp on my walking stick.

He steps forward a few paces. "Are you one of them tick folks?" His tone is polite and curious as if he's asking me if I prefer apples or peaches.

"What do you mean?" I reply, puzzled.

"The folk who keeps the big wood ticks on their backs. Are you one of them?"

He waits patiently while I gaze at him, wondering how to answer. It's not a yes or no question.

"We don't 'keep' them," I finally say. "We don't want to have them. We hate them. They control us. Use us to see and hear. And communicate with each other."

He furrows his brow and nods. "Are they—are they doin' that now?"

I shake my head. "No. I escaped. I mean, I neutralized mine and then escaped. Ten or twelve days ago. But it's still attached to me. On my back."

"So it's still . . . takin' a feed off you? Takin' your blood?"

For some reason, this question makes me shudder. One of the books Thorn and I took from the vault was about a man who slept in a box and sucked blood from people while they slept. Parts of it made the hair on my arms stand up.

"They don't feed off us. They don't eat anything. They don't even breathe. They're not like other—" I search for the right word—"not like other creatures. They're not from here."

I'm sure he doesn't really understand what I'm saying, but he nods. Then he asks, "Can I have a glim?"

"A what?" I reply.

"A glim. At the bug. Can I have a gander?"

"You want to look at it?"

"Aye. Can I have a look?"

His tone is still so polite, I'm surprised he hasn't been saying, "May I?"

Again, I'm silent for a long time as I consider his request. At Blue Ring, we mostly try to keep our Headmasters covered. Hidden. Asking to look at someone's Headmaster would be kind of like asking to see what they deposited in their slop jar before the darkening. Still, if he and I are aiming to build some mutual trust, it's probably best not to hold anything back. I turn my back to him and lift my shirt above my neck.

I can feel him staring at me. At it. I continue to hold up my shirt until he says something.

"Homely bugger, isn't he? I wager even his mum doesn't love him. Can't you pull him off? Now that you've stifled him?"

I shake my head as I lower my shirt and turn back toward him. "It'd likely still poison me. It's a reflex."

"Like how a goose head keeps blinking after you cuts it off?"

"I guess so," I reply.

"That's a pity. I'm sorry for it," he says. He seems to be studying me. "You know, when I was a nipper growing up in the mine, I heard stories from the buffers that there was people like you—I mean, people with—" He pauses and gestures over his shoulder toward his back. "I reckoned it was a lot of guff. They said you folks lived in a circle far up creek, and there might be more of the big wood ticks yonder, and that's why none of us is allowed to bushwalk up that far."

Now, it's my turn to try to make sense of what he's just said. I give up. Instead, I just blurt out, "Are you going to try to kill me?"

He looks as surprised as if—well, as if I've just asked him if he's going to try to kill me—and shakes his head. "I've killed four-footed critters for food and two-footed ones, too, if they had feathers. You ain't neither of them." He smiles again. Then he adds, more sombrely, "No, I pledge you, I ain't ever killed another person. There ain't enough of us left to spare."

I consider his response. There's something about him that makes me want to trust him. Maybe it's his gentle curiosity. Maybe it's that I can barely understand him. Maybe it's how he stands—relaxed but attentive. Or maybe it's that he doesn't seem to mind that I'm taking my time deciding about him—like we have all the time in the world.

I decide. "What's your name again?" I ask.

"Real name or friend name?"

"Friend name."

"Eccles."

"Here we are, Eccles," I say. "I'm Maple. I don't have any other names." I walk toward him, holding out my hand.

He takes it and gives it a hearty shake. "Pleased to have your acquaintance, Maple. We pitched a camp up top by the rail track and were fixin' to fire up some scoff when we heard you hollerin'. Come join. By the look of you, you haven't had much grub in yonks."

I hope he's talking about food, I say to myself. When I nod, this strange man with his strange words turns and heads back toward the bush. I follow him. He climbs the riverbank effortlessly and slips into the trees. He moves quickly until he notices I'm having trouble keeping up. He doesn't say anything but slows down and starts to hold back the branches so they don't slap me in the face. He's clearly had a lot of experience moving through the bush.

"Where do you live, Eccles?" I ask as we press forward.

"Not these parts," he replies. "Downstream another thirty clicks. We calls it Tamihk—a shaft mine. You know what that is?

diamond coal copper

"Yes," I tell him. "A really deep hole in the ground."

"That's right. Our old dears were there, in the mine, when the Big Out hit. Three clicks below, so they survived. Came back up and were gobsmacked to learn the world was ended."

"How many people?"

"Back then or now?

"Then."

"Forty-six. Twenty-seven gals, nineteen fellers—awkward ratio, but they somehow worked it all out, from what I've heard. Half of 'em came from Oz, here to learn some new mining craft. If they'd aimed to leave a day after, they'd have fallen from the sky with all the other aeroships. I'm here 'cuz they didn't."

"How many now?"

"Near two hundred and fifty."

"You all live in the mine?"

"In the winter, for the most part. Spring, summer, fall, we're up top, scratchin' a living from the dirt and stockin' up." He stops and waits for me to catch up to him. "Almost there— camp's t'other side of this crest. You can meet my mates."

I'm winded. The ridge has gotten progressively steeper, and eating not much more than minnows and frog legs for the past ten days has sapped my reserves. I'm also still trying to get my head around the fact that I'm talking to a stranger—and will soon be meeting more. When I woke up this morning, there were no such things as strangers.

Eccles sees me struggling and extends his hand. I take it, and he helps me up the last bit to the top of the ridge.

"For supper, you can have whatever you likes," he says with a grin, "as long as what you likes is rabbit stew and hardtack bickie." He stops and waves down at two figures sitting beside a smoking fire below. "Hey, mates!" he shouts. "Fill another bowl! I've brung a friend!"

They stand up and smile.

They're not strangers. They're Thorn and Lark.

PART FOUR

CHAPTER 56
A BLOODY MUDDLE

I throw down my walking stick and race down the ridge toward them, nearly tripping on the steep slope and tumbling onto my head. In another moment, my arms are around them both, and I'm hugging them, screaming their names and crying.

"You're alive," I say, "Lark and Thorn, you're alive!"

"You're squishing me," Thorn says as he tries to wriggle out of my embrace.

"Me, too," Lark adds. "Let me go, please. You smell bad."

I release them both and step back. Something's not right.

"Are you Eccles's wife?" Lark asks as she moves farther away from me.

Eccles's wife? I stare at them, dumbfounded. "I'm Maple," I tell them, my voice hollow and shaking. "I'm your sister," I say to Lark. I turn to Thorn. "And you're my—you're mine."

They gaze at me, puzzled, brows furrowed. Then Lark shakes her head and says, "My sister is just a little kid. She's still in the Aery. You're grown up."

"But she kind of looks like Maple," Thorn says, squinting at me. "Or like Maple's big sister."

"I'm Maple's big sister," Lark says angrily.

By this time, Eccles has made his way down the ridge and is standing beside me. He puts a hand on my shoulder to steady me. My legs are ready to give out, and I can feel the blood pounding in my ears.

"What's the rumpus here?" he asks. "You know these two?"

"They—they —" is all I manage to get out.

"Sit alongside me, Maple," he says, gesturing toward a log someone's pulled up near the campfire.

"She's not Maple," Lark tells him. Her words stab my heart.

"You two, go fetch more wood for the fire. Big sticks this time. But stay in sight, hear?"

Lark and Thorn hesitate, then nod and trot off toward the bush. Eccles gently tugs me over to the log and motions for me to sit down. Then he straddles the log so he's looking straight at me.

"What are them two to you?" he asks softly.

"She's my sister. He's my partner. They're from the same place as me. But they don't know who I am."

"Partner? You and him are married?"

I shake my head, still staring at the flames. "We don't call it that. But basically, yes."

Eccles nods as he ponders this. "They don't have the ticks on 'em like you. Are you sure it's really them? Maybe your glims are playing tricks on you? On account of you being so gut-founded? You haven't had a scoff to eat in days."

I cut him off. "No," I say emphatically. "That's them. That's Thorn and Lark."

He nods again. "That's the names they told me. But they don't reckon you. Quite a muddle."

"How did they end up with you?"

"Well," he replies, "that's a bit of a tale. Six weeks back, I left Tamihk to scout for deer. I does that every spring. They ramble, so I does a walkabout till I finds them browsin'. Then I double-time back to the mine, shouts up a crew, and we go like clappers to snag a dozen or more before they move on. We butcher 'em on the spot, pack the cuts in salt, and fetch it back with us.

"Anyway, a week into the lookin', I finally found a herd and was gettin' primed to hie myself back to the mine. Went down to the river to top my flask, and that's when I gandered these two. There they were, naked as jays, standin' on the shore of a bitty-sized island in the creek. I could tell they was in hard shape—piles of bruises and scrapes.

"I hollered over to them, and they hollered back. They started to wade in to reach me, but I waved 'em off—they wouldn'ta lasted another dunk, the way that creek was rollin'. I hollered I was goin' for help and was shockin' gob-smacked when they seemed to fathom me. *Two days*, I signalled to them, and then I left, followin' the rail track.

"I was back to the mine by the noon of next day, and then back to where I found 'em the day after that with four big blokes and a long run of rope. We got 'em off sound and took 'em back to Tamihk and passed a couple weeks tendin' 'em hale again."

He stops and looks at me, giving me time to process all he's told me.

"So why are they here now, with you?" I ask. "Instead of at the mine?"

"Didn't take long for 'em to gab out where they come from. They didn't recollect how they ended up in the creek but said their gang was back at a place called Blurring. Lark wanted to get home to Poppy and River and Maple—that's you, I guess. Thorn talked mostly about a missus named Halo. Is that who knit him?"

"Knit him? What do you mean?"

"Is that his ma?"

I shake my head. Then I add, "Sort of."

"They were so fretful about getting back home, we were fearful they'd slink off in the night by their lonesomes. So I told 'em I'd shepherd 'em back to their kin. We couldn't let 'em trek alone, seeing as how they are, of course."

"What do you mean?" I ask.

Eccles gives me a puzzled look. "The rail track follows the creek pretty much, so it's easy enough to trek upstream, but we reckoned they might still ramble off the way or land 'emselves in some scrape."

I look blankly at Eccles, still not understanding.

"The two of 'em's simpletons, ain't they?" he says quietly as he glances over toward Thorn and Lark. "Their bodies is grown big but their minds is like little ones. They don't know enough woods-lore to get 'emselves back safe."

I try to make sense of what Eccles is saying.

"Back at the mine," he continues, putting a hand on my shoulder, "Hank's the same way. Came out of his ma with the cord round his neck—stifled his oxygen for a while. He's a man now, but no more than a eight-year-old boy in the mind." He pauses, then adds, as if he's trying to reassure me, "Sweetest man you'll ever come across, though. We all loves him."

Did something happen to Lark and Thorn in the river? Did they almost drown? Or bash their heads on rocks? Did some sort of accident damage them?

Then it hits me—it's obvious. Zara's memories are in my Headmaster. Thorn's and Lark's memories—most of them, anyway—were in their Headmasters, and when Thorn got them to detach, they took those memories with them. Everything that ever happened to Thorn and Lark after they were harvested—after they were coupled to their Headmasters—all those years of memories—are gone. Lost forever. It's like they're ten again, or twelve, or however old they were when they were harvested. It's like they never grew up. It's like Thorn never loved me. It's like Lark never became a Breeder. Never became a Thankful.

I try to explain all this to Eccles.

"So your gran's memories is in—" he gestures behind his back again—"that thing."

"We call them Headmasters."

"And so you remember what she remembered? Your gran."

"Sort of. It's more complicated than that."

"But their memories," he says, nodding toward Thorn and Lark, who are on the edge of the tree line, still collecting firewood, "is now churnin' down the creek in two of them things."

"I think they still have their memories from before they were harvested," I tell him. "And whatever they'd learned by then. Like talking. But everything else is probably gone." *Like Thorn being able to read*, I think. "That's why they don't recognize me. As far as they remember, their Maple is a ten-year-old."

Eccles is silent for a long time as he considers this.

"What are you aimin' to do?" he finally asks. "About them, I mean."

"You mean, will I tell them what's happened to them? I don't know. Tell them they've forgotten most of their lives? Tell Lark the Headmasters turned her into a breeding machine and crushed her spirit? Tell Thorn I once meant everything to him, and him to me?"

Eccles shakes his head and sighs. "A bloody muddle, that's for sure."

"Maybe Papa will know what to do," I say, mostly to myself.

"Well, for now, let's holler 'em back to the fire and dig into some tuck. Ofttimes things seem clearer after a good feed."

"Can you tell them I'm one of your friends from the mine, and that I was just confused when I ran up to them? Until I decide?"

"Of course, luv. Of course."

CHAPTER 57
SHOCKWAVE

After we eat—or "tuck in," as Eccles says—I rub my skin with a pine-smelling cream that Eccles offers me.

"It'll keep the skitters off you," he says. With a small smile, he adds, "The itty-bitty ones, anyway."

I lie down near the campfire and cover myself with one of the blankets Eccles brought from the mine. Not nylar—it's a strange material that reminds me of Farley's fur.

"Wool," Eccles tells me when he notices me rubbing it between my fingers. "The old dears found a few sheep way back. Now the flock's more than two hundred."

I nod but don't reply. I'm too tired. Worn out in every way. Through my half-closed eyes, I watch Thorn and Lark as they throw pebbles into the fire, trying to make sparks fly up. Then, they each stick a dry branch into the flames until the tips glow. They wave them around in the deepening darkness, drawing luminous loops in the air that vanish in a moment.

I used to do that with Thorn. When I was a kid.

That night, after I fall asleep by the fire, I have a dream. Thorn and Lark are children again, and they're walking hand in hand in a wilderness, laughing and talking, but the odd thing is, they're walking backward, away from me. I wave to them, but they don't see me, and I call out to them, but they don't hear me. They're getting farther away, walking backward and backward, and I start to run after them, shouting, but they're getting smaller and smaller. Then I see a great hole in the ground opening up behind them, and I know they'll fall into it if I don't stop them, so I cry out again, "Thorn! Lark!" but now they're not Thorn and Lark, and they're not children, they're Orlando and Rosalind, from Virgil's tale, and they're still laughing and talking, oblivious to the abyss they're nearing, and I have to stop them somehow, so I lift my foot and stomp as hard as I can, and the ground shakes with the terrible impact, and a shock wave travels toward them, rippling the earth as it approaches them, and then I realize, *Oh, no, the shock wave is going to buck them right into the hole*, and then I hold my hands out toward them, pleading, and I see that my hands are not my own, the fingers are long and slender and bedazzled with golden rings, the nails are elegantly trimmed, the skin unblemished by pricks from thorns and brambles, and I realize these are Gunther's hands, and the shock wave keeps surging toward them . . .

CHAPTER 58
FILL YOUR BOOTS

The next morning, I wake up when I hear Eccles's voice. "Yer hands and mugs are all grimy with ash," he's saying. "Go wash up, or no brekkie for either of you!" He sounds stern, but he's grinning.

Lark and Thorn pick up a container—Eccles calls it a canteen—and trot over to a nearby dogwood tree. They dribble water on each other's hands, then use the tree's leaves to rub themselves clean.

"Sleep well, did you?" Eccles says to me.

I nod. "I was warm for the first time in more days than I can remember. Thanks for the blankets." I pause and consider whether to say anything else. "I had a strange dream, though," I finally add.

"Not surprising. You been through plenty. Your under-mind has to wrestle to make sense of it."

"My what?"

"Your under-mind. The part of you where most of you happens. Like a badger hole. You and me only see the hole, but the badger kens the whole maze of tunnels underneath. That's the under-mind."

I pause as I think, *That's the most remarkable thing I've ever heard.*

A moment later, Thorn and Lark are back, mostly scrubbed up. It's beyond strange to see the man I've loved—and love—sitting cross-legged by the fire and giggling at something Lark's just whispered to him. Lark abruptly turns toward me.

"Are you coming with us?" she asks. "And what's your name? Your real name?"

I anticipated this question. "Call me Luv. Haven't you heard Eccles calling me that?"

"He calls everyone that."

"Well—that's what you should call me."

She nods. "So—are you coming with us, Luv?" Eccles is off to the side, stirring something in a pot over the fire, but I can feel his eyes on me, waiting for me to answer Lark.

"I wanted to talk to you about that," I say. "You remember that at Blue Ring, everyone has a Headmaster? If you go back, they'll put one on you. You wouldn't want that."

"I didn't have a Headmaster when I was there," Thorn says, "so I don't think they'll put one on me when we get back. I think they ran out of them."

"And besides," Lark adds, "I want to see Papa and River and Maple again." She furrows her brow and gives me a stare. "The real Maple. I don't care about the Headmasters."

Eccles sidles over and hands us each a steaming bowl. "Here y'are," he says. "Trekker stew—rice, mushrooms, lamb jerky, and garlic. Hopes you like it."

I dig my spoon into the white mess in my bowl and swirl it around. It doesn't look very appealing—the little white things remind me too much of maggots—but I start eating it anyway, knowing I'll need energy today, no matter what happens. I'm instantly surprised by how much I like it. I finish what's in my bowl and glance at the pot hanging above the fire.

"There's more," Eccles says, noticing my glance. "Fill your boots."

I get up, ladle more of the stew into my bowl, and sit back down before continuing. "Lark and Thorn, I'm wondering what you think of this idea. Since I'm already on my way to Blue Ring, how about if I keep going by myself, and you two head back to the mine with Eccles? That way, I can tell Papa and River—and Maple—that you're okay. They'll be so glad to find out. Then, after I make it so the Headmasters don't bother us anymore, we'll come and find you."

Lark and Thorn are scowling. "I want to see them right away," Lark pouts. "I don't want to wait till then."

"We've already walked a long way," says Thorn. "And anyway, how could you make it so the Headmasters don't bother anybody? Nobody can do that."

I take several bites of stew before I answer, trying to decide what to say. I put down my bowl and stand up.

"Look," I say as I pull down the collar of my shirt, revealing the top of my Headmaster, its coils rooted in my skull. "I've got one on me. It's still there, but I've put it to sleep—forever."

They both look dubious.

"Think about it," I tell them. "If this Headmaster had me in its grip, what would I be doing right now? Look how high the sun is."

Thorn nods slightly. "You'd be toiling. They'd be making you toil."

"And am I?"

Thorn shakes his head.

"So, that proves it. I put my Headmaster to sleep, and it's not going to wake up."

"Then we should go with you," Thorn says, "so that we're there when you put the rest of them to sleep. It'll be safe for us if you do that."

Lark nods in agreement.

I sigh. Even now, Thorn's hard to beat in an argument. "Well," I reply, "I don't care what you think. The simple fact is that Eccles and I aren't going to let you go to Blue Ring right now. He's going to take you back to the mine till I come get you."

I glance over at Eccles, who looks like he's bracing for a storm to hit.

"No!" Lark yells, jumping to her feet and stomping. "I'm not going back to the mine! I want to see them sooner than that!"

"Me, too," says Thorn. He's more calm, but I can see the resolve on his face. "If we have to, Lark and me will just go on our own. You can't stop us. Eccles said we just have to follow the rail track."

"That's right," Lark snaps. "What are you going to do, tie us up like berserkers and drag us back to the mine? Put us in a box?"

I look at Eccles again, hoping for support, but he just shrugs. "Ya can't stop the tide from raisin' your boat," he says.

"Fine," I say, exasperated. "Then how about this? We'll all keep following the rail—the rail track—back to Blue Ring. But when we get close, you three will stay back in the bush and hide. I'll go in and find Papa—Lark's Papa—and let him know what I'm going to do. Then, once I'm done putting the Head-masters to sleep, you can walk right into Blue Ring through the big gate. And everyone will be glad to see you. Deal?"

Thorn and Lark glance at each other, then nod in unison. "Deal," they say.

"Sounds like a plan," Eccles says as he lifts a spoonful of steaming stew to his mouth. "A rippin' good plan."

CHAPTER 59
THERE BE DRAGONS

We pack up and load everything onto something Eccles calls a trolley, a flat, low-walled platform that rides on the two steel rails that stretch ahead and behind as far as I can see. It looks like a sledge, except it has wheels, and each wheel has a lip that hangs over the edge of its rail so it stays on track. Eccles shows me how easy it is to pull it, even after we've got it fully loaded.

"But mind you," he says, "once it gets rollin', it's a devil to stop. If you trip while you're pullin', it'll run you right athwart."

"Why not push it?" I ask.

"You can, and when I've had them two help"—he points at Thorn and Lark—"that's what I had 'em do. But I'd rather pull so I can cast my glims about for loose track. If the trolley slips off the rails, it's a bugger to get back on."

Before we start off, I kneel and put my hand on one of the cold rails, imagining that Papa is doing the same. There and here are connected.

Then we set off, Eccles pulling the trolley, me walking just behind him—the rails are too close together to easily walk abreast—and Lark and Thorn following behind the trolley, chattering and clanging together the big iron spikes they've picked up from between the rails.

"Have you been here before?" I ask as we trudge along. "I mean, this far?

He shakes his head. "No one has. I mean, no one from the mine." Then he lowers his voice as he glances back at me and says, "They say there be dragons."

"What do you mean?" I ask.

I can tell he's smiling as he replies. "That's a thing we says back at the mine when we tell spooksome yarns to the little gaffers on a winter's night. They say centuries ago when sailors rode the seas, they wrote that on charts to forewarn of the shoals and hazards."

"No dragons where we're going," I reply. "But I'd rather have one of them than this," gesturing toward my back.

Eccles laughs. "Either way," he says, "it sounds like you're fixin' to slay them, like St. George of old."

A memory—Zara's, of course—flashes into my mind: the cathedral where her grandfather once took her, the sunlight pouring through a huge window of coloured glass. A man dressed in metal on a horse, looking bored as he pushes a spear through the long, coiling neck of a giant lizard.

"I'm going to paralyze them," I correct him. "Put them into a kind of thinking loop. I don't know how to kill them." Then, for the next hour or more, I tell him about Zara, what she tried to do, how she used *Kinikatos* to enter their collective mind, how she broke Papa's heart in order to fill herself with anguish, how she was going to use that anguish to paralyze everyone's Headmasters—and how they killed her before she had a chance to finish.

Eccles listens to me intently, leaning forward, hauling the trolley, not saying a word.

"And you're after to pick up where she left off?" he asks

when I finally stop talking. "Finish her business?"

"I know how to do the *Kinikatos*. I know when to go in. I can do it."

He considers my words. Beads of sweat are trickling down his neck, soaking his shirt.

"Let me haul it for a while," I say.

"One more click," he replies. "Then you can take over. Or we can get them two to push for a bit. I've noticed you favouring one leg. Hurt your knee in your travels?"

"My hip," I reply. "But it's fine."

He nods again. We walk, and he pulls, and we walk, and he pulls, and finally, after a long silence, as if he's been pondering something, Eccles takes a deep breath and speaks.

"You and your kin have endured more than I can reckon. At the mine, we've had our own heaps of sorrow and hardship over the past sixty years—what with the world ending and all—but nothing like what you say the Headmasters have done to you. Your people," he says solemnly as if he's choosing his words with great care, "have suffered great and unrelenting subjugation." He glances over his shoulder at me. I meet his eyes, wondering where this is going.

"So I'm fair sorry," he continues, looking ahead again, "if this question treads upon your heartstrings." He takes another dozen steps in silence, then asks, "But what anguish will you carry into that mindful desert place when them Headmasters start their chin-waggin'?"

Just like when Jenna asked me, the memory of Thorn and Lark standing on the edge of the bridge, bound together, and then—gone—instantly flares in my mind. But a moment later, I suddenly understand—no, I *feel*—what Eccles is getting at: the depthless grief, the white-hot rage—the soul-twisting anguish—it isn't in my heart anymore. Thorn and Lark aren't dead. I can turn around and see them right there, fifteen steps behind me.

In its place, I feel something more complex, something with more colours: yes, I'm devastated that Thorn doesn't remember loving me—but I'm overjoyed he's alive. Maybe, over time— years, perhaps—he can even learn to love me again. And isn't it a blessing that Lark has forgotten her years of being a Breeder, the despair that drew her to the Thankfuls? That she has a new start? And Papa and River—imagine their faces when they see Lark walking toward them. And everyone else at Blue Ring when they learn that other people are out there, living and thriving at a mine. And if there are people at the mine, how many other pockets of humans might there be around the world?

And all this, I now realize, is why I might not succeed when I enter the Headmasters' collective mind. The anguish I felt— the anguish I was preparing to turn against them—is muddled, confounded, if not pretty much gone.

What anguish will I carry into that desert place where the Headmasters meet?

"I don't know," is my reply to Eccles.

The sun is high in the sky when Eccles lets the trolley roll to a stop so we can all sit down for a break with a bit of food and water. The track has more or less followed the river. Sometimes, we get glimpses of it through the bush, but even when it's obscured, we can usually hear its lively babble and taste its fresh scent in the cool air.

We snug close to the trolley, trying to get out of the chilly wind. Eccles passes around a flask of water and chunks of a whitish thing he calls hardtack, which he assures me is edible.

"How much farther?" Lark asks wearily. "I'm getting tired of all this walking."

"I reckon another day or two. You told me, luv," he says, looking at me, "that you'd been walkin' upstream for five days when we found you."

"When I found you," I correct him. "I spotted your footprints."

"Point taken," he replies. "Now, you weren't in the best of shape, and you were walking alongside the creek, which is slow going. So, I'm figuring you didn't make more than four clicks a day when you were trekkin' back to Blurring. Tallied up, that's twenty clicks or thereabouts. Six more this morning makes thirty. You told me, too, you clung onto that log coming downstream from early morning till midday."

"Where the sun is now is about where it was at then," I say. I'm beginning to wonder if Eccles' odd way of speaking is rubbing off on me.

Eccles nods. "Then, taking the speed of the creek into account, I don't cipher you travelled more than forty clicks on that log."

"So, ten more clicks to go," Thorn says. It's odd to hear him saying a word he's learned from Eccles. "That's not too far."

"Thereabouts," Eccles says. "It might be twice that, mate. Them's just shaggy estimates."

"Still," I say, gazing down the track to where the two rails converge in the distance, "just another day or two." My stomach tightens. Eccles sees me put my piece of hardtack back into the bag.

"Let's pitch camp here," he abruptly announces. "We made good travellin' today. We'll start out again first light tomorrow."

Thorn and Lark hesitate. Now, they want to keep going.

"And after we've set up," Eccles says to them, "I'll get my harp out."

Their faces light up, and they jump to their feet and start to unpack the trolley.

CHAPTER 60
HARP

"That's not a harp," I say.

"By golly, it is, too!" Eccles exclaims.

We've finished setting up camp under the broad canopy of a nearby walnut tree. Eccles and I are leaning against its rough trunk, watching Thorn and Lark as they roam along the edge of the bush, gathering more firewood.

"I know what a harp is," I insist. "Zara has a memory of one from her father's funeral. It's as tall as me and curved and has about a hundred wires and a beautiful woman with hair piled up on her head is playing it. It doesn't look like that little thing in your hand."

"Well," he replies, "this little thing in my hand is also called a harp. But you can call it a harmonica if you'd rather, till you get better acquainted with it." He grins at me. "Actually, I was gonna bring my other harp—along with a beautiful lady with hair piled up on her head—but they wouldn't fit on the trolley."

"How am I supposed to know that?" I say, feeling my face redden slightly. "Zara doesn't have any memories of that kind of harp—a harmonica. Or if she did, they haven't come to me yet."

"Try it out," he says, putting it into my hand. "Blow into it."

I hold it to my lips and get ready to exhale.

"Other side," Eccles says. "Give it a flip."

I turn it and gently blow into the silver box. It makes a sound like a squeaky door hinge but sweeter.

"Now blow while you slide it across your lips." I do, and the sound rises gradually from a mourning dove to a chickadee.

"Again, but suck the air in this time."

The mourning dove and chickadee once more, but they're a little sad.

"That's all there is to it," he says. "The rest is practice."

"It must be old," I say to him.

"It belonged to my gramps. I've had to swap out the reeds a few times, but it still plays true."

"Is he alive?" I ask.

Eccles shakes his head. "No, neither of my gramps, and neither of my grans. None of the other old dears either—the ones underground when the world went to hell in a handbasket —they've all passed on."

"They were gold miners? The old dears?" The mines in the books that Thorn and I had read were usually gold mines. Sometimes diamond.

"Some were miners," he smiles, "but not for gold. Nickel and copper. But the story is, some were down there for a different reason: to unravel what everything is made of. They called themselves astrophists. They built this machine to make little squibs—too small to see with your eyes—and made 'em smash into each other to see what knit 'em. Astrophists from all over were down in the mine the day the world changed—they'd come here on aeroships to learn about the squib machine. Ever heard of Australia?"

I nod. "It's on the bottom of the map."

"My gramps hailed from there, and a few of the others, too.

Some folk from Britannia, some from a city called Houston in Texas. Or a city called Texas in Houston. I never remember which way is which. Some from a faraway place called Joanna's Bird. Anyway, they were supposed to go down, learn about the squib machine, and come back up. But the Big Out happened while they were still deep under."

"Maybe that's why you talk the way you do," I say to him.

"I don't fathom what you're after," he says.

"I mean, a lot of the words you say—I've never heard them before. And the way you say them. It's different."

"I thought Lark and Thorn talked funny when I found them—and you too—but I wasn't gonna say anything. I reckoned you just didn't know any better."

"What I mean is that maybe your—your old dears had different ways of talking because they came from all those different places."

Eccles considers this as he turns the harmonica this way and that in his hand. "Well, there might be some sand in what you say. When I was a gaffer, I remember some of the old dears —especially the ones that come from Joanna's Bird—telling me they had trouble fathoming the mining folk who came from the rock."

"What rock?"

"Dunno."

We fall silent as I ponder the fact that other people were living and eating and sleeping and having babies and growing older and dying at the same time that all those things were happening at Blue Ring. *O brave new world* is what Zara would have said.

"They never left the mine? Your people?" I finally ask.

"They tried, a couple years past the Big Out. They sent a crew back to the city, ninety clicks far, to see what was what.

Four of six came back. But they weren't never the same. Changed by what they'd seen."

"What do you mean?"

Eccles pauses. The smile that so often plays around his lips flickers away.

"They said they found lots of townies. Mostly dead, but some alive. Said the ones alive were damaged. Not their bodies. Their noggins. They'd talk, but it was like their words had come undone from their things and then settled onto other things. Like *hand* now meant *under*, and *under* now meant *running*—but it was different for everybody. Nobody could fathom anybody else.

"My gramps was one of the crew that went. Said all hell was busting loose there. People fightin' and smashin' things and burnt up buildings everywhere. Said a woman ran up to them in a street, all smirched in blood. Had a little gaffer in her arms and kept pushing it to my gramps and cryin', 'Wagons rumble jumper from! Wagons rumble jumper from!' When my gramps took the babe, she scuttered off."

"What did your gramps do with the baby?"

"One of his crew cautioned they should leave it there. Scared it might have a blight that was makin' them all turn like that. But, of course, Gramps couldn't do that. So he brought it back with 'em to the mine. Brought her back, I mean. The little gaffer. Gramps called her Leida."

"It wasn't a disease," I say, guessing that's what he meant by *blight*. "It was an accident at Blue Ring. Where I'm from. Something went wrong with a big machine."

Eccles nods. "That's what the astrophists at the mine reckoned. Said it was a pulse from a big ring. Couldn't hold the flare —went haywire. I don't fathom what it means." His sombre look gives way to a smile. "Anyway, I don't hold it against you."

He pauses. I sense he's deciding if he should tell me more.

"My gramp's crew lost two of their mates on that trek," he finally says. "One of 'em got brained by a brick one of the crazed townies threw. I don't recollect what happened to the other. But they brought back to the mine someone else, too. The sweetheart of one of the crew. They found her just before her man got brained by the brick."

"Was she okay?"

"She was gabbling like the rest of 'em—like a thing most brutish, my gramps said. But once they got her settled back to the mine, they coaxed her language back. Took years. Gramps said it was like she had to unlearn all her words before taking to them again. He ever after grieved they didn't fetch more folks back to the mine. To save them. But they barely got back themselves."

"And they never went there again? To the city?"

"Years later, they tried again. And other crews trekked to other cities. But they all came back with the same tale. The cities were ruins, and the few folks still alive were more like beasts of the field than humans. Ever after that, we've stayed put near the mine."

He puts the harp to his lips and brings it to life with a gentle breath.

"Anyway," he says, nodding toward the edge of the forest, "back comes Thorn and Lark. They don't need to hear about any of this long-ago sorrow." I turn and see the two of them approaching, their arms filled with dried-out sticks and branches. Lark drops to one knee and carefully stacks hers to the side. Thorn tosses his down with a clatter.

"Gentle there, mate," Eccles says to him. Then he hands Lark the harp. "Now, sit down, the two of you, so Lark can show her sist—show our friend what she can do with it."

They sit cross-legged, side by side, and Lark puts the harp to her mouth. She closes her eyes, and a moment later, music—

strange and mournful, yet strangely familiar—begins to pour out of the instrument. After a few more moments, Eccles begins to softly sing words with the song. Then Thorn does, too, their voices wrapping around one another.

> From this valley they say you are leaving
> We shall miss your bright eyes and sweet smile
> For you take with you all of the sunshine
> That has brightened our pathway awhile.

Lark stops playing and opens her eyes. She smiles when Eccles tells her she's a natural and hands the instrument back to him.

"Now, your turn, Thorn," he says. "Let's see if you can recollect what I've been learnin' you along the way."

Thorn nods, leans over to grab one of the smaller sticks they've gathered, and begins to scrape in the circle of dirt where we'll soon start a fire. "H," he says, "A . . . R . . . P."

And there it is in front of him: HAЯP.

CHAPTER 61
ALMOST BACK

We wake at dawn, eat, load the trolley, and start moving again. Before long, the terrain ahead of us steepens, and Eccles has the three of us get behind the trolley to push.

"If you slip, or it starts to roll back," he says to me, "hop on quick and shove this bar through that hole in the floor till it bites the ground."

"Then what?" I ask him.

"Then hope like blazes it stops."

We start off, Eccles pulling and the rest of us pushing, and no one saying anything. After a while, Eccles calls out, "Midway to the crest! Getting tuckered?"

I glance over at Thorn and Lark, both of them dripping with sweat and panting. I don't know how Lark is keeping up—during her years as a Breeder, she lost a lot of muscle. But the time she and Thorn spent with Eccles's people at the mine seems to have revitalized her.

"Should we stop?" I ask them. I'm hoping they'll say yes—my hip is throbbing. But both shake their heads.

"We're okay," I shout up to Eccles. "Keep going." And so we do, pushing and pulling, gasping and straining, until Eccles finally announces we're almost at the crest.

"Maple!" he calls out. I wince as he says my name and glance over at Lark and Thorn, but they seem too exhausted to have noticed. "Hop on," he says, "and sink that bar in."

It's all I can do to jog ahead to the side of the trolley. I put my foot on a low metal step and twist myself over and in. I pick up the long metal bar lying beside the supplies and shove it down hard through the hole in the platform till it stabs the earth below. The trolley lurches to a sudden stop.

I look behind and see Lark and Thorn already lying on the ground, drenched with sweat and gasping. Eccles trudges around from the front, and then he and I do the same. The ground is cool and smells fresh and sweet.

"Good work, mates," he pants as we all stare at the grey sky above us. "I wasn't sure we'd make it."

"Then why didn't you tell us that?" I exclaim.

"Because then we wouldn't have made it," he says, turning his face toward me and grinning.

We rest for a long while, then pull out some dried meat and fruit. When we're done eating, Eccles leans over to me and whispers into my ear, telling me what he's about to do—and what he wants me to do. Then he addresses us all.

"You three bide here for a jiff while I go ahead." Thorn and Lark look puzzled but nod. Then Eccles steps between the two rails and starts walking down the slope, his head lowered as he examines the track. He walks for a long time, as if his goal is to reach the place where the two rails seem to converge. Finally, we hear him yell and see him waving back at us.

"Thorn—Lark—climb on," I say. They're up in an instant and then grab my arms to help pull me on. Following Eccles's whispered instructions, I wiggle the bar out of the ground and draw it up out of the hole in the trolley floor.

Nothing happens. Thorn and Lark both frown. Then

slowly—very slowly—the trolley starts to nudge forward, then begins to roll in earnest—"Hang on!" I shout—then picks up speed until we're flying down the track, and the landscape around us is flashing by in a blur. Thorn and Lark are laughing, their eyes wide with wonder, their hair streaming wildly in the wind.

Then, bit by bit, as the slope eases back to level ground, we begin to slow down. We can see Eccles up ahead, getting bigger as we approach him. By the time we reach him, we're almost at a stop.

We hop off, grinning at one another, and look back to the distant crest we rolled from.

"I didn't think anything could go so fast," I say to Eccles, grabbing him by the arm to steady myself.

But before Eccles can reply, Thorn yells—"Look! That's our wind tower up ahead! I recognize it!"

We're almost back.

CHAPTER 62
I LOVE YOU, MAPLE SYRUP

I seize Thorn by the arm to hold him back. I'm half-afraid he'll start running toward the bridge, and Lark, too, overcome with excitement. But neither of them do.

Instead, Thorn seems suddenly anxious and says, "Should we push the trolley back so nobody sees it? And cover it with branches?"

"Good thinking, mate," Eccles says, "but hold up for half a sec." He turns to me. "If I reckon rightly, the first thing you're after is to find your Papa."

I nod. "I want to be the one to tell him about Lark and Thorn. And I want him to know that tomorrow I'm going to enter the Headmasters' collective mind and—and that if I fail, I won't see him again."

"So you'll wait till the—what do you call it—the slackenin' to go see him?"

I shake my head. "No. If anyone saw me during the slackening, the Headmasters would realize I'm back as soon as it ended. And then they'd be ready for me. And, in fact, I'd probably be in danger even before the slackening ended. Someone there—her name's Ivy—wants me dead."

"She's roary-eyed at you, is she?" Eccles asks. "You cross her somehow?"

"Not exactly," I reply. "Anyway, I'm going to wait till the darkening—that's what happens after the slackening. Papa's Headmaster is like mine—it doesn't control him—so I'll be able to find him in his cubicle and talk to him."

"And then you'll do that *Kinikatos* trick after you parley with him?"

I shake my head again. "No, I'll come back here to you three and wait till tomorrow. I want to get into their collective mind exactly like I did before. First, I'll go into my own Headmaster's mind during the slackening. Then, I'll wait till the other Headmasters emerge during the darkening."

"And then you'll drop the kibosh on them," Eccles says. He's smiling, but I can tell he's concerned.

"Ummm . . . I think so," I say, as I wonder what a kibosh is. Even Zara doesn't seem to know that one.

The four of us then line up shoulder to shoulder in front of the trolley and push it back far enough that no one at Blue Ring can possibly spot it. It's not likely anyone will ramble out this way during the slackening, but we take Thorn's suggestion anyway and cover it with some branches we strip off the nearby cedars.

It's barely midday, but we set up camp to keep busy. Eccles would usually send Thorn and Lark to gather some wood, but we won't be having a fire this evening, so we settle down to rest. We're all too anxious to stay still, though, so Thorn and Eccles get up and walk back to the track, where Thorn uses a chalky stone to practice making letters on the shiny black surface of the rail.

Lark and I find a grassy patch where we lie flat on our backs. I watch the clouds scud by and listen as she blows softly into Eccles's harp. After a while, she stops playing and turns her face toward me, studying me.

"Are you really Maple?" she abruptly asks.

I turn my face to meet her eyes, but I'm silent, unsure how to answer. Finally, I say, "I'm not the Maple you remember, but I am Maple. I really am your sister."

She considers this. "Have I forgotten things?" she asks.

"Yes," I reply. "Some things. Thorn has, too."

"And I'm older than I think, aren't I?"

I nod.

"I thought so," she says. "My breasts are bigger. And I get tired faster." She pauses. "How did it happen?"

I sigh. "That's a long story. Almost as long as Virgil's. You remember Virgil?"

She nods. "He's the poop collector. Can we get them back? Our memories? Will you help me and Thorn?"

"I'll always help you, and you'll always help me. But I don't think you can get those memories back. But you're still you. You still have the same—the same under-mind. You can make new memories to put on top of it. Brand new, fresh ones."

"Fresh as a baby's butt," she says, grinning. "I've heard Eccles say that." She reaches over and takes my hand in hers. Before long, she's fallen asleep.

I lie there, trying to imprint the shape of her hand on my memory, the hand I haven't held for so many years.

I must have fallen asleep, too, because when I open my eyes, the sun has dropped low in the west. Lark is up and arranging a handful of flowers she's gathered. Thorn and Eccles are leaning against a couple of packs we carried from the trolley. They both notice I'm awake.

"How will you know when the slackening starts, Maple?" Thorn asks.

He used my name. I must look surprised because Eccles interjects. "I told them about your plan to go see Papa tonight. And I reckon Lark told Thorn about the talk you had with her earlier on."

I pause, taking in this moment. It feels so good to be known by them again. To be known by my name. Almost as good as when I first saw them by the tracks and realized they were alive. It makes me feel stronger. More whole. More ready.

"I'll just know," I reply. "But I'll wait extra-long to make sure. When I see Papa tonight, he's going to be so glad when I tell him that you and Lark are both okay."

Thorn nods, and we all fall silent.

"It's time," I say. Eccles is the only one who hears this. Lark and Thorn have dozed off.

"You're sure it's safe?" Eccles asks.

"Nobody at Blue Ring will be moving till morning. Except my Papa."

"Mind how you wake him," Eccles says. "You don't want him to keel over from the wonder of beholding you." I can tell he's joking, but I'm actually worried about that.

"See you in a few hours," I tell him. He steps forward with his arms wide as if he's going to hug me, then hesitates and shakes my hand instead. I turn and head toward the track. I reach it quickly and start walking between the rails toward Blue Ring. The moon is high and nearly full, the rails glinting in its pale white light.

Before long, I'm at the bridge. I stop for a moment and think of the hundreds of times I've sat here with Papa or Thorn or River, hanging our legs over the edge and watching the water pass below. And I think of the last time I was here—when Thorn and Lark disappeared into the river. I give my head a shake and keep moving.

I start across the compound, but I don't head to the Cube. Not yet. Instead, I make my way to the Deep, then feel my way around it to the back corner. I slip past the jammed door easily —I've lost so much weight since my escape. I reach into the cavity in the wall and take out the light cylinder. I don't turn it on yet. I want to save its light. I head back toward the Cube.

I tug the door open and start climbing the stairs to the third floor, where Papa's cubicle is. I move quietly, like a fox, even though there's no real need to do so. It feels like the walls are listening.

When I reach Papa's door, I pause to take a deep breath. Then I knock lightly, thinking it's the best way to wake him gently. I immediately hear steps—uneven—and the door opens. He stares at me for a moment as if he doesn't recognize me. Then, the walking stick in his hand clatters to the floor, and he throws his arms around me and squeezes me without saying a word.

"Papa!" I whisper into his shoulder as I hug him back. He keeps holding me and holding me. Finally, I say, "Papa, let's sit down. I've got a lot to tell you." He reluctantly releases me, and we sit on the edge of his cot, side by side. His face is still luminous with joy and disbelief.

"Lark is alive, too, Papa. And Thorn. Both of them."

He blinks twice, then nods, but still doesn't say anything, as if my words are in another language.

"And they're free of their Headmasters."

He nods again, more slowly. I'm not sure if he's actually taking all this in.

"But their memories—the memories they formed after they

got their Headmasters—those are gone. It's like they're children again."

His face darkens with bewilderment and concern.

"But they're happy, Papa. And I think over time they'll be able to—to grow up again. They're already learning new things." I stop talking. Now he's staring straight ahead. This is a lot for him to process all at once. As I wait, I glance around his cubicle. My gaze stops on his table—it's stacked high with books I recognize from the vault.

Finally, he leans forward, takes one of these books, and opens it to the front page. He begins to write on it with a short piece of pencil. At the bottom, below his moving hand, I can see printed

London
SECKER & WARBURG

He stops scribbling and then hands me the book.

Maple, I can't talk. Had a stroke, Jenna thinks. Twelve days ago. Left leg drags, too. But everything else still works.

"What!" I cry out. "Will it come back? Your words?" My heart is pounding. I want to hear his voice again.

He takes the book, writes again, and hands it back.

I still have words—they're in this pencil, waiting to get out. Jenna has lots more of them sharpened and stashed away for me. And River brought me these books from the vault to write on. I might even read some of them! Don't worry about me.

He takes the book back and writes.

Where are Lark and Thorn?

Then, for the next couple of hours, I tell him in detail everything that's happened. I try to anticipate his questions so he doesn't have to write them down. He's astonished to learn about Eccles and the people in the mine. But he frowns with concern when I tell him my plan to enter the Headmasters' collective mind tomorrow night.

Finally, I think I've told him everything. But before I leave him, there's one thing I need to find out. "Papa, what happened to Silex?"

He pulls the book toward him but stares at the page for a long while before starting to write. Then he turns it toward me so I can see.

They made us kill him. I'm sorry, Maple.

I shut my eyes, but the words are already emblazoned in my mind. Papa puts his arm around me as I begin to weep.

"How could they do that?" I sob. "None of the kids are old enough to be harvested." Papa gently squeezes me and rocks me back and forth. I want to stay here, held in his arms, but after a few moments, I force myself to straighten up and stop crying. I don't have time to be sad. Before long, I'll have to head back to Eccles and Thorn and Lark.

"Papa, I'm going to stop at the Aery to see Lark's kids. Then I'm going to head out before the darkening ends." I wrap my arms around him and murmur, "I'm going to see you tomorrow, Papa, after it's all over. I promise. I'm going to be fine. I love you."

He reaches again to the book on the table and writes.

I love you, Maple syrup.

I stand up and wipe the tears from my eyes. I pick up his walking stick from the floor and bring it to him. I'm about to step to the door when he holds up his hand. Then, he writes one more thing in his book.

After you see the kids, can you come back for one more goodbye?

I smile and nod. "Of course, Papa."

Then I'm through the door and hurrying down the stairs to the Aery.

CHAPTER 63
THIS GIFT OF GRIEF

By the time I reach the Aery, the moon has dipped low, almost touching the tops of the pines, its light angling through the open windows of the kids' sleeping room. I pause in the doorway for a moment, gazing at them as they slumber, listening to them breathe—Birch and Prairie, Fox and Lynx—then I quietly step into their room.

Their cots are arranged in a rectangle, one against each wall. I make my way around, leaning over each child in turn, softly pressing my lips against their warm foreheads, and whispering, "I love you." As I pull back from Birch, he doesn't wake but stretches slightly, then rolls onto his side. "Maple," I hear him murmur.

At that moment, I want more than anything to stay with them, to fall asleep beside their uncompromised warm bodies, but I can't. Without looking back, I turn and walk through the hallway to the front door and down the three crumbling steps. The night is passing quickly. I start to cross the compound but then stop in my tracks and stare: to the north, shimmers of light—white, pink, green, blue—are rippling across the sky. They flicker and pulse, stretching out like fingers, then falling back like water as if they take joy in their wild reeling.

These are the northern lights. Papa has told me about them, but, of course, I've never seen them—the darkening always comes too early.

I gaze at them in wonder for a few more moments. I'll tell Papa I saw them. Then, tomorrow, after I've beaten the Headmasters, he and I will stay up late and together, we'll watch them shimmer from the roof of the Deep.

I start again toward the Cube, then once more climb the stairs to Papa's floor. I'm halfway down the hallway when I see it: a white rectangle pinned to his door. Even in the gloom, I know what it is. A page torn from a book. I walk slowly toward it and pull it off. I turn on the light cylinder.

Maple, Silex isn't dead. I told you that because you said you need your heart brimming with anguish to beat the Headmasters. But I don't want the last thing I tell you to be a lie.

Take this truth instead: I'm more proud of you than words can say. I know Zara would feel the same.

Tell River and Lark—and Thorn—that I love them. And all the kids, too—Birch and Prairie and Fox and Lynx. I hope this gift of grief is what you need. I love you always, Papa.

Still not comprehending, I tap lightly on his door. "Papa?" I whisper. But, of course, there is no answer.

I push the door open. There he is, beside his cot, on the floor, on his side.

Staring up at me.

The worst part isn't that he's dead, his body slumped sideways on the cold floor. It's that his eyes are still open, rolling side to side. It's that his mouth is a wide O, his swollen tongue silently twitching back and forth, his fingers curling into fists, then straightening into a mindless blessing.

I watch as the Headmaster begins to stir beneath Papa's

shirt. It braces its lower legs against the middle of his back and starts to pull away from his skin. I hear it slowly peeling off as the suckers on its scaly abdomen release their grip with a slurping sound—like pulling your foot out of a wet bog. Then it begins to tug on the two sinewy coils burrowed into the base of his skull. They slide out sluggishly, slick and glistening. It retracts them into its shell, then wriggles itself out from beneath Papa's shirt and slips to the floor. It scuttles beneath his cot, waiting.

My body clenches with anguish, even though I understand that Papa has given me what I need to defeat the Headmasters. His gift of grief has made it possible.

Trembling, I step into the room, kneel beside him, and put my hand on his shoulder. Then, I gently roll him onto his back. I lay my fingers on his eyelids to draw them closed. I lift his head and slip his pillow underneath to stop his mouth from gaping. I stoop to pick up the walking stick that lies beside him —the one he used just a few minutes ago to pry at his Headmaster, to impel it to release its neurotoxin. The last thing he touched.

I sit on the edge of his bed, holding the stick, thinking about Papa, how he came to me after I was harvested, how he carried me to Jenna when I hurt my leg, how he drizzled sweet sap onto Zara's handful of snow, how he sat beside me and talked and listened so many times in so many places.

Papa.

Jacob.

CHAPTER 64
THE HAWTHORN BUSH

My thoughts are interrupted by noises echoing in the hallway: cots creaking, chairs getting shoved aside, coughing and grunting, cursing and groaning. The darkening has ended. I've stayed too long.

I jump to my feet to push Papa's door closed, then press myself against it, my heart pounding against its cold surface. What should I do? Hide until tonight's darkening, then sneak away? But Eccles will come looking for me if I don't get back to them soon. Run now and try to go unnoticed in the morning commotion? I barely escaped last time.

No, my only option is to wait till everyone's in the Meal House, then try to slip away while they're occupied with their biscuit.

It doesn't take long for the Cube to empty out and fall silent. I pick up Papa's walking stick, then open his door and turn to look at him one last time. "Thank you, Papa," I whisper.

Then I'm racing for the stairwell, running down it as fast as I can, two steps at a time. I push through the main door, then slide to a stop—which way should I go? If I skirt around the

Meal House, it'll take longer. Running straight across the compound is faster, but for a brief moment, I'll be in the line of sight from the open door of the Meal House.

I decide to cross the compound—it's still fairly dark out, and it's unlikely anyone will see me in the gloom. The rising wind will muffle the sound of my footsteps. I start off, but soon remember that "running straight" isn't really an option. The surface of the compound is littered with potholes and fragments of broken concrete heaved out of place by sixty years of heat and frost. I try to weave around these hazards, but they're hard to see in the dim light of dawn.

Suddenly, my foot comes down hard on a loose chunk, and a jag of pain shoots through my hip. I tumble to the ground, twisting my left ankle as I fall, barely a stone's throw from the Meal House. From within, I hear the low murmur of weary voices, dishes clattering onto trays, spoons clacking in dishes. I lie there for a few moments, panting, taking stock of the scrapes and bruises on my elbows and knees. Nothing too serious, but my ankle sings with pain when I put weight on it, even with the support of Papa's walking stick.

The first rays of the sun are beginning to slip over the tree-tops and onto the compound. I have to get past the Meal House and back into the shadows. I tuck my legs into a crouch, grit my teeth, and push myself to my feet with the walking stick. I'm up, wobbling on the rubble beneath me, but I'm up. Tears of pain well in my eyes as I start hobbling, leaning on the stick and shifting my weight to my left heel instead of the ball of my foot.

I stumble a dozen more steps until I'm past the doorway of the Meal House, safely out of the line of sight of anyone inside. But I'm not going to get past the gate before the others start streaming out to their various toils.

Change of plan: get to the big rock near the side of the Meal House and crouch behind it until everyone's left for their toil. Once there, I can take off one of my foot wrappings and bind it around my injured ankle to stabilize it.

I make myself take ten steps toward the rock. Then, ten more. Then another ten—I'm halfway. Suddenly, the rubble clatters behind me—someone's running at me! I twist my hips and swing the walking stick with both hands.

It connects solidly with Eccles's head.

"Ow!" he says—he somehow manages to whisper instead of yell—"That's my noggin, cub!" The momentum of my swing has me off balance, but before I can fall, he scoops me into his arms, one arm under my knees and the other under my shoulders.

"That big rock," I gasp, gesturing to it with a nod of my head. With a few big strides, he has me there. He lays me down behind it, then crouches low beside me.

"Lark and Thorn are still at the camp," he whispers. "I told them to hunker down till I get back."

"Everyone's in there," I tell him, pointing at the Meal House, "but they'll start coming out any second."

"And if they see us, their Headmasters will make 'em collar us?"

I nod and reach down to unwind the wrapping from my uninjured foot to bind around the ankle of the other. The effort makes me wince.

"Let me, cub," he says. He finishes unwinding the strip and then wraps it tightly around my ankle. "These'll help, too." He pulls off his boots and starts putting them on my feet.

"Don't," he says as I begin to protest. "Right now, you need these a sight more than I do. And if you stink them up," he grins as he ties their cords, "we'll just torch them on the barbie."

I hear benches starting to scrape the floor in the Meal House. They'll be heading out in a few moments.

"You can't outrun 'em," Eccles tells me, "not with your

ankle like this. But I reckon I can, even barefoot. So, I'm after getting their attention and leading them on a goose chase. Is there a place you can hide yourself till their head barnacles fall asleep?"

I think for a moment, but not about where I can hide. I'm thinking about what the Headmasters will do to Eccles if they catch him. Kill him? Or keep him and make him a host? There's a Headmaster available right now in Papa's cubicle. Maybe it's no longer impotent.

Eccles's voice pulls me back. "Where can you get to, cub?" he asks again.

"The hawthorn bushes," I reply. "I can hide in them."

Eccles looks puzzled at my choice but nods. "Which way?"

"That way," I reply, pointing to the east, where the sun is now well above the tree line.

"Then I'll go this way," Eccles says, and with a wink, he's off, sprinting toward the Meal House, deftly darting around upthrust chunks of concrete and other hazards on the compound. When he reaches the open entrance of the building, he stops to peer in for a moment, then shouts, "Oi! What a stink! You should skin those muskrats before you cook them!"

The Meal House falls utterly quiet. I imagine everyone turning to the door and staring at Eccles, their eyes taking him in, their brains processing his existence, their Headmasters becoming aware, their awareness leading to action—suddenly, I hear every bench in the building scrape across the floor as the Headmasters impel their hosts to push away from the tables and rise to their feet.

Eccles must take that as his cue because I hear him start to scramble away, followed a moment later by a storm of feet pounding across the floor of the Meal House, through the door, and onto the compound. I stay behind the rock, unseen, and listen to them race after him in wordless pursuit. All of them must be completely bewildered—who is this man, this *stranger*, where did he come from?—but their confusion, for now, is pushed aside by a single, collective impulse from the Headmasters: *get him.*

The commotion of the chase grows more distant, then becomes a faint clamour, as they reach the edge of the compound, where the loam-covered bedrock leading to the forest begins. I wait a bit longer to make sure that even the slow ones will be gone, then poke my head out for a look. No one in sight. But how long till the Headmasters give up on chasing him and turn them all back?

I stand up and try putting some weight on my ankle. It's not bad—the nylar wrap, along with Eccles's boots, provides good support. I look around but can't see Papa's walking stick—it flew out of my hands after it bounced off Eccles' skull. I could really use it, but rather than spend time searching for it, I start to limp slowly toward the east gate. I reach it fairly quickly, pause to catch my breath, then turn north and follow the familiar trail that leads to the hawthorn bushes.

Halfway there, I realize how thirsty I am—I haven't had anything to drink since I left the camp last night. In the shade, some of the long blades of grass are bent with quivering droplets of morning dew—I stop to lick them, but it doesn't help much.

I press on till I reach the thick, thorny hawthorn bushes. Silex and Rose and Twilight must have been picking here recently because the bushes are almost bare of hawberries—or maybe it was blackbirds trying to plump up before starting their long flight south.

I limp around to the other side, then get onto my stomach to crawl into a small clearing in the centre of a big bush. Sometimes, Thorn and I would come here when we wanted to be alone—somewhere no one would stumble upon us. I stay low as I squeeze in, but some of the thorns still catch the back of my arms and legs. Once I'm in, I sit up and wipe away the spots of blood from the small punctures and scratches. I glean a few ripe berries from the vines and pop them into my mouth.

Then I wait. Judging from the sun's angle, it's still only early morning. The slackening is a long way off. I sit with my arms wrapped around my knees and try not to think about Papa—not yet. I need to save that.

Instead, I let myself worry about Lark and Thorn. I'm pretty sure the camp is too far away for any of my pursuers to happen upon them. But what if the two of them decide to leave the camp and follow the rails back into Blue Ring? Eccles told them to stay put till he gets back. But what if Eccles doesn't get back to them?

But he will. I know he will. If anyone can elude the others, it's him—he doesn't know the terrain around Blue Ring, but he knows how to cover rough ground. He's like a—what were they called in one of the books Thorn and I read?—like a scout. Like Daniel Boone.

he was brave   he was fearless
and as tough as a mighty oak tree

As the sun climbs higher in the sky, a rising wind begins to gust through the bushes. I pick and eat a few more hawberries to moisten my mouth and throat. I promise myself that after tonight—after I paralyze the Headmasters—I'm going to drink the biggest jug of water I can find.

My butt is starting to get sore, so I stretch out on my side. I close my eyes and instantly see Papa on the floor of his cubicle, his eyes rolling back and forth. I open them again and choose one plump hawthorn berry to stare at. I keep my eyes focused on it as it bobs up and down in the growing wind.

Through the rustle of the swaying bushes, I listen for the thud of distant footsteps, the crack of breaking branches, possibly even voices—anything that will tell me that others are approaching. I focus on that.

CHAPTER 65
THE WIND TOWER

Suddenly, I become aware of Lark calling me. "Maple! Maple, where are you?"

I open my eyes—I must have fallen asleep—and call back. "Lark! Over here! I'm in the—" Wait. Did I really hear her voice, or was I dreaming?

I hold my breath and listen. Nothing. I breathe out—and then I hear it—the crackle and swish of someone stepping over dry leaves. "Lark," I call out again, "Wait there—I'll come to you!"

I throw myself back onto my stomach and crawl out of the bush, ignoring the thorns that again pierce my skin. As soon as I'm clear, I jump up and run around the bush—

—and straight into the arms of Ivy.

"Here we are," she says with a grim smile as the three others with her—Knot, Twig, and Raven—mechanically step around to encircle me. Unlike Ivy, I can tell they take no joy in what they're being made to do—they look haggard, not just physically but emotionally exhausted, their eyes dull and their jaws slack from trying to resist their Headmasters all day.

Maybe it's Eccles's boots, but Ivy doesn't seem as tall as before. But she's still an imposing figure, especially covered with dirt and scrapes from scrabbling through the forest. Then again, I probably look the same.

"Give me water," I say evenly, staring at her coldly, hoping to get her talking. Her eyes widen—surprised, no doubt, by my brash demand.

"That would be a waste," she replies, "considering what's about to happen." She gives a quick nod to Knot behind me. I sense him hesitate, then hear him step closer. Suddenly, I feel his hot, rough hands around my throat. They start to squeeze.

"Sorry, Maple," I hear him whisper. "I can't help it."

"Lark is alive," I rasp, "I'll take you to her. She's not far."

Ivy's eyes widen. She gives a quick nod, and Knot releases his grasp on my throat. Ivy's brow furrows. "You must think I'm as stupid as Knot. And are you such a coward that you'll exploit your sister's memory to eke out a few more moments of life?" She shakes her head in contempt, but I can tell I've unnerved her.

"Look at my feet," I reply. She frowns, then glances down. "Those are boots," I continue. "I got them from a man who pulled Lark out of the river. He's not from Blue Ring, and he's about to take her away."

Ivy's frown suddenly turns into a scowl of confusion. She raises her eyes to mine again, trying to read my expression, waiting for her Headmaster to tell her what to do. Am I telling the truth?

"So, if you want to know where she is, give me water," I say.

After a long pause, she nods at Knot. He takes the flask from his hip, unscrews its lid, and hands it to me. I take a deep drink, almost draining its contents. Ivy thrusts out her hand to take the flask. I tip it back and slowly gulp down the rest.

"Thanks, Knot," I tell him.

"Welcome, Maple," he replies, looking at me sadly. He hands me the lid, and I begin to casually screw it on. Under the dirt and smudges of blood, I can see Ivy's face growing rigid with rage.

I hold out the flask and take half a step forward, offering it to Knot. But as he reaches for it, I pivot on my good leg and slam it upward against the side of Ivy's head, right where her ear once was. It glances off—I should have swung it down instead of up—but it at least dazes her, and she stumbles to the side with a shriek of pain, creating an opening in their circle. I dart through it.

If I'm lucky, I tell myself as I run, their Headmasters won't send them after me until Ivy regains her bearings. That'll give me a bit of a head start, but not much. They've been looking for me all day—they'll be tired. My ankle is injured, but Eccles's boots are better for running over jagged rocks. Still, it won't take them long to catch up to me.

I glance up at the sun, well on its way to setting. Was I asleep that long? It can't be long till the slackening.

I keep running—more like a fast hobble—not daring to look behind me, loping over jutting rocks and weaving around tall pine trees, swaying in what has become a fierce gale.

Wait, I think. *The trees. What if I climb one? Even if they spot me, I might be able to keep them from getting up to me.*

I skid to a halt beside the first tree with branches low enough for me to grab. I begin to pull myself up, then stop as I remember: Knot is a Filcher. In the spring and summer, all he does every day is climb trees, stealing eggs from nests. There's no way I can outclimb him if his Headmaster is forcing him.

Shit! I only say it in my head, so it doesn't count.

I drop to the ground and start to run again. I still can't hear them behind me. Maybe I did more damage to Ivy than I thought. My injured foot comes down on a round stone that rolls away beneath me, making my ankle bend awkwardly. A stab of pain shoots through it. I can't keep running for much longer. Where to?

Then I remember. Just over that ridge is the wind tower. Does its door have a working lock? I can't recall. But there's no other option.

I veer to the left and start to clamber up the ridge. It's steep and tough going, but I know going down the other side with a throbbing ankle will be even harder.

When I reach the crest, I stop to catch my breath. From here, I can see the top of the wind tower peeking over the tree line. I turn and begin to make my way down the ridge sideways. Again, I miss Papa's walking stick, left back at the compound: it would come in handy here. I'm almost at the bottom of the ridge when I hear something—the ragged sound of feet scrabbling over rocks. I look behind me and see them off to the left, just coming over the crest—all four of them, Ivy in the lead.

I let myself half-slide, half-roll to the bottom of the ridge, then pick myself up. The tower—it's right there, no more than a hundred paces away over level ground. I lunge forward and start to run lopsidedly, making myself swallow the pain that sears through my ankle.

this pain is mine I claim it as my own
this pain is mine to do with as I wish

A few more steps, and I'm at the base of it, heaving open the metal door and ducking inside. I pull it shut.

No lock. I glance around, looking for something, anything, to fasten it closed. The floor is covered in ankle-deep wood shavings. Some pieces of braided steel cable are strewn around, but nothing long enough to secure the door handle.

No choice again. I have to go up.

I put my foot on the ladder and begin to climb, but the rusted rung snaps in two, and I tumble to the ground, gashing my arm on a jagged edge. I get back on my feet and eye the next rung. It looks more sturdy. I lift my good foot and step onto it gingerly. It holds, and I start climbing, expecting with every step for something to collapse under my weight.

I make my way up twenty or so rungs, then pause and listen. Still no sound of Ivy and the others. I tip my head back and gaze up the shaft, which stretches into darkness. Far above, I can see a small rectangle of light—the sole window atop the tower's gear cabin. It's dizzyingly far away. *Forty Maples from the bottom of the tower to the top*—that's what Thorn once calculated and told me a long time ago. And each blade another fifteen Maples. All in all, fifty-five Maples stacked end to end.

I was in the wind tower once before. Papa took me inside a few moon cycles after I was harvested just to show me where we got the invisible current that kept us warm. With its blades spinning, the entire structure hummed with energy—like having your head in a giant hornet's nest. I remember putting my hands on its curving walls and feeling the deep swoops of the giant blades.

But now, of course, the blades are nearly motionless, even with a strong wind blowing outside. After Knot smashed the tip off one of them, the Keeper angled them so the wind would slip effortlessly around them. It's eerily silent. So when Ivy and the others finally approach, I can hear the crunch of each footstep on the gravel around the tower.

I hold my breath and press myself against the ladder—if they don't hear me, maybe they won't enter.

But they do. The door crashes open, and a pool of light fills the bottom of the tower. They look around, then up, squinting.

I hold still, hoping the shaft is too dim for them to see me up here.

"Two eyes glimmering in the darkness," Ivy says loudly as she stares straight up. She adds in a mocking voice, "Probably just an owl. But I better go up and check."

She moves toward the ladder, then hesitates. She kneels and picks up an arm's-length piece of cable from the floor—long enough to swing like a whip. She drapes it around her neck, then begins to climb.

The others stay put—their Headmasters probably sense the rusted ladder might be too frail to support their combined weight. Instinctively, I begin to head further up. If I can just keep out of her reach until the grip ends—which must be soon —then maybe I can reason with her.

But probably not. As Eccles said, she's mighty roary-eyed at me.

My climbing is slower than hers. I can't push off my injured ankle, so it's my other leg that's doing most of the work. After another sixty rungs, I reach the first switchback platform— about a third of the way up—and step onto it. I pause to look down at Ivy. She's climbing steadily. Maybe I should stay on this platform—if she tries to pull herself onto it, I could kick at her head or step on her fingers.

But I know I couldn't really bring myself to do that. It's one thing to hit somebody in the head with a water flask as you're about to be strangled. It's another thing to make them fall to their death. Even if they hate you.

I take a deep breath and begin climbing the next section of the ladder. To take my mind off the burning pain that's creeping into the thigh muscles of my good leg, I start counting rungs. *Seventy-eight, seventy-nine, eighty, eighty-one, eighty-two, eighty-three . . .*

I have to stop—my leg is cramping, and my eyes sting from

the sweat dribbling into them. I look down and see Ivy still climbing. She's slowed, but not by much. She pauses when she notices that the cable she looped around her neck has slipped to one side and is about to slide off. She grabs it, puts it between her teeth, and clamps down.

Suddenly, someone at the bottom of the ladder calls out.

It's Knot. The grip has ended.

CHAPTER 66
THE LADDER

"Maple, I'm sorry for what I done." Knot's voice echoes against the walls of the tower.

Then Twig cries out, "Ivy, stop now! Leave her be!"

But Ivy keeps climbing.

"Ivy," Twig shouts, "if you don't turn back right now, the Thankfuls will never spend another slackening in peace. River and I will make sure of that!"

Ivy hesitates. I hear murmuring from the bottom of the tower but can't make out the words.

"And Knot and Raven say they'll help us! Knot says every slackening, he'll pour his slop jar on the floor where the Thankfuls sit."

More murmuring from the bottom.

"And poison oak leaves—Raven says she'll burn buckets of them on the fourth floor. Lots of others will help us, too! Do you want to take us all on?"

Ivy stops thirty rungs below me. In the dim light, I can still see rage in her eyes, but alarm now, too. Twig and Knot's threats have rattled her. She takes the cable out of her clenched jaw and shouts down, "Maple needs punishment! Lark is dead because of her and her man."

"Lark's not dead!" I yell. "Neither is Thorn."

"She killed her Headmaster!" Ivy continues. "And she's going to teach the others how!"

There's a long pause. Then Twig shouts, "If she can really do that, how about if she does it for whoever wants that and leaves you and the other Thankfuls alone?"

Ivy doesn't reply, doesn't move. She's stiff with fury.

"Start climbing down, Ivy," Twig yells, "or we'll come up after you."

"I think I'll send Maple down instead," Ivy snarls. "But don't blink, or you'll miss her." She lifts her foot to the next rung.

"Ivy, wait!" I shout. "Just listen for a minute!"

She tips her head back and turns steely eyes toward me.

"Ivy, do the Headmasters appreciate your thankfulness? Your loyalty? Do they love you? Do they know your name? Eventually, they're going to terminate you, just like everyone else. And when that happens, will they grieve for you?"

Ivy continues to stare at me, unblinking. Finally, after what seems like a very long moment, she replies, "Would you?"

And with that, she begins to climb again. So do I. I reach the second switchback platform and begin scrambling up the third and last section of the ladder, the section that reaches the gear cabin. That's where I'll have to make my stand.

Ten rungs, I tell myself. I can do ten rungs. Then, when I reach that goal, I start over. Ten rungs. Then, ten more rungs. Then, ten more. I close my eyes—I don't need to see the rungs to grab them. Ten more. Ten more. Ten more. My hand stretches for the next rung but seizes only air. I open my eyes— I've reached the platform of the gear cabin. No more rungs to climb.

I haul myself up and roll onto the platform, breathing hard, then turn to look down the ladder. As I do, Ivy's hand appears on the last rung—then, half a moment later, the top of her head emerges. Where I bashed her with the water bottle, I can see a deepening purple bruise beginning to mingle with the angry red lesion of her ear wound.

I freeze. What should I do? My eyes dart frantically around the cabin. All over the floor: more wood shavings.

Against the wall farthest from the platform's edge: the Keeper's cot.

Beside the cot: a wide grey panel dotted with switches and circles of glass.

In the middle of the platform, under the roof window: a chair and table.

On the table: a carved replica of Blue Ring—it must be the one the Keeper showed Knot when he climbed up to hammer on the blade. But I can tell at a glance, even from where I'm standing, it's not just the buildings around the Blue Ring compound. The carving is far more extensive and intricate, replicating the Shield around Blue Ring, the river, the trees, the rocks, the ridges, the bogs, the meadows, the coil, the wind tower itself—everything the Keeper has seen or remembered.

And finally, under the table: the Keeper, crouching, her arms clasped around her knees, her long grey hair fringing her face, her eyes staring at me in terror.

I nod at her and turn to Ivy, who's now pulling herself up onto the platform. I run to the table, grab the chair, and haul it toward the edge where Ivy is clambering up. I push it at her, aiming to drive her back down the ladder, but she seizes one of its legs and tries to wrench it from me, pulling me off balance and almost making me topple off the edge of the platform.

We continue this tug-a-war, fighting over the chair, fighting with the chair, till finally, she yanks it out of my sweating hands, and it goes sailing backward over her head. It seems to take a long time to fall, a couple of heartbeats before I hear it crash into the floor below—hopefully not onto Twig or Raven or Knot.

In one fluid motion, Ivy pulls herself up over the edge of the platform and jumps to her feet. How can she still have so much energy? She takes the cable from between her clenched teeth and dangles it from her right fist like a dead snake. She's breathing heavily.

"Is Lark alive?" she gasps. "Tell me the truth, and I'll let you live—as long as you leave the Headmasters alone and leave Blue Ring for good." She pauses and wipes dust and sweat from her eyes.

I know she's lying. I know she'll never let me live. I need time to catch my breath. Time to keep Lark and Thorn safe from her. So, I decide to make something up. A story.

I lower my head to appear defeated. "Okay," I say dully. "I'll tell you the truth. They survived falling into the river. Thorn slipped out of the rope you tied around them. But he kept it around Lark's waist and held onto it so they wouldn't get separated. He said they almost drowned. Twice. When they got swept around a bend in the river, he lunged for a rock close to the shore and held on to it. Then he tied the rope to Lark's hand and got to another rock and pulled her to it. He kept doing this—going from rock to rock—till they finally reached the shore. Then they started walking farther downriver."

"So they escaped, but they left you behind," Ivy sneers. "Both of them—your man and your sister both left you behind."

"They had to," I sob. It was a very good sob. "They knew they had to get away from here." I wipe away some tears—actually, beads of sweat—as I desperately try to think of what to tell her next.

"They walked for five days and kept themselves alive by

eating minnows and snails. But they were getting weaker. Thorn couldn't seem to shake out the water he'd got into his chest. That's when the man found them—the stranger who everyone was chasing this morning. He found them and gave them food, but then, when they were sleeping, he killed them both by biting their throats. He's crazy. Like a wild man. He told me all this after he sneaked up on me beside the river and tied me up. But I got away. He's been chasing me ever since. He followed me all the way to Blue Ring. He's still trying to kill me."

My hope is that Ivy won't go looking for Lark and Thorn if she believes they're dead.

Ivy scowls. "Oh? Then why did this man give you those boots?" she says, pointing at my feet. Oh, right. The boots.

"He didn't. He was washing himself in the river when I got myself untied. I took his boots to slow him down. I was going to throw them into the river but then thought they might fit me. So I've been wearing them ever since."

I can't tell if Ivy is believing any of this, but I rush ahead with my tale anyway.

"He had the two Headmasters with him. The ones from Thorn and Lark. He had them in a cage with a squirrel and a raven. He said he'd found them by the river. The Headmasters, I mean."

"The two Headmasters?" Ivy says eagerly. "He has them?"

I nod. "He showed them to me. And he said he was going to pull mine off my back and add it to his collection."

"He had both of them?"

I nod again. She slowly stalks toward me. *She wants to look me in the eyes,* I tell myself, *to see if I'm telling the truth.* I stay where I am, leaning against the turbine's ancient panel of dials and switches, trying to look sincere as she bends so close I can smell the salt of her sweat. Suddenly, she throws her arm back and whips the cable at me. I lunge to the right—it misses me but smashes into the panel. I dodge past her before she can strike again and run to the far end of the platform.

"You lie," she seethes, shaking her head and turning toward me. "You lie. One of the Headmasters crawled back to the compound two days after you escaped. They'll soon be coupling it to a new host. Maybe to Lark's oldest. His little back is still narrow, but he'll grow into it."

As she's saying this, a low-pitched, metallic groan—no, more like a whir, like something sliding into place—begins to resonate through the cabin. Then it stops, followed by a deep metallic click, like something locking. A moment later, a shadow sweeps across the floor of the gear cabin, then another. I glance up through the window: the blades of the turbine have begun to spin.

Ivy ignores this as she slowly sidles toward me, menacing, trying to hem me in against a wall. As she approaches, she spies a knife on the Keeper's table and grabs it. She moves closer, cable in one hand, knife in the other, but as she approaches, I notice for the first time that she seems slightly off balance. With each step, she drifts slightly to the right. Suddenly, I feint left, making her step in that direction. Then I dart forward and to the right, passing under her arm. She spins and slashes downward with the knife, slicing my shoulder, the tip grazing bone.

I race back to the other side of the cabin, pressing myself again against the panel. She runs at me again, and this time, I make a wide arc around her, coming precariously close to the edge of the platform. She swings with the cable but misses. As she pauses to get her bearings, I become aware of a growing tremor—I can feel it in my feet. A whining thrum has begun to reverberate in the cabin. The turbine's blades are picking up speed.

And the cabin is beginning to tremble.

"Ivy," I shout through the growing whine. "When you hit that panel, you engaged the blades. They're not balanced—not since Knot damaged one of them—they're going to shake to pieces!"

Ivy stops mid-step and stares at me.

"You can't survive the winters without the turbine," I yell. "And without us, what will the Headmasters do? Couple themselves to muskrats?" I'm not even sure she hears the last thing I yell, but she turns and is about to race back to the panel when she finally notices the Keeper huddling under the table.

"Keeper!" she shouts. "Stop the blades!" But the Keeper doesn't move, petrified with fear. Ivy takes two steps toward her, seizes the table, and sends it spinning toward the edge of the platform. "Keeper!" she shouts again, but the Keeper's eyes are locked on the table as it slides through the wood shavings, reaches the edge, and slowly starts to tip as one of its four legs slips from solid platform to empty space.

"Keeper, stop the blades," Ivy shouts again, but now the Keeper is on her feet and hobbling toward the tilting table. She reaches it just as the hundreds of tiny carvings on its surface begin to slide off and rain down the shaft. A moment later, the table tumbles over the edge, and then the Keeper herself begins to plummet, her arms outstretched as they grasp for the miniature, falling world she created.

Ivy watches the Keeper vanish, then turns and sprints to the panel. Saving the turbine is more urgent than putting the kibosh on me. While she stares at the panel of dials and switches, trying to figure out what her cable hit, I limp to the ladder and start climbing down. If I get a big enough lead, maybe I can reach the bottom before she does. Then Twig and Knot and Raven can help me. Because if she catches up to me on the ladder, I know she'll stomp on my fingers till I fall.

But that's not my only concern. As I descend, the whine of

the blades increases. The tower is beginning to shudder. The blades aren't disengaging. I need to get out of here.

I climb down faster and faster, getting reckless, barely grabbing one rung before I let go of the other. The ladder is shaking so hard my feet are almost slipping off the rungs. I reach the next platform as a new, ear-splitting screech engulfs me, the wail of metal slowly riving out of place. It seems to go on and on—then a silence—then a dull and rumbling crash.

Terrified, I look down. The bottom section of the ladder has sheared away and now leans crookedly against the inside wall of the tower, much too far for me to reach.

So much for getting out of here.

CHAPTER 67
THE CATWALK

All around me, the shaft begins to fill with billowing clouds of dust, decades of accumulated crud and grime shaken loose from the walls of the tower. After a few moments, I can't even see the ladder in front of me.

It's getting hard to breathe. I pull my shirt up over my nose, but it doesn't help much. I'm coughing uncontrollably but force myself to keep climbing down. Finally, I feel my foot make contact with the lowest switchback platform. I have to stop here. There's no more ladder for me to climb down the rest of the way.

As I slump heavily onto the platform, it occurs to me that I'm going to suffocate. I'm not going to defeat the Headmasters. Because of dust. Little squibs of dust.

Around me, the tower rumbles and strains.

I stop coughing. My lungs stop aching and straining for air. I'm not sure if my eyes are open or shut. If they're open, they're so coated with grime I can't close them. I'm starting to feel light-headed, almost giddy. This isn't so bad. I think I'll lie down.

But before I can lean back, I see, in the swirling clouds in front of me, a shadow approaching from across the platform. Did Twig climb up to help me? Or is it Ivy, here to kill me before the dust does?

Neither—it's Farley, padding jauntily toward me. And what's weird is, there's not a speck of dust on him—it's like there's a halo of clean air all around him. But then it strikes me: if a dead dog can suddenly materialize on a ladder in a tower that's about to collapse into a pile of rubble, he might as well be dust-repellent.

Farley saunters up and presses his nose against mine. Then he turns around and looks at me over his shoulder. He wants me to follow. Sure, why not? He's guided me before. Or maybe he'll lead me right off the edge of the platform, and that will be that.

As he trots ahead, the dust seems to disperse in his wake. I follow him, crawling on my hands and knees over the metal grill of the platform through the swirling passage of clarity he's creating.

As I inch my way forward in the near-darkness, I notice a rectangle of light emerging in front of us. Its glowing edges grow more distinct as I get closer, still crawling after Farley. Now I'm right in front of it, reaching out, touching it. It's cool and smooth, like polished metal.

It's a utility door to the outside of the tower.

I slide my palm over its trembling surface, looking for a latch. My hand bangs against it. I grab it and yank it up, but it won't budge.

Again, harder. It still won't move. It must be rusted shut. *Nice idea, Farley, but it's no good.*

Then, one last try, but this time, I push down on the latch. It moves easily, the door opens a crack—and then a fierce wind catches its edge, and it flies open, crashing into the outside of the tower. Beyond the door, there's a narrow catwalk. I throw myself onto it and take deep, gasping breaths.

I peel my eyes open. It's evening, but the light of dusk is still bright compared to the gloom in the tower. My eyeballs feel like they've been pelted with gravel. I turn around to find Farley, but the oxygen is coursing back into my brain, and I realize he was never really there. At least, not in the ordinary sense.

The catwalk runs around the entire tower, just below the attachment points of three thick cables that run diagonally from the midpoint of the tower to the ground, where they're secured to huge concrete footings. The tips of the turbine's blades sweep over the cables, but not by much.

The cables. *Grab onto one of them and climb down, hand over hand*, is what my brain doesn't tell me to do. *You were a Picker for ten years—you've got arms of iron,* it also doesn't say. My brain doesn't tell me these things because it can feel the burning ache in my biceps, my triceps, my deltoids and rhomboids. They're already spent from climbing the ladder. I couldn't get a quarter of the way down the cable before my arms would give out. And a fall of twenty Maples isn't much better than a fall of forty Maples. In fact, it might be worse: I might survive for a while as a crumpled sack of broken bones before I leaked to death.

What my brain does tell me is this: *Thorn could figure this out.*

So I can, too.

I close my eyes and think. And think. And think. And an idea begins to emerge.

I sit up and start undoing the boot strings that Eccles tied to keep them tight. But it's not the boots I want. It's the strips of nylar—the strip around my right foot and the one around my left ankle. It hurts to unwind it, but it's also a relief to feel the wind blow across the skin where it was bound so tightly.

Each strip is longer than I am tall. I take the end of one strip and tie it to the end of the other—not easy when the wind is making them billow like sails. Then, I do the same thing with the other two ends. Then I fold it all in half. Now I've got a band of nylar made of four parallel strips. I'm trusting it will support my weight.

The cable above me is just within reach. I pass the end of my nylar band over the cable once and then once more. I pull it tight so the nylar snugs around the cable. Then, I tie the ends of the band together so it hangs below the cable like a sling.

Above the roar of the wind, I hear a metallic ping. I feel a sharp, burning pain on my shoulder blade. I twist around, expecting to find Ivy, but she's not there. Instead, I see the catwalk beginning to pull away from the tower. The rivets that attach it to the outer wall spark and whip through the air as they shear in two.

I don't wait to get hit by another one. I jam my feet back into Eccles' boots, grab the cable, and pull myself up. Then I pass my legs and hips through the nylar sling I've made. I lower myself till it snugs under my armpits. I take one step forward to the very edge of the swaying catwalk.

And then I take one more—into empty space.

CHAPTER 68
THE CATCH

For a moment, as the sling stretches taut, I feel like I'm falling. But it holds. The wind buffets me, threatening to spin me around like a pile of dry leaves, but I stabilize myself by reaching up and grabbing the cable with both hands. Now, to see if my plan works.

I pull myself up toward the cable. The top of the sling loosens around it and slips forward an arm's length. I let my weight sink back onto the sling, and it tightens again around the cable. Then, I let myself swing forward until the top of the sling is once again above me. Pull myself up, swing forward, repeat.

This will work. I'll be able to reach the ground.

As long as I have enough time.

I keep moving down the cable bit by bit, pretending there's no raging wind, no howling of frenzied turbine blades, no cold rain beginning to pelt down, no flashes of lightning around me. I want to twist around and look back at the tower, but I don't—that won't help. I just focus on moving forward and down. I've got myself into a good rhythm, and my nylar sling is holding up well—only a bit of fraying where it wraps around the cable. I glance down, wondering when it will be safe to let go and fall the rest of the way if I have to. I'm still well above the tops of the highest pines—

—then suddenly, I'm upside down, tumbling in the air, above the cable instead of below it, my hands grabbing desperately at nothing—the band of the sling bites hard into my armpits, and then I'm back under the cable, jouncing around like a walnut on a string. As I spin helplessly in the sling, I catch a glimpse of the tower—it's pitching slightly to one side, the blades now whirling at a tilt. Something in the foundation must have given way, making the cable I'm hanging from suddenly go limp, then pull taut, turning my sling into a slingshot. I'm lucky I'm still in it instead of cartwheeling through the sky.

I manage to stop spinning by throwing my legs up and around the cable, one on either side. Then I lower them again so the sling unwinds slowly. It doesn't take long for everything to get straightened out. I take a big breath and get ready to resume my descent. But wait: the nylar strips around the cable are fraying—no, worse than fraying. They're coming apart like wet leaves. The wild spinning pulled them too tight, stretched the fibres, and broke their weave. They won't keep supporting my weight. I'm going to have to strong-arm it the rest of the way down.

I grab the cable and slip one arm out of the sling and then the other. Then, leaving behind the band of nylar to flail in the wind, I start to clamber down, hand over hand, left, right, left, right, my feet dangling over the rocks and trees below. It's agonizing, the strain on my arms and shoulders: left, right, a slow burn that grows deeper every time I grapple from one arm to the next. If the cable were horizontal, I could fold myself over it at the waist, drooping like a wet rag, and give my arms a rest. But I can't do that on a cable that angles down.

Left, right.

My palms and fingers are beginning to blister.

Right. Left. Right. Left. Right. Left.

The blisters are tearing open. I can feel the water from them trickle down my wrists. No more right, no more left. No more left. I can't do it. *Papa, I can't do it.*

I get ready to let go. I glance straight down: it's still a long way, and there's solid bedrock below me. Should I try to land on my feet? Does it matter? I don't want Lark and Thorn to see the mess I'm going to make.

"I've got you, cub!" is what I hear as my fingers loosen their grip, and I begin to fall. It's Eccles, of course—who else would call me cub—shouting up to me from down below. He's going to catch me! I'm going to crush him!

Except neither of those things happen. I get caught, all right, but when I open my eyes, Eccles is off to the side, sitting on his butt. The arms around me belong to Silex.

"Sorry for shoving you, friend," Silex gasps to Eccles, "but I didn't think you had enough meat on your bones to catch her."

Eccles is picking himself up and brushing sticky pine needles from his hands and trousers. "No worries, mate," he replies to Silex. "You made the right call."

Still holding me in his arms, Silex extends a big hand to Eccles.

"I'm Silex," he says as if meeting a stranger is something he does every day.

"Griffin Eccleston," he replies, shaking hands, "but mates call me Eccles."

"Eccles it is," says Silex.

Courtesies out of the way, they finally turn their attention to me.

"You're a mess," Silex says to me.

"Your palms," Eccles adds, taking one of my hands in his. "They look like raccoon meat."

"I'll help her wash and dress them," says someone behind Silex. It's Rose. She steps around in front and helps Silex set me on my feet. Then she wraps her arms around me and gives me a long hug. "We've missed you, Maple," she murmurs into my ear.

Behind us, the wind tower groans and shudders.

"That thing's gonna tumble down like Jericho any second," Eccles says. "We should strike some distance between—" He stops in mid-sentence.

I follow his gaze to see what's captured his attention. It's Ivy, trying to muscle her way down the cable. She's not using a sling to help support her weight. I can't imagine she's going to make it.

"Who's that?" Eccles cries out, pointing.

"Ivy," I reply.

"The one who's roary-eyed at you?" he asks. "The one who wants you dead?"

As I'm about to reply, Silex starts lumbering toward the tower.

"What's he after?" Eccles says, incredulous.

"He's going to try to catch her," Rose says matter-of-factly.

"Why?" Eccles says. "She wants Maple dead!"

"Because that's who he is," Rose replies.

"She's too high," Eccles protests. "And too big. He's going to get himself killed!" He looks from Rose to me and back to Rose. We both shrug.

"It's who he is," Rose repeats.

Eccles frowns for a moment, then sighs. "Maybe the two of us—" He sprints after Silex.

The raw flesh on my hands is stinging, but I'm not really registering it as pain. Instead, it feels like a distant noise, like a swarm of bees inside a hive. Rose and I watch as Eccles quickly catches up to Silex, and then the two of them run side by side toward the tower. By now, Ivy has given up trying to climb down. She's dangling helplessly, knowing there's nothing she can do, probably more concerned about her Headmaster than herself.

"Hang on, Ivy," I hear Silex shout. "Hang on till we get under you!" As they near the tower, it becomes clear that what they're attempting is impossible. Ivy must be three times as high as I was when I dropped. Maybe if there were more of them, and if they had a sheet of nylar to stretch below her—but there aren't, and they don't.

I blink twice in confusion: Ivy has suddenly vanished. In her place is a pinkish mist, and even that's gone in another moment, dispersed by the howling wind. Eccles and Silex seem just as puzzled—they've stopped running and are staring up at where she was. It's Rose who gets them moving again. "Silex! The cable snapped—it's going to collapse! Run!"

Rose is right. The cable that ran from the concrete footing that's behind us up to the midpoint of the tower—the cable I was dangling from just a few heartbeats ago—is gone. Only a short segment of it is still attached to the footing. When it broke, it must have whipped over us—just missing our heads—and then coiled into Ivy with the force of—

a freight train

Yes, a freight train.

Even as Silex and Eccles begin to run back to us, the wind tower begins to heave and swell as if it's taking its last, huge, dying breath. Eccles can run much faster than Silex, but he stays with him, one hand on his back, pushing him forward.

The tower begins to sway, leaning one way then the other as if it can't decide, then finally pitches forward, weighed down by the blades that are still madly whirling. One blade and then another slam into the bedrock, sending up huge showers of sparks, chunks of sheared blade ricocheting off the rocks and back into the air, some of them sailing overhead and landing in the trees beyond the ridge.

Then the barrel of the tower, now almost level with the ground, falls in on itself, sending a huge cloud of dust and debris over Silex and Eccles and, a moment later, over Rose and me. We stand motionless, Rose's arm still around me, my eyes closed to the dust settling onto us, as the rumbling of the collapse comes to an end. I open my eyes and wait for the roaring wind to clear the air—and for Eccles and Silex to appear.

I hear them coughing first. Then they emerge like shadowy figures in a fog, arms around each other, helping one another stumble back to us. They're caked with sweat and dust and gasping for fresh air but, otherwise, don't seem to be injured.

"She's gone," Silex says to us, his voice hoarse. "Couldn't get to her in time. I didn't even see her Headmaster fall."

"The cable smashed the bug to smithereens?" Eccles suggests.

"I'd like to think so," Silex says, "but that would be a first."

"We need to get you fixed up," Rose says, turning to me, "and then we need to lose you."

"What do you mean, lose her?" Eccles asks. "By the way, I'm Eccles."

"Rose," she replies, extending her hand and eyeing him cautiously. "I mean that once the slackening ends, Silex and I can't know where Maple is. If we do, the Headmasters will make us turn against her. And against you."

Eccles considers this for a moment. "What if I hogtied you and Silex till the next slackenin'?"

Rose shakes her head. "Won't work. As soon as the darkening starts, the Headmasters will be able to communicate with one another. If Silex and I know where Maple is, then our Headmasters will know where she is, and then all the Headmasters will know where she is. Whether we're tied up or not. And they'll send everyone else after her."

"Right, then," he replies. "But what if you were out cold?"

"What does that mean?"

"I mean, if you were . . . unconscious. From—say—a well-placed conk on the head? Could they still fathom what you know?"

Rose gives him a hard stare. "Interesting idea," she says slowly, "but I think Silex and I would prefer it if you and Maple just find a place to hide."

"I'm not going to hide," I abruptly announce as I wipe away the dusty grime that's caked on my face. "I'm doing this my way. All I need is some time." I turn to Rose and Silex. "I'm going to paralyze the rest of the Headmasters, just like I did mine."

They look at me like I've just told them I'm going to raise the crumpled wind tower.

"She can do it," Eccles says. "She's got this thing where she casts herself into their minds. Then she'll slap them into next Tuesday like so many mosquitoes. She calls it—" he turns to me —"what do you call it again?"

"*Kinikatos*. But I need to start before the slackening ends. And I'll need to be left alone for the first couple of hours of the darkening."

"So you *will* need someplace to hide," Silex says, looking puzzled.

"No. Like I said, I'm not going to hide. I'm going to the bridge. In plain sight. But I'll need your help once I get there."

"Okay," Rose sighs, sensing there's no point arguing with me. "Let's fix up your hands and go to the bridge."

"No time," I tell her, shaking my head. "My hands will be

fine. Also, Silex and Rose—" I stop in mid-sentence, trying to decide whether I should tell them about Lark and Thorn. If something happens to me—if I don't survive the *Kinikatos*—I want Eccles to take them back to the mine. Probably best if Silex and Rose don't know they're alive—not yet. I don't want to risk having the Headmasters find out. "Never mind," I say.

"Let's get going," Silex says, beckoning us forward. "By the way," he says to Eccles, "where are you from?"

Eccles grins. "I'm from down under."

CHAPTER 69
DON'T LET ME HURT HER

We're making our way to the tracks—following them is the fastest way back to the bridge—when it starts to rain again. I hold my hands in front of me, palms up, and let the cool drops fall onto them, washing away the dust and dried, salty sweat. It feels good—it takes some of the sting out of my open blisters. But it better stop raining soon, or my plan will fizzle out.

"Knot and Twig were with Ivy in the wind tower," I say to Rose as we sprint along. "Raven, too. Do you know where they are?"

"Safe at the compound," Rose says. "They found me and Silex—they'd just run back from the wind tower and said you needed our help, that Ivy was trying to kill you."

"They're okay?"

"Pretty much," Silex replies. "A bunch of the Keeper's carvings came hailing down on them. Knot has a big lump on his forehead, and Twig got whacked on the shoulder, but they'll be fine. A table came tumbling down, too, but missed them, and so did—"

Rose pokes him in the side and he abruptly stops talking.

"The Keeper?"

Silex looks grim and nods. I knew, of course, that the Keeper couldn't have survived her fall. I'm glad that the rubble of her wind tower has become, in a way, her cairn. But I feel heavy-hearted, too, to realize that I never knew her name.

"How much slackening is left?" I ask. "I've lost track of time."

"About half, I'd say," Silex replies.

Eccles turns to me. "That enough for what you're after at the bridge?"

"I hope so," I tell him.

"We're going to set it on fire," I announce.

We're at the bridge. I've gathered them around me so I can explain my plan. Actually, though, there's not much more to explain. That's the extent of my plan. Setting it on fire.

"So, I'll be with Silex on the far side, and you'll be with Eccles on this side," Rose says.

"With the fire in between," Silex adds.

"That's right," I reply. "You and the others won't be able to get across. And the river's still too fast for wading."

"But—cub, it's been raining. All the wood hereabouts is drenched."

"Not all of it," I reply. "We've got plenty of dry wood—"

"In the Jimsons' shed!" Silex interrupts excitedly. "They keep it there for their steam catcher!"

I turn to Eccles. "You've got your kindling kit with you?"

"Never without it."

"Then all we have to do is haul a shitload of wood here," Silex says. "Sorry, Maple," he then adds, looking me sheepishly.

"Don't worry about it," I tell him. "Lately, I've been cursing a lot myself."

"We'll use the sledges," Rose says.

We start moving again, heading across the bridge and into the compound. It's strangely quiet—almost nobody is outside. Then again, it would be more strange if they were. Everyone spent the grip scouring the shield, up and down, back and forth, looking for Eccles—and they know their Headmasters might even send them out again when the slackening ends. They're in their cubicles, exhausted, trying to get some rest, and wondering about the stranger they saw.

The few people who are still out stop in their tracks when they see us.

"Sister!" It's River's voice. I turn and see him sprinting toward me. He picks me up and hugs me. "She told us you were back, but I didn't believe her. But you're here! Alive!"

Over my shoulder, River suddenly notices Eccles. I feel him grow rigid.

"You're the one they made us chase this morning—the stranger." River lets go of me and steps between me and Eccles.

"River," I say, stepping forward again, "this is Eccles. He's from . . . elsewhere." I'm purposely vague—I don't want to risk the Headmasters finding out where the mine is. "He's been helping me. He's a friend."

Eccles holds out his hand. River nods but keeps his distance.

"River," I then ask, "who said I was back?"

"Ivy. After we lost track of him—" he nods at Eccles—"the Headmasters sent us back to the compound around midday to start our toil. That's when one of the Thankfuls found Papa's walking stick in front of the Meal House. She showed it to Ivy. She said you must have come back with him," nodding again at Eccles, "and got the walking stick from Papa. So the Headmasters sent us right back out to look for you instead of him."

He breaks off. His face twists from relief to grief.

"And, Maple," he continues, his voice breaking. "Papa is dead."

"I know, River," I reply, taking his hand in mine. "I was at his cubicle this morning—I was with him. I saw him."

We fall silent. After a few moments, Eccles clears his throat and speaks.

"My regrets for intrudin', but I'm—um—I'm just thinkin' about that scheme of yours, Maple, and—um—the evening is pushing on . . ."

I let go of River's hand. "Does Jenna know about Papa?" I say to him.

"I don't think so," he murmurs.

"Can you go tell her? And tell her I'm back, too."

He nods.

"And tell her I'm going to have a cup of mint water with her tomorrow."

River looks uncertain but nods again. He glances warily at Eccles, then turns on his heels and heads toward the Cube.

"Hurry," I say to the others, and we start running toward the back of the Meal House, where the sledges are kept. Once there, we pull them over to the Jimsons' shed, where we pile them high with chunks of dry wood. Then, Silex and Rose begin hauling one sledge to the bridge and Eccles and I the other.

"But your hands, cub!" he protests.

"It's not going to make things worse," I tell him, wincing. "It's only pain."

this pain is mine

He shakes his head, but I lean into my harness and start to pull.

The light rain makes it hard to keep our footing as we drag

the sledges forward. It takes longer than I expect to get back to the bridge.

"No time to unload," Silex gasps as we come to a halt midway on the bridge. We position the sledges end-to-end so they span the entire width of the wooden platform.

"I can start a fire, cub," Eccles says, "but it'll take a good while to get the whole thing going. More time than we have, I reckon."

"That's why I brought these from the shed," Rose says, lifting one of three big containers from her sledge. "Pure Jimson firewater—it'll light up the wood in no time."

Eccles laughs. "Now you're talking! But set some aside for a drink after Maple finishes walloping your head barnacles!"

They each grab a container and pour it over the two piles of wood. Then Eccles reaches into his pack and pulls out his kindling kit. He kneels down and gets ready to strike a spark.

"Wait!" I cry out. "Not yet—Rose and Silex need to be on the other side."

"Right," Eccles replies. "I forgot—our friends will fast become our foes."

"I'm not going to hug you," I say to Silex and Rose, my voice breaking, "because I'm going to see you again in a few hours."

Rose gives me a long and loving look. Silex winks at me and smiles. Then they turn and clamber over the piles of wood on the sledges. Eccles waits till they're clear of the sledges, then kneels and strikes a spark near a stick he's drenched with alcohol. It bursts into flame. He steps back and throws it onto one of the sledges. In an instant, the whole thing is ablaze. A moment later, from the other side of the flames, I hear a screech of bending metal.

"Eccles," Silex calls out. "Heads up!"—then one of the iron struts from the side of the bridge comes flying over the fire. "If anyone tries to get through, give them a poke with that. Try not to kill them. But if you have to—"

"Then I have to," Eccles shouts back. "Even if it's you."

"Especially if it's me," Silex says. "Don't let me hurt her."

"I promise, mate." Then he turns to me. "Go," he says. "Go wallop them."

I turn and run into the forest.

CHAPTER 70
THE SONG LOVES THE ROBIN

I don't run far. I need to get into my own Headmaster's mind before the darkening begins, before they begin to merge into their collective mind, which might be any minute. I veer off the path and find a toppled oak tree. I sit down on the forest floor and lean against the tree, close my eyes and take a deep breath.

The horizon seems closer than before as if the yellowed sky is rushing down to meet the barren surface of the desert place. At my feet, the turtle spins, its two heads and four legs still tucked into its grey and mottled shell. I turn around, looking for Farley, but he's not here. All I see are his paw prints on the dusty clay. They trace a circle around the turtle and then trail away, vanishing into the distance. This time, it seems, I'm on my own.

I keep standing, waiting for the slackening to end, waiting for the darkening to begin, waiting for the other Headmasters to appear on the terrain around me. It takes me a moment to realize I'm no longer in pain. I look at my palms: the skin is unblistered. Neither my hip nor ankle are hurting. Something else is gone, too: the sound of the wind in the trees—branches creaking, leaves rustling. Here, it is silent, except for the powdery sound of a turtle's carapace turning on clay, like two dry palms rubbing together.

I begin to count my heartbeats.

At 687, I hear a rumbling. It grows louder as the clay surface around me begins to tremble. A moment later, mounds of stones erupt through the surface as if pushed up by angry, subterranean fists. Dust fills the air. Then it dissipates as the emerging mounds—more than two hundred, one for every member of Blue Ring—grind to a halt.

I'm puzzled. These aren't the vats of maggots I was expecting. They're more like the piles of stones that emerged when Zara went into their collective mind. But they aren't tall piles— they're low, oblong mounds, like the rocky cairns we build over bodies in the boneyard. The very moment I think that, the stones begin to tumble away like a stack of eggs that's been jostled. As the stones roll off, each mound reveals a person.

The same person.

Papa.

Everywhere I look, I see Papa lying on his side, just like when I found him dead in his cubicle. But there's a difference. It's hard to tell with the ones further away, but with the nearer ones, it's obvious: his eyes aren't mindlessly rolling back and forth. Instead, they're staring at me, and I know that if I move, the eyes will follow me. Nor is Papa's tongue lolling about in the open mouths. These Papas have no tongue. Instead, each mouth is filled with a single, long, wrist-thick maggot. I can see the individual segments of their pale, slick bodies, the mouth holes at the end of their eyeless heads.

Zara pulled the snakes from the stone piles. I hauled the turtle out of the maggot vat. But what am I supposed to do now? Pry the maggot from the mouth of every Papa? Or do I have to reach in further, past the maggots, into his belly, and claw out something hidden deep within?

I take a step forward, then another and another, every eye tracking me, until I'm standing over the nearest one—over Papa. This one, I somehow know, is River's. His Headmaster.

I can feel the anguish swelling in my heart, the potent grief that Papa gave me, and I know that if I only stoop and grapple with the slimy creature writhing in this Papa's mouth, pry it out or slide my arm past it, I can release River, free him from the bondage that's held him almost all his life.

But I can't. I can't bring myself to do it.

I know that what I'm seeing isn't real. It's just a projection created in the space where my mind overlaps with the collective mind of the Headmasters. And yet, in here—in this desert place—it *is* real. As real as spit. I can taste the grit of the desert clay on my teeth, hear the slurp of the wriggling maggots, smell their oily secretions. And I can feel Papa's pleading gaze below me and all around me, a hundred plus a hundred times over.

I can't do it. I'm not up to this task.

The Headmasters must sense my resignation, my silent admission of defeat, because, in a single motion, all of the Papas roll onto their knees and rise to their feet. Their heads cock slightly to the right, as if they're considering me, studying me. They don't come closer, not yet. Their maggot tongues swirl.

As they study me, three memories emerge in the same instant, overlapping:

sonjas birthday party   a man with a tall black hat pulls
an egg from his pocket   cracks it open
shows a smaller egg inside its speckled shell   cracks it open
a yellow bird flies out

walking down a path with silex and rose

i don't know them well yet
we pass a pond filled with spring runoff
and chunks of ice
silex asks how far can i throw this apple
i hurl and it lands on the still surface of the pond
disappears
ripples move out in circles   radiate   to the edge of the pond
nice throw he laughs

this one I don't know whose or when
squeezing someone's hand
letting it go
letting it fall
turning and walking away

As the memories pass through me, I understand: I don't need to take on the Headmasters one by one. I don't need to grapple with their obscene projections of Papa. That's only what they want me to think, to make my task appear too enormous and grotesque to accomplish.

As this realization dawns, the sky darkens into a deeper, mottled yellow. Scowls appear on the faces of the Papas that surround me, and they begin to walk toward me, tightening their circle. Instinctively, I drop to my knees and press my palms against the clay surface of this desert place. Then I begin to release the burden in my heart, the grief I feel over Papa's death. It was less than a day ago that I found him dead. He'll still be in his cubicle, cold and stiff. River no doubt lifted him onto his cot, but they wouldn't have yet had an opportunity to take his body to the boneyard, to build a cairn around him, a real one, not like the obscene simulacra that have erupted here, in the desert place.

Tears begin to roll down my cheeks as I stare at the clay

beneath me, tears of grief, of rage. Frustration. Fatigue. My tears. Zara's tears. I let this pain pour from my heart, down my arms, through my palms, and into the clay beneath me, letting it radiate outward in circles, ripple after ripple, to the edge of this dry and barren place.

I look up at the blurred figures edging toward me. They've slowed and look hesitant, but they're still approaching. In a moment, the nearest ones will be close enough to lay their hands on me. This isn't working. Something is muting my anguish, tempering it, making it less pure and forceful. Am I too tired? Are there too many of them? Have they learned how to shield themselves? Is something happening to me outside of the desert place, in the forest where I sat down to enter *Kinikatos*? Am I going to be killed like Zara?

What's happened to my pain? Isn't my heart broken?

Then, as the first of them lays my Papa's hands on my head, I remember the necklace that Zara gave to Jenna, and Jenna to me: the fragment of maple leaf held and protected by the golden amber, like a bird within its shell. For a moment, I see myself as that bit of leaf, held and protected by Papa since I was a child.

But then a different understanding emerges: that bit of leaf is my anguish. My anguish is enveloped by something far stronger: love. Yes, Papa is dead—but he gave his life to help me. Because he loved me. He's gone, but I can still feel the intensity of his love. For me.

And for River and Lark. And Zara.

And Thorn and Jenna.

And Virgil.

And all them for him, and for me, and for each other. I can feel the love of Silex, who saved me, and of Rose, who's always looked out for me. Of Halo, who raised me. The love of Knot, who said he was sorry for having to chase me. And my love for him. And for Farley. And Eccles, who helped Lark and Thorn, and then helped me, only because he wanted to. I can feel love suffusing everything. The Earth and the moon are locked in orbit by love. The soil loves the rain, and the rain the soil; the wind loves the trees; the song loves the robin; roses and red are in love.

I know this vision will be fleeting. Other concerns and thoughts will eventually crowd in, and I won't feel all this love so clearly, so intensely. But for now, it burns pure and furious. It doesn't negate my anguish, doesn't displace it. Instead, it transforms it, makes it bearable—turns it into something almost beautiful.

And then, I realize it's not anguish that's going to defeat the Headmasters.

It's love.

All around me and beneath me, the cold grey clay is turning to warm black earth. Particles of soil tumble out of the way as green blades of grass begin to struggle through the surface, pushing higher and higher till they stretch past my wrists. I lift my head and see that the forms that were Papa are melting away, like icicles in the sun. In their place, different figures are emerging—River, Silex, Rose, Twig, Twilight, Fern, Knot, Canker, Chokecherry, Lichen, Raven—everyone—each Headmaster manifesting its human host.

But not quite.

These people resemble the people I know but with differences. They look like drooping, haggard versions of themselves. River, with the entire left side of his face disfigured as if the scar of his severed ear has cankered around his cheek and eye. Rose, her face blotched and wrinkled. Silex, bald and stooping. Twig, her mouth sagging, her teeth yellow and crooked. Another figure—his head hunched over almost to his waist, his face grey and bloated like an old potato—it takes me a moment to recognize as Knot. They and all the others, all around me: it's like seeing their reflections in a sheet of warped copper.

a fun house   the house of mirrors

This isn't how they look, I tell myself. *This isn't how I see them.*

But then I realize it's how they see *themselves*. It's the images of themselves that the Headmasters have seeped up.

As I stare sadly at their misshapen forms, I wonder: were people always like this? Before the Arrival, did people see themselves as lesser than who they really are? Does Eccles? Do I? Maybe we envision ourselves this way only because of our Headmasters. Maybe decades of servitude, of the grip, of enforced toil, of harm and the fear of harm, of having to literally wear our oppressors on our backs, has distorted who we think we are, made us doubt our self-worth.

Or maybe that's just what it's like to be human.

They all have Headmasters still clinging to their backs, but I know—I can somehow feel—that they've now been neutralized. Zapped, as Eccles would put it. The head barnacles.

The figures stare back at me. They stand where they are, but they're not motionless. They blink. Aspen, as always, is chewing at a willow stick hanging from the side of his mouth. Twig's hand moves from her mouth to her hip—then back over her mouth. Rose crosses her arms as if she's waiting for me to do something.

I walk toward River, take his hand in mine. I don't expect him to say anything, and he doesn't. Here, he's only a projection, like a shadow cast by the full moon. I move behind him and lift his shirt. I study the Headmaster, something I've never done before, not this close. I lay my hand on its shell. It's dry and smooth, except for faint striations—like the whorls on the tip of your finger—that I feel as I sweep my palm over it. It's perfect, the way a cricket is perfect. Each part of it, each segment, artfully joined to other parts and other segments to form a cohesive whole.

Gently, I put my hands on either side of its shell and begin to pull. The Headmaster lifts easily from River's back, and then its coils begin to slide out from the base of his skull—there's no resistance—it's like drawing a rope from a pail of water.

River once told me that he had one memory of our mother before she died. It was late fall. They were at the river's edge. The water was icy and low and slow. She looked at him as he put a pebble on a curled scrap of birch bark, then put the bark upon the water and let it go, let it drift away. He asked her if the pebble would feel lost. She told him it was floating to a better place.

His only memory of her.

I stop pulling. The Headmaster settles back onto him. Its coils glide back into his skull.

It's time for me to leave. I start walking.

CHAPTER 71
CAN I GET THEM BOOTS BACK?

When I open my eyes, I see Silex and Knot looming over me, their outstretched arms spreading a broad sheet of nylar high overhead.

"She's back," Rose says, releasing a deep breath. I can feel the relief in her voice.

I'm lying on my side with someone's foot wrappings rolled up into a ball and tucked under my head. I push myself up onto one of my elbows. My head is spinning, and I feel a bit sick to my stomach.

"What's going on?" I ask groggily. "Silex—Knot—what are you doing?"

"They're shading you from the morning sun," Rose says, kneeling down beside me.

"I've spent most of my life in the sun," I reply. "It's not going to hurt me."

"I know," Rose says softly into my ear, "but it gave Silex something to do while we waited for you to wake up. It was either that or have him wear a rut in the rocks with his pacing back and forth. Knot wanted to help, too. Said he needed to make up for chasing you into the wind tower."

I look up at Silex again. He's still holding the strip of nylar and squinting as if the bright sunlight is making his eyes water. Knot is smiling down at me sheepishly. On the side of his head, there's a lump the size of a hen's egg from when he was hit by one of the Keeper's carved figures.

"Thank you, Silex," I say. "And thank you, Knot."

Silex glances down at me and shakes his head. "No," he says, his voice quaking. "We need to thank you." I start to ask him for what, and then I remember: the desert place, the figures, the radiant love. I beat them.

"You beat them!" Rose says, extending her hand and helping me to my feet. "You did it, Maple. Look—it's mid-morning, and we're not doing toil!"

"Of course she did!" It's Eccles. He's pushing his way through the cedars and coming toward us. "Sorry I wasn't here for your grand awakenin'," he says, nodding at me. "I had to see a man about a dog. But anyway, you snuffed those big head lice just like you said you would."

"They're not dead," I remind him, still holding on to Rose for balance. "I only paralyzed them. They're still attached to everyone."

"Tomato, Tamahto," he says. "The point is, you've set everyone free."

Free?

When I hear that word, I'm not sure I really believe him. The trees and clouds look the same. The blackbirds are singing their usual song. Can things really be different?

"Where is everyone, then?" I ask.

"Far side of the bridge, of course," says Eccles. "Silex and Rose—and that feller Knot—climbed what's left of the iron frame as soon as the fire died down. You'd zapped the head bugs by then. But we told everyone else to sit tight on the other side. No sense riskin' somebody tumblin' into the hot embers or the cold river."

Eccles then saunters over to Silex and reaches up to put his arm around his broad shoulders. It looks a bit ridiculous—Silex is so much taller that Eccles is almost hanging off him. "I had my hands full for a while, keeping them all at bay, especially this one." He pokes Silex playfully in the ribs. "Had to give him a few good whacks with the iron strut when he tried to squeeze past the fire to get you."

Silex leans forward—I can see raised welts on his head through his close-cropped hair. "The Headmasters' grip was very strong," Silex says, grinning but also looking embarrassed. "I couldn't resist."

"None of us could," Rose says, sidling up to the other side of Silex and looping her arm through his. She adds, "We should have Jenna look at your head."

"Why?" Silex says with another grin. "It's still attached."

I'm starting to feel better, but I won't for long if I don't get some food. It seems like days since I last ate. Even the thought of biscuit is appealing.

"Can we climb across the bridge now?" I ask. "I want to see River."

"Of course, Maple," Rose replies. Then, more sombrely, "And then we can take your Papa to the boneyard. And build him his cairn."

I nod silently and turn toward the bridge. Some of the remaining wooden ties are still smouldering.

"I'll catch up with you all in a bit," Eccles says. "I need to fetch Thorn and Lark from our camp."

Out of the corner of my eye, I see Rose and Silex freeze in mid-step. Of course: nobody's told them yet.

"Thorn and Lark!" Silex cries out. "Alive? Since when?"

"Since I found 'em down-creek a few weeks ago. That's

how I met Maple—they wanted to foot it back to you folks, so I helped 'em make the trek."

Silex whirls around, grabs Eccles, and lifts him into the air. "You found them! You brought them back!"

Eccles laughs. "Well, let me go get 'em, mate," Eccles says. "I know they'll be glad to see you."

Silex sets him down. Eccles turns to me. "Now, can I get them boots back?" he asks with a smile. "That is if you're done with 'em?"

CHAPTER 72
WILL I STILL BE ME?

I cross over the river with Rose and Silex and Knot by clambering along the outside of the bridge's scorched iron skeleton, moving from one vertical joist to the next. The iron is still hot, so we wrap our hands in strips of nylar torn from the sheet that shaded me from the sun. The wooden platform of the bridge is almost entirely gone, consumed by last night's flames. It doesn't bother me that it's a charred ruin. With Papa gone, its purpose seems lost as well.

Now, we're heading down the path through the trees toward the compound, Rose in front, Silex at the back, and me in between. As we get closer, I begin to hear a hubbub. It's the murmur of people excited, astonished, frightened, of people trying to figure out what's happened and whether it portends good or bad. We come around the last bend in the path, and I see them gathered in clusters of varying sizes, most of them standing but some sitting cross-legged on the broken concrete.

When they see us approaching, their chatter abruptly comes to an end. They stare at us in silence as we walk to the middle of the compound. We stop, and Silex calls out to the crowd, his voice loud and hearty.

"Come closer, everyone! Maple is back—she's back, and she'll explain what's happened."

It's eerie to see everyone gather around me. They're so much like—and yet so unlike—the versions of themselves I beheld in the desert place just a few hours ago in the Headmasters' collective mind. I scan the crowd for River, but I don't see him. Then, a moment later, I spot him with Twig coming out of the Aery. He's holding Lynx in his arms; she's got Fox, and Prairie and Birch are straggling along behind them.

Gradually, everyone stops talking. Now they're waiting, gazing at me, expecting something. *Where do I begin?* Then I notice Virgil standing near the front of the circle. He nods at me and gives me an encouraging smile.

"I'm going to tell you a story," I begin, my voice catching in my throat.

Someone at the back calls out, "We can't hear you."

"Sorry," I shout back. "I said, I'm going to tell you a story. Some of it you might already know. It's the story that started sixty years ago when there were billions of people in the world. Most of them lived in cities—in thousands of cities like the ones in Virgil's tale. Back then, they had machines for talking to each other over long distances, and they could travel through the air in flying ships and go wherever they wanted. They knew how to do so many things that we've forgotten.

"Then, something happened. Something terrible. Something that we caused—we humans. Almost everyone died. Not the people here at Blue Ring. But something almost as bad happened to us. The Headmasters arrived from somewhere. We don't know where or why. And they made us their hosts. Their slaves. For three generations.

"But that's over now. There's not going to be a fourth generation of hosts. Because I—I found a way to paralyze them. To neutralize them. That's why you're here right now instead of toiling."

"You found a way to do what?" someone cries out.

"To neutralize them. I made them go dormant. Forever."

"That's impossible," someone shouts. "They're probably just testing us. Pretending to be asleep."

"No," I say. "I made them dormant forever."

"What if they wake up?" Violet asks. "We'll all get punished."

"They won't wake up," I reply. "I promise. You won't have to do what they want ever again. You won't ever be in their grip."

A deep and brooding silence falls over the crowd as they take this in. Finally, Briar asks, "So does that mean we can talk about the past now? About people who've died? About things that have happened?"

I take a deep breath. Time to tell them about the choice they'll each have to make.

"No," I say. "We still can't talk about the past. At least, not yet. Your Headmasters are paralyzed, but the memories of their previous hosts are still in them—still connected to your minds. I think those memories could still be triggered. And hurt you."

Throughout the crowd, I see shoulders slump. Somehow, they sense that without a shared past—a past they can collectively remember and celebrate and mourn and turn into history—without that, they're not fully free from the Headmasters.

"But I can do one more thing," I add. Heads tilt upward, and they look at me expectantly. "I can make them actually detach from you. Physically detach. So you'd be fully free. But there's a cost—" I pause and meet River's gaze and think about his only memory of our mother: the pebble on the scrap of birch bark floating away on the river, floating to a better place. "There's a cost. If you decide to get rid of your Headmaster, you'll lose all the memories you made ever since it was first coupled to you. Since you were children."

Silence again, but of a different kind—stunned.

Finally, Acorn asks, "If I lose my memories, will I still be me?"

I pause for a moment to consider the question.

"In some ways, yes. You'll still have the same body. You'll still have the same brain—but it will be mostly empty. Like pouring out a cup of water. But over time, as you do new things, you can fill it up again with new memories. And maybe that will make you into a different person. But you'll still think of yourself as *me*. A new me."

Acorn continues to stare at me blankly. My explanation had too much Zara in it. I try again.

"Dip your hand into our river," I say, "and take it out. Then, dip it in again. You're not touching the same water that you touched a moment ago. But the river is still the river."

Acorn nods. I can see a glimmer of comprehension in his— and others'—eyes.

"And that new me," he says, "he'd be able to talk about his new memories. Because he wouldn't have a Headmaster. The new me could talk about the past—my new past. Right?"

I nod, but before I can say anything, someone else cries out, "I don't want to stay me!"

It's a scratchy, crow-like voice. It's Fern. I haven't heard her speak since she brought me clean clothes the day after I was harvested.

"I want to start over. I want to be rid of every memory from the past forty years. All those jolts. All that punishment. The memories of that brutal man who called himself my husband."

Many in the crowd nod and murmur in agreement.

"If you can get this thing off me," Stump growls, "then get it off. And when you do, I'm going stomp on it, and slice it into pieces, and burn it. I don't care what it costs me. I want it punished."

"But consider, Stump," Virgil says, "that if you have Maple remove your Headmaster, you won't remember that you want to punish it."

"I'll get someone to remind me," Stump bitterly replies.

"My wife —" Briar begins to say, then breaks off. I'm certain he was about to say her name but caught himself. "My wife— she was terminated four years ago. After her eyes went cloudy. If you detach my Headmaster, will I remember loving her?"

"No," I reply quietly. "But maybe you—" I stop myself. I was about to tell him he could write down his memories before detaching from his Headmaster. But of course, he can't. He can't read or write. And even if he could, a thousand pages of recollections could never replace a heart full of memories.

Briar nods silently before turning and melting back into the crowd.

"If we give up our memories, we won't know how to look after ourselves," Laurel says. "We'd be like children."

"I know," I say. "But there are people beyond Blue Ring who could help us. Others. People whose ancestors also survived what happened sixty years ago. They've never had Headmasters. I've met one of them. The one the Headmasters made you chase yesterday."

"What are they going to do to us?" Spider asks in a fearful voice. "These other people?"

"Nothing," I reply. "They're not going to hurt us. Like I say, they'll help us. They're going to be our friends."

Now, the crowd begins to murmur excitedly, anxiously. After a few moments, someone at the back—Raven, I think— shouts out another question.

"Is this true?"

"Yes," I say. "It's all true."

"What do we do now?" someone yells.

My mouth opens, but nothing comes out. I'm actually not sure what we do now. And I'm beginning to feel dizzy.

Jenna must sense my quandary because she steps forward.

"We'll do what humans have always done," she says. "We'll figure it out. We'll start a new story. We'll get that other wind turbine up and running, like Thorn suggested. And Maple said that man—what's his name, Maple?"

"Eccles."

"Eccles and his people will help us. I know they will. That's another thing humans have always done. Helped each other."

The crowd murmurs softly, mulling this over.

"Now," Jenna continues, "I think you should all go and have something you've never had: a holiday. That's a day when you get to do whatever you want. Get used to being in charge of yourself. Tomorrow, we'll start making plans."

"But what about us?"

I turn to my left toward an unfamiliar voice. It's Dusk, one of the Thankfuls. She's standing with the other Thankfuls, who've slowly shuffled to one side. "Do we get a choice?"

"What do you mean?" I reply.

"The Thankfuls didn't ask you to make our Headmasters dormant. We don't want them that way. You chose for us. We want them back the way they were. We need them." She pauses. "Please."

"Wake up your Headmasters?" My words seem slurred. Jenna puts her hand on my shoulder to steady me. "I don't even know if I could even do that if I—if I even wanted . . ." My words trail off.

"But can you try? We suffer without them." Through blurring vision, I see her gesture toward the other Thankfuls around her.

Jenna steps forward. "We won't discuss that right now. Look at her," she says, taking my hand and holding it up for all to see. "Maple is a wreck. Cuts and bruises and blisters everywhere. We need to get her patched up."

"And I'd like a glass of water, too," I mutter, as my knees give way and I slump to the ground.

CHAPTER 73
LET IT GO, LET IT FALL

We built a cairn for Papa the next morning. We'd never done that before in the morning. Our dead had always been taken to the boneyard in the evening during the slackenings. Now, free of the grip of the Headmasters and with an unknown chapter in our lives beginning, it seemed like a good time to start some new traditions.

We wrapped him in his nylar bedsheet: me, River, Lark, Thorn, Jenna, and Virgil. When they saw his body, Thorn and Lark were stunned at how old he'd become. We paired our hands beneath him and then lifted him up and carried him to the boneyard. He was so light, as if any burden he'd ever held had been released. Almost everyone went with us—even some of the Thankfuls.

We covered him with stones we gathered from the bank of the river. I was afraid the ritual would remind me of the rocks tumbling from the cairns in the desert place—of the Papas that I saw there. Instead, it was healing, like leaves budding from a dry branch of memory. After the last stone was laid in place, Lark placed a ring of braided flowers on his cairn.

"Goodbye, Papa," she said.

Now, one by one, the crowd has dwindled away till only I am standing beside the cairn. Eccles stays in sight, wandering among the other cairns that dot the boneyard like anthills. I'm left alone with my thoughts.

> *Eccles says his community*
> *will welcome everyone.*

I don't know much about him,
but I trust him.

> *He cares about you.*
> *That's easy to see.*

Yes.

> *But you know that the ones*
> *who decide not to uncouple*
> *from their Headmaster*
> *won't be able to leave here.*
> *They can't live where the past*
> *is talked about. It could still*
> *trigger memories. They can't*
> *go to the mine where*
> *Eccles and his people live.*

But his people don't know
about our past, about the people
who've lived here. Nothing they say
could trigger a memory.

> *They might talk about something*
> *from the time before the Arrival.*

Something the first hosts
would have known about.
A shared memory from long ago.

Not very likely.

Do you want to risk it?

[sigh]

How many will choose to uncouple?

The ones who want
a fresh start. The ones who
don't want their memories.
The ones who just want
their bodies to be their own again.

What about the Thankfuls?
Will you reactivate their
Headmasters like they want?

I don't know if that's even possible.

Will you try?

They'd just attack us,
try to force me to reattach
the others, reactivate them all.
We'd be back where we started.
Where you started.

Will you try?

I don't know.

What about you?

I can't detach my Headmaster.
I need your memories
of how to do the *Kinikatos.*
Just in case.

*And you don't want to lose
your other memories.
Of the people who were here.*

No.

*So you'll be staying at Blue Ring.
Free, but still not allowed
to talk to anyone about the past.*

Yes.

*And Lark and Thorn
will be going to the mine.
To build new lives and memories.*

What will I say to Thorn
when he leaves?

*That you love him, that you love Lark.
Then you'll squeeze his hand,
and then you'll let it go, let it fall,
and turn and walk away.*

"Hey, cub." It's Eccles, back from wandering around the cairns. He sees me crying, and isn't sure what to say. "I—I wish I'd been around to meet your Papa."

I nod. "He would have liked you, Eccles," I reply. I manage a small smile. "Even though you talk funny."

"Crikey, wait till you hear some of the old codgers back at the mine. Sometimes, I can barely fathom them."

I don't say anything for a minute. Then, "I won't be going to the mine, Eccles. The ones who uncouple from their Headmasters will, but not the others. I need to stay here with them."

We both fall silent.

"Lark and Thorn were sometimes a handful on the way here," he finally says. "We'll need more than just me to shepherd all the uncoupled ones who'll be going to the mine. Before the day's over, I'll start heading back. When I get there, I'll explain what's up, and then I'll come back here with a handful of mates. We'll get your people back to mine safe and sound."

"You're sure they'll look after them at the mine? I mean, while they're growing up again?"

"I promise you they will."

"Then what? After you get them to the mine?"

"Then I'll come back here. To help out." He pauses and looks upward at a raven perched on the branch of a maple tree. "And so you'll have someone to talk to."

I nod and almost smile. We turn and start to walk through the boneyard to the path back to the compound. On the way, we pass a cairn, smaller than the others. Farley's. I stop beside it, kneel down, and touch its stones. Then, we begin again to walk to the compound.

"Eccles," I ask him, "can a woman be a mate?"

"Of course," he replies. "That's the best kind."

EPILOGUE

. . . my hands are not my own, the fingers are long and slender and bedazzled with golden rings, the nails are elegantly trimmed, the skin unblemished by pricks from thorns and brambles, and I realize these are Gunther's hands, and the shockwave keeps surging toward the oblivious Orlando and Rosalind, traversing the *terra incognita* on which they tread. In mere moments, it will toss them twig-like at twilight into the great gap, the huge hole, the awful abyss, that gapes behind their behinds like a yawning Cyclops.

But hark! They hear a distant cry—*Thorn! Lark!*—and raise their eyes to espy a far-off figure wordlessly waving, silently shouting, and at last descry the shuddering shock shrieking toward them. Aghast, they swivel and prepare to skedaddle but then perceive the prodigious pit that yawns before them.

Plunked between two perils, they peer about perturbedly, seeking salvation. Suddenly, a raven swoops from the shadows and circles them. Then, a squirrel named Bluebird jumps from one tree onto another on a tree. He shouts, "Blackie, help them!"

Then, the raven flies down and picks up Thorn in one claw.

And he picks up Lark in the other claw. So he has both of them in his claws. He starts to fly up. It's hard work, but the squirrel —his name is Bluebird—says to the raven, "Come on, Blackie, just a bit higher, you can do it." The raven flaps really hard. He gets them higher than the shockwave. It goes under them, just barely. Then he sets them down on the ground, and Orlando and Rosalind pet his wings and give him five pumpkin seeds.

Gunther is really mad when he sees this. He poops his pants and makes a fist at Blackie the raven. So, a cloud blows over him and starts to drop raindrops. And the raindrops land on him, and he starts to melt like an icicle. Finally, there's nothing left of him but some yellow rings in a dirty puddle.

And suddenly we awake, and behold, it was a dream.

ACKNOWLEDGMENTS

My friend Victoria Feth read an early draft of *The Headmasters* and provided insightful feedback that enhanced its narrative and characters. John Kennedy, of Radiant Press, kindly reviewed the manuscript of *The Headmasters* and connected me with Edward Willett, the publisher of Shadowpaw Press, who accepted the manuscript, provided eagle-eyed editing, and was a pleasure to work with. Tania Craan designed a splendid book cover that, to my mind, exactly captures the quiddity of the novel. I'm indebted to all of these gifted humans.

My children—Brandon, Laika, Rukhsana, and Matthew—have each embodied moments of resilience and courage that served as touchstones in my depiction of Maple, the novel's intrepid protagonist. To them I say, *Chlanna nan con thigibh a' so 's gheibh sibh feòil!*

The Ontario Arts Council supported the writing of this work through its Recommenders Grants program. Such programs are essential for artists working in all mediums, not only by providing needed financial support but also by affirming the merit of one's creative work when the knuckle of self-doubt begins tapping at the window.

The University of Waterloo, through its unique and innovative Staff Enhancement Grant program, provided funds that assisted in preparing the manuscript for submission to publishers. *Concordia cum veritate!*

ABOUT THE AUTHOR

 Mark Morton is also the author of *Cupboard Love: A Dictionary of Culinary Curiosities* (nominated for a Julia Child Award), *The End: Closing Words for a Millennium* (winner of the Alexander Isbister Award for nonfiction); *The Lover's Tongue: A Merry Romp Through the Language of Love and Sex* (republished in the UK as *Dirty Words*), and *Cooking with Shakespeare*. He's written more than fifty columns for *Gastronomica: The Journal of Food and Culture* (University of California Press) and has written and broadcast more than a hundred columns about language and culture for CBC Radio. Mark has a PhD in sixteenth-century literature from the University of Toronto and has taught at several universities in France and Canada. He currently works at the University of Waterloo. He and his wife, Melanie Cameron (also an author), have four children, three dogs, one rabbit, and no time.

ABOUT SHADOWPAW PRESS

Shadowpaw Press is a traditional publishing company, located in Regina, Saskatchewan, Canada and founded in 2018 by Edward Willett, an award-winning author of science fiction, fantasy, and non-fiction for readers of all ages. A member of Literary Press Group (Canada) and the Association of Canadian Publishers, Shadowpaw Press publishes an eclectic selection of books by both new and established authors, including adult fiction, young adult fiction, children's books, non-fiction, and anthologies, plus new editions of notable, previously published books in any genre under the Shadowpaw Press Reprise imprint.

Email: publisher@shadowpawpress.com.

 facebook.com/shadowpawpress

 x.com/shadowpawpress

 instagram.com/shadowpawpress

AVAILABLE OR COMING SOON

SHADOWPAW
PRESS

The Good Soldier by Nir Yaniv

Shapers of Worlds Volumes I-IV

The Downloaded by Robert J. Sawyer

The Traitor's Son by Dave Duncan

Corridor to Nightmare by Dave Duncan

The Door at the End of Everything by Lynda Monahan

The Sun Runners by James Bow

Ashme's Song by Brad C. Anderson

The Wind and Amanda's Cello by Alison Lohans

Hello by David Carpenter

Theories of Everything by Dwayne Brenna

Thickwood by Gayle M. Smith

The Emir's Falcon by Matt Hughes

One Lucky Devil by Sampson J. Goodfellow

Paths to the Stars by Edward Willett

Star Song by Edward Willett

NEW EDITIONS OF NOTABLE, PREVIOUSLY PUBLISHED WORK

SHADOWPAW
PRESS *Reprise*

The Canadian Chills Series by Arthur Slade:

Return of the Grudstone Ghosts, Ghost Hotel,

Invasion of the IQ Snatchers

Let Us Be True by Erna Buffie

The Glass Lodge by John Brady McDonald

Cupboard Love: A Dictionary of Culinary Curiosities by Mark Morton

The Lavender Child by Harriet Richards

Duatero by Brad C. Anderson

Phases by Belinda Betker

Blue Fire by E. C. Blake

The Legend of Sarah by Leslie Gadallah

Stay by Katherine Lawrence

Dollybird by Anne Lazurko

The Ghosts of Spiritwood by Martine Noël-Maw

The Crow Who Tampered With Time by Lloyd Ratzlaff

Backwater Mystic Blues by Lloyd Ratzlaff

Small Reckonings by Karin Melberg Schwier

The Shards of Excalibur Series, The Peregrine Rising Duology, *Spirit Singer, From the Street to the Stars* and *Soulworm* by Edward Willett